The Untouched

A Cord McCullough Western

by David and Marie Trawinski

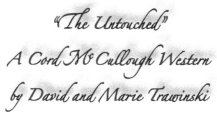

"The Untouched"
A Cord McCullough Western
by David and Marie Trawinski

Proudly published by DAMTE Associates.

Cover Image original artwork © 2023 by Kellen Churchill. All rights reserved - used with permission.

Cover Image Design and Layout© 2023 David Trawinski using Adobe Art Images as noted in Image Attribution listing.

Interior Images © 2023 David and Marie Trawinski except where noted in Image Attribution listing.

No text was generated by AI in the writing of this novel, although some images may have been AI generated.

Thanks to our longtime friends, Brian and Robin Tenney, who sparked the inspiration for this story with the tales of their visit to Palo Duro Canyon.

Dedicated to Our Good Friend,

Jim Dunham,

Who Through His Long Years

Kept Alive the Lore and Allure

of Western Heritage

Through his leadership at the

Wild West History Association

and the

Booth Western Art Museum

Amongst So Many Other Efforts.

The Llano Estacado...

Long before the Comanche came to the Southern Plains, the Spanish Conquistador Francisco Coronado lead an expedition across what he would call the "Palisaded Plains." Later others would come to call them the "Staked Plains."

Coronado was known to refer to the Llano as a "sea of grass." In 1541, he wrote upon crossing it:

"I reached some plains so vast, that I did not find their limit anywhere I went, although I traveled over them for more than 300 leagues ... with no more land marks than if we had been swallowed up by the sea ... there was not a stone, nor bit of rising ground, nor a tree, nor a shrub, nor anything to go by."

... And About This Fella' Cord McCullough

Cord McCullough is a character first developed in an earlier novel of ours entitled "Guns of the Yellow Rose."

In that volume, Cord's backstory is told in detail, including how he came to name his horse "Trouble," and how he chanced upon his canine companion, "River."

"Guns of the Yellow Rose" is the second volume in the Clay and Deekie series. It follows "Ever Blooms the Rose," mentioned here just in case any of the readers of this novel want to track the overall story all the way back to its trailhead.

The Comanche Nation

We have set this novel in 1874, a pivotal year in the history of Texas and United States. A line of forts stretched north from the Rio Grande all the way up to the Red River. West of these was the land of the Comanche, known as "Comancheria."

In that year, the ongoing slaughter of the Great American Bison population was being carried out by men known as "buffalo hunters" - a misnomer as the buffalo offered little sport to hunt and were readily massacred.

This work attempts to depict a balanced view of the Comanche tribe of Native Americans - a people whose entire culture was dependent on the buffalo. To the settlers of Texas, these natives were viewed as ruthless and savage raiders capable of inflicting the most inhumane deaths upon their families. Most often during these raids, adults were viciously killed, and their young children were often abducted.

To the US Cavalry that pursued them, the Comanche were known as the most expert horseman of the plains and were the fiercest of all mounted warriors.

To the Comanches themselves, in their language they were the "Nermernuh" or simply "the People." They proved to be a proud culture, resisting to being displaced from their land and its ways by the invading white men who recklessly slaughtered the animal essential to their existence - the buffalo.

We have included a list of source material used to develop our own view of these Native Americans in the appendix that follows this work of fiction.

Part One:

A Trailhand's Tale

Chapter 1: The Weatherford Stage Coach Holdup

The Event that Started It All

He noticed that the rhythmic swaying of the stage coach on its cradle of leather thoroughbraces appeared to be getting to the young girl, despite their nearing her final stop.

"Well, little Missy," the kindly old gent with the drooping mustache said to the child, "I guess after this gruelin' ride, you'll be more than happy to see your aunt waitin' for you in Weatherford. Won't cha' now?"

The girl only smiled at him warmly in response. It wasn't that she didn't like him, she surely did. They had sat side by side in the rear seat ever since leaving San Antonio. After the coach changed horses in Austin and rode through the night, she'd fallen asleep leaning into his side. Well, a small part of his side, for she was only fourteen and not very tall for her age. No, she liked him just fine. He had been nice, looking after her during the watering stops at Waco and Granbury. There, they stretched their legs, after which, the stage became full up with nine passengers for the ride into Fort Worth. During it, a fat man riding the middle bench dozed off, and leaned hard against the leather back-strap, crushing his full weight into her. It was the old gent who roused him roughly and told him in no uncertain terms to "mind hisself," which the fat man thereafter did.

When they arrived at Fort Worth, the old fellow's final stop, he dropped off his bags at his hotel, and then treated her to her first sarsaparilla. When the coach was ready to depart on to Weatherford, he rode along on that short leg just to make sure she arrived safely. No, she liked him just fine, but couldn't draw the words to thank him.

Even had she known what to say, there was still the issue of her heavy accent. It embarrassed her, and often she wished she could speak like any other child raised out here in the West. But it was always there, and the more she tried to hide it, the more it seemed to crawl out and betray her. So, unless absolutely necessary, she tended not to speak.

"It's okay, my dear," the old gent said to her after watching her crystal blue eyes gaze up at his, "you don't need to say nothin'. Your smile is quite enough. I figure I've come to know just how shy you are by now."

They had left Fort Worth with only five riders. The center bench had been removed. Near an hour later, the old gent stared at her warmly as the clatter of the stage coach's wheel outside his window slowed when the road dipped down into a gully washed out by recent torrents of rain. The girl's skin was nearly porcelain white, and her blonde hair, long kissed by bleaching rays of the Texas sun, capped the smooth, milky innocence of her face like a golden crown.

The old man felt the coach drop into the shallow gully. After a few minutes of a rough, slow ride it began to climb out. He figured them to be only a few hundred yards outside of town at that point. Then, he heard a ruckus up front - yelling that came just before a warning gunshot. A wagon coming in the other direction, from out of town, cut them off just as they pulled out of that gully wash. He knew from his younger days that this surely was a hold-up, with bandits figuring to catch them slowed to clear the wash out.

The stage coach had been forced to a full stop. All five remaining passengers stared at each other with great concern. Besides he and the girl on the backseat, three young men rode facing them on the front.

The old gent thought, *How could we have come so far, only to have this happen here, so close to town?* He did not liking how this was shaping up. The bandits were brazen enough to hold up a coach so close to town, in broad daylight, no less. He slid his arm around the girl. The door beside him sprung open with a wild jerk. Two barrels of a shotgun were thrust in by a man hiding behind a low black stetson and a high red bandana. The other door of the coach threw open, and there stood a large man in a fringed black leather long coat with flowing sleeves in the Mexican style.

"All right, all y'all riders," shouted the man with the shotgun, "everybody keep yer wits about ya' now. Y'all are to exit out that other door and line up alongside the coach. That man is going to free ya' of yer valuables, be they wallets, money-belts or any baubles he might find interestin'. Hand them over quiet-like, with no fussin' and everybody can go on to have a good rest of their day."

The old gent tightened his arm around the young girl and patted the fourteen year old's hand, hoping to calm her. He could feel her shaking with fear as he did so.

"We are goin' to do as these men say, and get off the coach," he whispered. "It's okay. You just stay with me."

He thought to himself, *How lucky was it that I come along to Weatherford with her? After all, I had only promised her poor nervous mamma back in San Antone that I'd make sure she got back on the right coach out of Fort Worth. Good damn thing I come along, if nothing else just to keep this poor young thing calm.*

"Git on out now, y'ole goat! The girl too!" The bandit with the shotgun had climbed into the coach and pushed the old gent along with the double barrels pressed hard in the small of his back. They obeyed, following behind as the three young men filed out ahead of them. They all lined up outside the coach as the man with the shotgun had instructed.

The Mexican, covered by the shotgunner, worked his way down the line, starting with the three men from the front seat. They gave up their wallets and pocket-watches. Not one of them seemed inclined to cause any trouble, and the one in the middle even surrendered a revolver that he carried. This made the old man hopeful that this would all end peaceably enough. Being the ex-lawman that he was, he knew it was his duty to observe all the detail he could to help the sheriff catch these bandits at some later point.

He counted six robbers in all. In addition to the Mexican and the shotgunner dealing with them, there were two up front taking possession of the strongbox from the driver and his partner, both of whom had simply surrendered without a fight. The final two bandits were in the rear going through the parcels carried in the boot.

They all seemed to be following directions from the man up front who was by then opening the strongbox. He wore a Slim Jim style holster. It was distinctive, the old man thought, and he marked the man as their leader. The Slim Jim fella had a pocket watch and kept glancing at it.

"One minute to go," Slim Jim shouted. It caused the others to work all the quicker. The old gent had spent his youth tracking this kind of vermin all over Texas. Most of these had bandanas pulled up over their faces, near to the rims of battered hats pulled low. Despite this, the old man figured them to be white rustlers. All except that Mexican.

The Mexican was the only one of them not bothering to cover his face. He had worked his way up to the old gent, and quietly relieved him of his wallet and watch. While he did this, the old lawman looked upon the features of the bandit's face and thought, *Mexican for sure, but something else was there.*

"Nermernuh?" he asked the bandit, then followed up with native word, *"Quahadi?"*

The Mexican responded by violently backhanding the old man, driving him to the dirt. The fourteen year old girl, who until this point the Mexican had shown no interest in, knelt down beside her fallen companion. As she bent over him, a medallion she wore under her dress fell free. It dangled in the sun, and caught the Mexican's attention.

He moved toward the girl, and the fallen aged gent raised his arm to stop him. The Mexican spun and kicked the old fella' hard with his pointed boots, again and again, until the man spat up thick mouthfuls of dark red blood.

Then the bandit dropped the sack of collected loot, grabbed the girl forcibly by the arm, and took the dangling medallion into his other hand, inspecting it closely.

"What this is?" the Mexican spoke his first words in butchered English. His face was cold, almost blank. His eyes seemed like dark holes that took in everything, but offered nothing in return. No emotion. No hope. His black flowing locks dangled from his forehead as he stared at the medallion of a bird carved in some sort of polished bone.

"Time!" yelled Slim Jim. "We're outta here!"

The bandits all began to move over to the wagon that blocked the stage coach. All except for the Mexican, who just held the medallion and the girl tightly in his grasp. He seemed lost in revelation, and stared at the carved bird.

"What this is?" he screamed louder at the girl as he shook her. "You tell, now!"

The girl's jaw quivered, she could not answer.

The Mexican unsheathed a knife, and moved to the old man lying on the ground. "You tell now, or I kill him!"

"An eagle." The words drained out from her in a wobble, streaming awash in a fall of tears from her eyes.

"C'mon, *Lobo*," said the shotgunner who had covered the Mexican throughout the holdup. "We're done here. Time to *vámonos.*"

"What kind of eagle?" the Mexican asked the girl, ignoring his partner.

"A White Eagle!" she cried over the fallen old man.

"White Eagle…" the Mexican echoed aloud. Then more firmly he repeated, "White Eagle!" His gaze then closely scanned her face, lingering on her blonde hair. He yanked the girl hard, saying only, "You come with me."

The bandit left the bag of loot next to the old gent, who by then had a river of blood flowing from his mouth. It was greedily retrieved by the shotgunner just before he scurried for the bandits' wagon.

The Mexican placed the girl on a horse, one of a pair the robbers had tied off to the wagon after riding up alongside it. Untying it, the Mexican began to mount, intending to ride in the saddle behind the girl.

The sight of the bandit abducting the young girl unlocked a rage in the coach driver, who until then had not resisted these robbers. He decided he could not stand to let this Mexican scum take off with the sweet little thing. He lunged forward, snatched up his horsewhip from the ground where it laid, and went to strike the Mexican from behind, but his whip's tip never came to fall on the bandit.

The gang's leader with the Slim Jim holster drew and fired his revolver, striking the driver in his chest. Then he screamed, "Lets clear on out of here. Now! Before the whole damn town comes a lookin' for us all."

The driver fell to the ground, dead before his body could raise up a cloud of dust. Shot through the heart. The Mexican lept down from the girl on the horse. He reached down for the dead man's horsewhip, and having coiled it in his hands, began whipping the corpse with a savage fury.

The death of the driver had everyone in shock as the six bandits withdrew: four on the wagon, two on horseback. One of those horsemen, the Mexican, with the little girl in his saddle, took off in the opposite direction from the rest.

The remaining passengers from the coach huddled together around the old gent. He appeared to be very badly injured, but still conscious.

"That Mexican took the girl," one said to him.

"Half-breed," the old gent fought to whisper through bloodied teeth. *"Half-Mexican, half-Comanche."*

"God help that poor li'l gal…" another mumbled.

Figure 1: A Colt Navy Six in a "Slim Jim" Style Holster (Courtesy Jim Dunham)

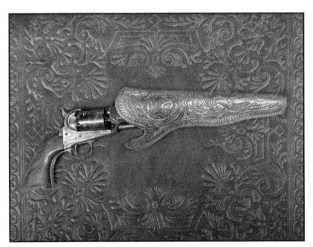

Chapter 2: A Man in Black

South Texas, Spring 1874

The countryside south of San Antonio had fully awakened from its short winter's slumber. The temperature was already warm enough that the lone traveler scanned the yards of barren dirt ahead of his gelding for rattlers. He feared less the strike of the viper as he did its telltale rattle startling his horse, less it rear up and throw him to the ground. He was getting too old to take another fall. That dirt path beneath him appeared hard and unforgiving. It led up to the ramshackle cabin sitting atop the slight, barren hill. It'd be kindly of anyone come a calling to think it more than a shack on a bald spit of a rise.

The man in black had passed the last tree a half mile back, and the ochre colored soil wound out ahead of him. It was parted only by sporadic patches of nettle grass and an odd growth of chaparral. The rider realized this all worked to the advantage of the dangerous man he sought inside the cabin. There was nothing to keep that gunman from sighting his rifle on those who approached, as he was likely doing so at that very moment. The rider's nerves were as taut as a banjo string; beads of sweat formed as he thought nervously of what lay ahead. The man he sought was known to be lightening quick with a gun, and any remorse he felt in using it lasted no longer than a roll of thunder.

Then, he was caught by great surprise. A mottled beast of a hound exploded from the shack's porch and ran toward him, growling ferociously at the unwelcome horse and rider. The dog scatted to and fro in front of them on hind legs which appeared to be spry and agile, contrasting with its forward pair which were thickly muscled and appeared to be planted steadfast. Its face was covered by a mask of two mirrored patches of russet brown, one covering each eye and ear, with both joined at the bridge of its nose. These colorings swept back away from powerful jaws that threatened to tear all intruders to pieces.

The rider's horse did indeed rear up onto its hind legs in fright of the dog, and the rider awkwardly lost a stirrup but maintained himself in the saddle by clumsily clutching onto the pommel's horn. The dog remained in front of the rider and his mount, defying them to take just one more step forward, which they did not.

"Vaquero desnudo borracho!"

Cord McCullough awoke to Lucia's jabbering away at him in her native tongue, spitting the words out at the devil's pace. Despite his hangover, he quickly came to recognize her three favorite Spanish words as of late to describe him, which he knew, all too well, meant "drunken, naked cowboy." She spat them over and over again as she pulled back the sheets as if to expose the evidence of her accusation. His head was splitting like the dirt of a dried out *arroyo*. His mouth was dustier than the empty whiskey bottle next to him, which he was prone to calling *budge*.

All the trailhands he knew called it *budge,* too, perhaps because after drinking too much of it they weren't likely to budge at all.

In the distance, Cord could hear River's agitated barking warning of an intruder. It seemed to produce painful throbs in his head, second only to the never ending shrill voice of the very excited Lucia.

"Eres solo un vaquero desnudo borracho!"

"Damn it, Lucia," he said over her screeching. "Enough already. I agree, I ain't nuthin' more than a drunken naked cowboy. Ya' done taught me that much Spanish by now. What's got River all riled up so outside?"

"Perhaps, *chust* because there is an *hombre* on a horse coming up the road," she seethed through her mangled Mexican-South Texas swill of bad English. She had escaped the deep poverty of Old Mexico. As a young, dark beauty, she had not far to look to find help sneaking across the Rio Grande. On the Texas side, she made her living riding cowboys for several years, which produced in her an amusing tangle of the two border languages.

"*Deese* is what I keep *jou* here all winter for, Cord, to tell *deese coostumers, deese hombres, dat* I am no longer a sportin' gal. *No mas! Jet,* here it is almost noon, and *jou* are still *desnudo!"*

"Alright already, just git my damn boots," Cord said as he reached to the floor to search for his clothes. *Desnudo noon,* he thought, *had a nice ring to it, once. She never minded it much when I first moved in, before the winter took full root. Then, when the cold nights hit in January and February, we spent many a night drinking and the next day drunk naked in bed. Those were definitely good times, but that friendly spell tween us wore off some weeks back...*

His head still pounded, and as such he was thankful to hear River's sharp barks decay into only a low menacing growl. Meant whoever was out there was behaving himself, minding the dog's threats.

"We ain't had any of yer gentleman callers here since before Christmas," Cord said as he shook out his shirt and pants. "I figured word done got out by now that ya' wasn't whorin' no more. Thought we'd seen the last of them waddies ya' used to enjoy gettin' paid to wrassle."

She came back with his boots as he slipped into his clothes. "Still, I reckon there's always likely to be a straggler or two. Either this one didn't git the message, or did but still figured it was worth the trouble to try more time to pay for a toss with ya'. I'll scare him off fer good."

Lucia held the boots a few feet away from him. *"Bastardo! Jou* never minded payin' for me. J*ou chust* want it for free now. *Steell dey coome.* Maybe *jou* not so much a *hombre malo* as *jou tink!"* She thrust the boots at him.

"Did ya' check 'em for scorpions?" Cord asked her.

"Jou chick 'em jouself," she spat at him, "and *git* out there and *git* rid of *deese* man. Run him off, if *jou* can, if *jou steell scere* anyone, my *chico suave!* Go! *Vámos!"*

Cord shook out his boots and then slid his feet into them. *Chico suave* - her *"soft boy."* When he first got there he was *chico duro.* But now she thought his hard body had gone lazy and soft. She forgot he had scared off some dozen clients of hers over his time there. Sure as hell, they were all scared off good. Not a one came back, had they?

They'd be even more scared if they knew my name, just who exactly they was dealin' with, he thought. Still, Cord never felt the need to tell them, just that Lucia was no longer sporting and best they not bother to come back.

Fact was that he had been very careful to make sure that his name had not gotten out. Cord had been lying low after that business last fall with the Stone Canyon Gang. He still had too many enemies looking for him.

"You inside there," a voice called from outside, as River ripped into a fresh cascade of threatening barks, "I am looking for a man, calls himself Cord McCullough."

So much for layin' low, Cord thought. *How'd the hell did he find me?*

Lucia burst into an uncontrollable giggle.

"What's so damn funny?" Cord asked.

"*Chust* for once," she said through her ripple of laughter, "*deese hombre* comes for *jour* ass, not mine. Maybe he is looking for an *amigo muy especial, eh?*"

Cord grimaced at her joke. "Well, more likely he's come for the man I used to be. But when he learns that, like yerself, I am also retired from my earlier profession, then I'm not sure that news will sit with him too well."

Cord had retired from working as an enforcer for the Drovers' Exchange. No more riding the Chisholm Trail for that group of cattlemen, taking care of those who rustled from their herds, like that gang up in Stone Canyon. Those outlaws were all dead now anyhow. But at least one of the Exchange's cattle ranchers, Vaughn Anders, still felt as though he had unfinished business with McCullough.

"You in there, Mr. McCullough?" the man dressed in all black asked in another yell from a distance outdoors.

Cord listened to the his voice and thought him to be older, and that he sounded not particularly threatening. Of course, this could be a ruse just to lure him out into the open. There might be others with him, but Cord reckoned not. It just didn't feel that way given River's reaction.

The hound would have acted differently if there were several men approaching. He would have pulled closer back to the front porch. No, Cord figured, best bet it was more than likely to be just the lone fella out there.

"Stay put with yer hands in plain view, I'm coming out," Cord yelled as he reached for his leather duster hanging from the peg by the door. In it was hidden his Colt Baby Dragoon in the special pocket Cord had sewn in at its bottom. He had already strapped on his Colt .45 Peacemaker in the holster under the coat. Just to be safe, he grabbed the twelve gauge, cracked open its breech and dropped buckshot rounds into each of its side-by-side chambers. After all, with Vaughn Anders' crew still looking for him, best he should play this safe.

"Lucia," he said as he headed for the door, "grab my rifle over there. If this bastard somehow gits the better of me, plug a round or two into him like I showed ya' how."

The instruction seemed to sober her as her laughing not only instantly came under control, but quickly stopped altogether. A tense second of silence preceded her saying, *"Chust jou* be careful, *amigo."*

Cord stepped out onto the shack's wooden porch and eyed the lone rider. He stood at rest as River once more swept back and forth threateningly before his horse.

McCullough glanced about the treeless hillside, still cautious that there could be more men hiding out somewhere on its open sloping grounds. Still, Cord knew River would, by now, be fully aware of them by scent alone. No, Cord was damn sure it was just the one old man dressed in black. That man held his hands up in plain view, palms out, but still had his head down watching the dog. The wide round brim of his hat hid his face from view.

"I'm McCullough," Cord hollered out menacingly as he stepped from the porch onto the dirt path. He then raised the shotgun and leveled both barrels at the intruder as he said simply, "State yer business, mister."

The man on horseback slowly raised his head. The brim of his hat cleared his face hesitantly, like the pass of an eclipse giving back the glow to a darkened moon. The skin of the face that was revealed was not of a rough weathered hide of a cowboy, nor did it sport the angular, taut-skinned sneer of an assassin, but simply the chubby, smooth skin of a life lived indoors, out of the elements.

The man in black could not speak at first, clearly frightened as he looked down the double barrels of the shotgun pointed directly at him.

Cord walked briskly toward the rider, shotgun leveled. "Ya' must be one dumb jack ass of a fella, mister, unless ya' were deliberately fixed on getting yerself riddled with buckshot today."

As Cord neared him, the rider turned his head away in fright, no longer able to face its twin barrels. In doing so, he raised his fleshy chin high enough to expose the white gap of the Roman Collar until then hiding safely beneath his low hanging jowls.

"Oh! Sorry, Padre," Cord said, but still not lowering the shotgun just yet. *After all, killers been known to dress out as preachers,* he thought. *That Pinkerton on the stage coach last fall had done just that, hadn't he?* Yet this man was far too soft, too gentle in his disposition to be a real threat in that way. That much Cord could plainly see.

"I didn't reckon ya' fer a man of the cloth," Cord continued. "At first, I thought ya' to be one of Lucia's old clients, ya' see she used to be a ..."

Suddenly Cord couldn't bring himself to say the word "whore" in the man's presence.

"Fff, Fff, Fffadder," the man stuttered with fright to Cord, "not Padre, my son, but *Fadder.* I am *Fadder Yerzy* and I come from *Panna Maria."*

"Panna Maria?" Cord asked. "Where's that?"

"It means *Our Lady Mary,* in our language*"* the priest said, "you know, the Blessed Virgin Mother."

This man had only spoken a few words in total, but Cord detected his speech was overlaid with some sort of an unusual accent. Cord could not place it. Certainly not Spanish nor Mexican, nor British. German? No. Swedish maybe? Cord had heard the Swedes were working the south Texas hills by then. There was only one way to find out.

"Just what language might that be, Father?"

"Polish, my son," the priest held his outstretched hands toward the shotgun. *"Pliss,* lower your *veapon,* I mean you no harm."

Cord lowered the shotgun cautiously. The air between them was still filled with the menace of River's continuous, ferocious barking.

The priest said nothing, instead he made a sweeping gesture with his hands, which were obviously shaking, as if to say, *can you do something about this beast?*

"River, down!" Cord yelled, and the dog stopped. He made a hand gesture and the animal walked off to the side of the dirt trail, where it sat and watched its master, a few steps away. It remained ready to pounce if needed.

"Ya' really need to be more careful," Cord said, "coming up on a man's spread like this. People get killed that way in these parts, Padre."

"Fadder," he said emphatically again. "Not Padre, but *Fadder. Fadder Yerzy.*"

"So ya' done said. Father *Yerzy*, is it?" Cord repeated without fully understanding the unusual name.

"Yes," the priest said. He recognized Cord's confusion, so he spelled it out. "J- E- R -Z- Y. *Yerzy.*"

"I don't know whereabouts in San Antone ya' learned to spell, Father, but where I did up north we'd pronounce that Jerzy, kind of like the state back east."

"I told you, I do not come from San Antonio," the priest said, "I come from *Panna Maria.* You have not heard of our settlement?"

"Down Karnes City way?" Cord asked, referring to the town that was fighting to become the county seat. He drew a nod from the priest. "Some kinda community of European immigrants living together out there, right?"

"Yes," Father Jerzy said, again nodding. "Poles. *Ve* are Poles. I fear even after our lands *vere* stolen from us in the old country, *ve* cling to our language, perhaps too proudly. In it, all letter J's sound like Y's. It is *vhy* my name is pronounced as *'Yerzy,'* not *'Jerzy.'* I am glad to have finally found you, my son."

"Well, *Father Yerzy*," Cord replied, "still, ya' best watch yerself coming up on a man's spread the way yer did. Some fellas woudda' just shot ya' from inside the winda."

The priest looked at McCullough carefully, as if he was deciding whether or not to even say aloud what was in his mind. He decided to, despite his reservations.

"I have been told that the property is not yours, but belongs to the young *voman,"* Father Jerzy said. "Not that it matters at all in the least to me." The priest then awkwardly flashed a nervous, knowing smile to Cord.

"Just how would ya', being a priest and all, come to know that?" Cord asked.

Father Jerzy just shrugged at him, then added. *"Vhen* a priest hears the sins of those of the flock he tends, he cannot help but recall who to go to for such information *vhenever* it might be needed. Let us say that your young lady friend has quite a reputation. It spreads so far as to even reach one of the Polish men in *Panna Maria.* As does your reputation, Mr. McCullough, even though you attempt to remain unknown. But that same gentleman you ran off from here not too long ago recognized you nonetheless. And it is exactly your reputation that brings me here."

"We been talkin' a spell now, Father, and I still don't see what yer gettin' at," Cord said. Standing out in the harsh sun was reminding him how bad he felt. His throat was nothing but a dusty gulch, his head still throbbed.

The priest shifted his weight in the saddle to reposition himself, and reached into his jacket to retrieve something. His movements drew a low growl from River.

"Freeze, father," Cord yelled as he swung up the shotgun again.

"*I, I, I* only reach for a *p,p,piece* of paper," the priest said, again stuttering nervously.

"Might as well be yer death certificate goin' fer it that fast," Cord said. "Now, pull it out as slow as ya' possibly can…"

Father Jerzy did so, producing only a folded piece of newsprint. "Last *veek,* there *vas* a stage coach robbery up in *Veatherford,"* he said. "Do you know this town?"

"I don't need yer newsprint, Father. I read up on that in the San Antone papers. Sure, I am somewhat familiar with Weatherford, just a bit west of Fort Worth."

Cord lowered the shotgun again.

"So I am told," Father Jerzy said. "I myself have never been so far north, at least in this country. But on that stage coach *vas* a young girl who *vas* abducted by one of the robbers. A half-Indian."

It was big local news, and Cord had indeed read about it on the front page of the San Antone papers the last time he went in town to buy his bottles of *budge*. Six men had held up the coach just before it entered Weatherford. Took the strongbox and passengers' valuables, and sadly, killed the driver and another man before abducting the young girl. But it only said she was a local girl - nothing about her being from *Panna Maria* or being Polish.

"*Comanchero,* it said he was," Cord said, "one of them Mexican bandits out of Santa Fe who trade with the Comanches. The law still ain't found her, last I heard. They believe he took the girl off into the lands of the Comanche. Whether she was taken by either a *Comanchero* or a half-breed, it don't matter none. Gettin' her back is gonna take a helluva lot more than the likes of yerself and me, Father."

Cord's words seemed to land on the rider with the weight of the oxen's yoke. A great sadness descended on the father. His entire demeanor appeared to change from business to bereavement.

"The poor girl *vas* only fourteen years old," the priest stated, "not yet a *voman.* You understand my meaning, Mr. McCullough?"

"I git yer gist, Father," Cord said, "but, in any case tracking down an Injun, even a half-blooded one, could take months. And if he takes her back into *Comancheria*, then all bets of getting her back just went south in a major way. Best ya' can hope is they decide to ransom her back."

"Vhat is this term, *Comancheria?"* the priest asked.

"Comanche country," Cord explained. "West of Weatherford and Fort Belknap. Out on *the Llano Estacado,* ya' know? *The Staked Plains.* Even the Texas Rangers and US Army won't wander out there without their being in great numbers. I sure as hell ain't goin' into *Comancheria* after any girl, even one as young and innocent as yer describin'. No, I figure yer best gettin' the Rangers involved. They're certainly more equipped to handle this sort of thing. Them boys been fightin' the Comanches for some fifty years now, learned their savage ways, and use it against them Injuns right fiercely. Least, I'm told so."

The priest looked at Cord with outright derision. His eyes searched the man, but failed to find in him a Christian soul to appeal to. Father Jerzy shook his head in disgust, only to slowly transition it into a knowing nod.

"I am sorry to hear you say that," he said in a sombre and sorrowful tone, "but, yes, others have already told the same to me and the girl's distraught mother. I *vas* told not to even hope to get the girl back until a large posse of Army or Texas Rangers could be raised. Even by then, they say, it might be too late. Sadly, they all seem to have given up on our poor little child. But as pitiful as her situation is, that is not *vhat* I have come to ask of you."

"It's not?" asked Cord, befuddled. "Then what are we jawing 'bout?' Whaddaya' need of me, Father?"

The priest shifted back into his business-like tone.

"I come to ask a much easier task of you, Mr. McCullough. The mother of the abducted girl is desperate to get her son back…"

"Son? I thought we was talking 'bout her daughter?" Cord said, softly shaking his head in confusion.

"As I said, the girl *vas* taken by the half-Indian," the Polish priest patiently explained. "A few days later her older brother *vent* against his mother's *vill* and took a horse and rode off alone to Fort *Vorth* to look for his sister in the area of that town called Hell's Half Acre. It seems the boy alone has not given up on her. I am here to ask of you a very simple task. *Vill* you please go to Fort *Vorth* and bring the boy back before any harm befalls him? His mother cannot bear to lose him as *vell* as her daughter. She has lost her husband to the *Vinter* Fever recently, and despite the tragedy of her daughter being taken, the mother fears most that she *vill* next lose her only remaining child, her son. The boy has quite a strong *vill* of his own, like a mule."

"Ya' mean the boy's a headstrong jack ass?"

"That is a more colorful *vay* to say the same thing, Mr. McCullough. He only *vants* to save his sister. *Ve* all fear he *vill* die in vain trying to do so."

"Well," Cord said, "at least the boy's got guts. Perhaps no brains to speak of, but lots of guts."

Father Jerzy then made a gesture asking for permission before he slowly reached into his jacket again.

"Slowly, Father," Cord answered, "just like before."

Father Jerzy cautiously produced a sack of gold coins, tied off with a decorative ribbon that seemed not to fit the sombre occasion. "Here is all the gold coin we could raise for your expenses to bring him back. *Vhatever* is left is yours to keep for your troubles."

Cord stepped up and took the sack from the priest. McCullough weighed it preciously in his palm. He was excited about what it contained. Not because he valued the gold within it, but more so because it contained freedom - a reason to leave Lucia behind and return to the open range.

"And what about the young girl who was taken?" Cord asked.

"Ve vill continue to *vork vith* the Texas Rangers and the army about finding her. But as you have said, even they *vill* not rush blindy into *Comancheria.* Too risky even for those brave men. I am sure they *vill* go after her in due time…"

Cord thought about the girl. If the man who took her was a half-blooded Comanche, he would most likely have taken her on a frantic ride deep into *Comancheria.* It was what they did. Ride hard with her for three days straight, until the raider felt safe out deep on *the Llano.*

Comancheria is an enormous place, he thought. Within it *the Llano Estacado* spreading out like an ocean all the way west into the New Mexico Territory and was bounded on the north by the Canadian River. It was a dry expanse of buffalo grass and not much else. It bore no real landmarks to navigate by. It held precious little water, unless you were Comanche and knew where to find it. They were *the Llano's* masters. The white man was prone to get lost in its expanse and die of thirst.

And that was just *the Llano,* Cord thought. *Comancheria* was even more vast. It spreads as far north as Southern Kansas, and south all the way down to Mexico. Its eastern end abuts the Indian Territories. Searching for a young girl across it was a near impossible task. And the Comanche did not take kindly to those who wandered into their homelands. That was proven a decade ago when some three hundred US Cavalry under none other than Colonel Kit Carson had been sent east from the New Mexico Territory to "subdue" the Comanches. The army expedition had been driven out after a battle at an outpost called Adobe Walls, located just north of the Canadian River.

Cord decided not to share all this with the priest. He knew there was little hope of getting the girl back, and sensed that the priest and the girl's mother most likely understood this. It was as hard a truth as anyone could ever be expected to accept. She, the mother, was forced to make the dirtiest deal of all with the devil himself. *You've taken my girl, just not her brother. Spare my boy.*

"How old ya' say this boy is that the mother wants back so badly?" Cord asked, weighing the sack of coins in his hands.

"*Piotr* is only seventeen," Father Jerzy said.

"Not the girl, the boy," Cord said, getting frustrated with the priest.

"The girl, Kalina, is but fourteen," the priest said. "Piotr is her brother. He is seventeen."

"The boy's name is *Pee Otta*?" Cord asked repeating the priest's pronunciation as best he could. "Sounds like a girl's name. Might as well named him Sue."

"*Piotr* is Polish for Peter," Father Jerzy explained.

"Well, he'll get run out of Hell's Half Acre damn fast if he uses the name *Pee Otter* up there. That is, of course, if he doesn't get himself shot first."

Father Jerzy opened his palms to the sky, as if in the depths of prayer. A great tension pulled tightly at the skin of his cheeks and brow.

"His mother fears exactly this, or even *vorse* that he *vill* go *vest* looking for his sister. She knows how dangerous the Comanches are. So you *vill* do this for us? For her?"

"For the mother," Cord nodded. The strain on the old priest's face melted away into a smile of great relief.

"Does the boy have any guns on him?" asked Cord.

"No, he does not have any *veapons,*" the priest answered. "He is a boy who *vorks* the land for his family. He knows plows and horses and mule teams, but not guns. If he has fired any at all, it *vould* have only been with his father before he died. The boy is a farmer, nothing more."

"Good Lord," Cord reacted. "Ya' say the boy is seventeen and yet has no guns? How long have yer people been in Texas? How on earth have y'all survived? How have ya' defended yourselves?"

"Do not take the Lord's name in vain, Mr. McCullough," snapped Father Jerzy, showing his anger for the first time. "Our people have been in *Panna Maria* since Christmas Eve of 1854. For nearly *tventy* years the men of *Panna Maria* have kept their guns at the ready, but these *veapons* are not shared *vith* our youths like Piotr."

"Well, here in Texas," Cord answered him, "a seventeen year old ain't a boy no more. He's considered a man, and knows how to shoot and ride."

"Piotr does not shoot, but the boy is an excellent horseman," Father Jerzy said. "He learned to ride from his father, who *vas* a Dragoon for the Prussian Army in the old country. Sadly, his father just died from the *vinter* fever."

Cord looked over at River, as if he was recapping the situation for the dog. "Okay. So we got a half-orphaned boy named *Pee Otter* who doesn't know which end of a pistol to point forward; he's nosin' round in the Acre, looking for a sister he'll never find there. Even if this half-breed bandit was lookin' to ransom the girl, he'd never do it there. It'd be the first place everyone will be lookin', includin' the law. But the boy is most likely to find more trouble than he can handle up there. I guess there's no time to waste. When did this *Pee Otter* leave for Fort Worth?"

"Three days ago," Father Jerzy answered, "but *ve* know by telegram that he has not arrived there yet."

"I suppose not," Cord said, "for even traveling light and fast, Fort Worth is a good week's ride. Perhaps before he stirs up too much of a hornet's nest in the Acre, I can catch up to him with Trouble."

"I do not understand *vhat* you mean," said Father Jerzy, "*vith* trouble."

"Sorry Father," Cord explained. "I know it's a bit confusin'. Ya' see, '*Trouble*' is my horse's name."

"Why would you ride a horse named '*Trouble*'?" the priest asked.

"It's a long story, Father…" Cord said, "and if *ya'* want me heading out any time soon after this *Pee Otter*, I'll have to tell it to *ya'* some other time."

Chapter 3: The Ride North

On to Austin and Waco

When the priest left, Cord McCullough went inside and gathered up his meager possessions. He reached for his saddle roll to ready it for the trip. He thought Lucia would be glad to be ridding herself of him, but instead she followed him around like a hornet, buzzing his head with questions as angry as a swollen stinger.

"So, *jou* are *chust* goin to up and leave me all alone here?" she yelled. "After all I have given to *jou* - a *rrrroof* over your head, food *frrom* my table, and *coomforrrt* in my bed." Her *r's* rolled like a wagon wheel when she was mad.

"Ya' know as well as I do, Lucia," Cord replied, "we both took a little too much of a shine to that comfort carly on. But truth be told, yer been gettin' a bit stingy with it as of late. I done what I promised ya' I'd do. Y'ain't had nobody come looking for a toss for several months now. I figure they done got the message."

Cord spread his saddle roll out flat on the bed. He looked down at it, focused like a hawk, as he decided how much to layer on his backside and how much to roll.

"And what if *dey doo coome?*" Lucia all but screamed these words at him. *"What am I to doo when dey doo coome, Cord?"*

"If," he answered her, "anyone does come along, all ya' gotta do is see just how bad they want it. Keep that shotgun o' mine, and fire off a round over the head of anybody coming up that path. I bet most 'em will turn tail and run. They'll forgit real fast 'bout what they come fer."

"And what if *dey doon't?*" Lucia asked angrily.

"Well, that's what the second barrel of that side-by-side is fer. Just let 'em get close enough to be sure ya' can wound them somethin' good, so ya've time to reload."

Lucia muttered something in Spanish under her breath. Cord could only make out the words *padre and hombre* and decided he didn't need to know whatever it was she was fussing over. Some things are best left unsaid, he reckoned, or in this case, left un-heard.

Cord had by then stripped off the few clothes he had thrown on to confront Father Jerzy. He needed to dress himself proper for the trail. He stood naked before her as he bent over to add the clothes he just took off to the bedroll.

"Chust look at *jou,"* she said. *"Jour* body was so hard when *jou coome* to stay with me. Now, *jour* belly is flabby and hangs from *jou."*

"Well, my lovely *Señorita*, that was all yer doin'," Cord replied. "Ya' made me take a liking to the indoor life a little more than I shouldda'. Still, nothing a few weeks in the saddle won't tighten up, I reckon."

Cord did not look at her directly, but in her dressing mirror he caught Lucia eyeing him in a way he did not expect. She had the look of a wolf who was not exactly hungry, but still took a fix on some easy prey, not knowing for sure when it might feast next.

"When are *jou cooming* back?" she asked, as the edges of her harsh tone softened.

"Truthfully, Lucia," Cord answered, "I don't figure that I am. I thank ya' for yer winterin' hospitality, but I am right sure that Trouble and River could use the rest of the spring and maybe a full summer out on the trail as much as I could. I reckon it's for the best, anyhow."

"Chust what do *jou* mean by *dat?"*

"Well, if that priest knew I was here," Cord reasoned, "then sooner or later some other folk are likely to come here lookin' for me. Bad folk. I don't figure them to bother ya' none if I'm long gone, but I don't want ya' gettin' hurt in any crossfire should I stay on here. Naw, best I just be moving on after I find this *Pee Otter* boy."

She walked up to him as he stood by the bed, pressed herself against his naked body, and threw her arms around his neck. Lucia raised her lips to where his strong neck met his rugged unshaven jaw and whispered into his ear, *"Adios, amigo. Jou will miss dis."*

Then she kissed him hard where the bone of his jaw ended in a jut below his ear. He turned to draw his arm up around her waist just before she broke back away to add, *"Jou* has been wanting to go back out on that trail for some time now. I could feel it in *jou* ever since the last heavy frost melted away. But *jou'* figured *jou* owed it to me to stay, I know *jou* did. But *jou* was not happy, and *jou* took to that whiskey a bit too *mucho.* No, *jou* always liked it best out there on the trail, free, just the four of *jou* all alone together: *jou,* riding on Trouble with River trailing."

Cord said. "That's only the three of us: Trouble, River and me. I know ya' can count, but ya' said four."

He didn't say what first jumped into his mind - that he had never met a whore who couldn't count. Especially one who saved enough to retire.

Lucia unfurled a wicked smile at him. "Nowhere that the three of *jous* will ever wander that *she* won't tag along. I could feel her in this bed with us a few too many times. When *jou arrre* quiet, I know *jou tink* about *jour* dead wife, *jour* Callie. She haunts *jou*, her and *jour* dead boy, too. But especially her. What did *jou* do, Cord? *Jou* never *rrreally tell* me what *jou* do to her."

"Yeah," Cord answered, "and I figure I don't owe ya' no reason to tell ya' now. Besides, ya' done ran as cool as a mountain spring the one time I slipped up and called ya' by her name."

"Jes, I deed!" she exploded, *"Chust* so *jou* know, Cord, no gal takes to being called by another gal's name in the *calor de pasión.* Not even a sportin' gal."

"Ya' mean an ex-sportin' gal, I hope. And was that what that was, Lucia? *The heat of passion?"* Cord asked, as he slipped his muscled arm tightly around her waist. His belly may have grown soft, that was true, but his arms remained strong, and his aim true. He wanted her to know just then what he was aimin' for. "I figured what we done was nuthin' more than our takin' care of each other's needs. Ya' got any last needs that need takin' care of, *Señorita?"*

Still naked, he pulled her close and kissed her deeply on the lips. She fought him playfully at first, but the swell of anger at being abandoned soon overtook her once more. Finally, she pushed him away with all her might.

"Look, Cord, *chust* go now. *Vaya con dios, amigo. Jou* want so bad to take to that trail 'cause *jou* can be with her whenever *jou* want. *Jour* horse and *jour* dog won't mind *jou* calling *dem* by *jour* dead wife's name, or always being lost in *jour t'oughts* of her. I will miss having *jou* here, but if *jou* must go *amigo,* then *chust* go now."

Cord's arms fell disappointedly by his side. She was right in that he often slipped into thinking of his dead wife in the freedom of the outdoors. Still, she didn't realize that those long hours on the trail, when he would pondered over Callie, were a form of penance, not of pleasure. But how could Lucia possibly know that? He had never told her how his woman and their son had died. All she heard was him calling out Callie's name a few times deep in his sleep, and just the once in the midst of '*love-making,*' or whatever what they did together should rightfully be called.

"Lucia," he said softly to her, "ya' been good to me. I know I wore away at ya' over the winter like a cockle-burr in yer saddle on a long ride. But yer right, best I just be goin' on my way. Should anyone come lookin' after me, just tell 'em I left and ya' got no idea where I was headin'. It's the truth, after all, once I git past Fort Worth, I mean."

Just when he figured he had somehow talked her out of one final roll, she proved to him he never could claim to understand women, whether they be Kansas farm girls or retired Mexican whores.

"I got a *burrr* in my saddle all *rrright, jou bastardo. Jou* can leave as soon as *jou* take care of it for me." Lucia then pushed him back on the mattress and pulled up her skirt as she climbed atop him. She straddled his body like it was the broad back of a Texas bull.

He happily welcomed her change of heart. She had always enjoyed toying with him. And even in this, their last time together, she had played him like a bottom dealt card. He would satisfy this, her last need, even if her thirst for it was only due to not knowing how far off the next watering hole might be. But if the girl wanted a final drink from the well, who was Cord to deny her?

What happened for the next two hours Cord would think about for the next two days. Lucia's movements were light and fresh like the first breezes of the Texas spring.

She's right, Cord thought, *I will miss this.* His leaving seemed to smooth away all the rough edges that had rubbed raw during their winter confined together. The easiness they found in each other during that final toss was due to their each knowing it would be their last time together for a while, if not forever.

Their final coupling was as indescribable as the flaming scarlets, pinks and blues of a western sunset; just as magical as how those hues of light could blend and diffuse into each other to create thousands more. With each pulse of her body, each glimmer of its sweat, Lucia tried her best to teach him that even an ex-sporting gal could give in to the heat of passion.

Cord rode Trouble down the dirt path as River scampered ahead of them. The old trailhand had a content smile upon his face. He was satisfied in more ways than one. His bedroll was tied down to the cantle behind him for the first time since coming to Lucia's spread. His Henry rifle was saddle-sheathed, and he wore his new pistol, the Colt .45 Single Action Army Peacemaker, in the holster on his right hip. True to his old ways, he kept the Baby Colt Dragoon in the hidden pocket at the bottom of his duster. On the other side he kept a piece of flint rock to balance out the weight. The gun had saved his life on more than one occasion, the rock not so much, unless you counted the many fires it had started for him out on the frigid cold nights of the trail.

The ride ahead would be a long one. He could cover no more than fifty miles a day, and even that was getting to be a press for the old mare, Trouble. Yet, if he was to make up time on the *Pee Otter* boy, he'd have to drive her hard.

Cord decided to break the ride up into three pieces. Austin was a hard two days' ride from Lucia's spread near San Antone, then from Austin to Waco was about the same. The last hundred miles or so up to Fort Worth would take two days more. He feared he might run the pads off River's paws, but deep down knew nothing short of a rattler strike would keep that dog from being left behind.

Along the two days of trail to Austin, Cord thought heavy on Lucia's last minute change of heart, and all the comfort she had lavished upon him in those last coupla' hours. It more than made up for what she denied him over the last several weeks. Funny how a woman's spite can turn to a spate of pleasure when there's a farewell involved.

Cord hoped Lucia would be fine. Now that word was getting out, the cattleman Vaughn Anders was sure to send some of his hands down to her cabin looking for him, so it was best he was away riding the trails. But would Anders' men get violent with the girl? Cord could only hope not, but these rough trailhands could be unpredictable.

Vaughn Anders was one of the founders of the Drovers' Exchange, the outfit that Cord had worked for ever since leaving his homestead in Kansas after his wife's death. Cord had made his way south on Trouble along the Chisholm Trail. He soon earned his pay tracking bandits who had rustled heads of cattle away from the Exchange's herds driving north. He brought in most of these bandits lifelessly draped over Trouble or some pack horse's back. All of which pleased the Exchange just fine.

They had paid Cord handsomely for doing their dirty work. If there was one thing cattlemen took very personally, it was some lazy-ass marauders rustling a few heads from their herds. It was too expensive for any single cattleman to pay for an enforcer, but when they all banded together as the Drover's Exchange, they could afford to hire a man like Cord McCullough to protect their various interests. This was exactly what he'd done for them for over a decade along the Chisholm Trail.

Vaughn Anders had been impressed by Cord's work for the Exchange, but that changed abruptly after that cattleman's son was shot in an argument during a card game. Vaughn's boy accused his opponent of cheating and was cut down in the gunplay that followed. Anders flew into a rage over his boy's death and sent one of his ranch hands to kill the shooter. But that wasn't near enough revenge for the cattleman. The murderer had gotten his gun from the Stone Canyon Gang - an old ball and cap Colt Navy Six converted by their gunsmith to a breechloader.

In his grief, Anders wanted revenge against that gang, but most especially the man who had smithed the gun that killed his son. Cord was dispatched to clear out the Stone Canyon Gang and to "retire" their gunsmith. He located the *Hacienda* the gang worked out of up by Silver Creek and wiped them all out. All except for that gunsmith. He came to learn the old-timer had been forced to work for them against his will. Cord just could not kill the man.

His clemency made no sense to Anders, who was furious. His son dead, he wanted frontier justice. Not only had Cord not killed the gunsmith, but had allowed the man to escape away back east. Anders swore no matter how long it took, he would hunt down Cord McCullough and take his life in exchange. He would have his revenge.

As far as Cord was concerned, Anders would be doing him a favor. After the tragic death of his wife, Cord's life was nothing but a wretched affair. He knew he could never bring himself to put a gun to his own head to end it that way, so instead he decided to satisfy his death-wish by putting himself in situations where he more than half-expected to die. Yet, that only taught him he was more skilled in killing other men than in getting himself killed.

So now, once again, Cord would ride the trails of the open countryside. He would rescue this Polish boy and return him south, after which he thought he might head off to the Cross Timbers country. That vertical line of forest ran north from Texas, up through Oklahoma and into Southern Kansas. It would give him cover. Anders might never find him so long as he kept moving, he reckoned. If Anders somehow did catch up to him, Cord figured he deserved to die for all the sins he had committed in his life.

After the first two days, the trio of Cord, Trouble and River made Austin. The town was busy, and perhaps a bit too much so for Cord's liking. He rode out of town a piece and made a trail camp alongside the Colorado River. There, he lay on the ground next to a small campfire in his unfurled bedroll, looking up at a canopy of unending stars overhead. Cord realized just how badly he had missed all this. The night's breath came on a brisk breeze, and River curled up next to him as the camp fire crackled. The scene reminded Cord of when he had nursed that dog back to health alongside another riverbank, the Cimarron's.

As Cord drifted off to sleep, he could not help thinking back even further, of his wife, Callie, and the terror upon her face when she lay dying in his arms. This had haunted him ever since that awful day twelve years ago when their Kansas farm was burned to the ground.

In the peaceful scatter of stars sprinkled overhead against the indigo sky, he thought he could hear Callie say, *Cord, I forgive you. So forgive yourself. The best way to do that is to turn your life around to help others in need.*

Under that thick swirl of heavenly lights overhead, Cord promised Callie that he would restart his wretched existence by saving this Polish teen from his own stubborn-headed search for his abducted sister. Though the girl was already lost, the mother would be forever thankful to have back her son, her only remaining child. Cord professed he would renew his own life starting with that simple act.

The next morning Cord, River and Trouble broke camp early and began their two day push up to Waco. It proved to be a peaceful and beautiful ride. Cord felt the Texas landscape open wide before him like the embrace of an old friend. But even old friends should welcome each other with a drink, he figured, and Cord made a deal with himself. When the three of them reached Waco, he would take care of the dog and the horse, and wander into the closest saloon he could find to buy himself a bottle of whiskey. The priest, Father Jerzy, had said, after all, that these funds could be used to cover expenses. Cord could figure nothing to be more necessary an expense to the completion of this task than some Texas *budge,* for medicinal purposes, he reckoned.

After another two days of hard riding, Cord set up camp just outside of Waco. He found a spot along the Brazos with enough grass for Trouble, hobbled her, and instructed River to stay and watch over the mare. Then he walked the quarter mile or so to the saloon he had spotted earlier when searching for a place to bed down. All he wanted was a bottle to ease the sting of being in the saddle for the two hundred miles they had covered over four days.

To procure his hooch, Cord soon found the Dry Creek Saloon. The place was not much to look at, inside or out. It was not more than a country log cabin with no signage. Had it not had the recognizable bat-wing doors, he might have mistaken it for just another settler's home.

When he pushed through those swinging doors, all eyes raised to stare at him. Inside, Cord saw no piano, no stage, just a rough oak bar and in its old mirror's reflection, a half dozen tables filled with men drinking for no other reason than to get drunk. They watched him walk over to the bar. When he ordered a bottle of *budge* from the bartender, he drew more than merely odd looks.

"You want a whole bottle of whiskey?" asked the barman, as if the purchase was outlawed in those parts.

"Yeah, and sometime while the moon's still shining, at that," Cord chirped at him. He pulled a single gold coin from the dusty pouch that Father Jerzy had given him. Then he slipped the cloth sack back into a pocket of his britches.

"Well, we got ourselves a big spender here, e'er'body," a voice called out in a mocking tone from one of the tables behind him. "Stranger, if ya' got 'nuff coin for a whole bottle of *budge,* I reckon ya' got 'nuff to buy me and my *pardner* a drink or two. Hell, maybe even a couple o' rounds for the whole house. Whadya' say, friend?"

Cord glanced into the half-corroded silvered glass behind the bar. The man speaking walked towards him while his *"pardner"* rose upright behind the table. Both were armed, but neither reached for their gun at that point. Cord could also see three men at the table nearest the front door slip out through it, fearing that gunplay was to follow. Cord remained calm; he did not turn to face the man as he neared. Instead, his eye tracked him in the mirror.

"Leave the man alone, Johnnie," the bartender said. "I don't want no trouble here in my place."

"Ain't no trouble at all," the man, Johnnie, said, as he walked up directly behind Cord, "so long as our guest here is hospitable and shares his wealth a bit."

Cord watched as the barman reached for something under the bar, most likely a scattergun. His hands had been clearly trembling before they disappeared under the bar's oaken surface. Cord could see the second man in the mirror undoing the hammer loop on his gun, so it could be drawn out quickly. The rest of the room had become like a pen full of scared sheep. Everybody realized that once the slugs started flying, there was no telling who might be hit.

Cord figured that the time had come to address the situation. When the barman placed the bottle and an empty glass on the counter near him, only then did Cord turn to slowly face these two trouble-making ramrods - *"Johnnie"* and his *"pardner."*

"Barkeep," Cord said loudly, "whadya' charge for a shot of whiskey in this place?" As he asked, he reached back for the glass with his empty left hand.

"A dime," the barman answered over Cord's shoulder.

"I figured as much." Cord stared hard into the eyes of the man Johnnie who had started all this business. He and his *"pardner"* were only twenty or so years old, each a good ten years younger than Cord. He then asked Johnnie, "Son, ya' had any schoolin' in 'rithmatic?"

"Don't call me son, y'old goat," answered Johnnie. "Y'ain't man enough to be my paw. He schooled me in bein' a man, in bein' tough, not in no damned useless fancy numbers."

Cord picked up the glass with his left hand and held it up to the oil lamp, rolling it in his hand as if it were cut crystal that might catch the light in some fascinating way.

"I much as figured yer paw never had ya' schooled proper," Cord said only to further agitate him, "so allow me. A shot of whiskey is called *'a shot'* because it costs about the same as a bullet - ten cents. A cowboy, if he's lucky, makes a dollar a day on a cattle drive. That's the same as only ten bullets or ten shots a day. So if ya' figure on puttin' two bullets in me for two rounds of *budge,* ya' might as well just pay for them drinks yourself."

"I figure to only need one shot," Johnnie said.

Cord slowly pulled back his duster with his right hand and hooked it behind his holster to show the Colt Peacemaker. "Now, I can pay ya' fellas yer two shots," he said as his voice stiffened, "in either whisky or lead, but the choice will be mine, not yers. Either way it cost me just the same, don't it? Ya' still want your couple o' shots each?"

In a swift, deft motion of his left hand he flung the empty glass at Johnnie's head while his right hand pulled and cocked his Colt. The man Johnnie had instinctively tried to bat away the flying glass and failed to even reach for his weapon. In being caught so exposed, he became timid as a sheep. His *"pardner"* had also failed to go for his gun. Cord stared him down, daring him to do so.

"I asked ya' a question, son," Cord repeated to Johnnie tersely, "do ya' boys still want yer two shots?"

A tension stretched across the saloon that everyone felt. As Johnnie looked down the barrel of the Peacemaker, Cord saw the bravado in his eyes melt into cold hard fear.

"A man who asks a question twice deserves an answer," Cord said in a clipped voice.

Johnnie stammered, *"Nnnoo, mista,* I reckon we don't any more."

"I thought not," Cord replied.

Cord continued to stare over Johnnie's shoulder at his *"pardner,"* assuring he made no move for his gun. He did not. *Pardner* merely dropped his hand slack, away from the weapon. Cord only then uncocked his Colt.

He said loudly to Johnnie, "Now git yer ass back at that table, beside yer *"pardner"* before I change my mind. Once yer both sittin' on yer brains, go ahead and hand me over yer guns."

Johnnie stumbled slowly to the table next to his *"pardner."* The men sat themselves down and slowly handed over their revolvers.

Cord, with his gun still drawn, but no longer cocked, watched them carefully. He followed Johnnie over to the table, then yelled out over his shoulder, "Barkeep, these youngsters had a good idea. Go ahead and set up the house with two shots o' *budge* for every fella in here. My friend Johnnie here and his *pardner* will be pickin' up the cost of it. Countin' these two, I'm figurin' fifteen heads."

Cord picked up the two revolvers, both cap and ballers. One was an old Colt Navy Six, the other a five round Remington New Model Police. Cord walked the guns over to the bar, and slid them across to the bartender. The barkeep picked them up, and looked at them with no idea what to do with them as Cord holstered his own gun.

"Barkeep, hold on to these boys' hoglegs. If they can't muster up the three dollars to pay for these two rounds on the house, sell off their guns. Even these relics should bring many times that. And should they want them back, remind them I'll track down and kill the both 'em."

"Damn, that draw was fast!" someone from one of the tables yelled out, piercing the tense silence that had settled over the bar. It being broken, a noisy commotion slowly buzzed up through the place.

Johnnie and his *pardner* sat stone cold silent as the laughter became louder and rolled through the saloon. They looked like school boys being punished in the corner, all they needed was the dunce caps.

"That sure as hell was a quick draw," agreed the barman. "I ain't never seen anyone stand up to those two like that." Then, in not much more than a whisper, he asked, "Who the hell you figure to be, mister?"

The question brought a flush of pride over Cord.

"Cord McCullough," he answered in a moment of weakness, having soaked in the man's flattery.

"Well, I'll be," the bartender said after a letting out a loud, high whistle. "I figured ya' to be somebody I'd heard of by the way ya' handled them two thugs, but Cord McCullough, *the Curse of the Chisholm Trail*, himself, right here in my saloon. Go ahead and take this gold piece back, your bottle is on the house."

"The what of what trail?" Cord asked in disbelief.

"*Curse of the Chisholm Trail,*" the barman repeated. "Ya' not know that's what folks been callin' ya'?"

"No," Cord answered. "I had no notion of that."

The barman slid the gold coin that Cord had given him as payment for the whiskey back to his guest. As Cord took the bottle and pushed through the batwings into the chilled night air, he could hear the barman shout out, "Hey, everybody, that there was Cord McCullough, the Curse of the Chisholm Trail, puttin' on a show right here in my li'l Dry Creek Saloon. 'Magine that!"

Chapter 4: Trouble in Hell's Half Acre

Fort Worth, Texas

Cord, Trouble and River came up from the south as they entered Fort Worth. They had been seven days on the trail by then. The first two days they had made Austin, the second two just beyond Waco. But the bottle of whiskey Cord had earned for his heroics in the Dry Creek Saloon ended up slowing him down, forcing him to get too late of a start the next day.

With the late start, it took them the better part of three days to make Fort Worth from Waco. Cord reckoned that was not the worst thing to happen as he had been pushing Trouble and River, and to be completely honest, himself, pretty hard up to that point. The only problem was that this meant the boy *"Pee Otter"* was still a couple if not three days ahead of him. Cord knew that the boy had just enough time to get himself in some serious trouble, and that his own travels could easily end with a visit to that town's notorious Hell's Half Acre. There, he would need all his wits about him, as the cowboys in the Acre wouldn't scare off quite so easily as the bar hacks in Waco. Cord would have to be on top of his game if he needed to rescue the boy from his own hard-headed stupidity.

Cord felt guilty for having given his name during the little showdown at the Waco saloon. It was stupid, he knew, but he was feeling so full of himself after being out on the trail again. After scaring off those two ramrods so easily, he wanted perhaps a bit too badly to be recognized by some fellow men. It felt especially good after being holed up all winter on that spread down south with Lucia.

Yeah, Lucia. Cord hoped his display of pride would not lead to her eventual downfall. If Vaughn Anders' sent his trailhands down south looking for him, after not finding him, they might take their frustrations out on the girl. Cord knew once that got started, it could lead to some dark consequences for her. All he could do about it now was to hope such trouble would never come to pass.

Late on the third day Cord entered Fort Worth proper. Once there, he headed for the address Father Jerzy had given him. The priest had sent a message ahead by telegraph to the home of one of the city's pre-eminent Catholics named Augustus Mueller. This was where young Piotr was to be staying. Mueller was a transplanted Bavarian from some place called "the Black Forest," which sounded to Cord like some made-up place from a fairy tale. Mueller had been told to detain the boy. The German was relieved to greet Cord, who arrived just as darkness was beginning to fall over the town.

Mueller's home was on Throckmorton and 11th Streets. It was a simple clapboard house with a small stable on an adjacent lot. It was only a very short walk away from the bars of the Hell's Half Acre carousing district.

"Where have you been, Mr. McCullough?" asked Mueller after greeting his guest. "I was expecting you yesterday, based on the telegram from Father Jerzy."

"We ran into a little issue in Waco that delayed us a bit," Cord said, referring to the bottle of *budge* by then long gone. "But Trouble, River and I are all here now, safe and sound. Where is the *'Pee Otter'* boy?"

A strange look came over Mueller's face.

"That is the problem, Mr. McCullough," Mueller confessed, "Piotr has gone into the Acre again tonight. He was to meet some men there who said they would give him his sister in exchange for one hundred dollars in gold."

"I thought ya' was to hold him here?" Cord said.

"He's a handful," Mueller replied, "far too young and strong for me to keep him here against his will."

"He has a hundred dollars?" Cord squinted at the German, as if measuring the man with his eyes. Mueller's clothes were plain and threadbare, as humble as was his spread. There was no way, Cord figured, that the Bavarian had a hundred dollars to give to the boy.

"No, of course not," Mueller replied, "Piotr has only one double eagle, all he had left when he arrived here three nights ago. Thinks he can trick these men to see her."

"Damn it!" Cord held the German in contempt in his thoughts. *Had this man not realized the danger he had allowed the boy to walk off into?* "He won't see his sister alive. Damn fool kid is likely to git hisself killed tonight. It's a set-up. No one takin' her captive would be dumb enough to bring her into the Acre. First place the law will look for her. These men likely heard the boy askin' round after her and figured him to be an easy mark to take a hundred dollars from. When they find out he's only got twenty, they're likely to kill him just outta spite. Where was he to meet them, exactly?"

"I don't know," Mueller said, "Piotr did not say."

"Damn it all to hell!" Cord cursed, realizing the sleep he had looked forward to would have to wait. "Take care of my horse, will ya'? River and I better go and look after this *Pee Otter* right quick. We can walk it from here."

"Piotr appears to be a fine boy" Mueller said in his thick German accent. "He just wants his sister to be safe, in the worst way."

"Yeah, and he's goin' bout it in exactly that - the worst way," Cord answered. "He's about as far out of his element as anyone can git."

Later that night in the Acre, Piotr sat at the front bar just inside the stenciled window of a saloon called *The Keg*. It was a rough and tumble gathering spot known to draw some of the most notorious of the town's lesser citizens. The boy awaited two men who the night before had said they could deliver his sister to him. They claimed to be acquaintances of those who had held up the stage coach.

The saloon was as wild a place as Piotr had ever seen. Liquor flowed like rancid water. The patrons around him were in various levels of drunken stupor. The saloon kept a live panther caged in the middle of the place, and every so often a customer who had become a little too drunk would forget himself and lean up against its cage. The panther did not take lightly to this, and was known to take a few swipes of flesh in revenge. The blood of those unfortunates proudly stained the nearest wall, and was left there uncleansed, like the sins of all who entered the joint.

Piotr sat at that front bar, cutting a pathetic figure. His clothes were weatherworn and soiled with the stains of the south Texas earth. His boots were those of a farmer, worn-through in places and heavily mended. His hat was a tattered number, scarcely enough of a thing to shade his face from the sun. He stood out like a cactus in a rose garden, or more accurately, given the situation, a potato amidst a field of Old Mexico agaves.

Piotr nursed his beer as he waited for the two men to arrive. He had a sporting gal working on him for a while, offering him pleasures he never dreamed of if he would just come upstairs with her. Her face was dusted white as an Easter lily. *That was where all the biblical comparisons ended,* the boy thought, *unless you considered Sodom and Gomorrah or the treachery of Lot's daughters.* But after a bit, the sporting gal left him there alone, figuring him to not be worth the effort, meaning either not having the funds required or the inclination to depart with them. She walked off to seek out other, drunker patrons.

All Piotr wanted was to get his sister back and return to *Panna Maria.* He just wanted to find her, to save her from a life of debauchery such as this woman was leading. Then Piotr shuddered from a truly awful thought. *If I fail in rescuing Kalina, then her ending up a sportin' gal was about the best she had to hope for. Whatever the Comanches would do with her was sure to be much worse.*

Piotr patiently waited for the two men to arrive. They had said the night before that the robbers would be satisfied with five double eagles to ransom the girl's safe return. The boy had only one in his trouser pocket, but figured it to be enough to buy him a glance at Kalina. After which, he thought, he could cut a deal with these bandits to pay the rest later.

The Polish teen had tried to get the rest of the funds from Mueller, who said he was sorry but he had no money to offer. He had recently bought the house and two lots at Throckmorton Street. He hoped to sell them as the site for the city's first Catholic church. Until that happened, Mueller was flat busted, forced to take on boarders to rent his rooms just to make ends meet. Piotr had been lucky to get his last vacant room to sleep in the past few nights.

Piotr had even tried all day to sell his horse, but no one in town would pay anything above a rendering price for the worn-out animal. Still, he was relieved not to sell her. He'd need the animal to take Kalina home to *Panna Maria.*

Piotr sat at the bar, a gold piece in his pocket and just enough other change to pay for the beer he nursed while he waited. He was not used to its taste, as his family made only vodkas from potatoes and rye grain raised especially for that purpose. That clear spirit he had tasted many times. Once over an Easter holiday, his uncle had given him too much. Piotr came to know what it was to be drunk. All around him here now, men were readily willing to pay the fare to escape, to steal away to that altered world.

The night darkened outside before the two men Piotr awaited entered the bar. They sauntered up on either side of the teen, wedging him in at his seat. Little did Piotr realize they had been watching him for the past hour through the bar's large stenciled window.

"You got the money, kid?" the tougher looking of the two asked. His face was etched with canyons of sun wrought wrinkles. *Looks to have been on the trail all his life,* the boy had thought upon first meeting him the night before. *His face looks like a mask made of leather.*

"Yes, I have it," Piotr lied.

"Okay, then, hand it over," said the younger of them, a small grimy man, who stretched out his filthy palm.

"Where is my sister, Kalina?" Piotr asked. "I need to first see my sister."

"Our friend has her just down the street in one of the stables," the younger man said, "you can not only see her, but ya' can take her home with ya', just as soon as ya' count out them five double eagles, boy."

"Not until I see my sister," Piotr replied without a single hitch in his voice. "I'll give you the hundred just as soon as I can see she's all right. Safe and untouched. Ain't no tellin' what you all might have done to her."

The two men looked at each other, as if they were weighing whether or not to agree to the boy's condition. Then, one smirked at the other, and they turned to Piotr.

"All the better," said the leather-faced man with a smile. "C'mon kid, we'll walk down there with ya'. You'll see her, then we'll collect the cash and everyone goes their own way, all happy like. Let's go see yer sister."

The three of them exited the swinging saloon doors onto the street and walked south. Then the two men began to walk across a series of vacant lots over to Rusk Street.

"I thought you said the livery stable was just down the street?" Piotr said, stopping in his tracks along the edge of the relatively well-lit Main Street. He knew better than to walk off into the darkness of the vacant lots.

"Y'ain't been in the Acre very long, boy," said the younger of the two men. "Ain't nothin' further down Main Street 'cept for more bars and whores' cribs. Best ya' follow us to the stables right now, or your sister might soon enough be working out of one or the other. She's just the right age to begin her career, now ain't she?"

Something about the lewd comment told Piotr these men had never laid eyes on Kalina. If they had, they would have known the joke wasn't funny at all. She was too precious, too innocent a girl to ever lead that type of life. Still, they tried to lure him off the street into the darkness. Piotr finally said to them, "I don't think either of you has my sister at all. I'm not following you another step."

As he said this, he felt the barrel of something he thought too large to be a pistol pressed into his back. From behind him, he heard a new voice - darker, grittier and unfamiliar - say, "Walk, my friend, or I'll blow a hole in ya' wide enough to turn a team of horses around in."

The gun barrel in his back pushed him forward into the darkness of the empty lot toward the two other men. After twenty yards or so, the third man, still unseen, pressed the gun barrel harder into Piotr's back.

"Son, ya' came to yer senses all but a little too late. Now it's best fer ya' to turn over them gold pieces."

Piotr nervously pulled the sole double eagle out of his pocket and handed it over to the leather-faced man. The weight of only the single coin shocked the thug.

"What the hell is this?" he cried out as it was pressed in his palm. "It's just twenty dollars. Where the hell's the rest?"

"You didn't think I'd be stupid enough to bring it all at once and have y'all take it and still run off with Kalina, now, did you? I got the rest in a safe enough place!"

The gun barrel pulled away from the small of his back and the butt end of the revolver crashed down hard upon the floppy farm hat on his head. The force of the blow felled Piotr forward into the dirt, leaving his skull feeling as though it was split wide open.

The leather-faced man bent down over the fallen boy to pat him down. Afterwards, he held up the lone gold coin, and Piotr heard him yell, "This, what he give me, is all he's got. C'mon, let's skat. What a waste of a night."

"Hold on, now," the younger, filthier man said, "this mamma's boy made us look like a bunch of dang fools. I say we leave him with something more than just a headache to remember us by. Maybe a finger or two missing to always remind him not to mess with them that are his betters." The young man flicked open a blade.

Piotr lay on the ground, still clutching his head when the younger man bent down over him with the knife. He grabbed Piotr's wrist and said, "Which two fingers will ya' miss least, boy? I'll give the courtesy of pickin' 'em."

At that point a sound rang out in the darkness from just about a foot or so away from the blade of the knife. It was the distinct sound of coins clinking together as the black cloth sack tied off with the festive red and white ribbon hit the ground. Not one of the three could see it in the darkness, but they all could hear it. The sound was of cold hard coins striking each other - the rattle of greed.

"The boy told y'all he had the rest safely tucked away," Cord McCullough said from behind them all, "and there it is. Now, before any o' y'all is dumb enough to go fer yer guns or reach for that money sack, we got to git something straight between us. Y'all tell the boy ya' don't have his sister, and then y'all can take the money and go."

Piotr lay on the ground, clutching his throbbing head. Above him, the third man who had pistol-whipped the kid, slowly cocked back the hammer of his revolver. The click might as well been a stick of that new-fangled dynamite going off for all the commotion it caused.

Cord yelled out, "River!" along with a gesture of his free hand. The growling dog pounced from the darkness. It leapt at the man clutching the pistol and took the wrist of his gun hand into its mouth. The man fired off a shot into the hollow of the night hitting nothing. The dog wrestled the gun free and then dragged him to the ground.

As this happened, the young man over Piotr raised his knife as if to stab the boy. Cord McCullough brushed back his trail duster and in a single fluid motion pulled and fired his Colt .45 revolver. The bullet found the ground just next to the filthy, younger one's boot and his knife froze.

"If yer thinkin' I missed ya' with that warning shot, then ya' need not drop that knife," Cord warned, "ya' sure enough will when the next round finds yer chest."

The young man quickly released the blade.

That left only the leather-faced man. In the moonlight, Cord McCullough could barely make him out. He moved stealthily to retrieve the sack of coins on the ground. Cord spotted him going for it and fired off his next shot in its direction, kicking up a spray of dirt over the black sack, stopping the sun-leached bastard in his tracks.

"That's enough," McCullough said. "Leave the coins where they lie. I'm feeling generous tonight, fellas. So all y'all are free to git on out of here empty-handed."

Cord called off River, who released the bleeding wrist of the gunman. The man caught his breath before starting to look for his dropped revolver.

"Leave that too," Cord said, "it's mine now."

"The hell I will," the man said, "I just got that gun."

"Ya' want me to have the dog retrieve it fer ya' then?" The man with the bloody, gnawed wrist shut his trap as Cord again said, "The three of y'all git on out of here."

"Hey, mister," the leather-faced man called, "your dog done chewed up our friend's arm here right good. He's bleedin' somethin' fierce."

The man held his arm, drenched black in the moonlight with blood.

"Than ya' best git' 'im to a doctor," Cord said. "Maybe he'll think twice before he ever again presses his iron in on anyone else from behind."

"Wait a minute," Piotr hollered out as he took to his feet and moved toward the leather-faced man. The boy reached into his pocket and extracted the double eagle coin.

"Grab that black sack of coins and the other one's knife while yer at it, kid," Cord yelled out. Piotr did so.

"What about Kalina?" The teen then asked. "Don't let them go. Have them take us to her, mister."

Cord waited for a response, but the trio that had assaulted Piotr stayed mum.

"Tell him," Cord said, pointing the gun at the leather-faced man in the moonlight. "I still got four rounds which is one more than I need for the three of y'all. Tell the boy the truth or each and every one of y'all will be bleedin' from somewhere new in a second or two."

No one spoke. Cord then cocked back his hammer.

"We ain't got yer sister, kid," said the dirty one, the youngest of them. "We just heard y'askin' round after her in the Acre. Ya' looked so damn gullible. We figured it to be easy money. That is till your friend here come along. We never figured on anyone gettin' hurt."

"No," Cord corrected him. "Ya' just never figured on any of y'all getting hurt. But cuttin' up this boy a bit, that just might be fun, huh?"

Cord then told Piotr to reach down at his feet for the liberated revolver. The boy moved slowly until he found it, with Cord never taking his eyes, or for that matter, his gun's barrel off the three men, who by then had all drifted together into a single close clutch of misery.

"I got it," Piotr said. "It's massive."

"Come on, kid," Cord said, "we gotta git out of here. We're 'ginnin' to draw a crowd."

The saloons on Main Street had indeed emptied out after the gunfire had started. A throng lined the street along the empty lot. Cord and Piotr brushed their way into the crowd and River followed after them.

"Aren't you afraid of them fellas coming after us, mister?" Piotr asked.

"They ain't the type," Cord said. "See how fast they all froze up once the real action started? They're just a trio of hustlers out for a quick score. Nope, I figure they had enough for one night. Still the young one would've enjoyed cuttin' ya' up just for spite. Let me see that gun."

Piotr handed Cord the enormous weapon. He stopped under the light of a street lamp to inspect it closely.

"Well, I'll be damned," Cord said, "it's an old LeMat Grapeshot Revolver. I ain't seen one of these since the war. That fella didn't lie to ya', this here could have blown a hole in ya' big 'nuff to turn a team of horses round in. This is the gun that General Beauregard's son-in-law designed and had made up in Paris, France. See, it says so in this fancy script right here on top. It was all the rage among the Confederate officers, yet despite that only a few hundred of them were ever delivered to the Rebs. It's a collector's item. Just never proved out to be too much of a reliable weapon for warfare though."

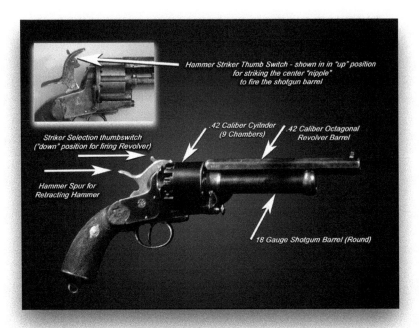

Hammer Striker Thumb Switch - shown in in "up" position
for striking the center "nipple"
to fire the shotgun barrel

.42 Caliber Cyilnder
(9 Chambers)

.42 Caliber Octagonal
Revolver Barrel

Striker Selection thumbswitch
("down" position for firing Revolver)

Hammer Spur for
Retracting Hammer

18 Gauge Shotgum Barrel (Round)

Figure 2: The LeMat Cap & Ball Revolver

"Why not?" Piotr asked. "All those rebel generals must have liked it for some reason. Sure looks pretty enough."

"I give ya' that," Cord replied, "but guns are like gals. It ain't always the pretty ones who are the best for ya. This one had some nice features goin' fer it, sure. For one, it carried nine chambers on its cylinder instead of only six. That's handy, but in .42 caliber that made this gun so big it weighs almost as much as a Colt's Dragoon. Ya' wanna try aimin' to hit a Yankee comin' dead on the run at ya' with four pounds of iron weight pullin' down at yer wrist? I don't think so. Also, those nine chambers were so close together that they was known to sometimes chain-fire."

"What's that?" Piotr asked. "What's a chain-fire?"

"It's when firing one bullet sets off more than just the one round, maybe all of them at once," Cord answered. "Very dangerous for whoever might be pullin' the trigger."

"And what's this?" the boy asked pointing to the big round barrel just below the octagonal main barrel.

"That's the part for blowin' a hole in yer hide. A full eighteen gauge scattergun. That big round barrel fires birdshot or buckshot, dependin' what yer stuffin' it with. Ya' just flip this thumb switch on the top of the hammer up and when ya' pull the trigger, it strikes down on the firin' nipple of that center barrel and *ka-boom!* But ya best be close, cause that short barrel scatters the shot like feathers on the wind after only a few feet."

"How on earth do you know all this?" Piotr asked. "Who exactly are you, mister?"

"I know a bit 'bout guns. As to who I am, let's just say I am a friend of *Father Yerzy, Pee Otter.*" Cord could see the boy's face react sourly to his pronunciation of his name. A quirky sense of satisfaction registered within Cord.

"My name is *Piotr,*" the boy said defiantly, "it is Polish and pronounced *Pyota.*" He pronounced his name that second time with an exaggerated lilt. Until that point, Cord had noticed the boy's English was overall very good, with only a light accent, unlike *Father Yerzy*, but when he pronounced his own name it became drenched with the pride and rhythm of the old country.

"Thats just what I said, *Pee Otter,*" Cord answered, having his fun agitating the boy with his flat tone.

"I ask again, who are you?" Piotr repeated. "So you say Father Jerzy sent you? What is your name?"

"Cord McCullough," he answered proudly.

"Never heard of you," replied Piotr.

"Well, I reckon ya' should just be thankful that *Father Yerzy* had."

They walked back to Augustus Mueller's spread on Throckmorton Street on the outer edge of the Acre. Cord watched River who trailed behind them. He knew how the dog would react had they been followed. They were not.

"Don't worry, that bunch won't bother us no more," Cord said to Piotr, who kept looking over his own shoulder. "They would have done ya' harm, no doubt, but a few rounds fired and they scattered quicker than their dreams of sportin' gals to spend that easy hundred dollars gold on."

"Yeah. Good thing you're some kinda trick-shot, mister," Piotr answered. "I guess you did scare 'em off something good. Where'd you learn to shoot like that, anyhow?"

"In the war, I figure," Cord answered, "but I always was handy with a gun."

"Did you fight in any battles?" Piotr asked him. "Kill anyone?"

"I fought in only one battle," Cord answered, "at Shiloh." He decided not to answer the question on killing other men, as it was at that battle that he first saw the senseless taking of life. To this day he still could not make sense of all the men he had killed since.

"Just the one battle? Why? Did you get hurt bad?"

"No," Cord answered, "I deserted. I couldn't stand that kind of senseless slaughter in the taking of other men's lives, whether they be our own or even Yankees. Even them Yanks were still just boys, like me. I reckon it just didn't sit well with the way I was reared."

"So you're a war deserter? Makes you a coward then," Piotr judged. "A trick-shot and a coward. No wonder you didn't shoot none of them men back there. You couldn't stomach the bloodshed, could you?"

"I ain't no coward, son," Cord said, "and I didn't shoot no one back there in the Acre cause it wasn't needed. Them boys scared off with no bloodshed. Always best to finish something with no blood lost unless it can't be avoided."

"When I find that man that took my little sister, Kalina," Piotr said, "there'll be plenty of blood shed to pay for what he done. Every drop of his."

"There very well may," mused Cord, "but not by yer hand, and not soon. Tomorrow, yer gonna be headin' back south to *Panna Maria,* from whence ya' come. That's why *Father Yerzy* sent me after ya'. I got my job to finish."

"No, I will not go with you," the Polish teen resisted. "I am not leaving here until I find my sister."

"Ya' best face up to the fact that yer sister Kalina is as good as gone," Cord said. "Them Comanches are known to raid and take pretty young girls to raise as their own. Ya' ever heard of the Parker Fort Raid? Of Cynthia Ann Parker and her cousin, Rachel Plummer, bein' taken off?"

Piotr and just about every Texas schoolboy knew all about that famous raid, even though it took place back in 1836, long before his own birth, almost two decades before his people had ever came over from Poland. In fact, most every pioneer family knew of it, and of the ferocity that the Indians had unleashed on that peaceful group of settlers.

"Yeah," Piotr said, "I know of it. The Comanche, along with some Kiowas, Caddos and Wichita braves attacked them. What's that got to do with us?"

"Them Injuns come up to that family's wilderness fort under the white flag of peace while the men folk of the Parker and Plummer families was working out in the fields. They was outside the protection of their fort's fifteen foot high wooden palisades. The fort's gates were wide open when them savages neared and asked for water."

Cord paused for effect before he went on. "When the family went to provide them some, them Injuns threw down the white flag and attacked. They got inside the open fort and killed five of the frontier men, cutting them up with the most brutal savagery imaginable. They attacked one of the older women right there inside the fort in front of everyone. In all, after many were slaughtered, five women and children were taken captive, including the two young girls. Miss Rachel Plummer was just seventeen," Cord drew his words out slowly, trying to shock the boy, "and Miss Cynthia Ann Parker was but nine years old."

"And they were both rescued," Piotr argued. "Ransomed. At least that's how Rachel Plummer was rescued two years later in '38. But I'm not waiting that long. I'm going after my sister, Kalina, now."

"My point is them girls and the others was taken deep into Comanche country." Cord stressed. "Sure, that Plummer girl was rescued, after them savages all had their way with her for near two years. She was sold off for horses to them New Mexico *Comancheros* who trade guns and liquor to the Comanches. By the time Rachel was ransomed by the *Comancheros* to a family in Santa Fe, she had suffered unspeakable abuse by both the Comanches and *Comancheros* alike. My point is there's no hopin' to find yer sister, as I'm sure she's already been taken deep into Comanche country by now." Cord let the thought of chasing after her seep into the boy's thick skull.

But the trailhand could soon see his strategy had backfired. It was exactly what the young boy did not want to hear, and only fired him up all the more. Piotr refused to believe his sister could not be saved, only that no one was brave enough to try.

"You don't know that for sure," Piotr screamed at him. "All I know is I am never gonna stop looking for my little sister. They eventually found Cynthia Ann Parker from that raid, didn't they? You know why? Because her family loved her and never stopped looking for her. I don't plan to stop, either! Certainly not before I even get started."

"Cynthia Ann Parker wasn't found until twenty-four *years* after she was taken," Cord answered. "And more by accident than her family's doin'. She was rescued at that *'Battle of Pease River,'* which was more of a massacre than a battle. Them Texas Rangers slaughtered a Comanche Chief and a bunch of Injun women and children as they were breakin' camp. The warriors had most all gone on ahead, as they tend to do, except for a few braves left behind with the chief. They were all butchered to pieces."

"It doesn't matter, does it?" Piotr said. "They still saved Cynthia Ann Parker."

"If ya' wanna call it bein saved." Cord felt like Piotr needed a dose of cruel reality. "By the time they realized they had found Cynthia Ann, she was already more Comanche than white woman. They only knew her to be a white woman by her blue eyes. She'd been married off to that dead chief and had bore him three children. Her youngest, a girl named *Prairie Flower,* was with her when she was *'rescued,'* so-called. No one knows what came of her two boys she put on a horse, but they likely escaped only to die out on the plains. The oldest was but twelve."

"What's your point?" Piotr asked. "Beside the fact that you're scared to go after them Comanches. Okay. I'm not. Just don't get in my way, mister."

Piotr was becoming visibly agitated with all this talk. Cord had intended only to show him how futile it would be to go after the girl, but instead had hardened the thought in the headstrong teen that he was his sister's only chance. Still, by then Cord felt like his main task was nearly complete. He had found and rescued the boy. Over the next few days he would babysit *Pee Otter* until he could arrange to get him back south.

"My point is yer maw needs ya' back in *Panna Maria,*" Cord said, "not off butcherin' Injuns in revenge like them Rangers done. I can see by yer eyes that yer seethin'. Ya' can't imagine the Texas Rangers doing something like what I just described? Well, I met a few of them Ranger boys while up on the Chisholm Trail. After a few fireside tugs on the jug, they'd shoot off their mouths about exactly what they done to them Injun squaws and kids at Pease River. They'd say, *'Ya' hadn't seen the savage things them Comanches did to those poor settlers at Fort Parker in '36, or the citizens of Victoria and Linnville in '40.'* Then they'd drink more to ease their conscience."

"I don't care!" Piotr exploded. "I don't care about what the Texas Rangers done to Indian squaws at the Pease River, or about any of those Comanche raids on white settler folk, neither. Those attacks were ages ago. Long before our people ever came here. and *Panna Maria* was ever settled. Ancient history. Besides, my sister wasn't taken on no Comanche raid. No, she was grabbed up during that stage coach robbery in Weatherford by a bandit that you *assume* to be half-Comanche. If you're not going to help me find her, then get outta my way and leave me to it."

The priest had said the boy was stubborn as a mule, and Piotr was proving to be every bit as hard-headed as what *Father Yerzy* had led Cord to believe.

"I'm just trying to show ya' what ya' might be in store for," Cord said. "Best ya' just do what yer maw and *Father Yerzy* want and go back home."

Piotr stopped in his tracks and looked squarely at Cord. "This is the last time I'll say this. I am no way going back to *Panna Maria* without Kalina. That much is final."

"I can make ya', boy," Cord threatened.

"Then get yourself ready to come and find me time and time again, because I will just run off once more each and every time you do, and keep doin' so until I find my little sister. If you're too much of a war desertin' coward to join me, then just leave me be. I'm not scared of a fight. Not even with a half-Comanche."

Cord let the coward insult run off him like the rain of a summer storm, but he could clearly see the stubborn streak in the boy harden into defiance. He feared it would get *Pee Otter* killed, and sometime in the very near future.

"Then ya' at least best stop looking in the Acre," Cord conceded. "Ya' won't find nuthin' else there but more trouble. That's fer sure."

Piotr looked at him, recognizing the slightest change in tone in this man sent after him. It was the first time he thought that this trailhand named Cord McCullough might just be inclined to help him.

"So, if not there, then where should I look to find her?" Piotr asked.

Cord grabbed at his stubbled chin as if in deep and reflective thought. Then, he decided to answer the teen.

"I reckon the most logical place to start is up in Weatherford," Cord said. "I'd git as much of the facts as I could gather, if I was ya'. I've come this far, I reckon I could ride out there with ya' to talk to the law."

"Settled!" Piotr declared. "First thing tomorrow, we set off for Weatherford. We'll talk to the sheriff there and see what he knows."

Piotr settled down somewhat after that. Cord had given in to the teen's request after he'd come to realize he'd have to hog tie Piotr to get him back south again, and even that would be a chore. Besides, Cord had grown curious himself as to what exactly had happened to the girl.

A quiet grew between them like an uneasy truce until they came just outside the door of Augustus Mueller's home. Piotr began to walk in when Cord reached out to grasp his arm, in effect saying, *just wait a minute here.*

"I been meaning to ask," Cord said, "what was yer little sister even doin' on that coach to Weatherford alone?"

"She wasn't alone," Piotr replied, "my mother said a retired Ranger was lookin' after her on the coach."

"Yeah," Cord acknowledged, "that was the old man who ended up giving his life for her. The one who first recognized the bandit to be half-Comanche. Why was she even goin' to Weatherford in the first place?"

"Kalina was on her way to be with our aunt," Piotr said. "She works on a quarter horse ranch up that way. After we talk to the sheriff, we can go over there and I can get myself a better horse for goin' west after Kalina."

Ya' won't need it, Cord thought. *I'll leave yer ass there with yer aunt and then I don't have to haul ya' all the way back south again to Panna Maria. Makes my life a hell of a lot simpler. And hers a lot harder, fer sure.*

Chapter 5: Calling on the Sheriff and Doc Blevins

Weatherford, Texas

"We ain't had a brouhaha like this in town here since as far back as anyone can remember," said the sheriff. "These bandits was bold as bluebonnets in bloom. Just pulled up a wagon in front of that stage coach right before it got to town. Yes, sirree, pretty damn bold. There was six of them in all, but the most fearsome of 'em surely was that half-breed that took the gal."

"How ya' so sure he was a half-breed?" Cord asked.

"One of the men killed was an old Texas Ranger," the sheriff explained, "Captain Dan Horton. Began Ranging when he was only twenty-three. He'd long been retired. He had business back in Fort Worth, but took the Weatherford stage anyway just to accompany the girl on to here. Was him that spotted the Comanche blood in that bandit. Captain said it was what set him off, when he asked the sonuva bitch in the Injun tongue if he was Comanche. The bandit slammed the old man to the ground, kicked him until most his ribs was shattered. Doc Blevins did what he could, but there was no saving Captain Horton."

"So, based only on the recognition of a seventy-some year old retired Texas Ranger," Cord followed up, "yer convinced this bandit was a half-breed?"

"No, not just that," the sheriff added, "Doc Blevins himself judged that bandit to be a half-breed, and I'd say any medical man got to be a good judge of that in these parts. Especially Doc Blevins, as he spent a lot of years in the US Cavalry as a medic, even rode with Kit Carson in the Battle of Adobe Walls back in '64. He settled down here in town a few years back. If anybody in Weatherford can spot an Injun', or for that matter a half-breed, I'd say Doc Blevins would be the best at it."

"And this doctor was on the stage coach?" asked the Polish teen in his softly accented voice.

"Whadya' say yer name was, son?" the sheriff asked in return.

"Piotr, sir."

"Well, *PEE-YAH-TA,*" the sheriff's mouth spit his name out painfully, like a woman given birth to triplets, "no, the good doctor was not on the stagecoach. Where d'ya say ya' and yer sister's people was from?"

"*Panna Maria*, outside San Antonio," the teen answered.

"I know that much from all the damn telegrams that came through after the holdup," said the sheriff, getting a little perturbed. "I meant where is it yer people come from originally? Where is yer Ol' Country?"

"Poland," Piotr answered. "My family and the others came over just in time for Christmas in '54."

The sheriff scratched his head and then re-directed his gaze at the boy. "I ain't never heard of no such a place as '*Poe-Land*'. Where is it?"

"Between Prussia, Russia, and Austria" Piotr said, his voice tinged with equal measures of accent and outrage.

"Huh!" The sheriff said, "didn't think there was anything between the three of 'em."

"Just greed," Piotr nearly spat at the lawman. "Those three empires stole our homeland from us. Sliced it up between them till nuthin' was left. Still, our culture lives in each Polish heart. We will win our lands back one day."

"Okay, but if ya' want 'em back so badly, then why are yer people running away from it by comin' over here? Go back to Europe where y'all come from and fight for it."

"How does this Doctor Blevins know the man who took my sister was half-Comanche?" Piotr demanded, ignoring the lawman's prejudice.

"Not till ya' tell me why your people come half way 'round the world to our good state of Texas, boy!"

"Sheriff," Cord interrupted, "can we git back to…"

"Ya' stay on out of this, McCullough, or I'll rustle up some John Doe paper that fits ya' to a tee and throw yer ass in one of these cells. Now, *Peeyata,* why'd yer people sail all the way over here from Europe? Bad enough we got Swedes, Czechs and are just 'bout drownin' in all type of Germans, now we got yer people, too."

"We come for the same reason as all the rest, Sheriff, " Piotr said. "Our people come for the land, and for the freedom and opportunity in this country. But not to have their children stolen by Indians. Now, how did this doctor get such a good look at this man who took Kalina?"

Cord was impressed with the boy's handling of the situation. The sheriff, on the other hand, was exasperated at Piotr's insolence and snapped, "Cause that half-breed mongrel barged in on him at his home that night of the stage coach robbery and demanded that Doc Blevins give yer sister an exam of sorts."

"What d'ya mean," Cord cut in firmly, "an exam of sorts?"

An embarrassed look overcame the sheriff. "The half-breed pointed a shotgun at the doc and made him tell him whether or not she was, err, *'untouched,'* if ya' get my meaning."

Soon enough the three of them were at the office of Doctor Carl Blevins. In other towns, doctors might take patients into an office space in their homes, but Doc Blevins kept a separate office in town to assure the sicknesses of his patients were kept out of his own living quarters.

"How can I he'p ya', Sheriff?" Doc Blevins asked as the three men filed into his otherwise empty office.

"Carl, these boys want to know about the girl," the sheriff said. "The youngin' here is her brother. I told 'em what the half-breed wanted to know. Still, they got plenty more questions."

"Let's start with the most important one: why didn't you save her from that bastard?" Piotr asked pointedly.

The doctor looked at the boy and instantly understood his agitation. "Son, I would've been dead in an instant and ya' would be here havin' a hell of a time gettin' answers from my corpse. Now, wouldn't ya' be?"

The answer caught Piotr off guard. He seemed to struggle for what to ask next. Cord McCullough decided to take up the role of posing the questions to the doctor.

"Sheriff here said the half-breed brought the girl to yer home," Cord asked in a calmer, more respectful way. "How was it he knew where ya' lived, Doc?"

"Thing was," Doc Blevins said, "I had the feeling someone was following me. I had just lost the Ranger Horton, here at the office, and was feeling right low 'bout it. Never knew the Captain professionally, but word had always been that he was a good man. He just had too much internal damage to keep him hangin' on at his age. So after he closed his eyes for the last time, I locked up the office and walked on home. I had a feeling like someone was shadowin' me. I reckon now it was the half-breed, 'tho I never saw anybody. But, if he's got even half of Comanche blood in him, I wouldn't have, would I? He showed up about an hour later with the girl. He must have had her tied up somewhere while he tracked me. He came back and burst in with a shotgun leveled at my gut, with the girl in tow. Scared me half out of my wits. I suppose yer some kinda law after this half-breed, too?"

"No," Cord answered him, a little surprised at the doctor's question, "just someone his people hired to keep an eye on the boy. I'm not goin' after this Injun, just gotta get this boy here back down San Antone way."

"I am not going home without Kalina," Piotr declared defiantly, as if going on the record before the sheriff and the doctor. "Everyone said the bandit would have high-tailed it straight out to Comanche country with my sister. Appears he did not. Waited a full day to come here with her, didn't he? Maybe they are still close by."

"Perhaps," the doctor said. "How can I help?"

"Well, Doc," Cord jumped back in, "to start with, what size fella' are we talkin' bout? What'd he weigh?"

"I'd say just under six foot. He didn't get on the scales for me, but I'd put him at a tad under 200 pounds."

"I'm sorry to hear bout yer losin' the Ranger and all," Cord went on, "but what exactly was it that made both him and ya' to figure this bandit to be half-Comanche? Maybe this was just some Mexican bandito strayin' north?"

The doctor looked at Cord strangely. For one who had no intention of going after the half-breed, he sure asked a lot of questions to help him identify the man.

"Son, both this dead Ranger and I spent a lot of time out in the *Comancheria,* that is, in Comanche country. I was a medic attached to the US Cavalry. Retired almost ten years ago after the Comanches and their Kiowa brothers drove Colonel Kit Carson and the rest of us back off the plains. I could spot the Comanche blood in this one instantly, just as Ranger Horton had. You see your average Comanche is built a little different than most other Indians. They got a fuller, more moon-shaped face, and shorter, paunchier builds as compared to the Kiowa or Apache. I could see the Comanche in him even though he was wearing that big old Mexican jacket, the kind with the flowing sleeves trailing all that fringe. He must have picked that up on a cross-border raid somewhere back. Ya' know them Comanches love to ride down and steal themselves a mess of horses, maybe kill some Mexicans while they're at it. All okay by me so long as they're not raiding our Texas towns. But ever since I settled down here, we've had far too many Comanche raids. Far more than our fair share."

"Seems to have lessened up just a bit, Carl," the sheriff added, "since the army put up that line of forts west of here. Not too much, maybe just a bit."

The doctor answered him with a disagreeing glance.

"Anyway," Doc Blevins went on, "this fella had decorated the sleeves of his coat with what appeared to be Comanche markings of some sort. I pegged him to be half-Mexican, half-Injun. Maybe they captured his mother on a raid when she was a young girl. They like to do that ya' know. They'll kill all the adults, men and women alike, but take away the children, especially the girls. I'm reckonin' this half-blood was born in a Comanche village after they all had their way with his mother. Damn savages." He only then realized everything he had said was in front of the boy and regretted it on the spot. He turned to Piotr, "Sorry son, but it is true. This is what they do with captives."

"Tell us about yer inspectin' of his sister," Cord said. "What did this half-breed want to know?"

"Just the one thing," the doctor said, "and I don't feel right talkin' 'bout it in front of the boy."

"Well, Doc, you done said more than a mouthful to run me off, but I'm not leavin', am I?" snapped Piotr. "So, say what you got to. I'm not a child, I'm seventeen. I'm a man. I can take it." There was a momentary standoff between the boy and the doctor. Piotr's face flushed red with anger and became as hard as his will.

"Doc?" Cord said, as a tilt of his head seemed to add, *it's okay, go on.*

"All right, but before I get into all that, there was something really strange that happened. The girl was as jumpy as a prairie dog, scared to all git out, as ya' can imagine. I tried to calm her down by saying how pretty her necklace was. It was a bird of some kind, maybe a hawk or a falcon, danglin' round her neck. Carved out of what I took to be bleached bone. I never really seen anything quite like it. Some real elaborate whittlin' on that thing."

Figure 3: Kalina's Polish
White Eagle Medallion

"It is an eagle," Piotr said. "A White Eagle. The symbol of our country. My father carved it for her before he passed away. It is very dear to her."

"Yeah, okay," the doctor said, "that is exactly what it looked like, a White Eagle, with a little gold crown on its head someone took the trouble to paint yella. Well, when I took it between my finger and thumb to tell the girl…"

"Kalina," Piotr said, "her name is Kalina."

"Okay son. Okay, just calm yerself down… I took it in my hand to tell yer sister, Kalina, how pretty it was. That was when this half-blood went mad with rage. Struck me hard with the butt end of the shotgun. Drove me to the floor. I thought he broke my dang ribs."

"Why'd he get so riled over it?" asked Cord.

"Don't right know," the doctor said, "once I got off the floor, he just said to me, *'No touch,"* like it meant something special to him too."

"So, Carl, you inspected the girl," the sheriff tried moving things along, "and then what?"

"Well, he just wanted to know if she had been *touched* or not," said the doctor, shrugging his shoulders. "You know what I mean by *touched?* That was the term he kept using."

"You mean as to whether was she a virgin?" asked Cord. "Is that what yer sayin', Doc?"

"Of course she was a virgin," exploded Piotr. "Kalina is only fourteen. Who would be sick enough to take any girl that young in that way?"

Cord, the sheriff and the doctor all looked at each other. It was clear that the boy was raised sheltered from knowing just how sinister life could be out on the frontier.

"What d'ya find, Doc?" asked Cord.

"Listen, mister," Doc Blevins said, "I am a country doctor who rode most of his life fixin' up the wounded of the US Cavalry and sometimes the Texas Rangers. I really don't have much experience in checkin' young girls out in this way. So I did what I thought was right, I took a cursory look and told the half-blood, sure, she was *'untouched.'* That was the term he kept using. I knew it was what he wanted to hear. He seemed relieved, I thought, when I said that. Somehow I got the feeling that his relief was tied to that White Eagle necklace he wouldn't let me touch."

"I 'spose she won't be *'untouched'* for long," the sheriff said crudely. Piotr exploded fresh into another rage over the comment. Cord had to forcibly restrain him.

"Well, I don't think so, Sheriff," the doctor said after the ruckus settled. "I got a feeling that he wanted her to stay that way, that he was saving her for someone or something special, but who or what, I can't raise a guess."

"So how'd it all end?" Cord asked.

"Well, once I looked her over," the doctor said, "he struck me again with the butt of the shotgun, this time from behind on my shoulder. Hard. Hurt like hell. I thought he broke my shoulder blade. He took the girl out back and stole my only horse and rode off into the night."

"What direction did they head off into?" Piotr asked, again in an overly excited fashion.

"Son, I wish I could tell ya', but I was still down there on the floor. My shoulder hurt so bad I done forgot about my achin' ribs. I couldn't pull myself up off them floorboards."

"Other than your ribs and your shoulder," Cord asked, "he didn't hurt ya' none?"

"That was plenty 'nough," the doctor said, "still hurts just sittin' here chattin' with y'all. But I reckon I was spared because of the girl bein' with us. Like somehow killin' or scalpin' me would have in some way tainted her. I figure he wanted her pure of all that too. You know *untouched* in that way, also. He spoke very little English, but that word *'touch'* kept coming up. He knew that word for sure."

The doctor's digression on the bandit's vocabulary annoyed Piotr to no end. The teen seemed to build up a head of steam like a kettle on a wood stove. Then, he blew.

"What kind of men do you both call yourselves?" Piotr burst out in disgust to the sheriff and the doctor. "Neither of you raised a hand to try and save my sister? And especially you, Sheriff, for not going out after them."

The sheriff glared at Piotr with a look that could take down a charging bull. "Go after them where?" He asked. "As soon as I got something more than a mouthful of words to follow up on, boy, ya' just watch me."

"I ain't no boy, damn it!" Piotr fired back. "I am seventeen, a man. Maybe the only real man in here."

"Well, I still consider myself lucky be alive," the doctor admitted. "I'm thankful that I could even pass on this information to y'all. I wasn't going to say this in front of the lad," - he stayed away from the word '*boy*' - "but what the hell? That half-blood also had a leather horsewhip with him the whole time they were here in my home."

"Must've picked it up after the driver was shot by his partner," said the sheriff. "Ya' know, the bandit that the captain said had the pocketwatch and the Slim Jim holster."

"Well," the doctor went on, "when I inspected the girl, she was covered with mud up the front of her dress. She was soaked from the hips down, as if they had been hiding out in the bed of a creek or a stream. But she also was striped across her hindquarters a good bit. Looked fresh, but of course it had to be, right? He had only taken her hours before."

"That doesn't go with all that '*stayin' pure*' talk, does it?" Cord thought out loud.

"That's what I thought, too. I wondered if she tried to run from him and he scourged her with it from behind, instead of runnin' her down. I'm telling ya' both this just so yer'll be very careful should ya' decide to go after him."

"Of course we are going after him!" Piotr snapped. "He has my little sister. He has Kalina."

Just then a messenger came crashing into the doctor's office from the street, out of breath from having run a long distance.

"Sheriff, that gang of coach robbers you're after is holed up in a ranch house outside of town. Yer deputies got 'em surrounded!"

Chapter 6: Surviving The Shootout

Outside of Weatherford, Texas

The sheriff, Cord and Piotr left the doctor in his office and quickly rode out to the surrounded ranch house. At first, the lawman had refused to allow them to ride along, but yielded when he figured he could use Cord's gun to add to those of his deputies. Cord, however, refused to leave Piotr behind, so all three rode out as the sun began to set. The sheriff had drawn the line at allowing River along, so the dog was left behind, closed up in the jailhouse.

"How many bandits ya' got inside there, Chet?" the sheriff asked his deputy upon arriving at the ranch house.

"Not sure," the deputy said. "Never got a real count. We heard they was holin' up here in Zeke Cutler's place. Zeke's been off a good long while down south below Cleburne to sell some colts. Took all his wranglers with him, left only a couple house servants behind. A while back a passer-by heard shots and screams, so we figured it might be these stage coach boys took over the place to lay low. They don't seem to realize we're out here. We been real quiet, makin' sure we ain't kickin' up too much trail dust. Keepin' our distance. We'll move in after dusk settles in."

"Y'even sure it's our stage coach bandits in there?" the sheriff asked.

"Oh yeah, It's them all right. We spotted one standin' guard out on the front porch who met the description of one the robbers - the one who killed the driver, right down to his Slim Jim holster. Don't see a whole lot of them 'round these parts. Kept checkin' his pocketwatch, like he was still expectin' someone."

"How many men ya' got watchin' the place?" the sheriff asked again.

"And what about the bandit that has my sister?" Piotr asked before the deputy could answer. "Is he here?"

"Who's this?" the deputy asked.

"Brother of the girl the half-breed took. His name is *Peeyahta* or something. Ignore him," instructed the sheriff.

"Peeyahta - what's that, Injun?" asked the deputy.

"Polish," Piotr said flatly, "it means Peter."

"Don't pay him no mind, Chet! Answer me damn it, how many ya' got watchin' in all?" snapped the sheriff. "How many men total ya' got coverin' this ranch house?"

"Five of us counting me," said the deputy, "and ya' round out a half dozen, Sheriff. Like I said, we don't figure they know we're out here just yet. But good thing ya' brought these two along, cause its going to be sundown soon, and we're gonna need the extra eyes in the dark, lessen' we allow these bandits to slip through our pickets."

"How many inside, ya' reckon?" the sheriff asked again, by then knowing it to be only a guess by his deputy.

"We seen three different ones come out on the porch. Might could be two or three more inside, not sure. I ain't seen hide nor hair of any girl nor the half-breed bandit that took her, but that don't mean they ain't in there. Maybe that's who the Slim Jim fella' is waitin' fer?"

"Okay, Mr. McCullough," the sheriff said, "consider yerself deputized. Where ya' want him, Chet?"

"What about me?" asked Piotr. "Deputize me, too."

"I wouldn't do that," Cord warned. "He ain't never shot no gun before."

"Have so," objected Piotr, "I've shot my fair share of possum and even a coyote, once."

"Despite all yer bluster, yer just a damn boy," said the sheriff, "and an immigrant one at that. No deal! Don't nobody dare give this one a weapon of any sort."

"I ain't no immigrant! I was born in this country," Piotr protested. "I'm a Texan just like you, Sheriff!"

The comment offended the lawman to the core.

"Son, ya' sure as hell may have been born here in yer little Polish village, but that alone don't make ya' no true Texan!" snarled the sheriff. "Takes more than gitten birthed on its soil to make a man a real Texan. First off, despite what ya think, y'ain't no man yet, yer still just a boy. Ya' dress like a damn sod buster. Yer likely to act like one and get yerself shot out here. I should be sendin' ya' back to town and git ya' clear out of the way of all this. I sure as hell don't want to have to send yer carcass back down San Antone way in a pine box."

"*Pee Otter* stays with me," insisted Cord, "or else I leave with him." His voice's tone left no room for arguing.

"Well, I reckon that settles that. We need yer gun," said the sheriff. "Where d'ya say ya' want them, Chet?"

"I guess out back somewhere past where Big Butch Patterson is takin' cover," the deputy said. "Just make sure y'all keep yer movements outta sight of the house, we don't want to rattle them boys inside in no way."

Cord and Piotr swung a wide arc on foot to make it around back of the Cutler ranch house as the final dusty traces of day settled into night. The posse remained sure that the bandits inside the ranch house were still unaware of their being surrounded. The sun had just dropped below the ridge and the air was a thickening haze of an orange-brown dusk. Cord and Piotr took up their place a good thirty yards downwind of Butch Patterson. All knew it'd be moonlight inside the hour.

"That fella's sportin' a Sharps fifty caliber rifle," Cord whispered to Piotr about Big Butch as they dropped in behind some rocky cover on the hillside.

"So what," Piotr whispered back, "have you seen Kalina or the bandit yet?"

"Whadya' mean *'so what?'* That's a damn buffalo hunter's gun," Cord explained. "That man means business with that *Big Fifty.* Just hope he don't plan on takin anyone in alive, or even in one piece, given the size of the rounds in that rifle."

They waited the better part of an hour before they saw any movement come from the house. Dusk surrendered hard to the deep black night while they kept watch. A pale yellow slice of moon had just cleared the darkened hillside behind them, casting just enough glow to make out moving shapes, but not much more. It was then that one of the bandits wandered out of the house and down the hill toward the outhouse, which was not far from where Piotr and Cord hid. The bandit, having no lamp, tread cautiously. What he did have was his pistol, pulled and at the ready to be fired.

"He's makin' to use that *Jake,*" Cord whispered to Piotr, referring to the outhouse. "These boys surely don't know we're out here. We can still git the drop on them."

Cord, Piotr and Big Butch Patterson each watched as the bandit opened the door of the outhouse slowly and made sure it was empty before he crept cautiously inside.

"He could have taken a piss anywhere, but as he made to the Jake, we're sure to have 'im with his trousers down. He'll never know what hit 'im, the poor bastard."

"To hell with you and your gittin' the drop," Piotr said, "I want Kalina and sitting out here in the dark ain't gettin' us any closer to rescuing her. Give me a gun."

"Boy, y'aint armed, and yer stayin' that way - I ain't fool enough to give ya' a hogleg. You're likely to end up shootin me with it." Cord knew even his whispering was too much jabberin' as sound carried long distances off the rocks on the still night air.

"Look, there's another one of 'em." Piotr stretched his arm out toward the ranch house. Cord thought the teen had said this a bit too loudly. He squinted in the moonlight but saw nothing except the house's silhouette.

"Where ya' seeing this?" Cord asked of Piotr in a whisper, but there was no response. It was then that he realized that the teen had intentionally distracted him with the comment only to sneak away. *Damn how he was quiet,* Cord thought as he looked down the hillside, and saw the gray silhouette of Piotr stalking directly toward the Jake.

He's got no damn gun, Cord thought. *What's he planning to do? Pesterin' that fellow to death? He's got the balls of a bull, but, fer sure, the brains to match.*

Cord began to move down the hill slowly after Piotr when the boy skittered a bit too loudly on loose footing.

Both Cord and Piotr were surprised as the outhouse door violently swung open wide. Cord's mind flashed, *Had the bandit heard the boy's call to me about the house? Or was it the sound of Piotr skittering on them loose rocks. Something had spooked him, that much was fer sure.*

Cord could only watch as Piotr froze in his steps ahead of him. The bandit, trousers up, walked out, gun drawn and looked up the hill at Piotr, who was by then only a few steps away. Seeing the sight of an unarmed youth saved Piotr, as the bandit hesitated momentarily.

"We got the law on us!" the bandit screamed out as loud as he could as he raised his gun to shoot. Cord had drawn his Peacemaker from his holster, but could not draw a bead on the outlaw as Piotr was directly in front of him and blocking his line of sight.

It was then that a peal of righteous thunder exploded behind them both from Butch Patterson's Sharps Big Fifty. Cord could see the silhouette of Piotr drop to the ground in front of him. At first, he thought the boy to be hit, but then saw, just beyond Piotr, the outlaw picked up off his feet and thrown violently back into the rickety structure that was the outhouse. *Yup, that's what a half inch slug of lead from a buffalo gun will do to a man,* Cord thought.

Then all hell broke loose. The shooting from the house came in response as thick as thieves. However, it soon became clear that those inside the ranch house couldn't see what they were shooting at out in the dark.

The lawmen took aim on the flames belching from the outlaw's barrels. Before too long had passed, they figured all the bandits inside to be hit and surely either dead or dying. Their instincts proved to be right. Then, they simply waited for the silvery clouds of gun smoke to clear.

Cord McCullough scurried the rest of the way down the hill to the two bodies, both lying lifelessly still in the dirt. As he drew near, he lept over Piotr to first check the bandit to assure that he no longer posed a threat. Cord reckoned not, as the bastard had been driven off his feet by Butch's buffalo slug, opening up his gut while throwing him backwards. He smashed into and through the Jake, before he finally rolled face down into a bed of red rocks.

Cord stepped through the rank smelling, scattered debris of the former dry rotted outhouse. The latrine stench overpowered him, but he thought just as well as it masked the fetid smell of death. One thing Cord never could get over, was that pitifully sour-yet-sweet scent of a man having just lost his life. The body was far too fresh a kill to reek yet. It was too soon for the corruption to have worked its way in, but the rancid rawness of the exposed wound Cord found disturbing all the more. *What men won't gamble their lives away on, their souls over,* he thought. He reflected for an instant on his own wretched soul, damn as it surely was over all the killing he had done during his own lifetime.

Cord reached down to flip the bandit over. In the quarter moonlight, he could neither find nor feel any pistol, nor for that matter did he detect any apparent sign of life in the man. What he did see in the pale moon's glow was the black stain of blood spreading slowly from where the man's gut used to be.

Cord crawled back up next to Piotr. He laid his hand on the boy's body. It was not lifeless, as he had first thought - it shook uncontrollably. The boy was surely alive.

"It's okay, son," Cord said, and instantly felt the shaking intensify. "Shootin's over fer now.'

"What the hell was that?" Piotr asked, no longer bothering to whisper. His ears were still ringing like a pair of clanging mission bells from that first shot.

"That was the sweet sound of a Sharps Big Fifty round fired off by that Butch Patterson fella. Did it hit ya'?" Cord knew it had not because the boy wasn't screaming out in God-awful pain. "Now just stay down low, *Pee Otter,* till I tell ya' otherwards, less ya' care to catch the next slug, should the firin' start back up."

Cord looked up at Patterson, who by then was shuffling down the hillside, his massive rifle in hand.

"Good shot not hittin' the boy," Cord complimented Big Butch as he came closer.

"What boy?" Patterson asked. "Only thing I heard was the bandit who was screamin' out and saw him raisin' his gun to shoot. What boy you talkin' bout?"

"Well," Cord said to Butch, "I think ya' done come an inch or so short of gettin' the both of them with one single round. Good thing ya' didn't."

Cord and Patterson then helped the still shakin' Piotr to sit up as the sheriff called out from inside the ranch house, "We got four dead bandits up here."

"And one down here, to boot," Patterson yelled back. Only after the last echo of the big man's words faded away did Cord hear the awful sound. It was the pathetic wheezing of a dyin' man trying desperately to pull his last breaths in this world.

Amazing! That bastard's still alive, Cord thought, *How on Earth had I missed that? I best get whatever I can outta him before he dies from that gapin' gut wound from the Big Fifty.*

"What's yer name, fella?" Cord asked. He looked down on the dyin' man, who still instinctively clutched at his Slim Jim holster, only to find it empty, as it was.

"Matteo,"...wheeze..."I am dyin'," he said, clearly in shock, in the faintest voice carried on the scantest breath. *"Death comes now" ...wheeze..."for me."*

The voice was so faint Cord could barely hear it. He knelt down next to the dying bandit and lowered his ear as close he could to Matteo's mouth.

"Dyin? No, we got a doc just over yonder," Cord lied in a soft compassionate voice. "Same one that your half-breed compadre visited after the hold-up."

"What?"...wheeze..."No doctor"...wheeze..."I am already dead," he strained to say through gritted teeth.

"The half-breed," Cord prompted, "where is he?"

The dying man drew a shallow breath that rattled in his chest eerily. He fought hard to get out the next few words, *"...Lobo,"...wheeze..."damn Comanche..."*

"Where is he?" Cord asked the dying man.

His chest heaved again, making a loud sickly sucking sound. Cord thought it to be his final death rattle, as he strained to hear what he thought might be the man's last words on his final breath.

"Bastard"...wheeze..."never come"...wheeze..."for his share..."

"Where's the girl?" Cord shouted frantically, as if the man's hell bound soul was already drifting away, but it proved not to be so for an instant longer.

"...Girl?"...wheeze..."Bad luck"...wheeze..."to take her" ...wheeze ..."take her to the..."

His body then shuddered one final time, and on the faintest breath that ever could escape from it came the one word that Cord McCullough wished desperately not to hear.

"*...Llano.*"

Cord watched as the last of all life eased out of this killer's body on that same shallow breath. All that was left of the man was the mangled corpse lying in the blood drenched dirt. Cord felt no sense of loss in the man's dying.

Piotr had calmed himself from the shock of the gunfight to the point of wanting to once again pick up the search for his sister. He rose slowly to his feet. "I'm going up to the ranch house to look for Kalina."

"No, yer not," said Cord. "Last thing I need is yer running up on some trigger happy deputy and gettin' yerself shot. That big bore round whizzin' past yer ear wasn't enough excitement for ya' for one night? Besides, she ain't up there no how."

"How can you even pretend to know that," the teen barked at him, shaking off his own near death. Cord noticed the boys accent had thickened in all the excitement, as if the scare had drawn him back to his roots.

"Cause this one said the half-breed never come for his share of the take. Seems like they made the mistake of waiting for him to show. Instead, he headed out with her for the *Llano Estacado.* That can only mean one thing. After havin' the Doc check out yer sister, he took her out directly to *Comancheria.*"

Cord could not bring himself to tell the boy the last of his thoughts, that which already haunted his mind. *That half-beed bastard has got something special lined up for that poor little girl.*

Chapter 7: An Unexpectedly Convenient Betrayal

Fort Worth, Texas

As the sun rose at dawn, under the its cleansing rays of light, the posse, having finished its slaughter in the dark, retreated back to their homes. That is, all but one member, Chet Blackman, the sheriff's deputy. Blackman made a bee-line to the ranch of Fort Worth cattleman Vaughn Anders. By noon, he arrived there with valuable news.

"Vaughn, Chet Blackman is out here sayin' he needs real bad to see ya'," said the herder's most trusted ranch hand, a nasty wrangler called Huck Hawkins. He served as both Anders' bodyguard and, when needed, his most reliable blackheart killer.

Vaughn Anders sat behind the English Walnut desk in the small den of his ranch house. He was as wealthy as any rancher in Texas, it was said, but despite this he lived modestly. The only two things he did indulge in were cattle and land, and for that reason his bunkhouse was bigger than his ranch house, although not nearly as well appointed.

Still, Anders did have one vice that he could never satisfy, that being his addiction to revenge. For nearly a year, he had mourned the death of his son, and was close to over his grief. But what he could not get over was the idea of Cord McCullough still being out on the loose.

McCullough had not killed his son, had not even armed the man who had. He simply had bucked Anders' order to kill that gunsmith. Instead, Cord had let the old man go. Vaughn Anders could not accept his order being defied so. For that reason, the cattleman demanded Cord McCullough must pay the ultimate price. And while Anders viewed the death sentence he had sworn out on McCullough as an act of revenging his son's death, it truly was nothing more than just an excuse for patching up his wounded sense of pride and damage to his own importance.

"Sure," Vaughn Anders replied to Huck, "show Deputy Blackman in. It will be a pleasure to see him, 'specially if his need is indeed urgent."

The ranch hand withdrew and the cowboy-turned-lawman entered the room a few ticks of the clock later.

"Ah, Chet," Anders said, "good to see you again. It's been far too long. What brings you by this fine day?"

"Well, Mr. Anders…"

"No, Chet, call me *'Vaughn.'* We go back too far…"

"Okay. Sure, Vaughn, I was just wondering if that two hundred dollar reward still stands for information on where Cord McCullough might be hiding out?"

The mention of the name was enough to cause Anders to stroke the hairs of his goateed face. "Of course. Cash on the barrelhead. You know something, Chet?"

"I saw the man last night," the deputy said. "We had the gang that waylaid that stagecoach in Weatherford penned up over at ol' Zeke Cutler's spread. We wiped them all out in a gunfight."

"And one of them was McCullough?" Anders asked, visibly disappointed. "He was among the dead?"

"No, ya' see…"

"Good God, Chet," Anders raged. "Don't tell me Cord was among the dead. I ain't paying a penny for his corpse. I want to watch that bastard be strung up, draw his last breath for what he done to dishonor the memory of my boy. Can't do that if he's already done dead."

"Cord wasn't one of that gang," Chet Blackman fought back to explain. "Ya' see, he was deputized by the sheriff to help roust out them bandits."

A wicked smile replaced the dejected scowl that had overtaken Anders' face. "Oh, so I see," the cattleman said. "Okay, so you saw him. But how did he come to the sheriff's attention in the first place?"

"Well," Chet explained, "ya' might recall that during that robbery a half-breed abducted a little girl."

"So I heard, Chet," Anders said. "They said he was thought to be taking her out west into Comanche country."

"Well, her brother done come up from down San Antone way looking for her. A boy by the name *Pee Otta.*"

"Pee Otta? What the hell kind of name is that?" Anders bellowed. "Comanche? Kiowa?"

"I thought it to be Injun too," Chet said. "Naw, turns out the kid's Polish. Can't be no more than seventeen or so. Stubborn as a mule. Nearly got himself killed last night. Looks like Cord's helpin' him find that girl."

"So, McCullough might be fool enough to wander off into *Comancheria*?" Anders mused. "Even if that boy turns out to be twice the crack shot McCullough is, they won't last a week out there on those God-awful plains. If the half-blood they're tracking doesn't turn back and kill 'em, then some other full-blooded Comanche surely will."

"That boy is no crack shot - the sheriff wouldn't even trust him with a gun. No sir. Word is Cord was hired by the Polish folk to take this *Pee Otta* boy back to his people down south. But by what I saw and heard, this boy's too headstrong to give up on rescuing his sister."

"Okay, Chet, this is all good information," Anders said, "and I'm going to count you out that couple of hundred in gold coins right now. But should I find you been pulling a fast one on me, my friend, I'll send one or two of my hands to pay you a visit - maybe ol' Huck himself, - whether you're wearing that deputy star or not."

Blackman looked in the direction from which Huck Hawkins had shown him in. He knew that wrangler was the man Anders had dispatched to kill the card sharp who had gunned down his boy. Chet Blackman, being the lawman he was, knew that Huck Hawkins was not to tangled with.

"No sir," Chet answered, "I ain't fool enough to lock horns and tangle with ya', Mr. Anders. I just knew ya' was looking for McCullough…"

"And you could use the two hundred dollars, I'm sure…" Anders interrupted the deputy. "Okay. I'll get your money, Chet, but remember, there's a lot more waitin' if you can bring me Cord McCullough alive. A lot more. And enough of this Mr. Anders silliness, it's *'Vaughn'* to you. I don't let many men call me that, but even among those I do, especially them, I won't cotton bein' made a fool of."

"Yes, Mr. And…" Chet stopped. "Sure, Vaughn."

Chapter 8: A Last Respite at the Trinity Quarter Ranch

Weatherford, Texas

Under the very same morning sun that had risen over the Anders' ranch outside Fort Worth, Cord and Piotr headed back to Weatherford to free River from his confinement in the sheriff's jailhouse. Having retrieved the dog, they then left to go to the Trinity Quarter Ranch on the other side of town. River sauntered behind them both while they rode, happy to be reunited with his master, Cord, and his pal, the mare called Trouble.

Weatherford was by then well known for being the source of some of the best quarter horses in all of Texas. The Trinity Quarter Ranch was one of the biggest quarter horse concerns in all the state.

"So, *Pee Otter,*" Cord called out to his fellow rider, "how is it that a successful Weatherford horse rancher decides to hire yer aunt, a Polish immigrant woman from all the way down south in *Panna Maria?*"

The boy did not expect the question, and took his time to figure out the best way to answer.

"You have seen me ride for a few days now," Piotr answered, "do I know how to handle myself in the saddle?"

"I'd have to admit ya' do," Cord answered. "How ya' can do so with those big clunky farmer's boots on is a mystery to me, but I must confess, ya' do ride well."

"Well, my aunt rides even better than me," he said. "She and the horse are like one together on the wind. She learned from my father who was the best rider in their town in the old country. Three years ago, when that horse rancher from Weatherford came through on his way to the Sabine River, he heard tell of a beautiful young woman who could ride like no other, my Aunt *Mieczyslawa…*"

"Myetch-a-slav-a" Cord echoed aloud. "Now that's a mouthful."

"Yes, I suppose so for you," Piotr said. "It is the female form of Milton, her father's name. Anyway, this rancher was so impressed with her skill in the saddle that he offered her a job to come work out his quarter horses on his ranch in Weatherford. Up here I understand they took to calling her Midge. I guess the Texans couldn't pronounce her Polish name, so it became simply Midge."

"I can certainly understand that," Cord said. "So your mother fights to get ya' back to your home village, but she allows her sister run off north to a horse ranch?"

"My aunt is very unlike my own mother, who is not her sister but her sister-in-law. She is quite adventurous and could not agree to take the job fast enough. Besides, the family needed money desperately, so for each of the past three years she made a small fortune and would send most of it back to my father at *Panna Maria.* The rancher's family was, and still is, so very kind to her, they treat her like one of their own. *Ciocci Mieczyslawa* loves the horses, so many beautiful horses, she would write to us…"

"Wait," Cord asked, "what's this word *chuchee*?"

"Sorry," Piotr said, "I sometimes slip between your English words and my people's own. *Ciocci* means *Aunt.*"

"Okay, then, go on," Cord said.

"Well, *Aunt Mieczysława* always favored Kalina. She had long loved to ride with my little sister. My aunt asked her employer if Kalina could spend the summer on the ranch. He not only agreed, but he said he would pay her to do chores around the ranch house. *Ciocci...,* I mean *Aunt Mieczysława* told him that Kalina could be of even more use in working with the horses. That is why she was on that stagecoach."

"That's quite a story," Cord said. "So yer mother who is so protective of her young son allowed her even younger daughter to come north?"

"Only because she thought it might be good for Kalina after losing our father to the winter fever," Piotr answered. "She thought a summer with her aunt on a horse farm would keep Kalina from sinking too far into her grief. And my mother has only become so protective of me since my sister was taken."

"And ya' say it was yer father who taught yer *Ciocci* to ride so well?"

Piotr turned his head away, as if to hide his face from showing the pain of all this talk about his dead father. Despite this, Cord could see tiny pools of tears begin to form in the boy's eyes.

"Sorry, there, *Pee Otter,*" Cord said, "I didn't mean to be nosin' around so deeply in yer family's business."

"You been *nosin' round like a hog in a slop pen,*" Piotr mocked Cord's heavy drawl, smirking playfully. It was the first time Cord had seen any levity at all come from the boy. He couldn't help but laugh out loud.

"But yes," Piotr said after the lightness of the moment had passed, "Aunt *Mieczyslawa* learned to ride from her brother, that is, or I should say was, my father."

"The famous whittler of that White Eagle medallion that Kalina wears?"

"Yes," Piotr answered, "my father had learned how to carve as a boy. He had a real knack for it. He did a lot of it when he served as a Dragoon in the Prussian cavalry before the family came here, I mean to Texas. He whittled to fill the many lonely hours he was forced to endure away from his family."

"Why was he ridin' for the Prussian cavalry if he was Polish?" Cord asked.

"Because they had stolen our lands decades earlier," the boy answered, "and then they tried to steal our culture, our religion, and our language. It is why our people left to come to Texas. It is very much worse now. The Prussians call it *Kulturkampf*, a struggle of cultures, with them always trying to force our fellow Polish souls to accept their Germanic ways, their language, and their culture."

"Struggle of cultures, huh," Cord repeated. "Kinda like us and them Injuns, I guess. I can certainly see that ya' cared a lot fer yer father. It hurts to lose family, I know."

"Kalina loved him so dearly," Piotr said, as if to drive home the point that his little sister's heart ached to no end over losing her beloved daddy. "That is why she never took off that White Eagle medallion he carved for her. Now, I am afraid it appears to have cost her dearly."

"Well, d'ya ever think just maybe it's what's keeping her safe from harm," Cord said. "I still wonder what that half-breed's fascination with that medallion is all about. Why would he become so attached to it?"

"Go with me to find her," Piotr pleaded. "I figure we can go into Comanche territory together to git her back. Safety in numbers, and all that."

"Yeah, well, ain't much safety in the number two, as in just yerself and me up against thousands of them Comanches. Ya' just don't git it, do ya'? We can't haul enough ammunition to kill off even one-tenth of 'em. Ten years ago the US Cavalry under Kit Carson tried to and got driven back out. Comanches are so damn quiet-like, they been known to steal horses from alongside our soldiers who slept right alongside their mounts, and that's only when there be too many riders to kill. They can sure as hell sneak up and kill us in our sleep. We'd be dead before the week's out." Cord then muttered under his breath. "Yer sister'd be no better off fer it at all. Best she stays lost fer now. That way the hope of her bein' ransomed is still alive."

"That's the whole point," Piotr said, becoming very agitated, with his words tightening and becoming more affected by his accent. "Kalina's not already lost, not yet. It's just everybody's given up on finding her just because the man who up and took her *might* be half-Comanche! Well, I'm not giving up so easy, so if you try and take me back home, I will just come back again unless they shackle me by the leg to that big live oak out by the church."

"So if I don't deliver ya' home, boy, ya' figure to go after her?" Cord asked. "Out on *the Llano* alone?"

"If I have to, I will," Piotr spat the words at him. "Dying that way's still better than doing nothing. I don't understand why it is that everybody thinks you to be such a tough, brave man. You're just afraid of dying, like all these other cowards. I keep thinking about how Kalina's gotta be scared to death being all alone with that half-breed bandit."

Cord was also haunted by the thought of the bandit-turned-kidnapper having a cruel fate awaiting the girl. It ate away slowly at him, but he refused to share this with Piotr.

"Chances are," Cord said to Piotr, "he won't kill or maim her. In a couple of months, he'll likely ransom her back fer a mess of horses if he's half-Comanche, or fer a pile of money if he's *Comanchero*. It's not worth riskin' one life, and less so two, just to keep him from turnin' her for a spell into a Comanche …"

Cord held himself back, as he realized far too late he could not go on with completing his thought. He choked on the final word that he feared was about to roll off his tongue. So he stopped mid-sentence.

"Go ahead," Piotr seethed, an icy edge taut in his voice, "go on and say it!"

"I won't!" Cord answered. "I wasn't thinkin' right."

"SQUAW!" yelled out Piotr, his face flush with rage. "No sense us risking our lives just to keep my little sister from becoming a Comanche squaw. Well to me, and certainly to Kalina, that's worse than dead. What kinda man are you, Cord? Haven't you ever had an opportunity to save somebody's skin other than your own?"

Cord took note of it being the first time the teen had called him by any name other than Mr. McCullough.

I reckon' I got the boy's dander up now.

"I thought I just did," Cord answered calmly, "I saved your skin the other night back there in the Acre."

"Yeah, and you've already been paid for that by Father Jerzy," Piotr said. "I'm talking about more than trick shooting to scare off some greedy cowhands. Have you ever done anything for anybody just for the good of it?"

The words of the last sentence seemed to prattle off the boy's tongue, but they struck hard with the force of an unexpected blow deep within Cord. He heard an echo in them as if they had come from his dead wife.

Is Callie sending me a message from the beyond through the boy's rancorous and unending bitchin'? Cord decided not, it was just his guilt at work on him.

Still, it made him think of her, all those years ago, not long after he had come home from deserting from the war. They were waylaid at their farmhouse. After the fighting was over, she lay dying in front of their home, engulfed in flames, as it crumbled to the ground.

In his memory, he saw the wicked dance of the flames' glow upon the pale skin of her tortured face. Callie spat up blood and forced herself to look up at him. With the last breaths of her life, she asked him, '*Oh, Cordell, what have you done? What have you done, Cordell?*'

The bitterness of that memory played itself out within him as a swallow of bile choked up in his throat. He could never think back on her passing without it doing so. Cord knew he would sink back into that darkness if he did not do something to heal that wound. Perhaps it was time to do that something…maybe he needed to try and save this girl. *Just not with this damned headstrong boy*, he thought.

They found their way to the Trinity Quarter Ranch. It was a beautiful spread and quite prosperous looking. At its gate they dismounted and walked their horses up the dirt road, Cord and Trouble led the way, passing two massive stables, a huge paddock, and a finely kept exercise ring for working out the quarter horses. They then approached the ranch house - a proud, handsome and massive all-stone structure.

As they came up to that ranch house, a man came from behind them out of the bunkhouse alongside one of the stables. He carried a shotgun, but with the breech cracked open over his arms. It was signal that Cord quickly recognized. *I mean no harm to you, stranger, but if you mean any harm to us, yer better be prepared for a fight.*

"How can I help ya' fellas?" he called out.

"I am here to see my Aunt *Mieczysława,"* Piotr yelled out before Cord could answer the man.

"You mean Midge?" the ranch hand answered. "She's the only woman on the ranch other than the owner's wife and daughter, and they're back East at the moment."

"Then I reckon so," said Cord, "if she's the one whose niece got taken in the stage coach robbery."

"Yup. That would be Midge, sure 'nuff," said the man. "So the boy's her nephew? We were told to expect him. And just who might ya' be, cowboy?"

"McCullough," he said, "Cord McCullough."

"Well, I'll be damned," said the ranch hand as he slung the open breech of the gun over his shoulder. He walked forward and extended his right hand. "You're the feller who cleaned out that Stone Canyon Gang last fall. They'd been rustlin' our horses for quite some time. We ain't lost a head since then. Let me shake your hand, sir. Ya' done made my job considerably easier."

He took Cord's hand and shook it with a broad smile beaming across his face. Cord felt the roughness of his hand, and the strength of his grip. Both said he was a hard working man, which to Cord made him trustworthy. "I'm Brett Sumner. I run this operation for the Scotsman."

"Scotsman?" asked Cord. "Who is this Scotsman?"

"That's the ranch owner," Brett explained, "Mr. Sinclair. He and his folks came over years ago from around Glasgow somewhere. Built all this up from scratch. Great man to work for. Richer than the Comstock Lode, he is. And not a penny-pincher like most Scotsmen. Generous to a fault - if he likes ya', that is."

At this point, on the front porch of the ranch house two figures emerged. The man was older and barrel chested. He was well dressed, more like a businessman than a rancher. His vest and jacket looked to be finely tailored, possibly from New York or maybe overseas.

Beside him was a much younger woman, some twenty-five years younger or so, dressed out in tight tan riding britches and a form-fitting white blouse. A matching tan colored Stetson with a curled-up brim and a braided rawhide hatband completed her outfit.

"I take it that's yer Scotsman," Cord said to the ranch hand, Brett, "although I doubt the young girl beside him is his wife."

"Naw, like I said, his wife and daughter are back East just now," Sumner repeated. "But he treats Midge like she was another daughter. They're both torn up something fierce about the young girl bein' taken in the way she was."

It was then that the ranch owner, Darraugh Sinclair, called out across the yard, "Who you got over there, Brett?"

But it was the woman that stood next to him who answered as she screamed out in joy, *"Piotek!"*

She exploded off the porch and ran as fast as she could across the dirt courtyard to her nephew as he stood in front his pathetic mare. Cord couldn't help but appreciate the sway of her figure as he watched her run. He thought her to be one fine looking gal.

"Piotek?" He whispered to Piotr, sounding out the word just as he'd heard it, *"Pee-Yah-Tek."*

The boy could see just how much Cord was enjoying watching his aunt run toward them. He explained, "Piotek is the diminutive form of Piotr. Just as Cord is the diminutive form of Cordell."

"Well, *Piotek,*" Cord answered, "I don't right like to be figured as *diminutive* in any way."

Piotr's *Ciocci Mieczysława* found her nephew, slammed herself against him and wrapped her arms tightly around the boy as she kissed him.

"That would be yer Midge," Brett said, as both men watched her embrace her nephew. They harbored the same thought, each wishing only to trade places with the lad.

"Mr. Sinclair," Brett then called out to his boss, "this here is one man you'll be more than pleased to meet. Calls himself Cord McCullough."

Sinclair's face exploded with surprise. The rancher clearly recognized Cord McCullough's name instantly.

"No, you don't say," Sinclair mused. "Well, don't just stand there, Brett. Bring Mr. McCullough on up here. The lcast I owe him is my hearty 'thank you,' but how about I throw in a wholesome meal of Maria's stewed chicken to boot. We were just sitting down to eat. Why don't you all come and join us? You too, Brett."

"Looks like it's gonna be a good day," Sumner said to Cord, "ain't often I get to dine inside the ranch house."

"Perhaps yer boss just wants yer shotgun close by," Cord said, "should things go unexpectedly awry."

"And he's got it," Brett agreed. "If it fills my empty gut with Maria's stewed chicken, I'm happy to oblige."

The four of them walked across the yard to the ranch house porch, with Piotr and *Mieczysława,* or Midge, arm-in-arm, speaking in an unintelligible mangle that Cord assumed to be the Polish language. Amid that sea of miss-mash he heard his name and noticed as Midge cast a welcoming glance back at him. A sluice of her long blonde hair drained out from under her hat like a golden silk waterfall. She cut him a smile, and Cord figured whatever the boy said had pleased her.

At the base of the porch, they stopped at the bottom of the steps just below the Scotsman's boots.

"Pleasure to meet you, Cord," he said. "Come on up here and let's get inside. You too, young man. I reckon I figured out precisely who you might be."

"This is my nephew, *Piotr,*" said Midge, "but it is perhaps easier if you call him Peter, or maybe Pete."

Her voice carried the same accent as her nephew's, but it sounded so much more pleasant coming from her lips. Her face was long, thin and adorable, with her cheeks set high. Her skin was as pale as that of a doll carved out of ivory, smooth and unblemished in any way. She carried herself with confidence. Midge appeared to have had none of her nephew's erratic behaviors. There seemed to be nothing nervous at all about her. She was a woman who was more than confident enough to live and work in a man's world.

"Okay, Peter," Darraugh Sinclair said, "welcome to the Trinity Quarter Ranch. Come inside and eat. After all, you must be famished."

As they climbed the steps, Brett and Cord trailed behind the others. Cord could not resist stealing a peek at the back of Midge's tight riding britches. *Very fine indeed.*

They all wandered inside and began to sit down to the lunch that Cord and Piotr's arrival had interrupted. A white jacketed steward raced in with extra place settings ahead of the guests. The smell of the stewed chicken was like a gift from heaven to Piotr and Cord, both of whom had not eaten a hot meal in days. They dug in, though not quite as fast as Brett, who ate cradling the open breech shotgun across his lap, just to be safe.

"So, Mr. McCullough, is your family name Irish or Scottish?" asked the rancher Sinclair.

"Irish," McCullough said. "My family came over to escape the potato famine back in the '40s."

"Didn't every Mick in this country, it seems," Sinclair quipped. "My own mother was from a clan that had been Irish, the Campbells. She even gave me this Irish name, Darraugh, after her own father. But don't let that fool you. My family was and is Scottish, through and through."

Cord could hear the man roll his *r*'s just like Lucita, only much more subtly, less angrily.

"We came over from Glasgow a bit earlier. I was a wee lad about twenty-five years old back then." Sinclair said. Cord figured him to be in his mid-sixties. If his math was right, it meant the man came to America in 1835 or so.

"I remember it well," Sinclair recalled. "It was quite an adventure for my being such a young lad. Our family left everything we owned in Scotland to come to this great open country. I suppose it was a slightly different situation then than young Peter faces now, Mr. McCullough."

At first Cord did not know to whom he referred, but then as if his mind were some sort of a mechanical gear, he cranked out that "Peter" had to be Sinclair's choice instead of trying to pronounce the boy's Polish name.

"Call me, Cord," McCullough said.

"Thank you, Cord, and you can call me Darraugh," the rancher said in turn. "I assume this horrible business with Midge's niece is what brings you to the Trinity Quarter Ranch?"

"Yup," Cord said. "*Pee Otter* here wanted to see his aunt and get himself a fit horse for going after his sister."

Midge could not hold back her smirk at Cord's attempt to pronounce her nephew's name.

"I think, Mr. McCullough, you should also stick to Peter, or maybe Pete," she said with a most pleasant smile.

"Naw," Cord smiled back at her, "I've become somewhat attached to the name *Pee Otter.*"

"Well," she said, "I am so very thankful you've decided to help him. You are very brave…"

"Then, you got a bead on them, Cord?" Sinclair interrupted. "I mean on that Comanche and the girl."

"Naw, I sure don't," Cord admitted. "The rest of the bandits all got taken out in a shootout last night, but the half-breed and the girl, Kalina, they wasn't with 'em. I figure he's already taken her well inside *Comancheria.*"

"Do you really think going into Comanche country is wise, Cord?" Sinclair asked. "Few white men have done so and came back to talk of it."

Cord noticed the question drew the gaze of Midge to him, as if she was already concerned for his safety.

"Don't worry yourselves none," Piotr nonchalantly said as he took a break from gulping down his lunch, "this man's too cowardly to go after our Kalina at all. I know. I've spent the last few days with him. He's just telling you all now what he thinks you all want to hear."

Before Cord could even think of a response, his host all but exploded at the boy. "Peter, I assure you that this man, Cord McCullough, is no coward. He near single-handedly cleared out a gang of rustlers and gun runners only a few months back."

"Piotr and Cord do not have any choice but to go after and save Kalina," Midge said, ignoring the outburst that had come from her nephew. "She is still just such a young girl. I can't imagine what those Comanches might do to her. It is all my fault for asking Mr. Sinclair to allow me to bring her here."

Cord watched as she folded her head down over her plate and the tears dropped from her lovely frame which shuttered with regret. Piotr sat next to her, reached out to comfort her, and laid his young hand on her shoulder. He said something softly in Polish to his distraught aunt.

"No, Midge," the Scotsman Sinclair said, "you can't blame yourself. Cord will see to it that Kalina is brought back here safely. But the way the Comanche ride and fight, Cord and Pete here will not be enough. They will need a crew of hands to travel out there with them. Even with an army of three hundred, the savages still were still able to drive off Kit Carson at Adobe Walls in '64. It's said if that army didn't have a few pieces of mountain howitzer artillery with them they would have been done in for."

Cord could no longer allow the discussion to go on further without jumping back in. "I was just explainin' that to the boy" he said, "but, then again, that was ten years ago. With the way these buffalo hunters have been thinnin' out the herds lately, I figure the Comanche bands are likely to be thinnin' out as well. I hear most of the them are living on the reservation at Fort Sill these days."

"That is true," Sinclair answered, "but even then, they only go onto the reservation to camp for the winter and get free Agency beef, then when the weather breaks, they slip across the Red River and raid us here on the Western edge of the Texas' frontier. But that's only the *Honey-eater and Yap-eater* bands. The ones they call *Quahadi, or Antelopes,* are still out west on *the Llano* and have shown no inclination of going onto the reservation."

"To answer your earlier question, Darraugh," Cord replied, "I don't think chasing them deep into *Comancheria* is smart at all. The girl's most likely been taken somewhere out on *the Llano* by now. But the only real chance to git her back is to track down that half-breed and wrestle her away by force. To have a chance of that working, I'll need a few things, including a mess of provisions."

"Like what, exactly?" Darraugh Sinclair asked.

"Well to start," Cord answered, "A fresh horse and clothes for the boy. Lots of ammunition and cold trail food for us both, and a small fortune in cash in case we find she is being ransomed."

Cord could barely believe the words that were coming from his own mouth, but he had to admit the thought of the young child in the hands of that half-breed had been cutting hard on him.

He was instantly rewarded with a warm, broad appreciative smile from Midge from across the table. The fact that he had stopped her crying warmed him to no end.

"Whatever you need, Cord!" the rancher Sinclair said. "Horses, men, ransom money. Whatever you need, I'll gladly provide it! Just bring back that poor, sweet girl to her family."

"Thank ya', Darraugh," Cord replied, "then we can git an early start in the morning."

Piotr was stunned with Cord's reversal, and clearly didn't believe it. "He's lyin'," the teen exploded. "He's been paid to take me back to *Panna Maria.* That's all."

"The boy's right," Cord admitted. "I'll need someone to smooth that over with his mother."

An air of excitement filled the space around the table. All felt it except Piotr, who remained skeptical.

"Just how might you go about finding them?" Sinclair asked, referring to the half-breed and Kalina. "They got a good many days head start on you, and those open plains are massive. Easy to get lost out there."

"Well, I'm gonna need a tracker," Cord replied. "I'm decent at it, but not near good 'nuff to track a half-breed out on *the Llano.* There's a fella up at Red River Station I need. Can ya' get a telegram off to him? I'll draft it up. I need him to meet us up by the Wichita River Falls day after next."

"You got it," Sinclair said, "but don't you think it's best to leave the boy here with his aunt?"

"Nope, the boy comes with me." Cord said firmly, while winking at the Scotsman out of Piotr's view. "He's my responsibility now."

Darraugh Sinclair caught the signal and understood. He'd seen what Cord had since meeting Piotr - that the boy was just too high spirited for this type of ride.

"There is no way I'm not riding out to find Kalina in the morning," Piotr rose from his chair, standing with his table knife in hand. He made his point with it, stabbing at the air for emphasis in the general direction of the rancher.

"That is if this coward and trickster even goes through with it. If I were you, Mr. Sinclair, I'd be afraid he'll just run off with the ransom money."

Brett softly snap shut the shotgun's breech, as if he was gonna need it. Cord noticed and slowly reached over to gently placed his hand on the gun to calm him.

"It's okay, Brett" Cord whispered, "the kid's just hot-headed. Let's not git carried away here. Besides, that scattergun would make one hell of a mess in here."

All the while, *Piotr* had not stopped his rant. "I'm tired of everyone treating Cord like he's some sorta hero. The man's nothin' short of a coward. I had to badger him into even going after Kalina in the first place. If he goes through with it, nobody's gonna keep me from heading out west tomorrow to look for her."

Cord knew his next few words would further antagonize Piotr, but wanted the boy's temper to flare in front of the Scotsman.

"Tomorrow we head north, not west," Cord corrected Piotr, "We head first to Jacksboro, and the day after I'll meet up with my tracker near the Witchita River Falls. Only then will we begin to swing westward."

"Why aren't we going now?" Piotr snapped. "We've wasted too much damn time already. All we do is sit and talk, and wait and talk some more. Then we wring our hands that the bandit is too deep into *Comancheria.*"

The boy was right in his words, Cord thought, but was way too erratic - he was as jumpy as a cornered coyote. It was the all-up effect of his having ridden too many days, survived gunfights and suffered from frayed nerves in general. But best that Sinclair and Midge both saw just how wild he could get. Best they think he should be left behind.

"First of all, we ain't wastin' nothin'," Cord replied. "We came here to roust up any provisions we could from yer Aunt Midge's employer, and thanks to Darraugh here, now we got 'em. As for Jacksboro and the Wichita River Falls, they're on the way. If we're to have any chance at all, we need that tracker to meet up with us. That means we gotta give him a day or two to git to the falls."

"But why so far north?" Piotr still stood over his pushed back chair, holding the knife high in the air. "And who's this tracker we're to meet there?"

"Yes, Cord," said Sinclair. "I also wondered just how did you come to know of this tracker? Are you sure this is a man who can be trusted in all this?"

"Darraugh, I know him from the years I spent workin' on the Chisholm Trail," Cord answered. "He was a trader there. He's a good man, and the only one I figure skilled enough to track an Injun. To answer your question, I just think of it as I am trusting him with my life."

"I will explain to Piotr's mother," Midge said, finally having collected herself. "I will send a telegram after you have both left in the morning. She will not like it, but will have no choice in the matter. But, I do have one condition of my own…"

As she said this, she reached up and gently took the cutlery from her nephew's hand and slowly pulled him back down into his seat. Cord nodded to Brett, who only then cracked open the breech of his shotgun once more.

"…I want to ride along with you," Midge said abruptly, drawing a look of astonishment from Cord.

"Might as well let her," Brett said. "She shoots as good, if not better, than me or any of the other hands on this ranch. She can also most likely outride even yerself, Cord."

For a brief moment, Cord saw himself riding side-by-side with Midge on the open range, and the thought pleased him immensely. Then, he returned to the reality of the situation. Having a woman as beautiful as Midge along would only open up many more problems for him.

"Midge," Cord said, "much as I'd like to take ya', I'd just be invitin' every Injun and buffalo hunter we was to come across to take ya' as a captive. No, sir, them wild lands is no place for a woman as breathtakin' as yerself."

Cord could see her cheeks blush after he'd said that. Midge was truly beautiful, he had no need to embellish that. It was the emotion that swirled like a storm in her eyes that convinced him he needed to go after Kalina.

"If you want to do something to really help us," Cord said to her, "take yer nephew out and teach him to shoot. Revolver, Rifle, Shotgun. As it is, he's a danger to have around a weapon. And once we're out on the trail, there'll be no opportunity to practice. We'd just be signalin' every Injun around as to exactly where we were."

Cord really wanted to get them out of the room so he could explain to Sinclair what he truly had in mind.

"Okay, then," the rancher Sinclair said, "Brett, you round up as many volunteers to ride with Cord as you can from the ranch hands. I'll pay 'em triple to go along."

"No!" Cord objected, "I appreciate it, I really do, but I need to keep this party small if we're to have any chance at all to catch up with the half-breed and the girl."

"Kalina!" Piotr all but screamed, pounding on the table. "She's got a name, it's Kalina. She ain't *'the girl,'* like everybody keeps saying, she's my sister, Kalina."

Midge bent over her nephew to console him. She seemed to be the only one who could calm the boy down.

"I will speak to Piotr in Polish now. Forgive me if this may appear rude. Then, if you will excuse us, we will go out to practice shooting guns. I will make sure he knows how to handle them for your trip in the morning."

She and Piotr began to speak in their native language for several minutes. Cord saw how Midge used the tongue's familiarity to soothe the boy's rattled nerves. As they got up to leave the room, Cord McCullough looked intently at Darraugh Sinclair and Brett Sumner. Only after Midge and Piotr were fully out of sight and earshot did Cord began his confession.

"I think ya' both can see that there is no way in this world that boy is headin' north with me in the morning. Still, I want him to think he is," Cord explained.

"So I figured as much when I caught your wink," said Sinclair. "Nice bit of deception with the shooting practice. Let the lad focus on something tangible."

"Darraugh, I hate to ask," Cord said, "but if I have to pay a ransom for that girl I'm going to need for that sum yer providin' to be damn near a small fortune."

"I already told you I'll take care of that, Cord," Sinclair said firmly without any hesitation.

"Brett, can ya' have someone keep *Pee Otter* busy today after he's done shooting with Midge?" Cord asked. "Keep his mind off of what's goin' on around him."

"Sure thing," Brett said, "I'll have one of the boys spend the rest of the day with him rustlin' up trail clothes, ridin' boots and fixin' him up with a decent mare."

"Good," Cord said, "just keep him busy. I reckon' he'll collapse come sundown and sleep all the night through. By the time he wakes, River and Trouble and I will be long gone."

The three men all looked at each other in agreement. Cord added, "Y'all just gotta keep him from followin' my trail. Then, send him back south by coach."

"Don't you worry about that, Cord, we'll take care of all that," the rancher said. "Tonight we'll load him up with enough whiskey for him to sleep it off over two days."

"Sorry to tell ya' the boy don't really drink," Cord said, "but I'll sure will take ya' up on that offer."

"Okay, then. I'll have Maria prepare that special tea she gives me when I have trouble sleeping," Sinclair said. "Lord knows what she puts in it, but it always does the trick. We'll pump the boy full of it."

"All right, Brett," Sinclair continued without wastin' a breath, "you get together what Cord is askin' for. Get the rifle cartridges and revolver rounds from our stores. You have any extra boots and hats to fool the boy with?"

Brett Sumner seemed like he needed to think on the last bit. "I got a couple of pair of old boots and a fairly decent hat that we took from them two drifters a while back. Remember they couldn't repay the salary advance ya' was kind enough to give 'em, Mr. Sinclair. We caught 'em tryin to sneak off the ranch that night, remember?"

"Sure I do. I guess those will have to do," the rancher said. "I know it's bad luck to wear a dead man's boots, but I guess the boy not knowing he'll be wearin' a deadbeat's boots is okay."

Everyone laughed except Cord. "Ya' know, I seen my share of Confederates at Shiloh stealin' boots off of Yankee corpses. Wearin' a dead man's boots never bothered them much as they was in great need. I reckon' yer right, though, cause maybe that proved to be the reason all that bad luck caught up with them Rebs in the end."

"C'mon, Cord," Sinclair said, "let Midge teach Pete to shoot and Brett chase down yer list of wares, while you and me retire into the den. You can tell me about that business of wiping out the Stone Canyon Gang last fall over a few glasses of the best Scotch whisky in all of Texas. No sense in waiting till after dinner, is there? At least not while my wife and girl are back East."

The two men retired to the den, and in the comfort of its leathered chairs and fancy paneled confines they imbibed in glasses of single malt over tales of gunfights and other adventures. Cord told the story of the Stone Canyon Gang as they drained a full bottle of Sinclair's favorite Scotch. The rancher paid dearly to have the stuff shipped in, including for a dedicated wagon to haul the cases of whisky from the nearest train depot in Dallas. As they opened a second bottle, they got down to the serious discussion.

"Cord," Sinclair said, "I consider myself to be a great judge of a man's character. I like yours. Any relation to that old Texas Ranger Ben McCulloch? Its the same name, just spelled out the way we Scotts are prone to pronounce it."

"No, Darraugh," Cord answered, "can't say I am any kin to him. Fact is, I never met the fella. In my line of work, I try to steer clear of them Texas Rangers as a general matter of practice."

"Well, damn it, I still like your judgement," Sinclair said. "I especially like how you're refusing to take Midge or her Peetey-boy nephew out on *the Llano.*"

Cord laughed to himself. *Peetey-boy. Sounded like the peat was gettin' to Darraugh a wee bit.* Cord felt as if he was starting to become a little smoked himself. It felt damned good, though. It always did. That was the problem.

"I won't say this in front of Midge," the rancher continued, "but these Comanches are nothing but brutal savages. That Ranger Ben McCulloch used to sit right here and share a drink or two just as we are doing now and tell tales of Comanche raids. Bad enough they'd kill innocent settlers, but they'd have their way with the women, then impale their bodies on lances. The men, their innards would be cut out while they were still alive and able to watch."

Cord had heard all the same stories from Rangers on the trail. He thought of what Midge's reaction might be had she heard them. He was convinced that after ditching Piotr, he'd have to go after the girl. That was what his dead wife had been whispering in his ear all along. Only after meeting Midge, did he realize he must act on Callie's call.

"Darraugh," Cord answered, "every man on the Southern Plains done heard those stories of Injun depredations. That's why *the Llano* is so empty. Comanches spread that fear on purpose. Everybody's scared to death to go into *Comancheria,* to face the Comanches on their own ground. I can only hope they treat their young captives better."

"I don't wan't to spoil your hopes, Cord," Sinclair said, "but you should know what prompted their War Chief Buffalo Hump to raid the towns of Victoria and Linnville in 1840. It was our killing three of their chiefs who had come into San Antone earlier for peace talks. One was Buffalo Hump's uncle. He led the *Penatekas,* the Comanches known as *Honey Eaters,* and his name was *Mukwahruh.*"

"You're talking of that Council House Fight," Cord said. "I heard the chiefs refused to give up the captives they had as part of the treaty they were tryin' to negotiate."

"Much worse than that," Darraugh explained. "The chiefs brought their braves, women and children to town with them. Even worse, they brought a captive white girl named Matilda Lockhart who had been taken two years before. When the town's folk saw what they had done to her they were outraged. She was cut and bruised and burned by the other women of the tribe to the point of being near unrecognizable. They said the tip of her nose was a nub of raw bone. Made the Army negotiators demand all white captives be released, regardless of which tribe or band held them. When *Mukwahruh* refused, the army went to arrest them and all hell broke loose. The result was the massacre that became known as the Council House Fight."

Sinclair's eye's were glazed, and he paused, so Cord figured he would finish the story. "And when Buffalo Hump heard of what had happened to his uncle and fellow chiefs, he retaliated with the raids on Victoria and Linnville later that year. They were so vicious that even today everybody's still afraid to stray into Comanche country."

"All except the Army," Darraugh countered. "President Grant is so tired of all these raids that he ordered Secretary of War William T. Sherman to step up the attacks on the remaining Comanches. They're supposedly going to stop the Injuns from coming off the Fort Sill Reservation to raid on us. And I hear they got a large group of some three thousand soldiers under Colonel Ranald Mackenzie getting ready to go in later this year and clear out the rest of the Comanches - to drive them all on to Fort Sill. MacKenzie supposed to be one serious son of a bitch. They call him Three Finger Jack. He lost two digits durin' the war."

"Well," Cord said, "it's gonna take a real son of a bitch to go up against them heathens. Good luck to 'im. I just can't wait for any army. Even if I could, I prefer not to move as slow they'll be. Only way I have a chance is to move light and fast. To move like the Comanches do."

Sinclair took a deep pull of his single malt. He was enjoying the company of a man like Cord McCullough, even if it was spent on discussing such a horrible problem.

The Scotsman had loosened up quite a bit in front of Cord. He said in a sloshy, slippery voice, with his words just beginning to slur, "Cord, I can only hope Mackenzie's troops are more vicious than those Comanche bastards he'll be tracking out west. I hope he shows them no mercy. In fact, I harbor no greater desire in all my being than for him to make their war chiefs cry out these words from my favorite poem:"

The Scotsman theatrically waved his arm in front of him, drunkenly mimicking an actor on a New York stage. He drew a deep breath before he loudly projected the following bit of verse:

"Our fatal day is come, my friend;
And all our wars and glories to an end!
Tis not this course alone we guard in vain,
Condemn'd to vultures on the open plain;
We too must yield:
the same sad fate must fall,
On thee, on me,
Perhaps, my friend, on all."

"Very well done, Darraugh," Cord said. "I have to say, that was beautiful. What's it from? Some Scottish poem? Robert Burns?"

"No, not *Rabbie Burns*," Darraugh mumbled with his Scottish burr on heavily, "It's my take on a passage from Homer's *Iliad*, written over two thousand years ago. It was that blind poet's massive epic about the Greek's obliteration of Troy. Very comparable - only difference is the Trojans hid behind their impenetrable walls, and these Comanches hide amongst the vast expanses of *the Llano*."

"Well," Cord said, raising his glass, "here's to *'Three Finger Jack'* Mackenzie. Let's hope he can bring about the noble defeat of such an ignoble people."

"Except these Comanches are not really people at all," Darraugh Sinclair seethed. "They're nothing short of animals. And they need to be treated as such. I'll give you that small fortune in case you have the opportunity to buy the girl back, but if not, I want you to use every penny of it to kill as many of those savages as you can."

The Comanches are not really people. Those words kept ringing all night in Cord's ears. He could hear the hatred in the Scotsman's voice, freed by the flow of liquor. Darraugh had been forced to live a life under the fear of their terror raids. But Cord knew a little about these Indians. *Comanche* was not even what they called themselves. That name had been given to them by the Utes, one of their tribal enemies, and it meant *he who wants to fight me all the time.*

In their own language, the Comanche simply called themselves *Nermernuh,* or *"The People."*

Part Two:

A Comanche's Story

Chapter 9: Running The Comanche Trace

Northern Mexico, 1848

Juanita lay down to sleep. Through the open window above her bed she could see the full summer moon rising in the night sky. It was what everyone in their village called a *"Comanche Moon."* Her father, her only remaining family, was a simple North Mexican horse herder. He had long ago taught her to fear its deceptively peaceful ascent.

"It could be under the glow of a moon just like this that the Comanche may one day raid our horses." Her father had spoken these words to prepare her many times over the years, but no Indians, Comanche or otherwise, had ever arrived to bother them. During that time, he had built up a modest remuda of horses. It was not extensive enough to accurately be called a "herd," but still it formed the largest corral of the animals in their poor, scant territory.

They had enjoyed several recent months of calm. The war with the Americans had ended in February. On this July night, Juanita had fallen asleep peacefully enough, but when she awoke, it was in an absolute terror. Outside, all she could hear was the whooping of Comanche raiders stampeding her father's horses. The summer sky, hot and dry, was well lit by the glow of that Comanche Moon.

"Juanita!" her father called out to her from the dark interior of their modest home. "I need you to run, my little one. Here, take my coat and run to the spot in the *arroyo* that I have shown you many times before. Cover yourself with it and stay as still and quiet as you possibly can. In the darkness they will not see you. They will not find you."

"*Papá*," the twelve year old said, "I am scared."

"Yes, I know," he said, wrapping the black fringed leather long coat around her torso. "Just run, *mi pequeña*, and stay hidden. I will come for you after they leave. Do not worry, they only want the horses, that's all. Now, go!"

That long leather coat was her father's proudest possession. It had been made by the hands of an artisan from the village, and its long tapered sleeves opened as they flowed, like bells at each wrist, and were fringed with long strands of leather. Despite it being crafted from the thinnest, lightest skins, she feared it would weigh her down.

"Remember," her father said, tears forming in his eyes, "cover yourself completely and stay as still and quiet as you can. *Papá* will come for you. I promise, I will."

He picked her up and lifted her out through the window, settling her gently on the ground beneath it.

"Wait until you hear my gun," he told her with tears streaming from his face, "then run, *mi querida.*"

"No, *Papá*, don't leave me," she sobbed, yet he then kissed her and did exactly that. She remained crouched alone in the darkness against the side of the house. After a few moments, long as a lifetime, she heard the boom of her father's rifle. It was a sound she knew well, having been with him hunting rabbits or killing coyotes. She exploded into her sprint as soon as she heard it, and ran as fast as her little legs could carry her, quiet as she could be.

Her father's ruse had worked. The rifle blast had drawn the Comanches to attack him at the rear of the house, away from his daughter. She ran toward the *arroyo*, which cut a small jagged canyon only several hundred yards in front of their little home. In it, concealed under his black leather long coat, hidden among its dark craggy crevices, her father prayed that Juanita just might be safe.

At first, Juanita believed she had not been detected by the Indians. Intent as they were on overtaking her father, and their stampeding of the small number of horses from the herder's corral, she guessed the savages were not aware of her movements toward the *arroyo*.

As she ran with the coat wrapped around her torso, Juanita could hear the Comanches crying out behind her in the distance. A second later, a man's voice screamed out in a high-pitched terror, that which accompanies excruciating pain. Juanita knew it to be her father, and without thinking stopped and yelled out, *"Papá!"* Instantly, she prayed her cry had not given her away.

Juanita stood flat-footed for a brief moment, frozen, unsure what to do next. Then she remembered her *papá's* instruction and headed once more toward the *arroyo*. As she ran the last fifty yards, she heard the drumming of a horse's hooves growing louder behind her. She knew not to turn to look, as this would only slow her. They grew louder and closer before she could make out that the drumming of the hooves was not of one, but two separate animals.

Juanita did not turn to look back, but still her heart beat so hard she feared it might burst from her chest. It was then that she lost her grip on the coat in one hand, and its sleeve dropped to the ground. She stepped on the fringe that trailed from it, which tripped her and threw her to the dirt. The two Comanche horses were almost on top of her.

She got to her feet, the coat no longer with her, and began to run frantically. The first rider was coming up on her at a full gallop. She knew in her heart he meant to run her down and trample her. But at the last second, she could feel his animal veer and a strong arm scooped down and wrapped itself around her as she ran. She fought, but to no avail. The horse never broke stride and the Comanche raider lifted her, placing her on the animal's back directly in front of himself. He cried out in pride, for he knew taking a captive earned him another eagle feather for his coup stick.

Juanita was terrified. She could not stop her chest from heaving with throes of horror. The second Comanche horseman pulled alongside. She could see that he had retrieved her father's black fringed leather coat.

The two Comanche riders returned to rejoin the others of their raiding party. As they came close, Juanita could see her father lying sprawled in the grass with three other Indians standing over him. *Papá* was not moving.

The girl then made out the shafts of arrows protruding from his chest and thigh. She saw a scarlet red slash across his throat. Juanita turned her head away instinctively, only to have the strong hand of the Comanche behind her turn it back. He said something in their language to the three raiders standing over her father's fallen body.

Then, among a great commotion of yipping and war cries, the three Comanches parted from the body of her father. The rider holding her father's coat dismounted and walked over to the corpse. It was then that he unfurled the coat, waving it like a flag of victory on a breeze over the dead man. The Comanche donned the leather coat, and the fellow Indians reached out in reverence to touch it. Then the savage pulled her father's head up by the hair and slashed his knife across his the skin just below the hairline.

Juanita broke her captor's grasp and turned her head away. The Indian gripped her jaw again in his strong hand.

"Tu miras!" the voice instructed her to look. It was said awkwardly, but still surprised her that he spoke any Spanish at all. While she feared his vise-like grip would break her jawbone, the real agony came from being forced to watch as her father's lifeless body was scalped in front of her. The fact that her eyes were flooded with tears, blurring out much of the unbearable details, did not matter. Just the realization that it was happening in front of her caused her body to quiver uncontrollably with revulsion.

As the cries of the scalping party reached a crescendo, she could see the warrior slice open the skin of her *papá's* forehead. She heard the Comanche ripping away the skin from the top of her *papá's* skull, producing a sickeningly wet tearing sound that she knew she would never forget. Wearing her father's long coat, the Comanche then wiped the blade flat on its leather sleeve. He attached the dangling scalp to his war lance and held the long weapon high before her. The nauseating metallic smell of her father's blood filled her nostrils. When the Comanche behind her joined in the war party's cries, it rattled her to the core, piercing her ears and heart alike.

What terrified Juanita most, even more than her *papá's* scalp dangling from that lance like his disembodied soul, was watching that Comanche's arrogant pride in being dressed out in the long leather coat. He swept his hands over its flowing sleeves, one which was smeared with her *papá's* blood. She sensed that her father's prized garment, would forever trail her, as if it had entrapped his ghost. One day, it would bear witness to her losing her own life among them. She imagined this happening not under a full summer moon, but what she thought to be a massive winter star.

There was a discussion in the Comanche tongue between the one who had taken her, and the other in her father's coat. The latter brave soon nodded in reluctant agreement, after which her abductor rode off alone with her. As they did, she looked back to see the others, under the direction of the Comanche wearing the coat, scatter away from *Papá's* body and mount to round up his horses.

Juanita and her captor rode north for hours before they came to and crossed the Rio Grande. She had been here once on a journey with her father so that she could see it, but she had never dared to cross it into Texas. Yet this Comanche knew exactly where to ford the great river. Once across, the Indian rested his horse, but only briefly. He allowed it to drink for a bit from the water.

He took Juanita a few feet downstream along the riverbank and in front of her relieved himself. In butchered Spanish he said, *"Lo haces, haz aqua!"* or *"You do. Make water!"* But she could not. Fear's grip was too powerful.

He repeated himself, but she could not do as he said. Off the horse, she stood side by side with him, and for the first time looked upon his war painted face. His eyes were lifeless, uncaring flat black stones. He reached his hand up to her face, and she feared he would strike her.

The Comanche grabbed her by the jaw, just as he had atop the horse over her father's corpse. In the moonlight, he inspected the smooth youthful features of her face. Then, he reached with his free hand to his own cheek and dragged his fingers through the heavy streaks of vermillion and yellow-ochre war paint. Those same fingers then smeared the waxen colors across the beautiful soft bronze skin of her cheek. Somehow, Juanita knew it meant she was his prize to keep. This unleashed a stream of tears to her eyes that, try as she did, she could not stop.

"Vámos!" He gestured with his arm, *"We go!"* before he climbed atop his horse and reached down to pull her up. She thought for a second to run off, but where would she run to? He would just chase her down again. She reached her hand up to his. He lifted her easily from her feet with his powerful arm. They rode throughout that night. Eventually, she got used to the horse's rhythm thrusting her backward, hard against his muscled chest. They did not stop again, and rode straight through until dawn. As the sun rose, he stopped only to again water the pony and "make water" himself. She still could not.

On the second day's ride, she finally learned to obey him. She would "make water" when he said, and drink fresh water from his animal skin when he offered it. The first time she attempted to relieve herself, she walked to hide behind a tall bush, but he grabbed her arm firmly and pointed her back to the open ground. She would not do this in front of him, so he angrily went to the pony and retrieved his lance. She feared what he would do with it.

He merely stirred the growth of high bush with it until she heard the unmistakable sound of a rattler's tail. It sent a shiver up her spine. Juanita then turned her back on him, raised her skirt high above her knees, and squatted out in the open, giving into her dire need for relief.

As they rode further that day, the terrain climbed and then flattened onto a great plain of grass and scrub. With the hills behind them, there were few trees and Juanita soon became very aware of the unrelenting breath of wind blowing across the plain. It seemed to pulse and heave, like the lungs of God Almighty, constantly scrubbing these lands clean. Her long black hair fluttered upon it and danced teasingly in the face of her captor, although she hoped it to stop, but the wind refused to obey her wishes.

The Comanche stopped his horse, and almost ceremonially, pulled from a leather sheath a large, sharp skinning knife. He gathered her hair from his face and pulled it hard, yanking back her head until her chin pointed skyward. The sun burned bright in her eyes. Even when she closed them, its ball of flames danced in the darkness.

A tremendous fear surged through her. Every nerve of her skin rose and tingled; all her senses peaked with a deadly anticipation.

So he has spared my life only until we reached this place? Here am I to meet the same fate as my father, to have my throat slit? Will I even feel it when he takes his prize of my scalp with my long black locks attached to it?

She felt the tight muscles of his chest flex, and with one swipe it was over. Her head was released. She clutched instinctively at her throat, surprised to find it still intact.

He extended his arm around her, his fist full of the long strands of her lustrous black hair. He opened his palm and, one by one, they came to life on the warm wind. Each strand peeled away on the breeze in its own distinct ways, not one wriggling quite the same way as that before it.

Juanita reached up to feel her barren skin of her neck, the remaining hair now barely covering its nape. She felt as if her innocence, her childhood, had been stripped away from her. Just as the last of her family had been in the savage killing of her *papá*.

"Comanche men hair long," he said in shards of Spanish, "our women no." His meaning stung tears in her eyes; she fought their release. He counted her among, "our women." Then, he swept his hand across the landscape before their view and spoke again. She heard him utter the single Spanish word, *"Llano,"* meaning, *"the Plains."*

When the sun rose high in the sky, it parched *the Llano* into a dry sea of grass. Her tears by then flowed freely down her cheeks, but that seemed to be the only water to be found. He guided them to a dry creek bed and followed its dirt upstream until it widened. As he trailed it, the soil became moist, and further beyond, fresh water trickled before them. They rested there for some time, then traveled more. As the sun dropped in the west, they stopped to sleep for a few hours. Juanita, sore from the ride behind her, remained terrified of what still lay ahead. She feared what the second night might hide under its dark cape.

The Comanche laid out his horse's saddle blanket on the ground and motioned for her to lay on it. She soon gave into the sheer exhaustion of the tiring ride. She couldn't escape thoughts of her *papá*, but even his death and scalping were not enough to keep her from slipping into the clutching fingers of sleep. She needed its rest to restore her fatigued body and soothe her tortured mind.

She dreamt that it had all been a nightmare. She was at home with her *papá*, telling it to him in great detail. He yawned and said, "It is a most terrifying story, *mi pequeña*, but you are safe with me here now."

It was then that the Comanche startled her from this much needed escape. He knelt over her, his knees parting her legs. A raw and inexplicable fear swept through her as she pulled back away from him. In response, he harshly staked one arm, and planted it firmly above her narrow shoulders, in effect pinning her down. She could no longer move away from him. Then, with the other hand he drew out the skinning knife.

The fear rippled through her uncontrollably. Once more, she thought that he had brought her to this specific place, for some unknown reason, to kill and scalp her.

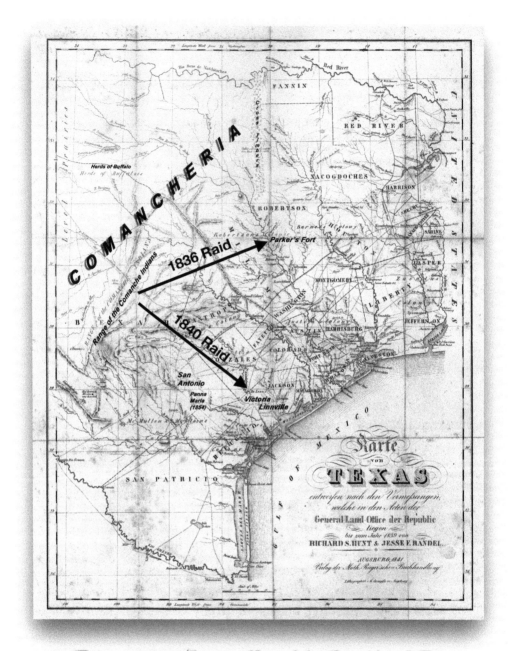

Figure 4: 1839 German Map of the Republic of Texas
With Author's Overlays Showing Comancheria and
The Raid on Parker Fort (1836) and
Raids on Victoria & Linnville (1840)

She trembled at his intention until she heard the predator's guttural growl, when an even more primal fear overtook her. Juanita arched her neck, her shoulder pressed hard against his staked arm, and saw the ravenous coyote only a few feet beyond. The diabolical vividness of its eyes pierced the darkness that otherwise enshrouded it.

A chorus of sickly howls came not from it, but from the other members of its pack nearby. Hearing their songs of hunger, the animal lunged. For Juanita, the assault was horrifying. The fear of her being taken against her will by the Comanche had in a split second been washed away by a wave of sheer terror - the thought of being killed and eaten by this beast. She screamed in a pitch so high, it was one she did not realize she even possessed.

The echo of her fright had not subsided when the Comanche stabbed at the lunging animal, sinking the blade of his skinning knife deep into its abdomen just as its claws ripped at her skin. The animal let out a blood-curdling yelp as the Indian violently twisted his wrist, carving out a swath of muscle and tissue that fell free from the blade upon her skin. It smeared the terror stricken girl with warm flesh engorged with seemingly still pulsating blood.

In just a few seconds it was all over. The coyote lay dead beside her. The scratches from its claws upon her skin were deep, but not physically crippling. She had not been bitten. Instead, it was the hysterical trauma that pierced her to her core. Juanita sobbed uncontrollably after the attack, shaking and heaving violently. The Comanche ignored her.

"Others not come now. We sleep," the Comanche said in broken Spanish. She knew he meant the other coyotes, scared off by the attacking animal's death cries. He left its carcass by their side to keep the others away. His knife's blade still pierced the dead animal's heart.

But Juanita knew no rest would come to her after that attack, with the snarling animal by her side, frozen in death. It was then she knew she had to fight a battle even deeper within herself, realizing that if she was to survive, she had to learn to trust this Comanche. He had kept her first from the peril of the rattlesnake in the brush. Now, he had saved her from a savage coyote attack. She had to conquer the fear of her captor and allow him to protect her.

The Comanche gave himself into sleep. Juanita had her hands and feet bound together by leather strips that were attached to a braid he wrapped around his own wrist. She could not sleep, merely stared up at the thicket of stars scattered across the night sky. In the distance, she heard the plaintive howls of the other coyotes as they retreated further under the glow of that Comanche Moon.

The next day, Juanita and the Comanche remounted his horse to again ride hard and long. She could see that the land had completely flattened out. All around her she saw only grass. *The Llano* appeared empty of all other living things, but she knew better. It was full of danger of many kinds. Still, she found it to be beautiful in a delicate way.

During that third day she finally gave into her burning hunger and accepted what he had to offer her to eat - dried meat and pemmican. The latter was the closest thing to bread the Comanches possessed. It was made from pounded fruits and berries and then infused with buffalo tallow. It tasted unlike anything she had ever put in her mouth, but the pain in her empty gut forced her to eat it.

The next night he watched over her as she fell asleep. He had tied her hands, but not her feet, for where would she run to? Once he was confident they would not be bothered by any beast, he rested next to her. But still, her leather braid stretched to wrap around his own wrist.

The fourth day, they rose well before dawn and rode through the hours until sundown, deeper into *the Llano Estacado.* She remembered from her schooling at the mission how these lands had been named by the Spanish explorer, Coronado. The words meant *the Staked Plains,* or some say, *Palisaded Plains.* She could see neither stakes nor palisades, only an unending flat sea of scrub grasses.

The long ride over this expansive landscape devoid of everything, even shadows, slowly ebbed away the terror that had filled her since her taking. *If this savage wished to harm me, he would have done so by now.* Yet, even with her fears receding, it left behind no calm, only a void that slowly became a reservoir for sadness and desperation. She still could not stop thinking of the body of her slaughtered, scalped father. How much she had loved him in life, only to keep seeing his body butchered in death.

Her own body ached in so many places that she could no longer even isolate individual pains. The ride had all but rubbed raw her legs inside her thighs. The cheeks of her buttocks were numb. Inside her, she ached from the hollows of morbid emptiness, a feeling she had never before experienced in her life. She longed only for her past; she had never before felt so alone.

They continued across that sea of grass, when in the distance she spotted what appeared to be a black crust scorching the plain. She stretched out her arm and pointed toward it, in doing so realizing it was her first attempt at initiating a discussion with her captor.

His strong arm reached up for her outstretched wrist, and gently pulled it down. Then, he reined the horse hard toward that dense black feature. Without a word, she realized she had asked what it was, and he, in turn, had volunteered to show her.

As they neared the darkened mass, it slowly transformed before Juanita's eyes from a solid stain to a gently shifting vapor. When they closed in further on it, the dark black mist-like cloud soon revealed itself to be a huddled slowly moving mass of many individual creatures, thousands of them, packed tightly together. They were so closely arrayed that it was difficult to make out any single animal. Instead, she noticed only the bobbing waves of tightly curled dark humps foamed with the occasional gleam of pale white horns.

"Cibolo," the Comanche said in her ear, naming the beast in his tongue. It was the twelve year old's first ever sighting of a buffalo herd. Then, in his broken Spanish, her captor said, *"Nos dan vida!"* which she understood him to mean, *"They give us life!"*

What came next opened a part of her soul. He charged his horse directly at the herd, yipping and hollering as he did so. The great mass slowly lumbered, then broke into a halting run in response. Great clouds of dust rose up around them, scattering the rays of the sun. The ground shook and rumbled in what Juanita thought an earthquake might be like. The Comanche took her so close to the edge of the herd she could look individual animals in the eye. Then, unexpectedly, she smiled. It stretched across her face, but it came from deep within her. She was not afraid in the least. Instead, the purest joy spread throughout her.

They rode along the edge of the herd of buffalo for a quarter of an hour or so. Juanita could see the curly tight fur draped like a cape over the great humps of the beasts. It gave them a deserved majesty. Their great numbers seemed to assure they would forever roam over these southern plains. It brought a deep happiness to her, just knowing that these proud animals roamed free in such massive herds.

A few days later, as they continued to ride north across the hot plains, she noticed ahead of her another sight that her mind also could not quite process. She thought it to be an illusion at first, the effect of many days of having the plain's high sun beat down unforgivingly upon her. She swore she could see the flat ground open up before her. As they neared, it proved to be no illusion.

In fact, the real illusion, from a distance, had been that the plains stretched on forever, when in fact, a tremendous canyon was carved out before them from deep within the flat earth. They rode up slowly to its ragged rim.

The ground dropped away hundreds of feet from the its edge upon which they then rested. The canyon gaped open a mile wide. Its walls were rocky bluffs that were dabbled in horizontal stripes of tan, ochre, and rust. Nestled deep inside the canyon was a silver ribbon - a winding creek that reflected the sun with a glint. It drew her attention as it snaked through the labyrinth of windswept canyon walls.

It was along the creek's narrow grassy banks that Juanita saw lines of angular Indian lodges, what she had been told in the mission school were *tipis*. Not far beyond those in the distance, she could make out a great heard of horses. She wondered how many of this herd had been stolen from the lands of Northern Mexico, from which she herself had been taken. Had her father's few horses already been brought ahead of them here?

Her captor waved his arm across the descending earth as it opened wide before them, as if to say, *take all this in*. Leaning back against him, she swore she could feel his chest swell with pride. He said to her in Spanish the word's *"Palo Duro"* or *"Hard Wood."* She took this to be the canyon's name.

Then he pointed with his finger to the settlement of lodges and said a single word - *Nermernuh.* Juanita would soon enough come to understand their language. When she did, she would learn *Nermernuh* was the name they reserved for themselves - meaning simply, *"The People."*

It was then that she thought again of her father, but remembering him this time in life, not death. She thought of how he would break the will of wild horses not in any single day, but over time by repetition to gain their trust.

It was only then that Juanita realized her great ride across *the Llano* over these many days had broken her own will. She had come to rely upon and even to trust her unnamed Comanche.

A great fear returned to the girl. *So is this the only reason I have been broken but not harmed for so many days and nights? Only so that I might be delivered unto another of these people?*

Then the warrior slowly began to ride down a path that was nothing more than an antelope's trail along the canyon's steep wall. It switched back on itself many times as they descended. Juanita feared the Comanche horse would misstep, and they all would be cast violently down the ragged canyon's side, but instead the animal's hooves remained true.

They reached the bottom and crossed over the creek's waters to the village. Even from a distance, Juanita could see just how massive each *tipi* was, many times her own height. It was then that all *"the People"* emerged from their lodges. They quickly swarmed and ran to him, welcoming him as a conquering hero. They called out her captor by his name. Unintelligible to her at first, she soon would learn it meant, *"Wolf of the Dark Night."*

The other thing she would learn was that many of the *Nermernuh* spoke fragments of Spanish. She soon discovered why, for even on that very day, in their camp, there were *Comancheros.* These were the New Mexican mixed-blood Mexican Indian/Hispanic traders who were allowed to deal guns, liquor and other goods to the Comanches. From them, the Comanches had over many years learned simple elements of the Spanish language.

As *the Nermernuh* collected around them, Juanita felt her returning terror peak. Many hands of women and children reached up to touch her. Their fingers swept over her, tracing out her body's features. Their touch was cold, she thought, curious, but not welcoming. After the days riding amidst *the Llano's* heat, she felt as if she was now being pulled through a sea of ice.

"Wolf of the Dark Night," or more simply said, *"Dark Wolf"* allowed this for a bit, but then suddenly made a fist and struck his own chest with it brutally, powerfully, as if to say, *she is mine.* The crowd of hands melted away, disappointed by his declaration.

In Juanita, there was only relief. She had feared being handed over to some other member of the tribe. In Mexico, stories were told of how Comanche women would abuse captives, especially young girls. They would punch them with their fists, hit them with sticks, burn them with hot coals, or even cut them with knives. *Dark Wolf's* fist thumping display gave her a feeling of protection. After the exhausting ride over what she would learn had been the *Comanche Trace,* she had become comfortable with him. He had made her feel safe. He had protected her.

It was clear to her then that her will, as angry and defiant as it had been over the death of her *papá*, had been broken, just like that of one of her father's wild horses.

Chapter 10: She Who Runs Like The Trembling Wind

Comancheria, 1851

Three years had passed and Juanita's former life had been fully sloughed away from her, slowly but thoroughly, just as the wind whittled away at the rock of the canyon walls that rose around them. Not long after her arrival, the young Mexican girl had been taken by *Wolf of Dark Night* to the medicine man, who would give her a new tribal name. She was surprised to learn that all the children were not named by their parents, but by the village through a ceremony overseen by the main medicine man. After *Dark Wolf* had told the details of his story of her capture, of how she had run to the nearby *arroyo* in a stop-start fashion, Juanita was renamed as *"She Who Runs Like the Trembling Wind."*

Trembling Wind then became the second wife of the brave *Dark Wolf.* His first wife, *Scent of Dawn*, had not given him any children. She had been full once with his child, but the medicine man with the power of the river otter was not in camp. *Trembling Wind* learned each village possessed many medicine men, each with a different "magic" or "power" taken from the spirit of different animals. The river otter was revered because it slid easily down the muddied banks into the river of life. This was the otter's special magic, its *"puha."*

But the animal's *puha* was not with them when his wife's time came to deliver his first child. The one who possessed the river otter *"puha"* was gone from the village on a raiding mission. *Scent of Dawn's* child did not survive birth. After that, even over several years, her belly was never again full with life. So, *Dark Wolf* took the young girl *Trembling Wind* as a wife with the hope to start his family.

Trembling Wind learned the Comanche ways. Men, even boys, did no menial work. They hunted, raided, went to war, or practiced such. Boys were raised only to fight and hunt. Women did all the chores, from cleaning and washing, to preparing food. Even the butchering of buffalo that the warriors killed on hunts was done by women.

The buffalo were only killed only in numbers needed to sustain the village. From a herd of thousands, only two or three, rarely more than single digits, would be taken in a hunt. Then, after the kill, the women skinned the carcasses and prepared the meat. It would be dried for the village to sustain itself on for the coming weeks or months. The women even processed the hides for a number of uses.

Trembling Wind soon learned what her new husband had meant when he told her that the *"cibolo"* gave them life. Every part of the animal was put to use. Nothing was wasted. Buffalo skins were used for clothing, even for shelter, as multiple hides were tanned, weatherized and stitched together by the women to make the exteriors of the *tipi* lodges. Buffalo robes made from the animal's winter furs protected the Comanche from the brutal freezing cold so common to the plains' winter. Thick buffalo skins were layered into stacks to build shields to protect warriors on summer raids from the weapons of the white man. The bones were used to make tools and other implements. The horns and skulls were kept for ceremonial purposes.

Trembling Wind also learned that the village would move every few weeks to follow the great herds. The entire village could be dismantled and readied to move in less than an hour. Each woman would be responsible for taking down the family lodge, using the long *tipi* poles and skins to fashion a *travois* to carry all their goods upon. For this reason, possessions were kept to a minimum. There were no clay jars or containers of any kind to lug. Water and other necessary fluids were kept in pouches made from the buffalo's organs, mostly stomach or intestines. Other items were stored in *parfleche* - bags made from the animal hide.

But if it was the buffalo that gave the Comanches life, *Trembling Wind* quickly learned that the currency of that life was the horse. For tradition told them that before the Spanish Conquistadors brought horses to the plains, the *Nermernuh* had no truly effective way to hunt the great *"cibolo."* True, occasionally they were able to run a few of the animals over a cliff, but once they took to horseback, the Comanche people were able to hunt buffalo on the run. For this reason, the Comanche cherished the horse, and collected as many as they could by any means possible. They accumulated great herds of the animals, and selected from them only the swiftest and most durable for their own use, especially for the buffalo hunt or raiding parties. The Comanche quickly became the most feared of all enemies mounted on horseback in battle.

It was during one of the great buffalo hunts when a very tragic, but not very rare, event occurred. Her husband *Dark Wolf* was away hunting the *cibolo,* when another of the village women began to mistreat *Trembling Wind.* It was early in the girl's days as a Comanche, and for some reason the other woman thought the young wife had slighted her. For this, the woman sought vengeance.

She took *Trembling Wind* into her *tipi* and used a hot ember from the fire to burn the skin of her forearms in scalding patterns. *Trembling Wind* fought free from the woman and returned to her own lodge where her sister wife, *Scent of Dawn,* tended to her burns.

When *Dark Wolf* returned from the hunt, he made his complaint to the elders against the woman. She just happened to be the wife of the raider who had recovered the Mexican long leather coat that once had belonged to *Trembling Wind's papá.* His name was *Raging Anger.* He was, like *Dark Wolf,* a war chief. Comanche villages had many war chiefs, and it was not unusual for feuds to crop up between them. These disputes were settled most often by a council of the village elders.

Dark Wolf was awarded by the elders two horses as payment from *Raging Anger* for having allowed his wife to unjustly abuse the young woman. *Trembling Wind* had to accept the terms of that payment, despite how unfair she found it to be. She learned that, in this culture, what she felt did not matter. All that mattered was that her new husband, *Dark Wolf,* was satisfied with the settlement.

Raging Anger's wife was shamed and ran off alone to the far edge of the village. There, she cut herself with a knife on her arms, breasts and thighs in response to the disgrace that had been thrust upon her by the elders.

Once *Trembling Wind* had been fully accepted into the tribe, she learned the Comanche tongue fluently. Languages had always come easily to her. She had picked up a fair bit of English along the border. She taught more Spanish to the braves and the elders who traded with the *Comancheros.* She was highly respected for this, but was never allowed to speak directly to the *Comancheros,* who were a very rough band of half-bloods themselves.

At the end of her first year with *the People,* the child *Trembling Wind* became a woman. On the night that her blood first flowed, she was sent to a separate lodge used to house village women in their unclean state. Her sister wife, *Scent of Dawn,* accompanied her, so she would not be alone, but also so that she could tell their husband when the girl was ready for him. When the girl stopped flowing, she was cleansed and given to *Dark Wolf* to mate.

She had by then been in the lodge many times when *Dark Wolf* had taken *Scent of Dawn* in that way. She knew what to expect physically. But emotionally, she proved to be totally unprepared. She had been without a mother for so long, there was no one in which she could confide. Even as kind as her sister wife had been to her, *Trembling Wind* sensed there had been a competition growing between them for *Dark Wolf's* attention. Becoming his new mate would only sharpen those pangs of jealousy in *Scent of Dawn.*

The first night that *Dark Wolf* took her, he was unaffectionate and mechanical. She ached for days from his having entered her, yet something in *Trembling Wind* desired another turn with her husband. Perhaps it was driven by the way *Scent of Dawn* clung to him afterward.

Soon, *Trembling Wind* learned to relax during her time with *Dark Wolf,* and given that, she began to enjoy when he selected her. She began to look forward to her encounters with him, most so those when they were alone in the lodge because *Scent of Dawn* was banished to the unclean tent.

As time progressed, *Dark Wolf* selected *Trembling Wind* more and more over *Scent of Dawn,* for his first wife remained unable to bear him children. This greatly angered *Scent of Dawn,* although she did her best to hide it from both her husband and her sister wife.

In her third year in the camp. *Trembling Wind* found herself with child. *Dark Wolf* had filled her belly with a son, so the otter medicine man said. Those who possessed the otter's powers were sought for all woman giving birth. Many wives were lost in childbirth, just as was the case for the white settlers and the Mexican villagers that the Comanches raided. It was believed that fewer wives or children were lost when the birth took place under the oversight of the otter medicine man. Because of this, the river otter's *puha* was highly prized.

Dark Wolf had already lost a child with his first wife, *Scent of Dawn,* because the otter medicine man was not present. This time, *Dark Wolf* made sure he was available for the birth. With the help of the otter *puha,* the fifteen year old wife, *Trembling Wind,* delivered to her husband a healthy son. Initially, *Scent of Dawn* enjoyed the child's arrival also, but over time became increasingly jealous of the boy, or rather the attention he garnered from *Dark Wolf.*

The child was given the name by the village's main medicine man of *Crying Hatchling* because of his chronic wailing. But this was merely a temporary name, for as he grew older, the child would be awarded a new title that would better describe his personality, once it revealed itself.

Chapter 11: The Legend of the Killer Owl

Comancheria, 1851-1858

Time passed and the child named *Crying Hatchling* grew. He was a lovely child, but soon differed in appearance from the other Comanche youth. These differences became more pronounced as he developed. He had much of his mother's natural beauty, and even though *Trembling Wind* was accepted, her looks differed noticeably from those of the native women. Her skin was smoother, more bronze than theirs. Her cropped black hair, no longer allowed to be kept in any length past her neck, was the same hue but more silken, less flaxen than that of the village women. Her nose was straighter, more European. These traits were all passed on to her son, where they mixed with traditional Comanche features. Still, even with all these features being apparent, *Crying Hatchling* was fully accepted by *the Nermernuh.* That was until he would make a series of decisions that would ultimately separate him from *the People.*

Crying Hatchling was raised as were all Comanche children. As an infant, he spent much of each day in a *papoose,* either upon his mother's back or on a standing frame built just for that purpose known as a *papoose* board. In this way, Indian children became independent from birth.

As they grew, boys were allowed to wander freely and engage in play fighting with the other male children. They began learning early the concepts of mastering the bow and arrow on simple weapons with flat-tipped arrow shafts. Comanche boys mastered these simple toys to the point they could knock hummingbirds out of flight.

By no older than five years old, children of both sexes were placed on their first animal's back - either a tame old horse or a mule. Once accustomed to riding, they would be given their first mount. Boys were advanced quickly to more capable ponies, faster than girls. Most boys were accomplished riders by the time they were eight.

Raised by their parents, all Comanche children were taught the necessity of obedience from an early age. Those who misbehaved were warned of the legend of the Big Cannibal Owl named *Piamempits*. Although Comanches did not believe in cannibalism, as was practiced by their enemy tribe, the Tonkawas, they used stories of that great owl to scare their young, telling them that if they did not behave, *Piamempits* would come and eat them.

Scent of Dawn, still jealous of the child of her sister wife, told this legend over and over to the toddler *Crying Hatchling* and throughout the years of his youth. The young child became terrorized by the thought, but after mastering the simple bow and arrow, he learned from his father how to spot owl roosts. In trees, this could be done by studying the owl's white droppings that discolored the leaves below their nests. The boy *Crying Hatchling* became proficient in identifying the nests of owls in the trees near their lodges.

When he was eight, *Crying Hatchling* heard for the first time the terrifying call of a screech owl outside their *tipi*. While hoot owls and burrowing owls were common on *the Llano,* screech owls were more rare.

The next day, after a night of hearing the owl's shrill, loud screeches, *Crying Hatchling* was sure the night predator was none other than *Piamempits.* The boy identified the roosting nest of the animal, and the next night stole away with sharp tipped arrows from his father's quill. When night fell, he waited for the owl's horrifying call, located it precisely and shot several arrows into the roost.

The boy had merely wounded the animal which fell to the ground flapping its wings and releasing an awful wounded screech. *Dark Wolf* was drawn out of his lodge by the commotion, just in time to see his young son killing the night bird with a large stone. The child explained to his father that he had merely killed *Piamempits* who had come to eat him. But instead of being rewarded for his bravery, his father merely bowed his head in great shame.

In the Comanche culture, all owls are revered animals, as they are in most other native cultures. They can see in the night, and as such are thought to commune with the spirits of the dead. Their wings are tufted, silencing their flight almost completely, making them admired as stealthy predators. Killing any owl was considered an offense not only against nature, but against *the People, the Nermernuh,.* This taboo act was considered to be an invitation for dark spirits to visit upon their village.

For this reason, the boy was chastised by the village. Before the elders, he lied and told them he had spoken with a coyote who told him to kill the cannibal owl. He thought this clever, as coyotes were taught in their culture to be great deceivers, makers of forbidden mischief. He expected to be forgiven the sin of having killed the owl, but having claimed to have spoken to *the Great Deceiver*, the elders considered the child to have coyote *puha.* Thus, he must be treated as a deceiver himself.

The elders' decision robbed *Dark Wolf* of his son. His child had not only taken on the shame of killing an owl, but had admitted he had been lured to do so by the coyotes.

The young boy was forbidden by the elders from ever becoming a raider or warrior, or to ever accompany his father or any other Comanche brave on the buffalo hunt. In an act of publicly humiliating the young man, his name was ceremonially changed from the simple descriptive one of *Crying Hatchling* to one forever connected to the shame of his taboo act. He would from that point on be known as "*He Who Kills Owls,*" or more simply "*Kills Owls.*"

The young boy lived in the village for several more years, but was never allowed to train for the raids on the Texas settlers or Mexican horse farms. In this way, the boy named *Kills Owls* would be forever dishonored.

Chapter 12: Gray Feather

Comancheria, 1858-1862

Having much idle time on his hands, *Kills Owls* found only mischief with which to consume it. The elder men of the village, long past their primes for raiding or hunting buffalo, spent their days making bows, arrows, and shields for the younger warriors. The elders' wisdom and long honed skills were highly respected. At night they entered into a special *tipi* called the smoke lodge, where only they could hold sacred smokes and speak of the news and village gossip of the day. Even the village warriors were not permitted to enter the smoke lodge.

One particular elder, *Gray Feather,* took pity on the wayward boy. He received permission from the others to guide the mischievous child. He would teach *Kills Owls* the ways of the Comanche people each day as the boy assisted him in his specialty - fashioning bows and arrows from selected hardwoods. *Gray Feather* would pass these skills onto the boy, he thought, so that the child could one day himself become a maker of bows and arrows, and thus a productive member of the village.

Soon, *Gray Feather* was looked on by the boy as a father figure. Given the child's disgrace, his own father would have nothing to do with him. *Kills Owls* came to cherish the hours he would spend with *Gray Feather.*

Gray Feather first taught the boy the history of the Comanche tribe. He taught *Kills Owls* how the *Nermernuh* had separated from the Shoshone tribe on the great plains east of the mighty mountains in the north.

He taught the boy how the *Nermernuh* then moved south and took up deadly battles with many other tribes - including the Utes and the Tonkawas - both of whom the the *Nermernuh* were victorious over for undisputed control of the great southern plains that stretched from the Canadian River south to the Rio Grande.

Gray Feather even taught the boy that it was the Utes who had given them the feared name *"Comanches,"* meaning, *"He who wants to fight me all the time."* It was this name that struck terror into all who heard it: the Texas settlers, the Mexican horse herders, even *the Nermernuh's* most dreaded enemy - the native tribe of the Apache.

The Apache had been for years, if not centuries, the lords of this great southern plain that the Spaniards called the *Llano Estacado*. While they also were mounted warriors, they did not possess the same level of skill of fighting on horseback that the Comanche had mastered. In a fierce nine day battle, the Comanche drove the Apache from the highly desired buffalo grazing grounds west to the lands that would later become New Mexico and Arizona.

Gray Feather also taught *Kills Owls* that the greater tribe of Comanche was separated into the various groups know as "bands." Each band was a separate entity from the others, and there was no one central leader over the tribe. While each band had several war chiefs, one was selected as the overall warrior leader. Still no band's chief spoke on behalf of the other bands. They were connected and shared a common brotherhood, but each band stood alone. Despite this, braves were allowed to shift between bands if needed.

Over the years that *Gray Feather* mentored *Kills Owls,* the boy learned his village was called *the Quahadi* band of Comanches. *"Quahadi"* meant *"Antelopes,"* so common to the plains upon which they lived. *The Quahadi* also took pride in the great distances their raiders could travel. They were known to travel far south deep into Mexico, and as far north as Wyoming. No other band had their raiding range. *Gray Feather* taught the boy that no other band possessed the warrior fervor of *the Quahadi.*

The other bands of Comanches were geographically dispersed. There were the *Penatekas, or Honey-eaters* in the east, nearest to the Cross Timbers area where many bees were to be found. This band was responsible for the great raid on Fort Parker. Also, there were the *Yamparikas or Yap (Root) Eaters* in the north. In the south were *the Penanes or Quick Stinging Wasps,* who like *the Quahadi* were great raiders. One band, *the Nokonis or Wanderers Who Make Bad Camps,* were so named because they broke camp and resettled so often that the quality of their encampments was decidedly poor. In all, there were as many as a dozen bands, comprising over seventy thousand Comanche warriors at the height of the tribe's power.

Gray Feather taught the boy how the Comanche had stopped the advance northward of the Spanish from Mexico, and the French westward from New Orleans. He warned the child that the white men coming into Texas were unlike the rest. These men wished not only to share the land, but to take possession of it. This was not understandable by them, for the land belonged to no one. It supported the *cibolo,* who in turn gave the Comanche life. They would fight with other tribes only over who could hunt on the land, but they could not conceive of anyone owning the land any more than owning the wind or the sky.

The white men, they taught their young, would keep coming until they *took* the land as their own, as they had in the East from other tribes. They would claim every *cibolo* that dwelled upon it. It was a dire threat to their way of life.

Gray Feather explained to the boy this was why such ferocious raids on the white settlers were needed. It was why Parker's Fort was invaded and the young children taken, just as his own mother had been taken away from Mexico. The white man coming to settle from the East had to be scared off, and brutally so, to make them never want to come further west and destroy the beauty of *the Llano.*

Gray Feather finally taught him how the white men could not be trusted. For years, the leaders of the white men who wore Blue Coats had called for the chiefs of the various Comanche bands to come in for peace talks. In the white man's year 1840, three chiefs went into San Antonio for that very purpose. As they were negotiating with the Blue Coats, they were told they had to turn over all white captives. When the chiefs said that they did not have control of all the captives, only the ones in their own bands, the Blue Coats told them they could not leave. They were going to hold our Comanche chiefs as captives in return. A great battle broke out and all three chiefs and their people were slaughtered, with only a few women surviving.

A single woman was released to bring the white men's demands back to the rest of the Comanche people. When it was learned of what happened, there was great anger. *Gray Feather* explained how the Great War Chief, *Buffalo Hump,* vowed vengeance. T*he Great Spirit* sent him a vision of driving the white men violently into the sea. This came to pass later that year when *Buffalo Hump* led raids on the white towns of Victoria and Linnville, where many white settlers took to the waters of the bay to escape.

"You see," *Gray Feather* said, "the mightiest medicine men and war chiefs receive visions from *the Great Spirit* of what is to come. It is the duty of the leaders to make *the People* believe, and to lead them into battle."

Gray Feather also explained that in the year 1860, another conflict took place, and used it to teach the boy just how treacherous the white men had become. "The eastern band of *the Penatekas or Honey Eaters,* were camped along what the white men call the Pease River. Most of the warrior braves had already left camp, while the Comanche wives were loading the lodges and buffalo meat onto pack mules. Only then did a group of Texas Rangers attack. They cut down everyone, women and children alike."

"The chief of the *Honey Eaters, Peta Nocona or Lone Wanderer* was chased down and savagely killed, as were the few of his warriors still present, left behind to protect the chief. *Peta Nocona's* wife, *Na'ura*, was chased and thrown from her horse, but when the Rangers saw she had blue eyes, they knew her to be a long captive white woman and they spared her. They soon learned that she was the girl for whom they had long searched - the one taken from Fort Parker twenty-four years earlier. They called her Cynthia Ann Parker. She had only her infant daughter, *Toposannah,* or *Prairie Flower,* with her."

"Her two sons survived that day's massacre only because of her. The oldest, twelve, was named *Quanah,* which means *fragrant.* At the onset of the raid, he and his younger brother, *Pecos,* were put on a Comanche pony by their mother. They were chased by the Rangers but the boys were able to outride them. The Rangers took their mother and sister away. Afterwards, *Na'ura* only wished to return to her Comanche life, but the white men would not allow it. Instead they kept her a prisoner against her will."

Figure 5: Cynthia Ann Parker nursing her daughter Toposannah, "Prairie Flower"

"After that massacre, came a golden period for the Comanches. For the next five years we lived with little trouble from the white men. This was said to be because of the Great War in the East, where white men killed white men, where the Blue Coats fought the Gray Coats. The few soldiers still here mostly left the Comanche to be. The *cibolo* were plentiful, and life was good."

Gray Feather imparted this wisdom on *Kills Owls* over several years. Much of it, including talk of the white men's Great War, had been discussed in the smoke lodge with the other elders. *Gray Feather* had taken a chance when he shared this news with the boy, for the talks held in the smoke lodge were considered to be sacred. Its secrets were not to be shared, but, by then, *Gray Feather* had bonded closely with and came to trust *Kills Owls*.

When *Kills Owls* was thirteen, he had the idea to plead with *Gray Feather* to ask the other elders to take up his cause with the chief and the main medicine man so that he could join the buffalo hunts and prepare to become a warrior raider. *Gray Feather* reluctantly did as the boy asked, but the elders, upon learning that *Gray Feather* had passed on information from the smoke lodge to the boy, would not consider honoring *Kills Owls'* request.

Kills Owls was furious with the rejection of the elders. A few nights after this, the boy decided to get even with them all for their decision with a harmless prank. He climbed the smoke lodge and sewed shut its vent flaps. Then he hid himself nearby and waited. That night, when the elders gathered there and lit a fire, it filled the *tipi* with dense wet smoke.

He laughed as all the elders came stumbling out, choking on the thick fumes. All but one, as *Gray Feather,* amid the mayhem, had tripped and hit his head hard on the stones around the firepit within the smoke-filled lodge. He was helped to his feet, but no sooner than he straightened up, *Gray Feather* collapsed and had to be carried out of the smoke lodge. Three days later he died. The elders were in agreement that *Gray Feather's* death was a punishment on him by *the Great Spirit* for revealing the truths of the smoke lodge to this troublesome boy.

After this catastrophe, *He Who Kills Owls* was no longer allowed to live in the village, not even in his family's lodge. His father, *Dark Wolf,* had him driven off to live a solitary life on the outer fringe of the village grounds. It was in this lonely existence that the boy's real troubles would only begin.

Chapter 13: A Most Unforgivable Sin

Comancheria, 1862 - 1864

As time went by, *He Who Kills Owls* lived alone on the most remote edge of the village. When his village moved, he moved also, trailing far behind them. All direct contact with *the People* was banned, although his mother was allowed to leave food and skins for him, provided they had no direct discussions or meetings. She gave him enough buffalo hides to shelter his own small *tipi*.

Every few days, she would lay dried meat out on a certain stone in the morning and would check later to make sure it was taken. The boy would stack a few smaller stones there to say thank you. His mother would look for the stack of stones, she told herself, only to confirm that a wild animal had not dragged the meat away. In fact, the stacking of those stones was the only contact she had with her son, who she still loved dearly in her mother's heart.

Kills Owls missed, most of all, their nights together in the family lodge around the fire, when his mother told stories of living in Mexico with her *papá*. She always spoke of how proud her father was of his long leather coat, lovingly recalling how it flared at its tailed bottom and at both of its gracefully flowing fringed sleeves.

His mother had also spoken to him of the night she was taken from her *papá*. She spoke of how *Dark Wolf* had chased her down as she ran, and scooped her up in his strong arm without breaking his horse's stride. She recalled the great ride across *the Comanche Trace* which she had endured after having been taken. She romanticized it in her telling, leaving out no detail whatsoever. It was the story of her conversion to the Comanche way of life that she had come to love so. It became her favorite story to tell.

She described the great expanse of *the Llano* and of the enormity of the herds of *cibolo* roaming freely over it. She detailed how on that raid, *Raging Anger* had been the party's war chief. She later learned from her husband that *Raging Anger* had wanted to take her for his own wife, but *Dark Wolf* had said no, she belonged to him because he had caught her. So *Raging Anger* instead took her father's long leather coat as the symbol of his own special triumph.

Although she never said it directly, *Kills Owls* knew it haunted his mother that *Raging Anger* not only still possessed that long coat, but had defaced it by adding Comanche beading to the fringes of its sleeves. To her, this celebrated the memory of her father's killing, and disgraced the purity of the man. It was bad enough she had been forced to watch *Raging Anger* scalp his lifeless body, but now the brave would wear his long coat during ceremonial dances held before raiding parties and before buffalo hunts.

At those events, even as a young boy, *Kills Owls* could sense the stirring of his mother's conflicted feelings as she was forced to watch while *Raging Anger* danced around the fire in that leather coat. She loved being Comanche, but the coat was her only link back to her first family. Now forced to live apart from his own family, *Kills Owls* decided he would steal it back to please his mother.

Kills Owls spent day after day devising some way to get his hands on the garment. He thought of how all the village warriors and older children would go out on a buffalo hunt. *Kills Owls* would wait and sneak into the village. The women would had gone as well, for they would butcher the bison in the field, then pack the meat and skins onto mules and bring it all back to the village. Only the old men would remain, and even most of them went out to watch the hunt in the distance from atop a rise.

This plan made sense because *Kills Owls* knew that *Raging Anger* would never wear the long coat during the hunt itself. It was too restricting a garment for the physical acts demanded on chasing down and killing the *cibolo*.

Kills Owls slipped into the village effortlessly the afternoon of the hunt. As was their tradition, the openings of all the *tipi* lodges faced to the east, toward the rising sun. This allowed *Kills Owls* to slip under the hanging skins of *Raging Anger's* lodge from the west, unseen by the few Comanche remaining. He quickly found the long coat and exited as he had come, confident he had not been seen. But he knew there would be a search for the stolen garment, so he made haste in finding an unexpected hiding spot for it.

Out on *the Llano, Raging Anger* was honored to lead the first charge against the buffalo. He would approach the beasts from the rear, always from the left side on the fringe of the herd. *Raging Anger* rode bravely with his lance alongside the stampeding beasts. He thrust the lance with both hands hard between the last rib and the animal's hind quarters to puncture its kidneys. While other warriors would aim for the heart, *Raging Anger* had been taught to aim for the kidneys, as the heart was often easily missed. A wounded *cibolo*, even with its lungs pierced but its heart untouched, could be great trouble to bring down.

Raging Anger's lance was true, and the animal lurched, ran a short distance with the weapon protruding from it before it hobbled to the ground. After the rest of the herd had passed, *Raging Anger* came in for the kill, to put the animal out of its misery. After the kill, he slashed open its underbelly and removed the intestines, which he would later give to the youngest village children. They would gleefully use their forefingers to squeeze out its contents and eat the buffalo's half-digested slurry raw like candy.

Raging Anger then thrust his arms into the slain beast's carcass as far as they would go. He located and pulled with all his might until the buffalo's liver separated away cleanly. *Raging Anger* held the massive organ high, and all of the youngest warriors of the village rushed over to the dead bison. *Raging Anger* then took the first bite of the raw, still warm liver, as was Comanche tradition. Then he passed it on to the young warriors who took it and waited patiently. When *Raging Anger* removed the animal's gall bladder and squeezed out its bile onto the meat of the liver, the young warriors then ate it heartily. It was a delight for these warriors, still too young to take their own kills, to participate in this second hand manner.

When the women made their way back to the village, *Trembling Wind* took some of their portion of fresh buffalo meat and laid it on the rock for her shamed son. The rock was far away from the village, and no one dared follow her as the boy was considered to be taboo. This bounty from the fresh kill she intended to be an unexpected gift for her son. But when *Trembling Wind* came back later in the day to make sure her son had taken the meat, she was surprised to find not only the animal flesh gone, but her *papá's* long leather coat laying out proudly on the rock. This she feared had been left as her own unexpected gift.

She was frozen by the sight of it. It brought tears to her eyes. Although *Trembling Wind* had long ago accepted her new life as *Dark Wolf's* second wife, the sight of the long coat flooded back memories of her father sacrificing his own life to valiantly try to save hers. For a moment in time, she was once again the little girl, Juanita, who needed to be protected, to be rescued. Little Juanita moved closer to touch the memory of her father.

As she traced her hands over the leather coat, she could once again see her *papá's* face, smiling proudly as he most often did while wearing it. But then, her mind's eye morphed into a lifeless mask as her fingers fell over the Comanche beading. All she then saw was the warrior *Raging Anger,* dressed in that coat as he scalped her lifeless *papá's* corpse. It was as if those damned Comanche beads spoiled everything about the garment, bringing the two worlds that she had separately grown to love into a brutal and unavoidable conflict.

Trembling Wind knew she could not take the stolen long coat, but stacked three rocks upon it so her son would know she had seen it lying there. She feared what punishment might befall him from *Raging Anger* or from the elders once this theft was discovered. Yet despite this, she realized that *He Who Kills Owls* did this for no other reason than to please her.

Chapter 14: The Thunderbird of the Great Spirit

Palo Duro Canyon, 1864

Theft of a prized possession by one Comanche from another was considered an act of dishonor, and was often thought to be done under the *puha* of *the Great Deceiver* - the coyote. For this reason, *Kills Owls* was instantly suspected of the crime. With the consent of the elders, *Raging Anger* and several of his hand-picked warriors went to the camp of the outcast boy and overpowered him. They staked him to the dirt, tied down by strips of leather, which they wet so that they would shrink as the sun dried them.

While the boy was constrained in torment, his limbs under increasing tension as the wet leather strips dried and shrunk, the warriors went through everything he possessed. The leather coat that *Raging Anger* had so long ago honorably claimed on that Mexican raid was not found. Having failed in their exhaustive search, the Comanches returned to the village, leaving *Kills Owls* staked in the midday sun. The boy was, at that time, still only thirteen.

There was a second suspect, another boy of the *Quahadi* band of Comanches, a few years older than *Kills Owls,* who had also earned himself a disreputable name. He was the only reason *Raging Anger* had even the slightest doubt as to whether *Kills Owls* was the thief.

This second boy was always boasting of his own greatness, but had never distinguished himself in either raids, battle or the hunt. On the day of the theft, this child had avoided the buffalo hunt and wandered deep into the canyon alone, making him as much a suspect as *Kills Owls.*

This boy had long ago been given the *Nermernuh* name *Isa Tai'i,* loosely meaning *Back End of the Coyote* or even more vaguely, *Coyote Dropping.* This name of disrespect had been given him not for any misdeeds, as was the case with *Kills Owls,* but because the child proclaimed his own importance with no deeds of valor on which to base the claim. Instead, he said he communed directly with *the Great Spirit* and from this derived great *puha.* He never did anything to warrant being outcast, as had *Kills Owls,* but was always considered to be a strange child. He would isolate himself from the other Comanche children, and would seek to be alone as much as possible.

When the long leather coat had been discovered to be missing, *Isa Tai'i* proclaimed he had created great magic that gave it life, and it would forever wander *the Llano.* He also was staked by *Raging Anger* as *Kills Owls* had been. All his possessions were searched. Again, the missing garment was not found. That evening, with the consent of the elders, his family freed him.

Later that same night, *Trembling Wind* slipped out of her lodge to free her son. She found him still staked as she had feared and cut him free. Her husband, *Dark Wolf,* had noticed her deception and knew she would go to tend to their outcast child, but acted as if he was asleep. He wished only for his second wife to not worry that wolves or other predators might attack their bound and helpless son. While *Dark Wolf* had given his son up for lost, he still held deep feelings for the woman who had bore him.

The mystery of the missing long coat became a great topic of discussion among the villagers, and especially of the elders in their meetings in the smoke lodge. Some believed the story told by *Isa Tai'i* of that coat wandering *the Llano,* and a fraction of *the People* came to believe that the boy had great medicine within him.

In reality, *Kills Owls* had the foresight to bury the long coat under a large flat rock near the base of a distinctive formation known as the *Thunderbird of the Great Spirit.* It was found on a high narrow mesa, so few people traveled there. Fittingly, it was this very place where *Isa Tai'i* was known to go to seek seclusion, where he claimed to commune with *the Great Spirit.* If the jacket was discovered there by anyone, surely *Isa Tai'i* would have been blamed for its theft.

Chapter 15: The First Attack of the Blue Coats

Adobe Walls, November 25, 1864

Soon enough, there was a more pressing issue for the *Quahadi* to deal with than *Raging Anger's* missing long coat. Word had come with the return of the *Comancheros* that the pony soldiers who wore the blue coats planned to attack them in their lands. A council of war was gathered, and the war chiefs of many tribes and bands attended.

Groups of soldiers traveling across their land was nothing new. In fact, the Comanches had attacked many army wagon trains over the years that dared to cross along the route that the white man called the Santa Fe Trail. Many soldiers had been killed and scalped, and much of the provisions they transported had been taken by the attacking Comanches back to their villages. Most cherished among this bounty were the soldiers repeating rifles, which then could be used in subsequent raids on the pony soldiers traveling along that same trail.

Word from the *Comanchero* traders out of Santa Fe was that the great White Father was tired of these raids, and that he would send soldiers not to cross, but rather to invade *Comancheria.* They knew from their experience that they would come to not only kill the Comanche braves, but also their women and children as well.

The Comanches also knew even if they drove the white man off, another disaster loomed. The ghosts of the men attacked and killed on the Santa Fe Trail had brought bad magic to their villages. Many Comanches - men, women and children - had died from the white man illness called cholera. It had decimated the lodges. Many warriors no longer died in noble warfare, but in the dishonor of this dark *puha.* An invading army of white pony soldiers in blue coats, even if they were killed, would bring more of this bad magic upon their sacred *Comancheria!*

Over the past four years, during the period of the white man's Great War, when Blue Coats fought Gray Coats in the East, there had been limited pony soldiers along the Santa Fe Trail. This period was good for the Comanches, as the buffalo herds grew large, and few white men dared to settle west of the line of frontier forts. When the Comanche did raid these white settlers, there were fewer pony soldiers to try and run them down. Even the Texas Rangers, who had learned to fight in the ways of *the Nermernuh* themselves, were fewer in number at that time.

It seemed to the *Quahadi* that the old *Nermernuh* ways were slowly being restored. The *cibolo* were plentiful, it was true, but not all the pony soldiers had left. The few settlers who remained on the frontier cried out for those remaining Blue Coats to protect them. Their cries were so loud it was said they were heard by the Great Father of the white man so far away.

Now the *Comancheros* from New Mexico warned them of many Blue Coats gathering there to attack from the West. The Comanche tribe decided to call in the assistance of their allies, the Kiowa along with a few other tribes. At this war council, it was determined the mixed tribes would band together to fight the Blue Coats.

The Blue Coats were just as motivated to cease the attacks on their supply wagons along the Santa Fe Trail as they were to protect the settlers living beyond the forts. In November of 1864, an army expedition of over 300 soldiers with 75 Ute and Jicarillo Apache Indian scouts traveled east along the Canadian River from the New Mexico Territory. They were under the command of Colonel Christopher "Kit" Carson. Their destination was the ruins of a trading post called Adobe Walls in the Texas Panhandle where Carson had once been stationed in the 1840s.

That 1864 expedition consisted of 27 wagons, an ambulance, 45 days of rations and munitions, and most importantly, two mountain howitzer artillery cannons. After enduring a fierce snowstorm, the Ute and Apache scouts, both among the most bitter enemies of the Comanches and their allies, the Kiowa, soon found a settlement for Colonel Carson to attack.

Figure 6: Colonel Christopher "Kit" Carson

At 8:30 am on November 25th, Carson ordered a surprise attack on a Kiowa village of about 150 lodges close to the Adobe Walls ruins. Under the Kiowa Chief *Dohasan,* or *"Little Mountain,"* the Kiowa were routed, but not before their chief could alert nearby Comanche villages. Within a mile was a Comanche village of over 500 lodges. Thousands of braves responded, and soon after, Kit Carson realized he had poked his fist into the hornet's nest.

The war party was led by the Kiowa Chief *Dohasan,* assisted by the chiefs *Satanta, or "White Bear,"* *Satank or "Sitting Bear"* and a chief known as *Stumbling Bear.* It grew to well over 3,000 braves, making the number of Indians ten times that of the intruders.

Satanta (White Bear) had a great surprise awaiting the Blue Coats. He had come to possess a US Army bugle and had learned how to use it. Whenever Carson would order his Army bugler to sound a "Charge!" call, chief *White Bear* would counter with a "Retreat" call. When the Army blew "Retreat," *White Bear* blew "Charge!" creating great confusion among the Blue Coats.

As the Indian numbers swelled throughout the day, Colonel Carson realized just how outnumbered his forces were and pulled his entire party back into the abandoned ruins of the old trading post of Adobe Walls. What was left of its thick adobe structures offered protection from the arrows, lances and the few rifles that the Indians possessed. Also, because the structures had no wood, they could not be burned out from their cover, a favorite native tactic.

The Comanches and Kiowas quickly realized their enemy was surrounded there. All they had to do was to wear them down and eventually overrun the makeshift fortification, then many scalps would belong to them.

As the native war party assembled to make its first massive charge against the soldiers at Adobe Walls, they heard a boom louder and more angry than anything they had ever heard before from the white man's arsenal. One of the mountain howitzers had fired its load which whistled as it flew toward them. Something truly unexpected then occurred. The incoming round exploded overhead and sent fragments of shrapnel in all directions. The pelting of the scattered debris showered great death and inflicted ghastly wounds upon both the warrior braves and their mounts. The Indians came to refer to these deadly mountain howitzers as *"the great white man guns that fire twice."*

Every time the Indians would collect in numbers large enough to mount a decisive charge, the howitzers would bellow and the Indians would disperse before the whistling canister charge it fired could explode overhead and rain down its deadly shards of metal fragments.

Had it not been for these two great guns, Colonel Carson would later say he and his men would have been completely overrun. Still, as the day's battle wore on, Carson realized he was running low on his canister stores, the lethal ammunition for the howitzers. He had no option but to plan a retreat back to the New Mexico Territory.

If there was one attribute of the Comanche that worked against them in battle, it was that the concept of besieging an enemy was foreign to them. Rather than surround an enemy and wait, they would repeatedly attack until they were no longer repelled. Then, having tired of this, it was not uncommon for the natives to withdraw at day's end back to their camp. Perhaps this was because it was dishonorable for warriors to die in darkness. Whatever the case, This was what occurred the day of this battle and it opened up an escape route for Carson's expedition.

The next morning, taking advantage of the lull in the Indian attacks, Carson cautiously withdrew his forces, only be set upon again as the natives returned for the day. Carson's Blue Coats fought their way back into New Mexico. Kit Carson reported to his commanding officer that there were still, in that year of 1864, far larger numbers of Comanche and Kiowa Indians in the lands of *Comancheria* than they had expected. To maintain an outpost at Adobe Walls would take upwards of a thousand troops, Carson estimated. Despite this, the expedition was welcomed back as conquering heroes by their commander, the military governor of the New Mexico Territory, General James Henry Carleton.

The joint Comanche and Kiowa war party knew they had achieved a great victory. They had driven off the massive invasion of the Blue Coats out of *Comancheria.* It emboldened them. The raids of the Comanche and Kiowa would continue for another decade. It would be the response to these deadly raids that would ultimately lead to the eventual downfall of both tribes on the open plains.

Chapter 16: The Message
Early November, 1864

In the days leading up to the attack of the Blue Coats at Adobe Walls, the Comanche warriors left the canyons of *Palo Duro* to travel north to the Canadian River to meet up with the Kiowa. The women and elders stayed behind, as did *Kills Owls*. He regularly checked on the stolen long coat he had buried under a large flat rock atop the narrow elevated mesa near the rise of the formation known as the *Thunderbird of the Great Spirit*.

It rose in stone vertically from the elevated mesa against the otherwise blue skies of *the Llano*, like the thunderheads visible along the distant western horizon. These clouds of thunder and lightning warned of the approach of conflict and war. Thus, many native tribes associated them with the great *Thunderbird* spirit. Like it, this formation was sacred - a tower of rock, etched by the winds of *the Llano*, the very breath of *the Great Spirit*.

As *Kills Owls* approached that day, he scanned the mesa and its surrounding area to assure he had not been followed. As he did, he saw a solitary figure standing at the base of the great *Thunderbird* formation. He knew it could be no other than *Isa Tai'i* who came there alone so often. *Isa Tai'i* claimed *the Great Spirit* spoke to him directly there, and had bestowed a great *"puha"* upon him.

Kills Owls decided he would sneak up on the young medicine man and scare him. As he approached, he carefully watched the back of *Isa Tai'i*, who continued to gaze up only at the *Thunderbird* formation rising before him. The young man seemed to be in a supernatural trance.

Kills Owls tread slowly, quietly, as he placed each step of his moccasins carefully, applying the pressure heel to toe in purest silence. He was about ten feet from the brave when *Isa Tai'i* surprised him by calling out.

"He Who Kills Owls," spoke out *Isa Tai'i* aloud, addressing him without turning around, *"the Great Spirit* watches your approach and warns me of your deception, but says it is to be expected of those with coyote *puha."*

Kills Owls was amazed, sure that his stealth had been such that *Isa Tai'i* could not possibly have detected his ascent and approach. He stood frozen in his tracks as *Isa Tai'i* turned slowly to face him. The young, self-proclaimed medicine man was dressed in a buckskin tunic and wore finger stripes of yellow ochre across his face. His eyes had a strange blankness to them, as if he had been awakened from a deep sleep.

"The Great Spirit has calmed my heart," *Isa Tai'i* answered the question that had not yet been asked, "and whispers many secrets to me. I am told there is nothing for me to fear from you. No spirits of darkness are within your heart to tell you to bring harm to me. *The Great Spirit* reminds me that we are brothers in our distrust of chief *Raging Anger.* Were we not both left staked to the ground, suspected of the theft of his garment? Were not both our bodies equally covered with the venomous bites of red ants and scorpions? Those wounds have since healed, yes, but not the indignity of their being thrust upon us by his hand."

"Why do you claim to speak to *the Great Spirit?*" asked *Kills Owls.*

Isa Tai'i took a step towards the young outcast brave. *"The Great Spirit* leaves me now because of your presence. He will visit me no more this day, as your approach has disrupted the bond between us. But he assures me you are here for a purpose."

"Why does *the Great Spirit* bother to commune with you?" *Kills Owls* asked. "You, of all braves, the one named *Coyote Dropping?"*

"The Great Spirit has conveyed a powerful *puha* upon me," *Isa Tai'i* responded. "It has been shared with me that I will lead *the People* in the final battle against the white man's coming invasion upon *the Llano.*"

"You practice false magic," accused *Kills Owls.* "I know this. You tell *the People* that the missing long coat belonging to *Raging Anger* has the power to walk upon *the Llano,* which I know to be untrue."

Isa Tai'i's defiance rested confidently in his face, and radiated strongly from his eyes. *Kills Owls* remained unimpressed. He would need more than faraway gazes to assure him that this brave spoke to *the Great Spirit.*

"Your *puha,* is false!" *Kills Owls* repeated.

"You say this because you have hidden the coat under that stone," *Isa Tai'i* said pointing directly at the very rock where *Kills Owls* had hidden the coat. "My words were misunderstood. I said not that it walked upon *the Llano,* but that it would be cast out upon the wilderness, beyond *the Llano.* It will not return until it finds a great sign among the whites. A sign so pure, so untouched that it must be brought back and offered up to *the Great Spirit* in the days of before the final battle with the white man."

Kills Owls was amazed by his words. Did the young boy really believe all this? Did he believe *the Great Spirit* spoke to *him?* It was no wonder that he also wandered alone, not befriended by anyone from the village. He always came to this formation, so long as the *Quahadi* were camped in any of the canyons of *Palo Duro.*

"You have many doubts," *Isa Tai'i* said to *Kills Owls,* "but you will come to understand all this. You will learn that the power of *the Great Spirit* works through me."

"You speak of this final battle with the white man as being far in the future," *Kills Owls* said, "but do not the chiefs of *the People* prepare now for just such a battle? Do the *Quahadi* braves not join the Kiowa upon the Great Northern River to prepare for this fight?"

"Yes," *Isa Tai'i* replied, "but this battle will only be with the white man in Blue Coats. It will be a great victory. But another battle is to follow, against not only the Blue Coats but also all white men - including those who will come to slaughter the *cibolo* in great numbers. These men mean to steal our way of life from us. At that time, the long coat stolen from *Raging Anger* will return from its wandering to this very spot to offer *the Great Spirit a gift so pure, taken from, but untouched by, the white man."*

"A gift so pure, taken from, but untouched by, the white man." The young Kills Owls replayed these words in his mind. *A coat that would wander beyond the Llano? It is all so fantastical,* he thought, *so unbelievable!*

"Why the future?" he asked. "Why not now?"

Isa Tai'i stared at him with a penetrating look, as if he wondered if the boy could stand the weight of what he was about to be told. Then, after studying *Kills Owls* in earnest, *Isa Tai'i* revealed the rest of the prophecy to him.

"Before the great final battle against the white man, there is to first come another great leader to *the People,*" *Isa Tai'i* revealed. "He will be a great Comanche warlord, but in his blood he will understand the ways of the white man. He will lead us to victory."

"You said *you* would lead *our People?*" *Kills Owls* argued.

"This war lord, with me as his connection to *the Great Spirit* - we will lead our people together," *Isa Tai'i* said, "but he must come to *our People* first."

"So this leader is Comanche but not among *our People?*" asked *Kills Owls.*

"He is *Nemernuh, yes*" *Isa Tai'i* answered, "but is not yet among *the Quahadi.* But he will come soon to us. Now, let us discuss what lies deep in your heart."

Kills Owls was surprised at this last statement. He somehow felt as though his inner thoughts had been read by the boy in the yellow war paint.

"What lies deep in my heart?" *Kills Owls* asked, challenging the young medicine man to demonstrate the *puha* given to him by *the Great Spirit.*

"Above all else," *Isa Tai'i* replied plainly, *"you* desire death to befall *Raging Anger* for what he has done to us. I know that you do."

...For what he has done to us. US! Kills Owls noticed the use of this collective term.

"As do you?" *Kills Owls* asked.

"As do I," *Isa Tai'i* admitted with no reluctance. "Together our wish will be offered up to *the Great Spirit* and *Raging Anger* will fall in the battle that is to come."

"I can not agree to this," said *Kills Owls.*

Isa Tai'i searched the eyes of *Kills Owls*, although it felt to the boy that this medicine man examined his very thoughts. *Isa Tai'i* then stated, "I know you are deceiving yourself of the truth. Do not resist me. I have been given a most powerful *puha* from *the Great Spirit.*"

The young medicine man's words were penetrating. His ways were confident and very convincing. *Kills Owls* desperately wanted for the boy's *puha* to be real. He wanted nothing more than to use it to punish the war chief *Raging Anger.* He felt this desire in every muscle of his young body.

Isa Tai'i stepped forward and took the young brave's hands in his own. and led him through an offering to *the Great Spirit* of burnt sage in exchange for the death of the warrior *Raging Anger* in the upcoming battle. After this was completed, neither boy said anything further. They simply separated from each other in a shared, complicit silence.

Figure 7: Authors' Photos of Palo Duro Canyon
from Rim (upper) and the Canyon Floor

Chapter 17: The Departure

Early December, 1864

In the days that followed the great victory over the Blue Coats at the ruins of Adobe Walls, *Kills Owls* kept watch over the village from afar. Among the returning warriors, he could not find his father, *Dark Wolf,* whom he still loved very much. To his great joy, the warrior chief *Raging Anger* had been brought back from the battle badly wounded on a travois dragged by *Dark Wolf's* own horse. He assumed *Raging Anger* would die from his wounds, as was the request made through *Isa Tai'i* of *the Great Spirit.*

Several days passed, and then finally one night his mother, *Trembling Wind*, came to his solitary camp. She carried great sadness upon her. She told her son that her visit was permitted by the elders so that she could inform him that his father had fallen in the tremendous victory of the battle against the white man.

"But *Raging Anger* still lives?" the boy seethed.

"He is very weak," *Trembling Wind* said, "but it appears he will grow stronger and live."

"Where is the justice in this?" her son raged back at her. *Kills Owls* could think only of the false *puha* of the self-professed medicine man, *Isa Tai'i.* His own father, *Dark Wolf,* had fallen instead of *Raging Anger*.

"You should be proud," countered his mother, *"for Raging Anger* lives thanks to the bravery of *Dark Wolf.* A Blue Coat's bullet struck *Raging Anger,* and threw him from his war pony. *Dark Wolf* rode to him and seeing his wound was severe, put the warrior across the back of his own pony. He then swatted it, sending it out of harm's way. As he attempted to leave the battlefield on foot, one of the rounds from the white man's devilish weapon that our braves call *the great gun that shoots twice* exploded near him and took your father's life. But thanks to *Dark Wolf's* bravery, *Raging Anger* will heal and live to fight in other battles for *our People."*

Her face streamed with tears as she told her son this. *Kills Owls* wanted only to hold her, but resisted as he knew it was a sign of weakness to embrace her.

"There is more," *Trembling Wind* said, "the elders have determined that since your father saved his life, *Raging Anger* is to become responsible for me from this point on. I am to become *Raging Anger's* second wife."

Kills Owls became confused. She would be forced to become a wife of the warrior who still carried the scalp of her own father on his coup stick? His mother's body began to heave, trying to expel this vile idea from her heart. Still, *Kills Owls* would not allow himself to comfort her.

"I am sorry, Mother," was all he could say.

"No, it is truly I who am sorry, my son," she said, "for the young medicine man *Isa Tai'i has* confessed to the elders that he had heard you making a sacrificial offering to *the Great Spirit* for the death in battle of *Raging Anger.* Please tell me, my son, that this is not true."

Kills Owls was stunned and could not speak, but his face told her that it was the truth.

He thought to tell her that the deceiver *Isa Tai'i* had not only also made this request of *the Great Spirit,* but that he had coaxed him as well into also doing so. Then, he realized it mattered not. *Isa Tai'i* had entrapped him with his false magic, just as a hunter ensnares an unwary animal in the field.

Kills Owls knew the elders had accepted the story of *Isa Tai'i.* They would not give his explanation any weight. They would not change their decision. They had spoken.

"Oh, my son," *Trembling Wind* said to him, "don't you see what you have done? If you had not asked for this from *the Great Spirit, Raging Anger* would not have been wounded, and your father would still be alive?"

Not said, he thought, my mother would have avoided becoming the wife of the warrior who scalped her own father.

"Perhaps *Raging Anger* will still die," he wished.

"No!" his mother objected harshly. "There has been enough death already! Now I must share with you the saddest news of all. The elders have decreed you may no longer live in the shadow of our village. You are to leave *the Llano* completely, for if you are discovered by any *Quahadi* upon these plains where the c*ibolo* graze, you are to be killed on sight."

The news penetrated the boy in a way he could not have possibly expected. He had been living as the outcast half-blood son of a fearless Comanche warrior. *Dark Wolf* was now dead due only to being fearless in battle. But his son, *Kills Owls,* was to be punished for this. He was to be fully expelled from *the Llano* on penalty of death.

"Where will I go?" he asked. "I know no other life. I have no other family, no other *People.*"

His mother cried all the harder upon hearing him say this. She slowly overcame her emotions to say, "Tomorrow, by the moon's light, the *Comancheros* will depart back to the New Mexico territory. The elders have shown mercy, and you will be allowed to leave with them. You are to meet them along the canyon trail at the great tree split by lightning. Please, child, never attempt to come back, or you will be killed. Of this the elders were clear. You can never be forgiven for the death of *Dark Wolf*."

"So be it," he said bitterly. "In no way could I ever stay and watch you lower yourself before *Raging Anger*."

He knew not what was to become of him. Surely, the *Comancheros* would never fully accept him. No white man would ever trust him. He was to be a man without either a family or a home, doomed to forever wander alone.

"And will you, my mother," he asked, "heal the wounds of *Raging Anger* only so you may one day bear him many sons, my half-brothers?"

"Oh, my son!" She rushed to embrace him, but he merely pushed her away, and spoke to her no further that night. His heart was enraged by her acceptance of the village elder's denial of him. Even more, it was bitterly soured upon the false magic of the deceiver, *Isa Tai'i*.

The next night, before the sun had set, *Kills Owls* retrieved the long coat he had stolen from *Raging Anger* from under the stone near *the Thunderbird of the Great Spirit*. Wearing it, he slipped into the village as the glow of the moon began its climb high into the sky. He found his father's war pony tied just outside the warrior *Raging Anger*'s lodge. It was the tradition of a brave to keep his war mount close, and as this animal, *Dark Wolf's* horse, had saved his life, it was given this spot of high regard.

"*Raging Anger* has taken away my freedom," he said under his breath, "and will heal only so he can steal away my mother from me. But I will at least deny him the pleasure of also taking my father's war pony - the horse that saved his life."

Kills Owls pulled out his skinning knife and slit the animal's throat, dropping it to the ground. It was his last act of defiance. To kill a warrior's prized horse was a grave crime, as heinous as the murder of another member of the tribe. As his father's mount kicked on the ground in its last throes of life, the boy *Kills Owls* wiped his blade on the remaining clean sleeve of the long leather coat. The other sleeve was long ago stained by the blood of his mother's father.

As he saw it, the animal's blood was traded for that of his father, *Dark Wolf,* and his mother, both of whom were now forever denied to him. *Kills Owls* then slipped into the darkness to move swiftly to the great tree split by lightning where he would meet up with the departing *Comancheros.*

Chapter 18: Enduring A Decade Wandering Alone

1865 - 1874

Having sealed his fate by the slaying of *Dark Wolf's* war horse, merely to deny it to *Raging Anger, Kills Owls* knew his life among *the Nermernuh* was over. He was to lead a new life, one which would demand a new name. Out of respect for his father, he would call himself *Lobo,* or *"the Wolf."* The Comancheros would expand that name to be *"Lobo Solidario,"* or *"Lone Wolf."*

Lone Wolf departed *the Llano* when he was approaching his fourteenth birthday. Had he stayed on with *the Quahadi,* he would have witnessed perhaps the most important years of their history. Instead, he would be forced to travel outside *the Llano,* hearing only echoes of the *Quahadi* culture upon the winds that scoured across it. These echoes were often distorted, relayed by second-hand sources who did not fully understand the ways and customs of the Comanche. This cast him into a great isolation. He became a solitary soul, and vowed one day to get back to *the Quahadi, his People.* Those unjustly denied to him.

He thought of *Trembling Wind,* and how he, like she, had been ripped from the comfort of their birth families. The thought only sewed more bitterness in him, for his mother was, by then, he knew, wife to *Raging Anger.*

The first several years he spent in Santa Fe with *the Comancheros* were good. They found his knowledge of *the Quahadi* to be most useful, and thanks to his mother, he spoke fluid Spanish. The conversations with them were easy. However, as the years went by, after his knowledge was fully passed on to *the Comancheros,* his utility to them quickly waned. *Lone Wolf* was not allowed to travel back and trade with *the Quahadi,* and *the Comancheros'* knowledge of the Comanche band soon surpassed his own. *Lone Wolf* had simply outlived his usefulness to them.

On top of this, *Lone Wolf* encountered another problem living in Santa Fe. His mixed Comanche and Mexican blood had produced in him a most attractive young man. He was soon delivered fully into manhood by one of the local Mexican prostitutes who looked with favor upon him. She enjoyed his youthful fervor, and taught him the ways and local customs of the mixed Mexican, Spanish and white cultures that co-mingled there. She helped him learn a little English, and how to dress to fit in. Her name was Yolanda. She spent many days, as well as many more pleasurable nights, with the young *Lone Wolf.*

The problem was that Yolanda was already claimed by the head of *the Comancheros,* a vile man known as Criado. Despite her being a known prostitute, Criado saw Yolanda as his own woman, his possession. *Lone Wolf* refused to stay away from her. He looked upon Yolanda as the only person in his life who cared for him. During his third year in Santa Fe, *Lone Wolf* was given a message by Criado to carry south into Old Mexico. He was also told to never return north of the Rio Grande again. Once more, *Lone Wolf* had been isolated and then rejected by the people he had thought of as his own, for *the Comancheros* were, like him, a race of half-bloods.

Nonetheless, there was nothing for this just-turned seventeen year old to do but comply. Before he left Santa Fe, Yolanda had one last gift for her *Lone Wolf.* She took the teen to an especially gifted woman she knew that told the future of other people's lives. She was a wrinkled old *anciana,* deeply steeped in the Old World Spanish culture. She burned a lock of his hair, and then held the teen's hands as she stared into the dance of the candle's flame to make her predictions. What she said excited him greatly.

The Spanish woman told him that his destiny was clear to her, and that he had a great role to play in the future of the Comanche band from whence he had come.

"The winds of fortune will carry you first South, where for three years you will stir in your great bitterness. Then, you will sail East across the blue waters before you will stumble upon a great gift, one which will allow you to return to *your People.* You will be welcomed upon your arrival, so long as you are bearing the great and pure gift."

Then he asked, "How will I find this wonderful and pure gift, and how will I know it?"

The Spanish woman replied, "this gift, which is to be taken from the enemy of your people, you will know by the crown of gold it will bear. It is to be given to the great chief who will lead *your people* against them."

Then, *Lone Wolf* pressed the woman further for more details, and she replied only with the words, "This is all that has been revealed to me. The rest is yours to live."

Lone Wolf could not believe the luck of having his fortune told. He made a gift of money to her, and went away holding close to his heart the fact that a path back to *the Nermernuh* not only existed, but due to his finding this great and pure gift, he would, one day, be welcomed there.

Her words soon enough came to pass. *Lone Wolf* traveled south on the command of *the Comanchero* Criado. He kept west of *the Llano* until he came to El Paso and entered Mexico into the state of Chihuahua where he lived for a year. He made his living there as a bandit, until he was driven east by other bandits claiming the area as their own.

In that year, his bitterness increased, for he wished nothing but to return to *the Llano* and *his People.* But he knew he could not yet, for he had still to cross the blue waters. He had not yet found the great but mysterious gift.

Lone Wolf made his way east to the Mexican region of Coahuila where he stayed for another year. Again, he survived there as a bandit. He learned that it was the land from which his mother had been taken when the long leather coat he wore was recognized as the master work of a local leather-smith. *Lobo Solidario* traveled to the artisan's town. The leather-smith confirmed the coat was, indeed, the work of his hands, although in his opinion it had been defaced by the addition of the Comanche beading and the smeared streaks of dried blood staining its sleeves.

The leather-smith gave *Lone Wolf* the location of his mother's home, and after much soul searching, the teen decided to go there. He waited until a Comanche Moon rose and under its soulful luminance, visited the modest house. He spotted in the front of the abandoned burned-out structure the *arroyo* to which his mother had once fled in the story she had told and retold so many times to him. He walked slowly toward it and descended into its dry banks.

In the moonlit darkness, he took off the black long leather coat. Given the thinness of its hides, he could wear it even in the heat of a Mexican summer night. This night, he would answer a question that had long haunted him.

Lone Wolf laid the long coat in the crevice of the *arroyo* and watched it in the moonlight. It blended into the shadows, truly swallowed by the darkness. He knew then if his mother had reached this place unseen, she would not have been found, and he would never have been born.

In the silence of that night, under that Comanche Moon, he thought only of *Trembling Wind.* He wondered how she was being treated by *Raging Anger.* Had she bore him any children? Did he have brothers or even sisters by this man he hated so? Not knowing only sharpened the blade of bitterness which stirred everything vile within him.

Later when he returned to the local village, he stopped by a cantina that stayed open all night. He wanted only to have tequila, a drink he had developed a taste for during his years in Santa Fe. He was approached by another known bandit, a white man, a fugitive from south Texas named Matteo. In excellent Spanish, Matteo asked about the distinctive long leather coat that *Lobo Solidario* wore. They drank tequila together and shared tales throughout that night. For the first time since leaving *Yolanda, Lone Wolf* did not feel completely alone. He then began referring once more to himself as merely *Lobo,* or *the Wolf.*

When *Lobo* was about twenty years of age he and Matteo moved east into the Nuevo Leon area south of Laredo. There, he and Matteo joined a gang of bandits who had developed a special reputation as horse thieves. The two became cross-border raiders, sneaking into Texas and stealing herds of horses. This was very dangerous work, as it was a hanging crime to steal horses in Texas, but given his hard and unforgiving upraising as a Comanche, *Lobo* soon learned that stealing horses came natural to him. He even wondered if his mother's father had stolen any of the horses she remembered his having as a young girl.

Trouble found them again in the summer of 1873, when a large party of Texas Rangers crossed south over the Rio Grande and stole back all the herds which for years they had stolen from many Texans' corrals. Not only did the Rangers take the herds, but they killed every single *vaquero* that worked for the gang that they found that night. They would have killed Matteo and *Lobo* also, had the two men not escaped eastward off into the night.

Lobo's Comanche blood served Matteo well that night. The two men had barely escaped the onslaught, taking with them only two possessions: a saddlebag of gold coins they kept always at the ready for a quick escape, and Matteo's six shooter in his beloved Slim Jim holster. *Lobo* had selected two of the best horses and under the moonlight they rode across North Mexico to the shores of the gulf.

The next day they bribed their way onto a steamer headed for New Orleans. There, they again bribed their way past customs. The two young men lived in the French Quarter in a life of decadence until the money began to dry up. Then, they had heard of a struggling gang of bandits up north in Shreveport, so they headed there to join them. But it was in Baton Rogue where they stopped for the night that *Lobo* had his future read by a Voodoo Priestess using Tarot cards. As she slowly flipped over and carefully read the cards, she shared with him what she foresaw.

"You have already come a great distance," said the priestess, who like himself was of mixed blood, "but the further you travel the greater you yearn to return to the lands and people from where you started. You will have a great revelation, and from it will spring forth a great gift, the key to open the door for your final return. I see a great power, rising like a warbird over your future. But it is your past that will mirror your future, always remember this."

This concluded the third prophesy he had received of what was to come. The first came from the lips of *Isa Tai'i* upon the narrow mesa of *the Thunderbird of the Great Spirit,* after which they had condemned *Raging Anger* to death. The second came in Santa Fe at the hands of the old woman from Spain, and now the third being this Voodoo Priestess. All predicted his return to *the Llano* bearing a great and pure gift. An *untouched* gift. But none could or would say exactly what that gift would be.

The next day Matteo and *Lobo* pressed on to Shreveport, and after a bit met up with the gang. It was late 1873 and history awaited them. In Shreveport they first began to hear of all that had been happening in Texas over the past several years. After the Civil War had run its course, the great warrior Ulysses S. Grant ascended into the White House as the new Great Father of the white man in 1869. His most famous general, William Tecumseh Sherman, had been named Secretary of War and was tasked with cleaning up all that was going on in the West. Namely, Sherman was given the order to force all remaining tribes onto the reservations in the Indian Territories. Especially the marauding Kiowa and the Comanche tribes.

They learned that Sherman had a very personal interest in doing so. He and his small party of just seventeen soldiers were on their way to Fort Richardson near Jacksboro in north Texas a few years back when they came upon many braves under three Kiowa warrior chiefs. *Lobo* recognized the names of two from the raid of the Blue Coats just before he departed *the Llano* - those two chiefs being *Satank, or "Sitting Bear,"* and *Satanta or "White Bear."* The third chief was named *Adoette or "Big Tree,"* but *Lobo* had never heard of him. Of the three, only the one he had never heard of, *Big Tree,* would live much longer.

These three chiefs allowed General Sherman and his small band of soldiers to pass without interference, even though they had more than enough braves to overtake the Blue Coats. Then, just hours afterwards at the same spot near Salt Creek, the Kiowas massacred an Army supply wagon train that had left Jacksboro headed for Fort Griffin. Seven of the twelve teamsters working that wagon train lost their lives, including the leader of the party, Henry Warren. The Warren Wagon Train Massacre of May 18th, 1871 outraged Sherman, who at the time of the attack rested comfortably, safely nestled inside Fort Richardson. Sherman was infuriated, and vowed to respond.

General Sherman was quick to use Tonkawa scouts, bitter enemies of the Kiowa and Comanche, to track down the three chiefs. They led him to Fort Sill, the massive reservation in the Indian Territories. It had become a great trick of the Indians in those parts to raid the white man and then return to the reservation where they would boast about their conquests. Sherman was steadfast that they could not use the reservation as a criminal sanctuary, and over the objections of the agent in charge of the compound, physically removed the three chiefs. They were taken by force back to Jacksboro to stand trial.

Satank, or Sitting Bear, told Sherman's Tonkawa scouts to tell his people to look for his body along the trail back to Jacksboro. He refused to be tried on charges in a white man's court, an unbearable humiliation, which the old chief Kiowa would not allow to take place.

When the Army threw him in the jail wagon, he hid his head under a blanket. The soldiers guarding him assumed it was from shame, but underneath the old chief gnawed away at his wrists, down to the bone, so he could slip out of the shackles.

Satank freed himself from the shackles and wrestled a rifle away from a guard, but before he could even get off a shot, he was killed by the bullet from another soldier's gun. Then, they stopped the wagon and laid his body along the trail, just as the chief had foreseen. Yet, his people never came to reclaim his body, fearing retribution from the army, even though Sherman assured there would be none.

The other two Kiowa chiefs were brought back to Jacksboro and stood trial in the courtroom there. In three days both were found guilty, and sentenced to death. It was the first time that any Indian chiefs were ever tried, found guilty and sentenced to die in a white man's courtroom.

But they did not hang, for when President Grant heard of this, he knew the Indians could not get a fair trial in any white man's court. So, Grant called upon the Reconstruction Governor of Texas to commute the two chiefs' death sentences. *White Bear and Big Tree* were sent to a state prison in Huntsville, Texas. *White Bear* was released and later participated in the second battle of Adobe Walls. After that, he was returned to jail, only to throw himself to his death through a prison upper story window. *Big Tree* was later resettled back to Fort Sill, where in his final years he converted to Christianity.

Lobo learned that these and other raids recurring near Weatherford, Jacksboro and the surrounding areas had led to the formation of a massive army group of some three thousand soldiers who were being prepared to go out onto *the Llano* to subdue the last of the Indians remaining there. These were most notably *the Quahadi,* the Comanche band from which *Lobo* came, and their Kiowa allies. *Lobo* recognized this coming conflict between the white men and his people to be the predicted last great battle. Now, he had only to find the great and untouched gift.

There was even more significant news that *Lobo* was greatly excited to hear. It was reported that two new figures had assumed leadership of *the Quahadi* and their allies against the invading Blue Coat army. A war chief named *Quanah,* who was the escaped son of the war chief *Peta Nocona* killed at Pease River, had joined forces with a very powerful medicine man named *White Eagle.* These two leaders vowed to attack not just the Blue Coats, but also the new breed of white man who came to *the Llano* only to slaughter the *cibolo* in great numbers. These buffalo hunters were drawn only by one thing - greed. They killed the animals to sell their hides back East. The skinned corpses were left to rot wastefully in the sun scattered across *the Llano.* It was these buffalo hunters that posed the greatest threat to *the Quahadi* and all life on *the Llano.*

Lobo knew from his three prophecies that his fate was tied to all these recent developments. The two great leaders were now in place for *the Quahadi,* and the great army of Blue Coats was forming to do battle with them. Still, all the prophecies predicted he needed to find the pure, untouched gift which he should offer up to *the Great Spirit.* He would stay with this gang of bandits until he understood just what that gift might be. He had gained faith in the trio of prophecies, including that of *Isa Tai'i* which he felt had been confirmed by the other two readings.

Lobo had only to wait for the discovery of the untouched gift, but he was confident it would present itself - a rising warbird, crowned in gold, of the greatest purity.

Chapter 19: Discovery of the Untouched Gift

Spring, 1874

The band of marauders made their way west from Shreveport into Texas. First onto Tyler, then up to Dallas and its access to the Cross Timbers. There they learned of a stage coach that carried payroll shipments of cash overland to the town of Fort Worth, where there still was no train service. Afterward, the stage coach went on to Weatherford.

Matteo had taken overall control of the six man team of bandits after the untimely death of their leader in a bar fight back in Shreveport. Matteo scattered the bandits at each end of the route to track and log the coach's arrival times and note their levels of defenses. He determined that the attack should take place after the Fort Worth stop, but before the coach arrived in Weatherford. It presented less cash to plunder, but also a lot less risk for this small team as the routes between Dallas and Fort Worth were more heavily guarded. The Weatherford ranchers still had to pay their hands, so that leg of the trip became their target.

Word came from the watchers in Weatherford that a storm had washed out a section of road near town. Not deep enough to cause a detour, but enough to slow the coach to where it could easily be overtaken by their team. This was exactly what was planned for the day of the robbery.

The bandits pulled a wagon in front of the coach just as it struggled to exit the washed out gully in the roadway. Everything went well for them. *Lobo* and another bandit were in charge of relieving the passengers of their valuables. He remembered thinking how easy this would be as they entered the coach, especially after they hustled out the three young male passengers. He expected no trouble from the old man traveling with the young girl. None of the passengers put up any real resistance.

Still, as the hold-up went on, *Lobo* felt the old man watched him closely, not to initiate trouble, but enough to perhaps later describe him to the law. The old man continued to stare at his face. Then, surprising him, that gray haired passenger asked *Lobo* in the Comanche tongue, *"The People? The Antelopes?"*

Lobo was angered to hear this old man dare to speak Comanche to him. He knocked the old geezer to the dirt, who the young girl then rushed to lean over. She had barely drawn *Lobo's* attention until then, but when she knelt next to the old man, the medallion hanging around her neck slipped out from under the neckline of her dress. It caught a glint from the sun and the bone carving shined brightly.

It was a bird rising. A white bird, but not pure white. More of a blend of darkened, mottled shades of white and gray, like the colors rising within distant thunderheads. Twisting streaks of gray and white seemingly forced together in a slow dance of conflict. The words of the Voodoo Priestess from Baton Rouge burned in his brain: *"I see a great power, rising like a warbird, over your future."*

Then he noticed the bird on the medallion wore a crown that someone had taken the trouble to paint gold. He recalled the words of the prophecy of the Spanish woman:

"This gift, which is to be taken from the enemy of your people, you will know by the crown of gold it will bear. It is to be given to the great chief who will lead your people against them."

To *Lobo,* that very moment was a revelation. Not only did the rising bird of the medallion wear a crown, but the girl herself was crowned in golden locks that framed her innocent pale white face. Could it be she herself who was the untouched gift?

"What this is?" *Lobo* asked the girl, who appeared full of terror. When she finally replied, "A White Eagle," *Lobo* recalled the news regarding *the Quahadi.* They prepared to fight the white man in a final battle under the recently arrived war chief *Quanah* and the *puha* of his all-powerful medicine man, *White Eagle.*

Lobo confirmed now this was the great revelation of the untouched gift! The girl herself is that which *Isa Tai'i* had long ago foreseen. Her face was framed by golden locks and she wore a medallion of a crowned White Eagle. She was the gift to be taken from among their enemy - a daughter of the white man. This was his chance at returning to *the People;* just as *Dark Wolf* had returned to them once with his own mother! *Lobo* would be accepted back into *the Quahadi* once more; he would be reunited again with his mother. This was his chance to finally gain the respect of the elders. Somehow this girl would allow him to contribute to that great final battle with the white man.

"Time!" was called by Matteo, who had stressed the importance of robbing this coach in under ten minutes in order for them to quickly make their escape. *Lobo* knew he had a decision to make. Either he would continue on with this gang of thugs, or take the girl out to *his People.*

Then and there, he knew the girl as far more important to him than any amount of bounty to be gained. She was his future, his life's renewal, and his purpose. He took the girl and abandoned the rest of the bandits to head west. He would travel across *the Llano* with nothing else than her alongside him, armed only with a shotgun, his knife and the dead driver's horsewhip.

He found a copse of three cottonwoods along a creek and tied the girl to one of them. He stood over her and constantly rubbed the White Eagle medallion between his fingers. This was all coming to be exactly as the three prophecies had predicted. But before he took the girl off onto *the Llano,* he had to be assured she was *"untouched."*

Too often, *Lobo* thought, he had been fooled in the past, doing what he thought to be right, only to lower his standing among *the People*. There had been the killing of the screech owl, the smoke lodge incident resulting in the death of *Gray Feather,* the stealing of the long coat, and the calls for death upon *Raging Anger. Lobo* knew he had to assure that this gift of a girl with the crown of golden locks was indeed pure before he took her back to *the People.*

He gagged the girl and left her tied to one of the cottonwoods. Then, he went into the town and located the office of the doctor. He arrived to watch from afar just as the old ranger he had assaulted on the coach was brought in. The old man would die, he thought. In any case, he must get the doctor to look over the girl and confirm she was pure, indeed *"untouched."* The word burned in his brain - she must be and remain *untouched* to assure his victorious return to *the People.*

Late in the day the doctor left the office, and *Lobo* stalked him from a distance. He made his way to a home, and watching him, *Lobo* knew it was his dwelling place.

Upon returning to the copse of cottonwoods by the creek, *Lobo* noticed two shadows among them, not one. He cautiously drew closer and noticed a cowboy untying the girl. Apparently she had worked one hand free, removed the gag and called for help. *Lobo* was lucky he had returned just in time. He knew he had to kill the man silently, as a shotgun blast would draw far too much attention.

Lobo came down the bank and picked up the horsewhip he had left there just as the girl was freed by her rescuer. The cowboy saw him and told her to run in the direction behind him. Then, the man stood between him and the escaping girl. As *Lobo* approached him, the cowboy went for the six shooter at his hip. *Lobo* could only react by snapping the whip at him.

If *Lobo* missed with the whip, he would be shot dead at such a close distance. Yet the horsewhip fell true on the cowboy's wrist while he was in the process of drawing his gun. The weapon fell free and into the creek. *Lobo* charged him and worked his way behind the man. Soon cnough, he had the braided leather horsewhip tight around the man's neck. He pulled it tighter and tighter still until he could hear the small bones in the man's neck snap. The cowboy fought violently, but *Lobo* was too strong for him, and soon strangled him to death.

Panting heavily, *Lobo* floated the dead body in the creek, then dragged it under a tangle of exposed roots where it would not soon be found. Then, he headed back to track the girl. Her footprints in the muddy bank along which she ran made this easy enough.

Lobo caught up with her as she attempted to climb up and out of the creek's steep bank. She had raised herself halfway over the bank when she began to scream for help.

Lobo drew the horsewhip and snapped it across the dress covering her rump. He tried not to do so too forcibly, but the snap of the whip's fall cut into her hind quarters. She cried out again, this time in pain, when he whipped with a second lashing. She broke down in a cascade of tears as she slid back down the muddied bank to him in defeat.

"Come!" he said, taking her arm. "We go."

At the doctor's she was declared to be *"untouched,"* and once she was, he thought about killing the man. He decided it to be unnecessary. Yes, the doctor could identify him, but he thought the old man most likely had already done so to the town sheriff and possibly others before he died. Besides, *Lobo* wanted only to head out westward across *the Llano,* and the sooner he did so, the safer he and his untouched gift would be.

Part Three:

The Deadly Pursuit –
A Clash of Cultures

Chapter 20: Kalina's Image

May, 1874

Cord McCullough traveled along the dusty, desolate road from Jacksboro to Wichita Falls. In his mind burned the image of the young he girl sought, but who he had never laid eyes upon. It was true, he had spent a few hours with the girl's Aunt Midge, who he had found to be quite lovely. Cord was aware that he had merely rendered Kalina's image as a younger version of her beautiful aunt. For instance, he knew Kalina had last worn a calico dress for her travels along with a simple straw hat, yet he saw her in Midge's riding clothes and two-toned leather Stetson. The image that drove him on, he knew, was an idealized version of the young girl. Still, it had been her aunt who had convinced him to go after Kalina, so what was the harm in projecting some of Midge's features onto the girl until he found her? That was, of course, if he ever found her. For *the Llano* was a vast and unforgiving place. Cord worried given the late start, that she might never be found.

Cord had left Kalina's headstrong brother, Piotr, behind for his Aunt Midge to look after. He was glad to be rid of the boy, although he had to admit he admired Piotr's unfailing determination. The boy had pluck, he'd give him that. Yet, perhaps unfailing was not the right word, because his headstrong will would surely not only one day fail him, but would likely get the teen killed.

Cord, Trouble and River had passed through the town of Jacksboro the night before. It was as Cord had last remembered it - a low sprawl meandering along the waters of Lost Creek. The town had once been called Mesquiteville after the thick tangles of those brambling trees there. It wasn't until the Jack Brothers came and went from this world that this place would come to bear their family's name.

The West was prone to make myths of men like Patrick Churchill Jack and William Houston Jack. They were great men, the both of them veterans of the war for the Independence of Texas. William fought with Jim Bowie, Patrick went on to be on the Texas Supreme Court. They both died in '44 of yellow fever, within weeks of each other. Patrick was only thirty-six, his older brother William merely thirty-eight. Their lives were prairie storms, violent and intense, dying out as quickly as they'd blown up.

Jacksboro had been the site of many brutal Indian raids until Fort Richardson was built nearby in 1870. Even afterwards, there were raids upon the supply wagons that traveled to and from it and other Texas frontier forts. *Only three years back had been that vicious Warren Wagon Train massacre near Salt Creek,* Cord thought. *The one that got General William T. Sherman so riled up that he drug those chiefs back here to Jacksboro to stand trial. Guess he didn't appreciate being attached to that massacre in any way.*

Cord tried to focus on the meeting ahead with his tracker at the falls of the Wichita River. Together they would determine a plan forward. As he rode atop Trouble, they cleared out of the mesquite woods and soon River romped through a bloom of bluebonnets that called to him invitingly from the sunshine. He wondered if Midge had ever seen a swath of the Texas wildflowers as large as this.

Cord's thoughts continued to wander, from his idealized version of the girl, Kalina, to the long stretch of blooming bluebonnets, but always back to the natural beauty and the inescapable allure of the girl's Aunt Midge.

Cord, Trouble and River pressed on to the small waterfalls of the Wichita River. It was not much of a display, as it stood lower in height than either Cord or Trouble, and only twice that of River. It was befitting the community that had grown around it: stubby but industrious. Not yet large enough to be called a town, it had become a favorite trading site of the Kiowa Indians.

Cord, Trouble and River came onto the falls just after noon. The place had grown considerably since Cord's last visit. More permanent store fronts had been thrown up, and the place was growing into more of a frontier town than an Indian trading village. The swarms of traders were near equally mixed between Kiowas and white men.

The Kiowas were like that, they would trade peaceably enough with the white man one day, and then brutally raid and kill them and their families on another. Often they would ride alongside the Comanches on these raids. The Comanches traded primarily with only two groups - *the Comancheros* out of Santa Fe and the Kiowas from the East. Cord knew, as always, he had to tread cautiously in dealing with the Kiowas here at the falls.

When they came upon the falls, Cord dismounted from Trouble and allowed her to water. River waded into the water pooled beneath the falls and squatted, so that his belly submerged, to cool himself off. A Kiowa trader came up quietly enough behind them, although Cord had sensed his movements and was tracking his every step. He knew the Kiowa all too well to do anything less.

"You should not allow your animal to wander into that water," said the Kiowa. "Warm enough for cottonmouths to be about, you know."

Cord turned slowly to face the native. "That dog ain't fool enough to let a snake get close enough to strike at him. I've seen him kill rattlers with my own eyes. I think he could make short work of a water moccasin."

"Those snakes much faster in water than he is," replied the Kiowa. "I hate to see anything bad happen to a dog that special."

Cord looked directly into the folds of wrinkled skin shrouding the eyes of the old Indian trader.

"Why, ya' fixin' on makin' a meal of him?" Cord asked. He knew that, unlike the Comanche, the Kiowa were known to favor dog in their diet.

"No," the Indian trader laughed almost imperceptibly, "River too old and too tough a dog to eat. Maybe if he mated and his bitch produced a litter of plump little puppies, then there'd be a feast."

"Ya' can be a real son-of-a bitch when ya' want to, *Sulking Crow,*" Cord scoffed. *"Damn y'all Kiowas and yer eating them innocent pups!"* A smile eased onto Cord's face as he said these words to his old friend. It was met by a knowing twinkle in dull black eyes of the Kiowa.

"I'm damn glad to see ya' got my telegram," Cord said. "I'm in a jam and need yer help."

"Not everyday in Red River Station a Kiowa gets a telegram hand delivered by white boy. He looked scared to death. Must have thought me and my family gonna eat him, too."

Cord could not help but to laugh to himself.

"Well, I'm glad he got up a pluck of nerve to deliver it, cause yer by far the best tracker I could think of. I'm in dire need of yer skills. I hope yer'll help me out."

"That depends on who we're to be tracking, my friend," *Sulking Crow* said.

"A half-breed that took a little girl from the stage coach hold-up a bit back in Weatherford," Cord explained.

"Half-blood?" *Sulking Crow* corrected. "You sure? I don't hunt my own people."

"Doc Blevins rode *the Llano* as a medic with the army for years, so I figure he would know," Cord replied. "Doc pegged him to be half-Comanche and half-Mexican. He's fond of wearin' one of those big Mexican leather long coats, the kind with the flared sleeves. He took the girl. I need ya' to track the pair of them across *the Llano.*"

"How many horses?" *Sulking Crow* asked.

"Two." Cord answered. "One bein' the Doc's."

"How long ago did he take her?"

"Near two weeks or so," Cord answered.

"Fourteen days?" *Sulking Crow* said sourly. "Not much sign left to follow after that long."

"Gotta be some sign left to cut for, something left behind to track," Cord argued. "Two horses, after all."

"Not after two weeks strong weather," *Sulking Crow* said. "Spring storms blow through this area over that time. Besides, he likely well out on *Llano* by now. Best chance be to follow the Red River upstream, or maybe the Canadian. The only Comanches still not on the reservation are *the Quahadi,* and they are partial to the buffalo hunting grounds between those two great rivers. But it be very dangerous time to go there."

"*Sulky,* I never known ya' to be fearful of the Comanche before," Cord said.

"I am not scared for myself, but for you. Kiowa and Comanche are friends, and I hear our braves gather there to listen to Comanches speak of attacking white men who slaughter the buffalo in great numbers. *Quahadi* have new war chief - big courage, big fight - named *Quanah*. He is son of the *Penatekas Chief, Peta Nocona.*"

"The chief killed at Pease River?" Cord asked. "The one who took the white girl Cynthia Ann Parker as his wife? This *Quanah* is one of their two boys, the only survivors said to have escaped that massacre?"

"Yes, them his parents," *Sulking Crow* answered. "Yes, he outrode Rangers and escaped that killing at Pease River over a dozen years ago. He only twelve then. Now, he full grown man, leads *the Quahadi.*"

"That makes this *Quanah* a half-breed himself…" Cord figured before asking, "…Ya' think the Comanche warriors will follow a half-breed?"

"Yes! When he handle white man like *Quanah* does. In '71, *Quanah* and his village of *Quahadi* surprise by Blue Coats while moving between camps. *Quanah* lead braves to fight them off, but then lure white man's army into Blanco Canyon. Make fool of them when they tracked them. Full village, women, children, lose army of soldiers there."

Cord could not imagine losing the US army, even in Texas canyon country, once they had a bead on a full village of Comanche. *That was quite the trick,* he thought.

"Well, the bandit I'm tracking is a half-breed who likely has decided to take the girl back to deliver to *the Quahadi*. If we can't track the two of 'em, then just how will we ever find 'em?"

"They make camp near *Palo Duro Canyon,*" *Sulking Crow* said. "I go ahead and find them. I pretend to be trader. I bring along many war supplies to trade with them."

"*Palo Duro* is not just one, but a massive series of canyons. They could be anywhere in that maze. How y'ever gonna find 'em?"

A broad smile stretched across the Kiowa's face. "As Kiowa always do, I read the sky!"

"I don't follow ya', *Sulky.*"

"They kill buffalo or antelope to live," *Sulking Crow* explained. "No matter how few they kill, circle of buzzards always fill the sky. Kiowa read the sky. Follow buzzards, find *the Quahadi.*"

"Damn that's simple," exclaimed Cord. "So damn simple I'd never have thought of it, myself."

"That is why you send for me, my friend," *Sulking Crow* said. "I will help you find this bandit so you can rescue girl, but I give no information to hunt *Quanah and the Quahadi.* You understand?"

"Yup," Cord answered. "That's fair enough. I definitely understand. Where will I find ya' and when?"

"Meet me noon, same day in two week time at ruins of old trading post at Adobe Walls. It near north shore of the Canadian River, near Bent Creek. If bandit has girl with *the Quahadi,* I know by then."

"Good. That will work for me," Cord replied. Then his friendly glance at his tracker melted into a deadly serious stare. All the playful camaraderie between them dissolved away. What he was to speak next had to be said, and had to be said with the respect of total seriousness.

"Sulking Crow," Cord began, "I need ya' to know that if the girl has been turned over to *the Quahadi* or their friends, the Kiowa, and I have to kill a few of 'em to git her back, I intend to do so."

"You do what you must do, Cord," the Kiowa said, "Just do not expect me to help you kill or hunt any Kiowa or Comanche. I find out only if they hold the girl. Rest you do, not me. I leave you now. Must travel up Red River in morning. Suggest you travel later on Red or Canadian River trails, my friend. To travel across open *Llano* on horseback is invitation of death for any white man."

The next morning Cord saw *Sulking Crow* off, confident in their plan forward. He knew he could not join him. He must make his own way out west, but decided he could wait the better part of a week to depart. He argued to himself that he could use that time to gather all further supplies he might need, as well as any information that might assist him in finding the half-breed, should *Sulking Crow* be unsuccessful. Still, Cord did not really know where to begin this search in Wichita Falls.

That was when he spotted the nearby saloon. Cord kidded himself that his decision to stay in that town for several days more was not to take advantage of its abundance of whiskey. But since he had some time to kill, a drink or two was not that bad of an idea. He made his way into the saloon, where he wrapped himself around a bottle and opened his ears to listen to for any discussion of the half-breed or the girl buried deep in the bar room chatter.

Cord worked his way through half that bottle of *budge* but had heard no bragging or even low whispers related to the Indian or the girl. The whiskey had thoroughly warmed him when he imagined Midge entering the bar accompanied by two men. At least he thought he had only imagined it until he saw every man's head in the place turn toward her. She spotted him and strode over, ignoring their hungry stares. Her two escorts trailed behind.

"Cord McCullough!" she abraded him. "Shame on you sitting here drinking whiskey when you should be off rescuing my niece." Her face was flush with her temper up. Her cheeks glowed like red hot embers in a campfire pit. Her fiery look was already better than any of the few memories of her he had squirreled away.

"What are ya' doin' here, Midge?" he asked plainly. "This ain't no place for a woman."

"No place for a woman?" she seethed. "Well, then, you don't stand much chance of finding my niece Kalina in here, do you?"

Cord looked up at her two companions. One was Brett Sumner from the ranch, the other man was familiar to his eye, but Cord could not exactly place him.

"Last I heard," Cord replied, returning his eyes to Midge, "yer niece Kalina wasn't exactly a woman yet." No sooner had he said this than he judged it to be a stupid thing to say. It was the *budge* talking.

"Just when I need you most, I find you here half drunk, squeezing yourself into a bottle," she said. "Don't think I don't see you sizing up my escorts. You know Brett from the ranch. This is Chet Blackman, a sheriff's deputy."

That's where I know him from, Cord thought. *Deputy Chet from the night of the shootout.*

"Gents," Cord said, as he offered the bottle he held aloft, "how bout a shot or two o' budge on me? What brings ya' fellers to Wichita Falls?"

Neither man responded, they merely glanced at Midge. She clearly was leading their little party.

"We're lookin' for my nephew," Midge said tersely.

Cord loved the iron showing in her now. The woman was a fighter, he could see that clearly. Damn if it didn't suit her.

"Well, Midge, yer about two towns too far north" Cord said. "I left him in Weatherford for y'all to send back south to *Panna Maria*. Don't ya' 'member?"

"He got away from us," Brett said, perhaps figuring the Polish woman was about to explode at Cord's mockery. "Acted as if he would take the coach back home, but when we went to git him in his room, all we found was a note to say he borrowed a horse and that he was coming to catch up with you."

"He won't be hard to find the way he was dressed," Cord said. "He'll stand out like a scarecrow in a field of half-grown corn. 'Cept the scarecrow would be better dressed for sure…"

"I am glad you find this to be so amusing, Mr. McCullough," Midge snapped, straining the words through her gritted teeth to allow them out. Despite that, her adorable accent crept out with them. "I can see you take Piotr's safety as seriously as you do my niece Kalina's. Perhaps you'll also find joy in mocking her modest style of dress when you finally sober up and get about to finding her. That is, if by then, the Comanche has left any clothes on her discarded, dead body!"

Damn she's fired up, now. I'd best back off a bit.

"Well, as it is, Cord," Brett tried to calm things down, "I done fitted him out with new duds, boots and even powder and balls for that relic of a gun of his, just like y'asked. Remember? Keep the boy busy."

"Not for that damn old Lemat revolver," Cord said, sobering up at the thought. "Fool kid will blow his own foot off with that wretched piece."

"No, he won't," Midge protested, "cause I taught him how to handle it. I'm not worried about that."

"Then he'll blow his hand off when it chain-fires on him," Cord quipped. "They're prone to do that, too."

"I taught him how to load it properly as well," Midge said. "How to make sure the fit is so tight it scrapes off a little sliver ring of lead from the ball when he levers it in. I'm not worried about that either."

"Then, just what do ya' worry yer pretty little head about?" Cord quipped.

"About you. You're drunk," she said. "And about why it was I ever thought you were just the man to go on out save my niece from that savage."

"Still ya' come here begging for me to round up the *Pee Otter,* again?" Cord said, playfully exaggerating his mispronunciation of Piotr's name. He expected Midge to correct him on it, but she merely looked down at him with disgust. Brett avoided his eyes altogether, only the sheriff's deputy looked at him intently.

"No, the three of us will do that," Midge brushed back at him. "I don't want Piotr to see you in this state. It would only serve to confirm the thoughts he already has of you: a war deserting coward, looking for a fast score of cash to purchase some courage in the bottom of a bottle. I was such a fool to try and convince him otherwise."

"Naw, Midge, ya' got that ass backwards," Cord said most seriously. "Courage is easy 'nuff for me to find. It's the absolution for the sins caused by my findin' it that I'm lookin' fer down in here."

He held up his empty whiskey glass as he looked hard into her eyes when he said these words. Somewhere deep within her, he saw something give just a little, like a gunman's flinch just before Cord was to shoot him down. But her flinch was not of fear, but of recognition. Perhaps she realized deep inside, despite his being drunk, those last words were the God-awful truth.

He felt empowered by his recognition of it in her. "Yup. Ass backwards all right. By far not the worst sight I ever seen, though."

Then she hardened herself again. "I refuse to be spoken to so vulgarly by a drunkard. Come on, fellas."

Midge and the two cowboys left him there, as if there was no value in wasting their effort to get him to stop drinking. Cord thought over what she had said, and decided she was right. He needed to sober up. Right after he finished off the rest of this bottle of *budge.* After all, it just might be his last for a while, he reckoned.

Chapter 21: A Respite on the Llano

May, 1874

The young girl wearing the White Eagle medallion slept soundly. *Lobo* watched over her as the moon rose, casting its luminous glow like a silken stream spreading across the barren lands. They had been on horseback across *the Llano Estacado* for many days. It had been as strange a journey for the Comanche-turned-bandit as for the frightened child. *Lobo* found himself recalling his own childhood as the boy, *Kills Owls*, when he was banned from joining his father or any other *Quahadi* out onto the Staked Plains.

He was never taught the full measure of *the Llano's* secrets. Survival on it was spared only to those who knew its hidden treasures - how to find its reserves of water being foremost. It had been many days since they slipped out of Weatherford, and the water they carried had all but run out. The little that remained was not near enough to quench the dire thirst of himself, the girl and their pair of horses.

Lobo knew to use the setting sun as his western mark. Each night as it dropped, he stood resolute watching it slide away beyond the horizon as the unrelenting wind of the plains blew into his face, taunting him. He did this each evening not to observe its beauty nor its majesty, but rather to seek out and memorize the promise of its path.

Lobo would carefully study details of the land under its golden-red glow to identify multiple features he could use to navigate true west come sun-up. Sometimes, there was nothing but the pattern of gaps between stalky growth of grass to remember, but even they could provide direction to guide those who studied them closely.

The bigger issue was the water. This night they would run out. He had not yet found a source. So *Lobo* had to resort to an old Comanche trick that was always a last resort. He feared he might have taken to it too quickly, but the girl's horse, the one taken from the doctor, was by then completely played out. He gave the girl water, and after she drank, he gave the last of it to his horse. He offered none to the dried-out mount. Then, he left the girl alone briefly with his own horse hobbled nearby by the small fire he had built. He remained parched as he rode the girl's mount out of the her sight. Once there, he had no option but to take the animal's life, and chase away his own thirst by drinking the blood he drained from its open, flowing vein. He knew to do this in dire need only from the tales of *the Llano* that his father *Dark Wolf* had told him as a boy.

Lobo walked back toward the glow of the camp's fire with two steaks of horse flesh he had butchered from the dead animal with his knife. He would cook them over the flame and nourish the girl and himself, which he would need to stand watch throughout the night. He knew the scent of the sacrificed animal would draw predators. It was his responsibility to assure they attacked neither the girl, nor their lone surviving mount. Loss of either would keep him from delivering his "untouched" gift to the new medicine man, *White Eagle.* That would mean an end to his hopes of rejoining *the People,* and thus, his mother.

Chapter 22: The Long Reach of Vaughn Anders' Revenge

Late May, 1874

The simple click of the hammer being cocked might as well have been as loud as a rolling peal of thunder. It roused Cord from his drunken sleep. He respected more than feared that sound, because even in his inebriated state, he recognized it to be the augur of death.

"Git up, McCullough," the gruff voice with the familiar ring to it said to him.

He tried to focus his eyes. They resisted at first, defied by the glow of the nearby fire, blurring the image before him that seemed to dance with a hop like a chorus girl. Yet as he watched closely as that image skipped forward and kicked at him, he felt the sharp tip of a boot explode painfully into his ribs.

"I said to git up, damn it," the voice was angry now. "We got a ways to travel today, and we don't want to keep Mr. Anders waiting, now do we? He's a very busy man."

Cord struggled to his feet. *How had this man from Vaughn Anders outfit found him? Only one? Where the hell was River?* he wondered. *Why hadn't the dog attacked?*

"Okay, okay already," Cord said. "Just throw me my duster and we'll git going."

The man all but laughed as he said, "Sure. Yer duster. Ya' was usin' it as a blanket when I snuck up on ya' and pulled it away. Here ya' go…"

The intruder pitched the long overcoat at Cord whose heart instantly sank. The coat caught the slight night breeze and ballooned like the cover of a Conestoga. No weight to it all. It floated to the ground upon which Cord still kneeled. McCullough dropped his head in defeat.

"Ya' surely figured that Mr. Anders would have warned me about that little surprise gun ya' keep in its secret pocket, didn't ya'?" The man's words mocked him. There was something both strange yet known to its quality. Cord's mind still pounded, and as he was suffering from the pain of his aching ribs, he couldn't quite place the voice.

"Did ya' kill my dog?" Cord finally asked it.

An ominous silence prevailed for several seconds. Cord could feel a sorrow swell within himself.

"Nope," the voice finally said. "I was fixin' to, for Anders had warned me about it, too, but when I came upon ya', it wasn't to be found. Just yerself and the bay mare."

"Her name is Trouble," Cord said, stalling for time as he slowly rose to his knees. He could now see the legs of the man emerge into focus from the darkness.

"I know," the man said. "I know all about ya', Cord McCullough. Who goes and names a horse 'Trouble,' anyway? I guess only someone who goes around by a name as strange as 'Cord.' What, did yer mother name ya' after some pianer player she had given herself to? Too drunk to remember his name, so she just went with 'Chord'?"

The laugh that followed angered Cord to no end. *He can 'muse himself over my naming the horse Trouble, even at my own name, but I'll be damned if I'm gonna let him mock my mama like that.*

Cord was up on one knee when he launched himself in the direction of the intruder, intending to wrap his arms around the man. He figured, *if Vaughn Anders wants me, he'll get my corpse shot through with a few rounds of lead. I don't intend to give him pleasure of makin' me suffer.*

But the intruder didn't shoot at the onrushing Cord, he merely stepped deftly aside, like a Mexican matador from a charging bull. When Cord went to wrap his arms around him and drag him to the ground, his limbs did not respond to his intentions. Instead, he lunged straight as a bullet past the man. A split second later, he felt the butt of a gun grip crash into his skull as the intruder pistol-whipped him as he went by.

Cord fell to the dirt again, his head throbbing from the combination of the gun hammering upon his skull and his own lingering inebriation.

"Damn, Cord," the voice said with a lilt, almost laughing, "yer so damn drunk ya' didn't even realize I handcuffed yer wrists together. By the way, that was yer Baby Colt Dragoon I slugged ya' with. If ya' want to make another pass, I still got yer Peacekeeper too. Ya' can have matching lumps from each of yer hoglegs."

Cord rolled over onto his back and gathered his first full glimpse of the man. He looked as familiar as his voice sounded. Then, it all came together for him.

"Ya' was with Midge last night," Cord said. "Ya' and that ranch hand, Brett Sumner, with Midge. But I know ya' from somewhere else, too."

"You really are a boozer, ain't ya?" the man said. "Ya' don't 'member me from the shootout the night we took down that stagecoach gang? Ya don't remember Midge tellin' ya' I was the sheriff's deputy last night?"

"Yeah, that sheriff's deputy," Cord said, as if he had remembered on his own. All the while his head beat out a raging pulse like a war drum.

"Bingo," the man said, "Deputy Chet Blackman at yer service. Hey, 'Bingo!' That makes a much better name for yer mare. Yeah, 'Bingo' rather than that lame-ass name of 'Trouble.' Come on, Cord, y'already done made me two hundred dollars from Vaughn Anders, and when I deliver ya to him in a few days, yer gonna make me a hella lot more."

"So ya don't figure to kill me?" Cord asked. "Anders won't be just as happy to git my corpse?"

"Not hardly," Deputy Chet said, "Vaughn Anders was very specific on that point. He wants to watch ya' die, boy. Ya' see, it ain't the death but the dyin' he wants, to see all the sufferin'. I reckon he wants to hear the wobble in yer voice when ya' plead for his forgiveness, which I assure ya' in advance won't be forthcomin'. I don't know if he'll pull the trigger himself that ends yer agony, but be sure that the last thing yer ever gonna see will be the light of the muzzle flash bouncing off the skin of his smiling face. And by that point, you'll be begging to see it."

"I figure ya' got that all right," Cord said, " 'cept for one thing."

"And just what might that be?" Chet asked.

"I don't figure to be doing no begging for my life," Cord answered, like a man confessing a long kept secret. "It don't amount to enough of a thing to beg fer."

Chapter 23: The Finding

Late May, 1874

Three days later the sun rose over them. The day before *Lobo* had found a dry creek bed and walked it upstream until it stingily gave away the little water it had held hidden. Water that was both muddy and chalky, not fit to drink unless you had ridden two dry days on *the Llano*, and been scorched red by its unforgiving sun, whipped raw by its unrelenting wind.

Lobo faced two major issues. The sun had only a scorching effect on his dark reddish-brown skin, but the girl's skin was the palest shade of white he had ever seen, like the polished horns of a *cibolo*. The sun had raised blisters on her face and hands. Everything else was covered by clothes, but the blemishes raised made her look impure.

He had heard this was a condition common to some white men, especially those called Irishmen. He applied mud from the creek-bed over her blisters, which only gave her the appearance of having the pox. He feared this would ruin his presenting her to the medicine man, *White Eagle*.

The other problem the Comanche outcast faced was that he had lost his bearings. *How far had they meandered, following the twists and turns of that dry creek bed, like the mangled fingers of a branch of mesquite? How far off course had it dragged them?*

Sure, he knew to go in the opposite direction of the rising sun, but even being just a slight bit off his bearings could mean missing the Texas canyon country altogether.

Having applied the creek's mud to her blisters, he reached down and took her medallion in his fingers. By then, she was used to him doing so, and put up no resistance. Yet no sooner had he looked down to rub its pale bone surface with the pad of his thumb, she let out a scream that caught him by surprise. Looking up, he saw pure terror on her face. Her eyes looked past him, and darted back and forth like willow branches on the winds of a rising storm.

He turned slowly to see four Comanche braves standing over them. They wore war paint, but bore no coup sticks or weapons other than their bows. He could see they were all young, likely in their early teens, out for a hunt of small game. Yet to the girl they must have been terrifying.

"I am *Lobo*, once called *He Who Kills Owls*," he said in their tongue. The girl hid behind his strong frame.

"We know who you are," said the one acting as leader. "You are a one who is *the Great Deceiver*. You carry with you the leather coat that is forbidden on *the Llano*. We were told to kill you on sight. We thought your tale to be nothing but folklore from our fathers, but here you now stand before us. We will kill you, and then we will share the girl among us."

Three of the braves drew back their bows, their sharp tipped arrows aimed at *Lobo*. He thought, *I have come too far to die here and allow these children to violate my untouched gift to White Eagle.*

Despite their young age, he knew these braves were dangerous, especially if only because by killing him, it meant they could prove their own courage to *the People*.

"Why do you wear the paint of war?" he asked them. "To hunt antelope or worse, rabbit? Are you too young to know it is only to be worn in battle or on raids?" *Lobo* stood defiant and upright before them.

"There is a great battle looming," the leader said, "and when we drag your body back we will be recognized as brave warriors, and will be allowed to fight in that final encounter with the white man. Now, give us the girl."

Lobo remembered the prophecies. *At the time of the final war with the white man, an untouched gift crowned with gold will allow you to rejoin the People.*

"Who speaks to you of this final war with the white man?" he asked.

"The medicine man who communes with *the Great Spirit,* who visits him in the sky. He who foretold of the coming of the comet in the night, and of its leaving. He who told us to beware of the wandering soul of *the Llano* shrouded in the long coat. *'He who wears the coat is under the puha of the Great Deceiver.'* He warned us that you were coming soon. Your return is the last omen that must appear before the final war with the white man can begin."

"What does this great medicine man call himself?" They hesitated, but *Lobo* demanded an answer. "If you are to take a Comanche's life, for I am your brother, then you must answer me, by whose authority am I to die?"

"He is called *White Eagle,*" their leader said proudly, "medicine man to our great war chief *Quanah,* first born of the *Great Chief Peta Nocona* slain unjustly by the Blue Coats of the white man. Now, give the girl to us."

Lobo placed his arms on the girl and gently pushed her further behind himself, shielding her from the path of their still drawn arrows.

"The girl is a gift to your medicine man who calls himself *White Eagle*. She wears his image around her neck. She is untouched and much stay so until I can present her to him. You wish not to be the one to defile her, not only fearing the wrath of *White Eagle,* but also because she carries the pox of the white man."

The four braves looked quizzically at each other.

"As we are warned," their leader said, "you are under the power of *the Great Deceiver*. We will not be fooled by your words. How can the girl be both untouched and carry the pox?"

"It is to keep her from you," responded *Lobo* "and any others who would desire to take away her purity. Only *White Eagle* can cure her of the pox, and then decide who should obtain the gift of her innocence. Most likely she will be offered up to *the Great Spirit*. But do not believe me, instead if you think she is not for *White Eagle,* then come close, look at the medallion she wears around her neck."

Lobo made a sweeping gesture with his arms inviting the leader to come close to the girl. The bows of the young braves were still arched and their arrows aimed at his chest. Cautiously, their leader wandered forth to stand over the terrified girl.

"It is good," *Lobo* said to her in English, "he look at *White Eagle.*"

The young leader scooped his finger below the neckline of her dress, hooked the chain and raised it until the medallion lay in his hand. An eagle wearing a crown of gold carved in bone bleached white, just as *Lobo* had said.

"We take you to *Palo Duro*, to *White Eagle*. He will know what to do with you." The leader made a signal and the three young braves lowered their bows.

Chapter 24: Cord McCullough's Day of Reckoning

Late May, 1874

The road back to Jacksboro was dry and dusty, but even for the end of May, the day was not particularly hot nor cold. May was one of the months that could play with a man. It could range from a particular nasty cold lick to some honest-to-God soul scorching heat, depending upon just how the aforementioned God was feeling at the moment. This day, He was peaceful. The two men lumbered along, side by side, Cord on Trouble, the deputy on his own mount.

"When we get into to Jacksboro," Deputy Chet Blackman said to Cord, "I'll send off a telegram back to Anders to let him know I'm bringing ya' in."

So, Cord thought, *Vaughn Anders isn't even aware yet that I am in this man's custody. If I can somehow get out of this mess, I won't even have to look over my shoulder for his men coming after me. But I best be quick about it.*

His words had been the first bit of chatting the two had done for a good spell since leaving Wichita Falls. With this new bit of information, Cord suddenly found himself feeling strangely talkative.

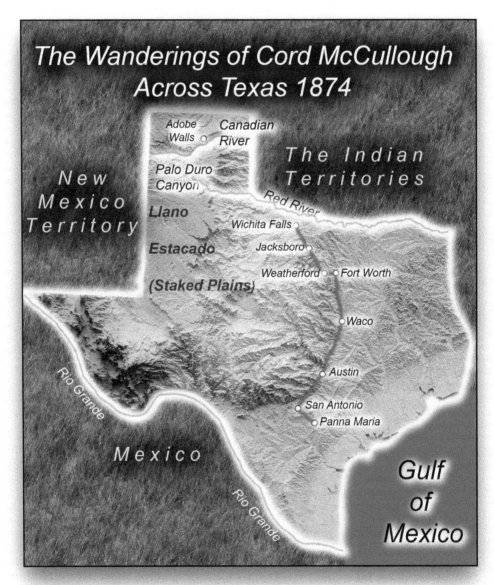

Figure 8: Cord McCullough's Wanderings

"How much ya' figure that cattleman is goin' give ya' fer me?" Cord asked. His wrists remained handcuffed but the shackles were also tied to the horn of his saddle by rope. Every so often when the deputy looked away Cord would give the knots a solid tug, but the braided rope would not yield; the knots held firm.

"More than ya' can possibly afford to match," Chet answered, "but even if ya' could come up with a small fortune, I'd never go against Vaughn Anders in that way. Very bad things tend to happen to those who do."

Cord picked up on the words "small fortune" and tried to lure the deputy into returning to the Falls.

"As it turns out," Cord answered, "I was carrying a small fortune in case I had to ransom the girl. Take me back to my camp and I'll show ya' where I hid it."

"It ain't there," the deputy said with a knowing grin. "Midge done told me 'bout it, being a man of the law and all, just how much ya' was carrying. She wanted to take it away from ya' last night after finding ya' drunk, but I told her it was best not to, with yer being sotted, ya' just might end up shootin' someone. Ya' never hid it. I found it in yer saddlebag before I rousted ya'. Now, it's right here in mine." Chet patted his saddle bag and grinned.

"So yer just gonna keep it," asked Cord, "git yer reward too, then watch Anders' boys go to work on me?"

"Not me," Chet answered, "I don't have the stomach for that. I can't stand to hear a grown man scream. Sends shivers through me. Nope, I'll get the reward money, and be on my way. I'll leave ol' Vaughn to his degenerate delights. As for this bounty, I never found it on ya'. Figured ya' hid it somewhere to come back and dig up later. At least, that's what the Scotsman will come to believe."

"Well, Chet," Cord smiled, "ya' got this all figured out, don't ya'?" They then passed into a mottled tunnel of light draining through a tangle of mesquite woods when Deputy Chet held up his hand to stop.

"I just saw something moving in the woods ahead," Chet said.

"Could be Comanches," Cord said, hoping to plant a seed of concern in the deputy's mind.

"Not unless they grew four legs and a tail," the deputy quipped. "More likely a lone coyote."

There from out of the shadows lurked an ominous canine figure onto the center of the road. Cord instantly recognized the silhouette of River, as a blaze of sunshine from beyond the trees backlit the image of his fearless dog.

"I never heard of a coyote coming out in front of riders in the daytime like this unless it was rabid," Chet said as he reached for the rifle from his saddle sheath. He took aim on the animal, still not recognizing it as Cord's dog, but as soon as he drew a bead on it, the animal scurried off and out of his sights.

Cord had trained the dog to do so. A couple of hits with bird shot from a 28 gauge shotgun was all that was needed to convince River never to allow so much as a broom handle to be pointed at him. It was cruel training, but in the long run, it served the animal well. Today it would save its life. *But how did River get here?*

"Damn thing won't let me draw a bead on it," the deputy said. "Damn it, this is frustratin'."

While the deputy was obsessed with taking aim on River, Cord drifted Trouble closer to Chet's horse. They were near side by side with the distracted deputy when McCullough made his move.

He allowed his leg closest to the deputy to fall free from the stirrup. As Chet remained fixated on trying to shoot the scurrying animal, Cord readied himself. Finally, Chet squeezed off a round, missing River well wide of the mark. But before the echo of the shot died out, Cord stood up high on his outside stirrup, leaned forward onto his shackled hands which remained bound to the horn. The metal cuffs bit hard into his wrists as he grasped the pommel. He ignored the pain. With all of his weight leveraged forward, he whipped his inside leg as hard as he could into Chet's hip. With both the deputy's hands still on the rifle, Cord's kick was barely forceful enough to drive him from his saddle, but it proved to be sufficient to do so. Chet's mount, already excited from the rifle shot, took off as soon as his rider began to fall free.

The deputy landed in the mixture of horse shit and thick mud covering the road. Its softness broke his fall somewhat. Lying on his back, he pointed the rifle up at Cord, who had made no attempt atop Trouble to run off.

"Damn it, Cord!" Chet protested, "I got every right to shoot ya' down here and now."

"I don't reckon Vaughn Anders would take too kindly to it if ya' did," Cord answered with an impish smile. "Relax, Chet, I was just having what I figure might amount to be my last bit of funnin'."

Chet Blackman stood up, making sure he was clear of Cord, even though he appeared to still be firmly bound to the saddle.

"Real funny," Chet said, "now we gotta go after my horse. Just how we gonna do that?"

"I figure ya' got bigger problems than that, Chet," Cord said chuckling.

"Oh yeah," the deputy said, "if ya' think you're gonna get me to look away again, I ain't that dumb. So I got other problems, like what?"

"Like that LeMat grapeshot revolver," Cord answered, "pointed square at the center of yer back from only a foot away…"

"…which will blow a whole in you wide enough to turn a wagon around in," added a youthful, accented voice.

Piotr's words took the deputy by surprise. The sight of him coming out of the underbrush behind Chet had also amazed Cord, but he managed to hide his astonishment.

Neither Cord nor Piotr could have expected Deputy Chet's physical response to his being waylaid. He spun around hard and butted the teen violently with the rifle stock in the shoulder, driving him to the ground. Cord was in no position to help the teen as he was still tied to the horn of the saddle's pommel.

When Chet leveled the gun at Piotr, Cord whistled out and River broke into a full-out run right at the deputy. By the time Chet realized the dog was on the move it was too late. He raised his rifle from its bead on Piotr to shoot at River, but before he could get off a single shot, the dog was on him, having lept from the stride of a full run.

The impact of the canine smashing into the deputy sent the rifle flying. River's teeth found Chet's right arm and ripped away at the flesh of his wrist. Cord and Piotr heard the deputy scream out a cry that seemed more fitting for a woman than a supposedly big, tough man.

Piotr shuffled to his feet and pointed the massive revolver at the deputy, but River showed no interest in giving this man a chance to recover the rifle. His attack on the screaming deputy was unrelenting.

"Hey, *Pee Otter*," Cord yelled out, "don't go and shoot my dog now. Git over here and untie my hands while River keeps the deputy occupied. Quick, like!"

Piotr, whose chest had been beating with indecision as what to do, then moved to free Cord from the rope tying his metal bracelets to the saddle horn. As Deputy Chet wrestled with the savage animal in the muddy and manure covered road, Cord dismounted from Trouble and had the boy mount her to go chase down the lawman's horse.

"We need to get that Scotsman's money back," Cord said urgently, "if we're going to use it to ransom yer sister."

While he fought on the ground with River, Chet had managed to use his left hand to draw out his revolver. As he raised it to quiet the animal, he felt something drive his arm back and then to the ground. Cord McCullough, his hands still cuffed, stood over him. The sole of his boot pinned Chet's left arm to the ground. Cord pointed the LeMat he had taken from Piotr at him and then called off River, only to expose the deputy's badly mauled right forearm.

"Deputy Chet," Cord said, "I see ya' finally met my dog, River. He's a little pissed off, I'd say. Must have heard ya' telling me how ya' had planned to kill him back at the camp. Looks like he got the last licks in, though."

"Yer damn lucky, McCullough," Chet spit the words out at him. "Had this boy and dog not come along, ya'd be dead in a matter of a couple of days, maybe less. What ya' plan to do with me? I need a doctor something bad."

"That scream ya' let out when River attacked did indeed send shivers down my spine, just like ya' said. Problem is, just what do I do with ya'? I believe ya' said ya' was takin' me to the end of my life, and a miserable one at that, so maybe that's the right answer for ya' as well."

"You can't kill a lawman," Chet said, "the sheriff will draw up a posse and hunt yer ass down."

"Might just have to, Chet," Cord reasoned aloud, "cuz if I let ya' go, ya'll likely cook up some tall tale how I waylaid ya' along the road. No tellin' what ya' might get some crooked doctor to attest to, let alone a sheriff to believe. Let's face it, Chet, yer too damn stupid and too much of a liar fer me to let live."

A mask of sheer terror crept over the deputy's face.

"I swear I won't say nuthin' to no one." The pitch in his voice wobbled between regret and fear. "Cord, this ain't gotta end this way!"

"Toss me the keys to these cuffs," Cord instructed, as if he was considering sparing the deputy. Chet fished out the keys from his pocket and pitched them to Cord.

"There," Chet said, "I done just like ya' said. And I will be keeping my mouth shut, too. Just leave me here."

"I don't see no other way out of this," Cord reasoned as he rejected the deputy's plea, "since ya' came against me once, ya' surely will again. Just with a hell of a lot more guns with ya' next time."

"I'm begging ya' Cord," Chet Blackman was on his knees in the muddy bog of horseshit, pleading for his life. "Let me live. I'll play it your way, I swear. I swear on my wife and kid's lives…"

"I got one last question for ya', Chet," Cord said. "Did ya' even spend the two hundred ya' made off me yet?"

"No, not a penny, Cord," he answered, "I still got every bit of that money Anders gave to me."

"Damn shame. Ya' shouldda enjoyed that Judas money," Cord said. "Shouldda spent it while ya' could."

Piotr watched the two men from a distance as he returned on Trouble leading the deputy's horse, but he could only hear snippets of the discussion. What he did hear loud and clear was the shot from the LeMat that took the deputy's life. It shook the boy to his core. He had never seen a man killed before, and especially not one already badly wounded, posing no real threat to them any longer.

"Why did you go and do that?" he screamed as he ran the horses toward Cord. "What are you, some kinda cold-blooded killer?"

"Some kind of killer, yeah," Cord said as he used the cuff keys, "but this man had done sealed his own fate."

"You had his life in your hands," the sickly pale Piotr said, "and you murdered him. Why was that necessary?"

"Ya' still want to git yer sister back?" Cord rubbed the skin of his newly freed wrists. "If the answer is yes, and I suspect it is, then it was necessary. I can't take on a half-breed in *Comancheria* while havin' to look over my shoulder for a corrupt lawman to come at me again, can I? Where the hell did ya' and River come from, anyway?"

Piotr began crying, but tried hard not to show it.

"I asked ya' a question, boy."

"I been tracking you for quite a while, now. When you went into that saloon I figured you'd be a spell, so I slipped back to your camp and lured your dog away as a joke. You didn't even notice when you came back last night, you were so drunk. I was bringing him back this morning, and saw the deputy overtaking you. So me and River followed you both. I remembered these woods and thought they would make a good place for an ambush."

"I guess it all worked out in the end," Cord said.

"You think no one is gonna miss him?" Piotr cried out. "Didn't he have any family? I heard him say he had a wife and kids. Surely the sheriff will be lookin' for him."

"Don't matter," Cord answered coldly, "they won't find him, I'll make sure of that. But just figure things this way - had ya' not run off from yer beloved *Panna Maria*, none of this would ever have happened. But it did, and yer sister is still out there somewhere, so let's git on with it."

"So, do you figure to kill me, too? Just to keep this all from eventually gettin' out?"

"Well, *Pee Otter*," Cord joked, "I figure if I don't reunite ya' with yer sister, I just might have to. Won't I?"

Chapter 25: The Revelation

Early June, 1874

The four braves drove *Lobo* and the girl - *White Eagle's* gift - doubled up on their mare before them. They had no fear of the pair bolting, as their ponies could easily run down the double mount. They led the pair back to *Palo Duro Canyon,* where a great encampment of Comanche was gathered along the creekside.

It wasn't the sight of the massive canyon that drove the emotions to rise within *Lobo* when they crested its rim, but rather the sight along their descent of the lightening-split tree. A decade ago, after having been driven from the village, he had joined the *Comancheros* on their departure at this very tree. Tears formed in his eyes at the bitter sight of it, which he fought to hold back until the prairie wind dried them away. But the girl, riding in front of him, made him think of his mother. *Trembling Wind* had once ridden the same way with *Dark Wolf* as they approached these lands. *Lobo's* mind returned to when he left all those years ago, when she was forced to become wife to *Raging Anger*. Would his mother even recognize him upon his return?

Something about that question made a muscle deep within him flinch. The girl felt him shudder, and turned to see a single tear tracking across his cheek. She reached up and with the gentlest move of her hand, wiped it away.

"Why is the canyon village crowded with so many braves?" *Lobo* asked the leader of the four captors as they rode down the switchback trail.

"The Dance of the Sun was recently held," the young leader replied. "Many tribes come: Kiowa, Arapaho, Cheyenne…"

"Comanches do not practice *the Dance of the Sun,"* *Lobo* answered.

"Now, we do," replied the youth, "on the direction of the medicine man, *White Eagle.* It is needed to complete his great magic for the last battle with the white man."

"What is this great magic?" asked *Lobo.*

"Those warriors painted with his yellow war paint will become immune of the sting of the white man's bullets. A great victory is assured under his *puha."*

"Take me and the girl to him," *Lobo* directed.

"When he is ready to receive you," came the answer, "he will call for you."

"What has become of *Raging Anger?"* he then asked regarding his mother's husband.

"He readies for this great battle," the leader answered. "*White Eagle* said he was too old, but *Quanah* said no, he could still ride."

"And his woman, *Trembling Wind?"* A tangle of emotion rose up in him, expecting to hear she had died at *Raging Anger's* hand.

"She is thick with the warrior's child," came the response that shocked *Lobo.*

"When will she give it life?" he asked.

"Soon. Save your questions for *White Eagle.* He has gained great knowledge and *puha* from *the Great Spirit."*

They were paraded proudly through the village, and many came out to view the captives brought in by these young boys. Several of the older women recognized him and called out his former name, *"He Who Kills Owls."*

An older warrior brave stepped forward and asked them if this was *the Great Deceiver,* who was ordered to be killed on sight if he was ever found on *the Llano.*

"It is he," stated the leader of the Comanche boys.

"Yet, he still lives?" the warrior brave argued.

"Only because he brings a gift of great *puha* for *White Eagle,"* the boy said, removing the girl's hat and allowing her golden hair to flow free like a waterfall.

The warrior brave reached out to touch her locks, when *Lobo* grabbed his hand and said, "She is untouched, and shall remain so until she is presented to your powerful medicine man."

The warrior brave defiantly pulled his hand free from *Lobo's* grasp. "What are these markings on her face," he sneered, pointing to the dried mud covering her sun blisters.

"Just something *White Eagle's* medicine can cure," said *Lobo.* "He will know what to do with her."

"As I know what to do with you," the brave replied, "when the elders agree the time has come to take your life."

Lobo did not back away from this warrior brave. His stare did not break lock with his eyes. He only said in response, "I assure you, when my time comes to die, it will not be at the hands of you or any other brave."

They were led to a lodge, *a tipi* where they were to wait until they could be taken to the medicine man. The swollen village was busier than anything *Lobo* had ever seen as a child. There was an energy that seemed to pulse throughout the encampment. Even the braves too old to fight excitedly prepared the weapons: bows, lances, coup sticks and thick buffalo hide war shields. They even cleaned the barrels of the rifles bought from the *Comancheros.* These rifles were relics, nothing as modern as what *Lobo* had been accustomed to using over the last decade, but any rifle in the hands of attacking warriors was still very valuable.

The fear in the girl had risen like the smoke from the fire she watched climb within the lodge only to be sucked out as it neared the vent flap. She wondered how this occurred so effortlessly. That thought was quickly lost among a thousand others of what was to happen to herself. She knew enough that this man had taken her to the doctor to learn if she was pure. Now she wondered what it all meant. Why was it important to these Comanches?

The one who had taken her had not attacked her in any way out on *the Llano,* but instead protected her as vigorously as she ever had been throughout her life. Why? To what end? She could only hope he would continue to defend her, here among all these natives, as he had since the moment he had ripped her away from her world.

Figure 9: White Eagle

Night fell outside the lodge, and *Lobo* and the girl were taken to another *tipi,* the lodge of the medicine man. They entered it only to see *White Eagle's* back as he finished his business with an old Kiowa trader.

As the Kiowa was escorted from the lodge, *Lobo* caught him staring at the girl as he passed. Surely it would not be unusual for such a beautiful young white girl to draw the attention of a Kiowa, or any other tribesman, in this setting, but *Lobo* saw something dangerous in his eyes. It sent a worrisome feeling through him, as if somehow he had been betrayed by the intensity of the Kiowa's glance.

"I do not trust that Kiowa trader," *Lobo* caught himself saying aloud. The medicine man replied, but for whatever reason, did not yet turn to face *Lobo* or the girl.

"That Kiowa trader has delivered a great supply of arrows and black powder for our cause," the medicine man said, as he slowly turned. *Lobo* felt ashamed, reprimanded as he was by *White Eagle*. He watched for the face of the man of great magic, of the most powerful *puha,* as it turned to him. He gently nudged the girl a step ahead of himself with immense pride, hoping his comment had not ruined the moment. Then, the face of the man was revealed.

"You!" Lobo shouted, as he pulled the girl back. "You are but the child *Isa Tai'i* with whom I was raised!"

"The Great Spirit with whom I commune," the medicine man said sternly, "has renamed me *White Eagle.* Just as you are no longer *He Who Kills Owls,* I am no longer *Isa Tai'i.* Yes, it was the voice of *Isa Tai'i* that prophesied that you would return before the last great battle against the white man, but now you stand here before me, *White Eagle.* You have returned to fulfill this prophesy and return to *the People?* You bring the gift of great purity?"

Lobo was unsettled, caught off guard by the unexpected revelation of who *White Eagle* proved to be. He could only think to say, "I bring you the most precious gift ever taken from the white man. I knew her to be the predicted gift, because she bears your image."

Lobo reached his hand below the collar of the young girl's dress, and hooked his finger around the chain of her necklace. He then slowly pulled it free until the bone carving of the White Eagle dangled in front of the medicine man who bent over to inspect it closely. He used his nails to catch the edges of the fine detail carved into the bone.

"It is my image," *White Eagle* said proudly, "and it wears a crown of yellow. Yellow is the color of victory over the forces of the white man in the coming battle. I am very pleased with this gift. It is that which *the Great Spirit* foretold would arrive just before the start of the final war with the white man."

Lobo reached behind the girl's shoulders. "Allow me to hang it from your neck, *White Eagle.*"

"No," the medicine man objected, "it must stay with her. You remember the place called *Thunderbird of the Great Spirit?* On the morning of the first battle of this war, I will be by *Quanah's* side leading our people against the white man. You will remain here and take her there to present her to *the Great Spirit.* He will know she is the gift of highest purity from me because she bears my image."

"And what will I do with her there?" *Lobo* asked.

"After you take her to the base of t*he Thunderbird,*" *White Eagle* instructed him, "dressed in the clothing of our tribe, you will present her. Show my image that she wears. You will then look up and read the rising sun. Through the image it raises in you, *the Great Spirit* will instruct you."

"Yes, *White Eagle,*" *Lobo* complied, by then over his initial shock as to the medicine's man's identity. He thought, *After all, had it not been Isa Tai'i who so long ago had prophesied all that had now come true?*

"This is the final sign, there can be no doubt," the medicine man *White Eagle* said. "Return now to your lodge with the girl. She must remain untouched and pure until the morning of the battle, which will begin very soon."

Chapter 26: The Ride
West Along the Canadian
June, 1874

After Piotr and River had rescued Cord from the hands of Deputy Chet, they made their way back to Wichita Falls, where they rejoined Piotr's Aunt Midge and the ranch hand Brett Sumner. There, Cord was surprised to hear Piotr tell the story of his rescuing him. The boy told it truthfully enough, until the end, when the deputy, according to the boy, escaped unhurt off into the tangle of mesquite trees.

"And the dog didn't run him down?" Brett asked.

Piotr looked for Cord to answer, having no response of his own at hand for the unexpected question.

"I called River off," Cord lied, "but that deputy had so much fear on his face as he run off that I don't think we have anything to worry 'bout. He's in hiding. He'll hole up and not move a muscle for quite some time."

The last statement by Cord was anything but a lie. The corrupt lawman was hidden in a hole, true enough.

"I am just overcome with joy that you both returned unhurt," Midge said. "The good Lord above answered my prayers and provided for your safety. Let us hope He extends His blessings over us as we begin our travel back in the morning to Weatherford."

It was then that Cord announced that he would be taking River and Trouble upriver, then westward to *the Llano.* He revealed to the group the arrangement with his friend *Sulking Crow.* Cord needed to get to the ruins of Adobe Walls to meet the Kiowa trader to see what, if anything, he had learned about the girl.

"Well, *Ciocci Mieczysława,*" Piotr said to his Aunt Midge in English so that all could hear his declaration, "if he is going after Kalina, I am sure as hell goin' with him."

The boy had lived through too much by this point, having witnessed death in the form of a revenge murder. The sight had sickened him to his core, but even its brutal reality was not enough to keep him from going on to rescue his little sister, Kalina.

"Piotr! Your language!" his aunt snapped tersely. "I forbid this. How could I ever explain it to my sister that I allowed her last remaining child to wander off after his abducted sister into *Comancheria* with a drunken trailhand. We don't even know if Kalina was taken there."

"Well," Cord said, looking into the eyes of Midge, once again sparkling with the flame of insistence, "this not-drunk-enough trailhand is goin' anyway to find out whether she is there or not. The die's done been cast. My friend *Sulking Crow* has risked his Injun' neck for me. I've got no other path forward than to show up for our meeting as we agreed. Doin' anything else would be dishonorable."

Piotr's head snapped at Cord's use of that last word. He was ready to call the man a hypocrite but instead bit his tongue and allowed his scalding glare to send the message. *Dishonorable! From the lips of a cold-blooded killer!*

"I'm going with Cord" Piotr declared instead, "and no one will stop me."

Then, in Polish, Piotr said to his aunt, "*Ciocci Mieczysława*, I certainly love you very dearly, and I understand you worry how you will justify your actions to my mother. But consider this, I cannot live the rest of my life justifying my own inaction. If I don't value Kalina's life enough to risk my own, then my life will never be worth risking for anybody or anything. I must go with this man, as hopeless a soul as he is, but I have seen a ruthlessness in him that makes him, perhaps, Kalina's only real chance."

Cord did not understand a word of what was said in this unintelligible tangle of guttural sounds. But what happened next he knew must have been tied to *Pee Otter's* message to his aunt. For immediately afterward, the remaining dominoes fell one after the other.

"I will allow Piotr to go with you, Cord McCullough," Midge declared to him, "but only under two conditions."

"Which are?"

"That you take not another nip of whiskey until we are all safely back in Weatherford…,"

"Agreed," Cord interjected, knowing he could easily sneak a drink if he needed to once they were all out on *the Llano*. "And?"

"… and that I travel along with you both," she said.

"No dice!" Cord snapped. "*The Llano* ain't no place for ya', Midge. Yer'll have me fighting off Injuns on one side and drunken, really drunken, buffalo hunters on the other. Spreads my sand too thin. Too thin by far. No deal."

Cord looked at Brett Sumner, expecting the ranch hand to back him up, and to talk her into returning to the *Trinity Quarter Ranch*, but instead he got more bad news.

"And if she does go," Brett Sumner said before Midge could object, "then I'm goin' too. I promised old man Sinclair that I would look after her and help her find the boy. I aint going back without her, that's for damn sure."

"Y'all don't understand just how much yer puttin' yer lives on the line," Cord said as he stood and began to pace. "This ain't some cattle drive or mustang roundup were talking about. These Comanches are as savage as any tribe on the southern plains. They don't just kill, they git pleasure from it. Y'all done lost yer minds. Midge, anyone as fetchin' as yourself surely will be offered up to the chief, once the rest of the braves had their way with ya'."

"And you, Cord," she replied, "are a crude man. But you also just made the case for my going along. You expect me to leave my innocent little niece, Kalina, out there alone amongst all that savagery? No, either I go, or no one does."

"Fine," Cord said, "then y'all stay behind and leave it to me to find the girl."

What happened next was totally unexpected. It caught Cord finding himself backed into a corner.

"Either I go along," Piotr said, "or I leave here right now and go find this town's sheriff."

No one else understood the implied threat except for Cord. The others likely thought Piotr simply meant that he would appeal to the sheriff who might allow him his freedom to travel westward. Cord knew Piotr threatened to report the murder of the deputy lawman from Weatherford along the Jacksboro trail. He knew he would surely be immediately arrested and held in lockup as they looked for the body. Of course, Piotr could lead them to the grave in the mesquite woods, having helped Cord bury him there.

Cord recognized the boy had him over a barrel. So when Midge declared it was all or none going out west, she was more right than even she could have known at the time.

The next day they made provisions to travel westward upriver on either the Red River or the Canadian. They decided the safer route, although it was further from them at Wichita Falls, was to follow the trail along the south bank of the Canadian River, as it was more heavily traveled. It was also known that Indian attacks had recently been reported along the Red River, possibly by native raiders slipping off the reservation at Fort Sill for that sole purpose, and then returning afterwards. The four of them travelled north, through the Indian Territories until they came upon the Canadian River trail.

It proved to be a beautiful time of year to travel alongside the Canadian, or South Canadian as it was often referred to just to keep it separate from the North Canadian. That river was in truth just a tributary that ran parallel before flowing into the Canadian downriver far behind them to the east. The Canadian rushed past them swollen proud, fueled by the waters of Spring rains upcountry. A canopy of leafy trees gave shade, and as Cord was prone to thinking, lots of cover to anyone wishing to do them harm.

They took to a formation, as directed by Cord, with Brett and Piotr riding side by side up front, and Cord and Midge tight behind them. Piotr and Midge were always closest to the river, with Brett and Cord on the trail just to their left. Indian attacks from across the river were unlikely, as it was far too wide for arrows or rifle rounds shot from the far shore to be a concern. Indians or bandits would rather attack from the woods on the south bank. Cord and Brett could protect them from any such ambush. Or from travelers passing along in the opposite direction.

They rode all day and cold-camped at night. Brett and Cord took turns keeping watch, always accompanied by the keen senses of the dog, River. All was quiet, and the travelers were undisturbed.

As they proceeded up that river trail, on the third day they passed a sprawl of buffalo skins washed from an overturned wagon grounded on the sandy curl of the far bank. It had been loaded with hulking stacks of the animal hides. Its cargo was now scattered along the shoreline. As they passed it, the powerful stench proved unbearable.

"That is one gawd awful smell," Piotr yelled out. "You'd think that river water would knocked it down a bit. Must have been out here a while to stink so badly."

Cord answered, *"Pee Otter,* 'em skins smell that bad as soon as they come off the buffalo. These could'a been field-skinned as much as a week or two ago."

The mounds of hides clung to the far shoreline, with only a few floating loose past them in the current. Those caught the attention of Midge. She looked forlornly upon the skins, as if the sheer quantities defied comprehension.

"The hunters float these hides downriver, Cord?" she asked, raising her hand to cover her nose.

"I don't reckon so," Cord answered. "They likely lost control of this wagon load crossing the river to freight these skins north to Dodge City and the railroad there. The Canadian is too long and windy to use for shippin' these skins. Too many sandbanks to get caught on. Besides that, it flows through the Injun Territories, where the sight of mutilated buffalo skins floating past wouldn't be tolerated for long. No, I'm pretty sure they lost this load crossing upriver. That being said, what yer looking at is a lot of wasted work by some buffalo hunter and his skinners."

"What I see is the reckless killing of beautiful animals of our blessed Lord's creation. What is it that draws these buffalo hunters to this slaughter?" she asked, raising her other hand with the reins to cup her face as if it might further diminish the fetid, penetrating smell.

"What draws 'em out? Money," Cord answered. "Easy money. These hides sell for up to two dollars each. A good buffalo hunter can keep ten or more skinners busy. So for only the cost of a bullet and maybe two bits a hide for the skinner, there's a lot of money to be made."

"But these men didn't even come this far west just until just a few years ago," Midge asked through her funneled beak of fingers. "Why? What changed?"

Cord looked at her. She's a sharp one, that's for sure. As bright as she is beautiful. Curious. And Piotr was right, she could ride like the wind when it proved necessary.

Cord answered. "A few years ago there was no white man's market for these buffalo skins - they were too porous to be of any real value. But in '71, some leather worker came up with a new process for sealing 'em, and now the eastern merchants can't get enough of 'em. So, the buffalo hunters closed in on the plains like a plague of locusts."

"From where?" Midge asked.

"From the dregs of humanity," Cord replied. "buffalo hunters don't exactly possess any real talents. They only have two skills - to shoot defenseless animals dead and to fight off Injuns. The buffalo are too damned stupid to run even when they are under fire from these Sharp Big Fifty rifles at long distance. They just stand there like bottles on a fence post waiting to be shot at."

"That's horrible!" Midge replied. "And these men must defend themselves constantly against the Indians?"

"Only if they want to stay alive," Cord answered. They rode the trail at a walking pace as they talked. With both hands cupped over her face, the skin-tight riding clothes clung to Midge's every delightful curve. Cord couldn't help but take the opportunity to admire her form.

"The Comanche are angry," he continued. "They risked everything to fight off the Apache and just about every other Injun tribe to take these plains as their own hunting grounds. They have fed generations livin' off these animals. They only kill what they need and don't waste any bit of the few animals they do kill, right down to the organs and bones. Now, all these rough as hell, pardon my language, buffalo hunters, most all white men, come out onto their hunting grounds to slaughter as many of these creatures as they can for nuthin' but the price of their hides alone. Worse, they field-skin the dead animals and leave their carcasses to rot under the sun. And not so slowly over the past few years, the Comanche come to realize that the buffalo had begun to disappear from *the Llano.*"

"I thought you said these animals didn't run off," Midge said.

"They don't run off," Cord agreed, "they just die off. These buffalo hunters kill thousands of them at a clip. That's how these overloaded wagons clutter the trails north to the railheads as constant as each day's sunrise. They get loaded there onto the iron horses to be delivered to places like Leavenworth, Kansas for processing before gettin' shipped east. Naturally, the Injuns don't take kindly to their way of life bein' stolen out from under them. So, yeah, the Comanches attack these men quite regular like."

"And the US Army doesn't interfere with all this killing of these helpless creatures?" Midge asked.

"Oh, sure they do," Cord told her, "as much as possible, but always in support of the buffalo hunters. Army figures the faster the buffalo are cleared off the plains, the faster the Comanche can be brought to heel and moved onto the reservations in the Injun Territories. As it is, *the Llano* is home to the last of the Comanche and some Kiowa and Arapaho, but mostly the Comanche, and of those, most all are from the band known as *the Quahadi.*"

"Who are these *Quahadi?* Midge asked him.

"They are the last of the Comanche still out on the plains," Cord explained. "Their name means *'the Antelopes,'* but don't let it fool ya', fer while they are as graceful on horseback as those animals, they are a hell of a lot more vicious. The man killed at the coach hold-up tryin' to protect your niece was a retired Texas Ranger, and he pegged our half-breed to be a *Quahadi*, or at least half so."

"That poor old man," Midge said, bowing her head out of respect. "Giving his life in that way for Kalina."

"Well," Cord replied, "let's hope his was the last life that needs givin'."

Midge cast him an agreeing glance. The wagon of buffalo hides was now well past them, and it slowly disappeared like a shrinking dark brown stain in the distance along the shore of the waterway. The smell lingered, however, taking forever to drain down from being overpoweringly obnoxious to being merely revolting.

"So Cord," Midge asked, her hands finally lowered away from her nose, "why is it that you seem to have so much contempt for these *Quahadi,* but yet you put so much faith in your Kiowa friend?"

"Sulking Crow?" Cord said. "Just for that reason. He is a true friend and been so all the time I spent on the trail. Injun or not, he's been there when I needed him."

"Yet, despite that, you hate the Comanches?"

"Ain't so much I hate 'em," Cord answered her, "as I simply see 'em for what they are. Ruthless warriors. And that means killers. It's their culture, to fight and to kill. They always had to do so just to exist. I respect 'em in that way. Ya' see, Midge, when ya' live out on these trails like I have, ya' learn to spot men for what they are. Cheats, crooks, and thieves. Ya' learn quick to root out the deception in a man, and being able to do so is the main reason I still live and breathe today. In these Comanche, there's no deception, they are true to themselves always. They are warriors. They are killers. And as it turns out, it is now the white man's turn to be at war with 'em."

The next day as the party of four rode further west along the Canadian, they neared closer to the point where they would have to cross over to the north shore to go on to Adobe Walls. Brett Sumner called out from the front row, "We got two riders approaching!" River was already running up the trail barking at the two men on horseback.

"I see 'em, Brett" Cord said. "Don't go for yer gun, I've got them covered from behind ya. We don't want to spook 'em now, do we?"

"No," Brett agreed, "we certainly do not want to do that. Let's everyone stay real calm."

The two men came upon them slowly and appeared to pose no threat.

"Howdy, folks," the larger of the two men hailed to them. "Nice mutt. Don't see many out here."

The second rider was more slightly built and was shielded from them by the first. He kept his hands low, and for the most part, out of sight, while his larger more talkative companion kept his own in view. Cord called for River to settle down and to stop his growling and barking.

Cord removed the leather loop up and over the hammer of his Colt .45 Peacemaker, just in case. He had a nervous feeling about these two.

"Name's Isaiah, and this here's my brother, Elijah," the larger of the two said, introducing themselves. Then he added almost apologetically, "Daddy was a preacher man, of sorts. Who might y'all be?"

Cord and Brett were slow to respond, but hearing the dead silence, Piotr shot off his mouth. "Were from *Panna Maria,* down San Antonio way. Looking for my sister, she was taken by a Comanche bandit in a stagecoach hold-up near Weatherford."

"We're just travelers headed to Adobe Walls," Brett called out, talking over the boy.

"What, y'all figure to ransom the girl back?" the rider calling himself Isaiah said. "If ya' do, yer gonna have to go all the way to Santa Fe. Them Comanche don't trade in captives directly with the white man. They'll sell her to *the Comancheros* for some horses, rifles, or firewater. They'll up the price and maybe sell her back to you. That is if neither the Injuns nor *the Comancheros* don't just decide to keep her for their own. And if she's as comely as this one, I reckon they gonna have a hard time letting her go."

The man's head nod told all he referred to Midge. She blushed as the filthy stranger washed his eyes over her.

Piotr began to say something else, when his aunt spoke in Polish to him, saying, "Piotr, allow Brett and Cord to speak to these men. You are telling them more than they need to know."

"Whoa!" The one calling himself Isaiah cried. "I done heard people speaking in tongues at Daddy's revivals that didn't sound as strange as that. What she saying?"

"She's just speaking Comanche to the boy," Cord said, speaking for the first time. "They're our interpreters."

Isaiah turned to Elijah and said, "Well, I'll be. I ain't never heard no Comanche prattle on like that." His brother agreed by shaking his head in the negative.

"You fellas headin' back east?" Cord said, changing the subject quickly.

"Us, no, not us," Isaiah answered. "We be mule skinners. Lost a wagon load of skinned hides yesterday morning. The river was too high and the wagon floated off. Just headin' down river to see if there's anything left of the wagon to recover. Figure all them hides to be worthless by now. Did ya' see anything like that? We've already come further than where we thought it might've washed up at."

Cord looked over the two men, paying keen attention to the smaller man. *He's positioned himself just as I would have if I was inclined to draw down on us.* But as it was four on two, he didn't expect this to happen.

"Yeah," Cord answered the man, keeping his gun hand by his side, refusing to turn to point downriver. "Passed by it yesterday. Still a half day's walk along the trail. That wagon looked to be pretty smashed up though, given how fast the river been runnin'."

"Thanks, kindly. Much obliged. We can still hope to harvest some parts for spares. Maybe a wheel or an axle," the man Isaiah said, touching the tip of his hat. "Keep in mind as ya' wander up the trail from here, be careful where ya' go to draw yer water. This stretch of shoreline is known to have pockets of quicksand. Just as dangerous as them Comanches. But if y'all gonna make contact with any of them *Quahadi,* and I hope ya' don't, there's a couple of other things ya' need to know."

"Like what?" Brett asked.

"Well, for one thing, *the Quahadi* have themselves a new leader, a half-breed," Isaiah continued. "Calls himself *Quanah*, but I understand lately he's taken to follow that with his white mother's name - *Parker.* This *Quanah Parker* is supposed to be some kind of a masterful war chief. The US Army has been chasing him and his Comanches across *the Llano* and through Texas canyon country with little success over the last few years. I hear now the US Army is regrouping for one final push. Been told they are amassing some three thousand soldiers to come out after *Quanah Parker's Quahadi."*

"Parker?" The name caught Midge's ear. "Like Cynthia Ann Parker? Taken in the Parker Fort Raid?"

"Well, well! Our pretty lady of tongues speaks English, too!" the big man said. "Yup, the one and same. She's was our *Quanah's* mama."

"Anything else?" Cord asked bluntly.

"No, no," Isaiah said, "just mind the quicksand. It's likely to be gettin' dark by the time ya'll reach the river crossing to the north shore and Adobe Walls. Best ya' wait till morning. Hate for any y'all to get swallered up in it. Wouldn't we, Elijah?"

His brother merely nodded in the affirmative.

"Well, then, we'll be going 'bout our business," Isaiah said. As the two men passed them, Cord spun Trouble such that he was always facing them. It was a telltale sign, and he knew the two fellas were sure to recognize it. *I don't have an ounce of trust for either of the two of ya',* Cord thought.

"Pee Otter," Cord said from behind Brett after they had gone up the trail further, "tellin' those two our business was the dumbest thing ya' done so far."

Midge glared at Cord, and her look said not to be so harsh on her nephew.

"I didn't say much…" Piotr replied.

"Just that we were lookin' to rescue yer sister," Brett chimed in, "and ya' saw how fast they asked about a ransom."

"Those two figure we got ransom money with us," Cord added, "and my bet is they'll be doublin' back as soon as the sun starts to go down. They're itchin' to count just how much we might be totin'."

"They're just a couple of mule skinners," Piotr argued.

"They're as much mule skinners as they are Ol' Testament Prophets," Brett said. "Boy, ya' don't even know what a mule skinner is, do ya'?"

"Someone who skins mules, I guess," Piotr said sheepishly. "Maybe skins buffalo, too."

"Why on earth would anyone want to skin a mule?" Midge asked.

"They don't," Cord answered. "Mule skinners is just another name for freighters. Ya know, someone who wears the skin off a mule with a whip. And Brett was right. Those two are not freight haulers. The big man's hands didn't have a single callus or scar on 'em. And they didn't reek of mule shit, either. No, I'd bet those two were the reason that wagon didn't make it across the river. Likely they waylaid the real mule skinners as they crossed. Goin' down river to see if there was any cash on the wagon that floated away. And all that bit about the quicksand was just to keep us on this side of the river tonight. I'd bet they're plannin' to come visit us a couple hours after sundown."

"You believe all that talk about the *Quahadi?*" Midge asked. "About Cynthia Ann Parker being the War Chief *Quanah's* mother?"

"I see no reason not to believe 'em on that," Cord said. "We'll find out fer sure when we get to Adobe Walls. There's a new camp there set up to supply the buffalo hunters with provisions and ammunition. They'll know."

"That poor woman." Midge said, "to be ripped away from her children in that way. She lived so much longer as a Comanche's wife than she ever did as a white man's child. I heard all she ever wanted was to go back to that Indian way of life again. I read where she died in 1871, not knowing if either of her two boys had even survived that Pease River Massacre. Bad enough that her husband was cut down while she was supposedly 'rescued.' And now one of her two boys is a great Comanche war chief. If that's true, she never even knew of it. That wondering always about her boys must have been such torture."

"That's where ya' and I are different, Midge," Cord said, "I got no sympathy for any white woman who would rather be a brave's squaw, even a chief's bride, than to be with her own kind."

"That's because you're a man," Midge said. "She gave that chief at least three children. You might expect her to just abandon her two sons, but I wouldn't. Like I said, it's because you're a man and not a very good man at that."

"I'm hurt that ya' can say that never havin' tried me out, yerself."

She slowly nudged her horse as close to his as she could. The slap across his face came quick, with explosive force and left a red mark that he thought might leave a welt.

"Don't you ever talk to me like that again, Cord McCullough," Midge seethed at him. Her anger only made her all the more appealing in his eyes. "I don't let any man talk to me in that desirous tone of voice, do you hear me?"

Not waiting for an answer, she reined her horse away from him and as close to the river's edge as she dared. That was the last thing that she said to him until they reached the crossing as the sun went down behind the steep hills that banked the river.

"She's still running pretty fast," Brett said about the Canadian, knowing the hard decision before them. "Do ya' believe that business about there bein' quicksand about?"

"I don't right know what to believe from them two fellas," Cord said, "except that we'll be seeing them again. Look downriver on the far bank over yonder, is that a fella's hat snagged over there?"

Sure enough, washed up on the far rocks was a floppy man's hat. There appeared to be an easy enough footpath on that shore for any one to go and fetch it.

"Both them prophets had hats on," Cord reasoned. "Why would any man, especially a mule skinner, not walk down there and get his hat back?"

"Given the strong sun out in these plains," Brett figured, "there can be only one real answer. Because he couldn't."

"I think our preacher's sons," Cord said, "are nuthin' but cutthroats out here preyin' on some of these skinners and haulers. I'm sure they'll be back tonight, if not for the money, then maybe for Midge."

Brett looked out over the darkening river waters rushing by them. Cord instead looked up at the hills rising over them. He seemed to be figuring something out in his mind.

"That river's too swollen for us to try and cross now," Brett said. "It wouldn't be safe."

"That's not exactly what I'm workin' my way thru, Brett," Cord answered him.

Chapter 27: A Mother and Son Reunion

June, 1874

The warriors began to ride out of the village along the creek in *Palo Duro Canyon*. They had been preparing themselves for days, awaiting the final battle with the white man. Now they would go to a gathering ground along the Red River to join the Cheyenne, the Arapaho and the Kiowa warriors. From there, they would move north to their first objective - to attack the white man buffalo hunters who mercilessly, wastefully slaughtered the *cibolo*.

Once the warriors left the village, only the elders and the young braves were left to defend the women and children. This meant freedom for *Lobo*. He was free to visit his mother, *Trembling Wind*.

He called on her the afternoon after the warriors departed. As he had been told, he would find her full with child. *Her time will come very soon, Lobo* thought.

"Mother," he said from outside the entrance flap to her lodge. "It is your son, '*Lobo*,' once called by the name '*He Who Kills Owls*.' I have come to be with you again."

"My son," she said, very surprised, "you are forbidden to enter. I am too close to giving birth. You must go away."

He went in, despite her command, saying as he did. "I have spent ten years beyond *the Llano* thinking only of this moment. I will not let some superstition of the elders keep me from seeing you again, my mother."

She was on her back, resting, swollen full with child. The young girl attending to her left the lodge as soon as *Lobo* had entered. This left them alone. His mother's eyes filled with tears upon seeing him, and for the first time in a decade, he could not keep from kneeling next to her so that he might embrace her.

"My son," *Trembling Wind* said, "you wear the long leather coat of my father."

"You mean of your husband, *Raging Anger*," *Lobo* replied.

"My husband did not come to take it from you since you returned?" she asked.

"No," he said, "I was surprised that he did not."

"It is because *Raging Anger* considers it now to be a garment of shame," she said. "It is of no use to him now that it is associated with *the Great Deceiver.* Instead, he went off to the great battle and left me here to die."

"What?" *Lobo* was truly shocked. "Why would you die? You have given birth before…"

"It has been foreseen by the medicine man of the *puha* of the river otter. He has said it would be so before he left with the braves for the battle." she explained. "He said the child will live, but I will die giving birth to it. Of course, *Raging Anger* has accepted this. He has another wife. He grows old now. This will be his last great battle. He needs only one wife. It will not be *Trembling Wind*. He only awaits the birth of a son, even if it must occur upon my own death."

"This is untrue," *Lobo* said. "I will not allow it. I have come to be with you, Mother, and with *the People*. I will not allow you to be taken from me now."

"Did I ever tell you," she said, stroking the face of her long exiled son, "that the night your father took me, when I was forced to watch the scalping of my own father, that even then I knew that his leather coat would follow me and haunt my days? I have foreseen that it would loom over me under a Comanche star at the moment of my own death. It has always been my secret fear, and now you return wearing it as my death approaches."

Lobo stood up and backed away from her. "I will not allow it. I will stand between you and this so-called death. Have you thought that the river otter medicine man knew he would not be here while you gave birth, so he predicted the worst thing that could happen? Then, if it did, he was not responsible. If it did not, he could claim to have made great magic on your behalf. You will not die, Mother, I will do everything I can to assure this."

"But you are just *the Great Deceiver*," she said through a veil of tears.

"No! I am *Lobo*," he said proudly, "the one who has brought the untouched gift that will allow *White Eagle* to create his magic over our warriors and finally defeat the white man. Don't you see, it is why I was cast out in the first place. It was foretold by *the Great Spirit*. I was sent out into the white man's world to find the untouched gift. It is true. There is no deceit in my bones, there could be none, for they were formed from someone as pure and loving as yourself."

Chapter 28: Return of the Sacrilegious Prophets
June, 1874

Brett and Cord had it all planned out. Cord and the dog would leave the rest of them and head up river a bit. Given the curve of the bank, it would afford him a good firing position on the camp. He took his Henry rifle, sure that he would have enough rounds to take care of Isaiah and Elijah, or whoever these fellas really were. Brett was armed as well, and even Piotr had his LeMat revolver loaded in all chambers. He could only hope the boy would not end up shooting anyone by mistake.

Darkness descended, but unlike the other nights on the trail when they had a cold camp, tonight they had a fire blazing. This was for no other reason than to give Cord light by which to find the two men who they all knew would be coming along soon. The lure of the ransom money and Midge's delicate feminine form would be too much for these two to resist.

Cord and River had reached their outpost just as dusk thickened. He spent the next ten minutes collecting fallen branches to fashion a solid enough rest on which to place the rifle. Just as he had finished doing to, he spotted movement down by the river bank. It was the man Isaiah.

As he sighted his Henry on the man, he saw the one called Elijah climbing the bank slowly, stealthily toward the fire and the campers gathered around it. Brett had intentionally made the fire out in the open so nothing would obscure Cord's sightlines.

Then, something Cord did not expect occurred. Piotr stood up over the fire, warmed his hands, and began to argue with Brett. Cord was too far away to hear any of it, but the body motion said the boy was being obstinate. Then Piotr walked away down towards the river. *What the hell was he doing? He was walking right towards the big man!*

Cord kept him in the sights of his Henry, but the further he got from the fire, the harder it was for him to see. Then, he stopped, almost to the river, and unbuttoned his britches and began to relieve himself. Damned jack-ass was pissing in the river. That likely was what he had fought with Brett about, who probably told him to do it nearby. But Cord could almost hear the boy argue that he would do no such thing with his aunt present.

Cord watched him in the rifle's sight, and no sooner had he buttoned up, than the hulking image of Isaiah descended on him. Cord couldn't get a good shot on the man because Piotr was obscuring his line of sight.

Cord raised his head, looked to the fire and saw the smaller of the two men shoot from the woods and hit Brett Sumner. His friend doubled over, but then straightened up clutching his arm. Cord figured the prophet aimed for Brett's chest but only ended up winging him in his right arm. The result being it took Brett's gun hand out of play.

Cord thought to shoot the man calling himself Elijah, but if he did, Piotr was surely a goner. He returned to the Henry's sights, only to find Piotr and Isaiah gone.

Cord looked up from the Henry's sights and found Isaiah walking Piotr along the bank at gunpoint. He led the boy out onto a large flat stone, surrounded on three sides by a sand spit. Isaiah then raised his leg, settled it on the boy's hind quarters, and pushed Piotr off the rock. As soon as he did, the boy went into what turned out to be sandy muck up to his waste. *That bastard knew exactly where that quicksand was and had thrown Piotr into it,* Cord thought.

Cord took aim on Isaiah, who was standing on the rock, belly laughing as he watched poor Piotr struggle and slowly sink into the mire. Cord then glanced up from the rifle's sights at the fire-lit camp and saw Elijah drawn down threateningly on Brett, asking him questions. Midge had moved to Brett's side to try to stop his arm's bleeding.

Cord decided to fire on the quicksand prophet first, as Isaiah was still alone on that rock. Piotr was up to his stomach now. Cord figured he'd have a good second shot on Elijah given the firelight. But could he take out Isaiah and find Elijah with the Henry before that second man might kill Brett or Midge?

Cord turned his Henry's sights on Isaiah, and drew a deep breath, held it, and squeezed off the first shot. He watched the man fall, and from the way he did, didn't figure he was any more of a threat. He then lifted the rifle, found the fire-lit camp, but before he could locate Elijah, heard the sound of a revolver fire. First shot. Second shot. His heart sank, because he knew as close as Elijah was, it meant the end of either Brett or Midge, or both. When he pulled his eye back from the Henry's sights and took in the bigger view, he saw Elijah sprawled out by the fire. Standing over him was Midge, a gun in her hand, its barrel smoking. Not just any gun, but Piotr's LeMat revolver, which Cord could tell even from this distance given its size.

"Come on, River," Cord yelled out. "We got real trouble going on down there in that quicksand."

Cord scurried his way to the rock just as Piotr was up to his neck, screaming at the top of his lungs for help.

First, Cord checked the body of the man calling himself Isaiah. He was shot clean through the heart, deader than a coffin nail. Then, Cord stepped out to the edge of the rock to attend to the boy.

"Get me outta here, Cord!" Piotr screamed.

"I guess these two weren't fibbin' about the quicksand, were they?" Cord laughed, seeing that the boy was close enough to him to use his belt to retrieve him. "I thought you'd be under the surface by now."

"I would be," Piotr said, "but I'm standing on something solid, but my feet keep slidin' off it."

"I reckon that to be the owner of that hat Brett and I saw on the far bank earlier," Cord replied. "Likely the real mule skinner these two killed and threw in there. This Isaiah fella seemed to be enjoying watchin' yer squirmin' a bit too much. Well, it cost him, staying out here in the open. I guess they didn't figure we was waitin' fer 'em."

"Will you stop jawing and git me out the hell out of here!"

"Keep yer britches on, *Pee Otter.* I gotta find a branch big enough to wrap this belt around," Cord said.

"Just use your damn rifle," the boy said frantically, balancing himself on what must be that corpse beneath him.

"There just ain't no way in hell I am gittin' that sludge down the barrel of my Henry," Cord insisted. "After all, it did just save yer life. Just give me a minute. I 'spect ya' can likely hold yer breath that long, if ya' need to."

Cord walked off and quickly came back with a fallen bough that he looped his belt around its center. He then tossed it out to the boy, who was only a foot or two away from the rock, to grasp on to.

Cord slowly pulled him over to the rock, and once Piotr could get a grip, he helped him out of the muck. When he did, Piotr rolled over flat on his back and started to shake violently. He refused to cry, but he could not suppress the shaking.

Finally, he asked Cord if he'd gotten the other man.

"Looks like yer Aunt Midge took care of him. Looked like with that LeMat ya' was fool enough to leave behind. Two shots and the other prophet was fallen."

"I didn't want to take it with me," Piotr explained. "I was afraid I might accidentally…" The boy paused.

"Ya' was afraid ya' might shoot yer pecker off," Cord laughed. "Well, it turns out to be a good thing yer so fond of that thing and left it behind. Everybody appears to be all right, assuming these two didn't have no friends joining them. Now, let's find y'a bit of firm footing into the river so ya' can wash away this God-awful slog."

Cord took the bough and walked upriver stabbing it into the sand. "Here, this is pretty solid footin' here."

"Poor *Ciocci Mieczysława,*" Piotr said, following him in a trance, "now she's killed a man."

"That's a might easier to do when they're trying to kill you, son." Cord said. "She'll be fine. Now, come on and let's git yer hide in this river water. I still gotta go up and check to make sure Brett ain't too badly hurt. Then, I reckon your Aunt Midge is gonna need some consolin'."

"You leave that to me, Cord," Piotr snapped. "She don't need none of your kind of sympathy, that's for sure."

Chapter 29: On to the Camp at Adobe Walls

June, 1874

The next day, when the dawn broke, none of the four of them had slept. After getting Brett's wounded arm tended to, and Piotr washed clean and settled down, Cord stayed up talking to Midge. She was rattled, all right, having put two of the LeMat's nine balls into the man calling himself Elijah. All Elijah had wanted to know from her and Brett was where the ransom money was.

"You had every right to shoot him," Cord said, as he touched the back of his hand to her face. She was deeply disturbed by it all, and he knew she needed comforting.

"That man shot Brett without so much as a call," she said. "Good thing he only hit his arm. I'm sure he was aiming to kill him."

"He would have killed ya', too, after he got what else he wanted." Cord did not elaborate, but she knew his meaning, and it was not solely the ransom money. "I had a bead on him, but with Piotr in the hands of that Isaiah fella', I had no choice but to go after that other one first."

"Both these men are dead," she shuddered. Cord wrapped his arm around her, half surprised she allowed him to do so. "Two lives just wasted, and I was part of it all."

"Midge," Cord said, "these two were nothin' but bad news. No tellin' how many men they victimized out here. Any wastin' of lives was done by themselves. Consider what ya' was forced to do as bein' nuthin' but cleaning up the countryside."

She removed his arm from around her shoulders and looked into his eyes. "You really are one cold hearted son-of-a-bitch, aren't you, Mr. McCullough?"

"Watch that language!" Piotr called out from down the hill. He had been listening to every one of their words.

The sun came up and not long afterwards Brett, his arm in a makeshift sling, yelled out, "Cord, we got more company. Down at the rock looking at the body of that Isaiah fella. He's spotted us and is sure to head up here."

Sure enough the man did. He was a thin, wiry fella and carried a large rifle. As he neared them, Cord could make out its double trigger. Just as he thought, a Sharps buffalo gun.

"Well," the man said as he neared their camp, its firepit now nothing but cooling embers, "I see y'all made the acquaintance of the Maddox brothers. Shot 'em both dead, did ya'?" He had spotted Elijah laid out by the firepit.

"It's not like they gave us much of a choice," Cord said. "They trailed us and made their move last night."

"Well," the man said, "Ya' done the world a favor. They been killin' and causing mayhem from here on up through Chicken Creek. We were hopin' they might fall to some Comanche, but dead is dead, all the same."

"Just who might ya' be, fella?" Brett Sumner asked.

"My, my, where be my manners," the wiry fella said. "Billy Dixon, buffalo hunter."

"I figured that from the Big Fifty yer totin'," Cord said.

"This? Naw, its only a .44/90," Dixon corrected him. "I had me a big fifty, but lost it and a mule in a river crossing a while back. Anyway, the Sharps .44 is the next best gun for hunting buffalo."

At that point Cord introduced himself and the rest of his party. Then, he pointed to the body of Elijah.

"We figure these two killed a mule skinner two days back and threw his body in the quicksand down by that rock. We spotted his hat across the way there. We had passed a wagon full of skins overturned downriver."

Dixon looked hard at the hat across the river and said, "Damn if that don't favor old Jesse Morton's hat. He just left me on *the Llano* with a wagon load of hides. Damn these fellas. What are y'all doing this far out, anyway?"

"We're trying to find Adobe Walls," Cord said.

"Well, you're not far a t'all. Come with me," Dixon said, "happens to be where I am headin' off to. Gettin' to be too dangerous campin' out at the field hut I built on *the Llano.* Too many Injun attacks goin' on. Best we all hurry on up to the safety of the Walls."

"Do we need to bury these two first?" Midge asked.

"Ma'am," Dixon said, removing his hat as he addressed her, "every hour we're out here we're more likely to join them. I reckon they got what they deserved. Ain't a man out here gonna think otherwise. Besides, Mrs. Olds is gonna be ever so happy to see ya'. She's the wife of one of the store owner's and is fixed on openin' up a restaurant in the camp. Being squirreled up with all these stinkin' dirty fellas, she's gonna be happier than a pig in slop to have another young lady to talk to."

Dixon then led them all to a shallow ford in the river. It had receded overnight, and their crossing was uneventful. Cord pulled River up onto Trouble's back to make sure the dog wasn't swept away.

"When we get to the camp at the Walls," Dixon said to Cord, "there's always wild dogs about. We never had any trouble from them, but I don't know how they might take to yer animal."

"Don't worry about River, here," Cord replied, "I ain't ever seen him back away from another dog."

"Okay, just lettin' ya' know," Dixon answered.

They were on the north shore, and after Billy Dixon retrieved his friend's hat, an act of sheer respect, they headed inland. They soon came upon a creek.

"This is Bent Creek," Dixon explained, "though some as of late been takin' to call it Adobe Walls Creek."

"What are those?" Piotr asked pointing to the remains of the some adobe structures.

"Them's the ruins of the original Adobe Walls site," Dixon answered. "It was where Kit Carson and his 300 man outfit was thrown down on. They drew into these old adobe structures to survive their tanglin' with the Comanche in '64. These original buildings go back to the 1840s. Our new camp is just another mile up the crick."

Cord made a mental note of the ruins. This was where he was to meet his Kiowa friend *Sulking Crow*. They had arrived only the day before they were to meet.

"Why make it all out of adobe?" Piotr asked.

"Cause walls made from adobe don't burn," Dixon answered. "Pisses off them Comanche to no end - adobe walls topped off with sod roofs. They can't torch us out."

Soon enough the party of five came onto the new "town" of Adobe Walls. To call it a town was being overly generous. It was little more than a saloon, a blacksmith, a corral of horses and two storefront mercantiles for the selling of supplies. The place was crammed with twenty-eight men - buffalo hunters, skinners, and freighters. All were a hardy bunch who settled in there. Other than the store owners, the men had no rooms so they took to sleeping outdoors near the buildings. Midge was pleased to see there was also one woman, as Mr. Dixon had said, the wife of the mercantile owner, William Olds. Midge introduced herself and Mrs. Olds quickly invited her inside. Mrs. Olds no doubt noticed Midge was already drawing the lustful gazes of the buffalo hunters and skinners.

"If yer going in there to chit-chat with Mrs. Olds," Cord called out, "I'll be in the saloon getting the latest on the Comanche and such."

"Remember our agreement, Cord," Midge called out to him. "No whiskey. You promised."

The saloon owner was a man named James Hanrahan. He had moved down from Dodge City, Kansas, some one hundred and seventy-five miles to the north. But upon entering his adobe walled and sod roofed saloon, it was another face that caught his attention. Sitting at a table, having his morning coffee was an old acquaintance from his days on the Chisholm Trail, specifically from the town of Wichita, Kansas.

"Bat," Cord called out. "Is that you, Bat?"

"Cord McCullough, you old cur," Bat Masterson replied. "Of all the faces I never imagined would walk through that door, yours is the most unexpected. What are you doin' out this far west in *Comancheria?*"

"I could ask ya' the same," Cord replied. "Can't be much gamblin' goin' on out here…"

"…Only with our lives," Masterson replied. "Comanche ain't too happy with our slaughterin' off their *cibolo* herds. Seems we been gettin' sniffs of somethin' big going on with them. In any case, it can't mean too much of anything good for us all. But despite that, the buffalo hunting has been bountiful."

"I'm here tryin' to track down a half-Comanche that ran off with a fourteen year old girl from a stage coach robbery in Weatherford. The bandits have all been killed except for him who took the girl and headed this way."

Bat arched his eyes in surprise, even though Cord was sure he would have heard about it. Word would surely have drifted in on the supply wagons from Dodge City.

"You might want to try *Palo Duro Canyon,*" Masterson said, "that seems to be the Comanche's favorite place is to set up camp. But be forewarned, it is one massive hole in the ground. A practical maze of canyons and *arroyos* splinterin' off of it. Suggest you not go on your lonesome wanderin' in there. Few white men have done so and survived."

"I got something better," Cord smiled at him, "an Injun trader in there with 'em, I hope, anyway. I'll find out tomorrow when I meet 'im at the ruins near here."

"Kiowa?" Bat asked. "I figure that other than the *Comancheros* out of Santa Fe, they're the only traders the Comanche will deal with. And I'm sure you didn't come from the direction of New Mexico, did you?"

"Nope, never been to Santa Fe," Cord admitted, "but I hear they got some lovely brown skinned beauties out there. Gonna make my way out there soon enough…"

"Well, you were preceded only minutes ago by word of a light skinned beauty you were bringin' in with your group," Bat said. "I had a peek out the window. She's quite the looker. How bout an introduction?"

"Oh, Midge," Cord replied, "she's the captured girl's aunt. Her and the boy's brother and a ranch hand are with me."

"Just the four of ya'?"

"Truth be told, I rather it was just me," Cord admitted, "but I lost that fight."

"We let parties of four go out to kill buffalo," Bat said as a whistle of disbelief left his lips, "but only with their Sharps rifles and not less than a thousand rounds of ammunition. You best watch yourselves lest your scalps end up on some Injun's coup stick."

"That I'll keep in mind," Cord said, "as I'm fond of havin' it to keep my hat from sliding off my head."

"And I'd watch that Kiowa trader friend of yours, Cord," Masterson added. "The Kiowa and Comanche are known to be pretty tight. I'd hate to find out he turned out to be better friends with *Quanah Parker* and his pals than with you."

The four of them stayed in the camp town of Adobe Walls overnight that evening. Midge bunked down with Mrs. Olds, while Cord, Piotr and Brett camped outside the saloon with Bat and most of the other buffalo hunters and skinners. Amazingly, Cord kept his promise to Midge and stayed off the *budge.*

The next morning, Cord rose early and left them all there as he and River walked the short distance to the ruins. He arrived just as the sun was rising overhead to find *Sulking Crow* patiently awaiting him.

"Hello, my friend," Cord said, "it is good to see ya' in one piece."

"You as well, my friend," the Kiowa replied. "Comanche and Kiowa good friends, we make smoke together. I bring both good news and bad for you, Cord."

"Is the girl with *the Quahadi?*" Cord asked impatiently.

"Yes, that is the good news," *Sulking Crow* answered. "I have seen her with my own eyes."

"Is she hurt in any way?" Cord probed.

"No, she look good, but the one who take her present her as special gift to powerful new medicine man, *White Eagle.*"

"*White Eagle?*" Cord repeated aloud. "So that is why the half-breed was so obsessed with that medallion. He thought it was some kind of sign.*"

"Yes," *Sulking Crow* answered, "medicine man, *White Eagle,* has convinced *Quahadi* that he has gone into sky to commune with *Great Spirit*. He prepares them for war, claims to have a *puha* more powerful than any have ever seen. That his *puha* can make them not fall to the white man's bullets."

"And this is the bad news?" Cord asked.

"Many warriors head to this place, Adobe Walls," *Sulking Crow* said. "Comanche, Cheyenne, Kiowa and others. They all come to kill white men in camp who have slaughter the *cibolo*."

"They prepare to move against the men in camp! In how large a number?"

"Many hundreds," the Kiowa answered, "perhaps a thousand warriors."

"Against less than thirty buffalo hunters?" Cord said, "Oh, my God, it'll be a slaughter, all right. And yer sure the girl is still untouched?"

"*White Eagle* not touch her until after the attack," *Sulking Crow* said, "for he fear betraying great magic. But afterwards, who knows what he do with her?"

"When is all this to happen?" Cord asked.

Suddenly the Kiowa became quiet, which greatly disturbed Cord. The very last thing he needed was for *Sulking Crow to* keep anything about the attack from him.

"*Sulking Crow,*" he said, "I need to know when!"

"I say too much already," the Kiowa answered. "I betray surprise of my brothers. All I can say is if you wish to take back girl from half-blooded one, the time to do so soon upon you. We go now to *Palo Duro.* It is only a day's ride from here. Warrior braves already departed from canyon to meet brother tribes at Red River, then they come to this place. Find half-blooded brave in long leather coat, and you will find young girl. But do not make idle in your ways."

"Thank ya', my friend," Cord said as he extended his hand, "I know I've put ya' in an awkward position with my request. I cannot ask ya' to take us to *Palo Duro,* ya' done risked enough already. If the Comanches find ya' with us, they'll certainly kill ya'. No, we will make our own way there without yer help. Here, please accept this as payment for all ya've done for us. We are all much obliged."

Cord offered the small black cloth sack with the intricate red ribbon. Inside it he had placed the two hundred dollars in gold coins he had taken from the saddle bag of Deputy Chet Blackman.

"No! If you stumble onto Comanche while looking for *Palo Duro,*" Sulking Crow said, "they kill you all. No, I lead you there before I return to Red River Station. Then, you will be on own. As for this, I cannot accept. It is blood money."

"Damn right it is," Cord confessed. "Money that had been drawn upon my own blood from the cattleman Vaughn Anders. It's all right to take it my friend. Ya' can come with us. We will leave in the morning."

Chapter 30: Approaching the Canyons of Palo Duro

June, 1874

That night Cord went to the Hanrahan's Saloon looking for Bat Masterson to warn him of the imminent attack. But when he arrived in the sod covered structure it was empty of everyone except for the proprietor.

"Well," Big Jim Hanrahan said with surprise, "an honest to God payin' customer. I'll be damned."

"Where are all the fellas?" Cord asked.

"Out shootin' and skinnin' buffalo," Hanrahan said. "After all, that is what they come to do, ain't it? A herd was spotted not far off and cleared the place out. You'd think these men would still be worried about the Comanche, but apparently all they're worried about is their buddies baggin' all the hides before they do. They'll be back soon enough. Whiskey for ya?"

"No thanks," Cord said, "but I got somethin' for you, Jim. I got word that the Comanche and their Kiowa and Cheyenne brothers are fixin' on attacking this camp of yours sometime over the next few days."

The words, so boldly stated, echoed through the saloon, seeming to crush every other sound in the place.

A troubled look befell the proprietor. Hanrahan wrestled with the news before even trying to appear calm again. Then, the saloon owner put on a brave face.

"Well, thanks for that, partner," Hanrahan said with a faux nonchalance, "but why do ya' think all these buildings are adobe walled and covered in sod. It don't burn. We've weathered our fair share of Injun attacks out here. They don't take lightly to our killin' and skinnin' their *cibolo,* but we're always able to hold our own."

"You don't understand," Cord said, "this is gonna be the mother of all Injun attacks. Up to a thousand warriors on horseback. Many with repeatin' rifles that them bastard *Comancheros* sold them."

"Hmmph!" Hanrahan said, "that's trouble fer sure. But that mercantile next door just been stocked from Dodge City. We kill a lot of buffalo around here, Cord. We got just shy of eleven thousand rounds of Sharps ammunition stashed away in there. I'll put it and our hunter's up against a thousand Injun anyday. How do ya' claim to even know any of this?"

Cord could feel the wobble of false bravado mixed in with Hanrahan's words. "Because I had a Kiowa trader in their camp over the last couple weeks. Said it was swamped with Kiowa, Cheyenne and even a few Arapaho. They all had a Sun Dance back in May. They're goin' on one hell of a warpath against the white man, and y'all just happen to be the first whites in their way."

"Come on, Cord," Hanrahan nearly laughed at him, "ya' been fed a bunch of bullshit. The Comanche don't even do the Sun Dance. Everyone knows that."

Cord could see the man grasping at the hope that he was right, like a gambler clutching at his last few chips.

"They do now," Cord said. "Them *Quahadi* got a new war chief, *Quanah Parker,* coupled up with a medicine man calls hisself *White Eagle* tellin' them braves his magic is strong 'nuff to make yer bullets bounce of them."

"That's a recipe fer trouble all right," Hanrahan said again, "but soon as they charge and 'em buffalo rounds tear into their hides, they'll pull back."

"You best hope so," Cord said, sensing the beads of sweat forming on the barman's forehead. "But if I was ya', I would be ready for them to ride in here before sun-up and kill yer buffalo hunters as they sleep outside in the street."

"Yeah, yeah," was all the man could answer with a faraway look in his eyes. Then, Hanrahan produced a full bottle of Kentucky bourbon from behind the bar and offered it to him.

"Listen, Cord, ya' done yer part in tellin' me all this. I'll manage it from here. The boys are likely to be coming back into town early 'morrow, and I sure as hell don't need ya' gettin' 'em all riled up. We got less than thirty of us here. If half of 'em pack up and ride off, we don't stand a chance. So keep yer mouth shut, and this bottle's on me."

Cord reached for the bottle.

"We got a deal?" Hanrahan said, pulling it back.

"Depends," Cord said, "let me see exactly what yer offerin' for my silence."

"Only Kentucky's finest. Last bottle I got," Hanrahan said. "None of this frontier *budge* bullshit. So, deal or not?"

"Too good to be true," Cord said. "Ya' waterin' it?"

"C'mon, it's still sealed," Hanrahan objected. "What ya' take me fer, anyway?"

"Someone who would take me fer anything he could," Cord answered. "Pour me out a glass. Just a small taste to base my decision on."

Hanrahan did so, and Cord thought of his promise to Midge as he raised the glass to his lips. He could smell the sweet hills of Kentucky before the golden liquor even reached his lips. This was surely the real deal. Then, he felt its smooth burn as it slid down his throat.

"Looks like we got ourselves a deal, Jim," Cord said, reaching for the bottle.

"Ya' won't breathe a word to any of the men," Hanrahan said, pulling it back. "Ya' swear to me, Cord?"

"Okay, Jim. I swear," Cord answered as he leaned across the roughshod bar and grabbed the bottle. "Won't be hard, as I'm pullin' out in the mornin."

"Yer a son-of-a-bitch," Hanrahan shouted, reaching for the bottle. Cord pulled the whiskey close with his left arm as with his right he pulled his Colt .45 Peacemaker in a flash. He did not cock it, but the sight of metal caught the full attention of Big Jim.

"Now, Jim," Cord said, "a deal is a deal. Next time ya' might ask a few more questions before ya' make a man an offer. But as I see it, this bottle is legally mine at this point. But even if I was to run across any of the boys out on *the Llano,* I'll keep my end. Don't ya' worry none."

"Damn ya', McCullough," Hanrahan seethed. "Good riddance to ya'. Where exactly ya' headin'?"

Cord saw the question coming. He had a mental image of Jim being tortured by Indians in the days ahead.

"Best I keep that to myself for now," Cord said.

"I don't take ya' to be one to run away from a fight," Hanrahan baited him, "and if what ya' say is true, this will be one massive fight. I sure don't take ya' for a coward, Cord."

"And I never took ya' fer a fool, yet y'are," Cord answered as he poured himself a second glass of bourbon. He swallowed half of it in a gulp, then was sorry he had acted so wastefully. "I'm gettin' a might tired of bein' called a coward, Jim."

"Stay, Cord," Hanrahan nearly pleaded. "We need yer gun."

"I really wish I could, Jim," Cord replied, "but I got another commitment. My only advice to ya', my friend, is to beware the Comanche Moon."

With this, Cord took the bottle and the glass and headed back to the ruins to offer *Sulking Crow* a taste of his newfound treasure.

The next morning, Cord McCullough was reduced once more to a useless heap of snoring drunken trailhand flesh. Midge and Piotr came to the ruins mid-morning, where Cord had camped with his Kiowa friend, only to find him sleeping off the bourbon.

"How dare you give him whiskey?" she snarled at the Indian.

"Not me," *Sulking Crow* said. "Man at saloon. I not even take any when Cord offer. Not a drop."

"Well," Midge said, holding the empty bottle upside down, "that's exactly what appears to be left - not a drop. Cord promised me not to touch the stuff. What'll we do?"

Sulking Crow looked up at Midge's distraught face. "His promises no good when fire water involved," *Sulking Crow* said. "Me and the boy load him in wagon. Mostly empty now. Cord sleep as we travel."

That was when Brett Sumner showed up. He had slept outside the Mercantile inside which Piotr and Midge had been invited to bed down overnight. He rejoined them at the ruins, not surprised to find Cord sleeping off a binge.

"The man didn't even think to offer me a nick of it," Brett said. When Midge shot him a disgusted glance, he defended himself, saying, "What? I wouldn't have taken any, but the man should at least have offered."

"This man, no," *Sulking Crow* said. "I sell him fire water many years on Chisholm Trail. He never share."

With Brett's arm still slinged, it was left to Piotr and *Sulking Crow* to lift Cord into the wagon. Then, they tied Trouble to the back of the wagon, alongside the two horses that the Kiowa had taken in trade from the Comanches.

With the dead weight of Cord McCullough in the wagon bed, *Sulking Crow* carefully led the other three riders, each on their own horses, south to *Palo Duro*. Given their late start, he knew they'd never cover it all before darkness fell. Especially as they needed to swing far out of the way of the seemingly endless stream of warriors heading north to Adobe Walls from the Red River.

That night they cold-camped about a mile from the canyon's rim. No fire, no hot food, just the unending wind of *the Llano.* It was the only constant. Whether the sky was clear, overcast or full of rain, the wind blew relentlessly.

Chapter 31: Abandoned at the Canyon's Rim

June, 1874

In the back of the wagon that night, Cord awoke, with his head pounding hard. He was alone. Even River seemed to have abandoned him. He made his way to look for Trouble, who he was sure *Sulking Crow* must had hobbled nearby. But there was not a single horse to be found, all were gone, even the two taken in trade by *Sulking Crow.* Not even the Kiowa's other pair, the horses that pulled his wagon, were to be found.

Neither did Cord find any of his companions. Only the near empty wagon. It had all the signs of a Comanche attack, except no dead bodies left behind. *Why not? And if it truly was an attack, then why had I not been killed?*

When the sun came up, Cord began to cut for sign. He thought he could make out three or four tracks from unshod Indian ponies. Four, not three, he was later sure of. As the sun climbed up into the sky, he saw no buzzards overhead, so he figured no corpses were nearby. That was the best news the morning had to offer him. The next best being that while his Colt .45 was gone, hidden away in his duster was still the Baby Colt Dragoon. He kept the hammer on an empty chamber, so with it holding just five shots, it left him with but four balls of lead for any hostiles.

Cord followed the tracks of the group as it moved toward the canyon rim. It was not hard as they had a dozen horses in all: four Comanche ponies, riding point on the four captives on horseback- *Sulking Crow,* Brett, Midge and Piotr - and trailing behind were the four horses of the Kiowa. That many hoof prints left behind a mangled mess of sign. But Cord could clearly make out a few of Trouble's tracks, as one of her shoes had a telltale nick in it. Overtop all this, Cord could make out River's fresh imprints. The dog appeared to be trailing them at a distance. Cord knew it was unlikely the Comanche would kill the dog, as it was a relative of the wolf they revered. They would not even unnecessarily kill the coyotes, those "makers of mischief."

Cord followed the tracks as they led to a trail leading steeply down the canyon wall. He lost what detail the sign had as it became trampled by the dozen horses fighting for footing as they half-slid down the descending trail. He began to work his way down on foot when he spotted the first buzzard overhead. Then another. Then two more, circling as if waiting impatiently for something to die. Cord hoped that "something" was not a "someone."

Soon he came upon a trail of blood, and followed it off into the brush. He found the arrow riddled body of Brett Sumner. He was lying face down, and as Cord turned him slowly over, he was surprised to hear a soft moan escape from the man. One arrow had pierced through his sling, pinning his arm to his torso. The man never had a chance to defend himself.

Upon flipping him onto his backside, Cord saw that Brett had been scalped while still alive. He was near enough gone, and barely responded to Cord's calls. Finally, on a whisper of a breath he strained to say, "I failed her, Cord…I mean Midge…the girl too, I s'pose."

"No, no. Don't talk, Brett," Cord said, as he laid his hands on this dying man he barely knew. Still, he was a good man, one Cord would have like to have gotten to know better.

"They was just kids," Brett said, as he closed his eyes. "Injun boys … only li'l boys."

"Let go of it all, Brett, git on to yer maker," Cord answered. "I give ya' my word, I'll get Midge and the rest of them all back home, safe like. Ya done more than yer part, brother, the rest is on me now."

Cord cursed himself for having taken that bottle from Hanrahan. Had he been sober, he convinced himself, none of this would ever have happened. Now, Sumner was all but dead, Midge and Piotr captives, and God only knows what would become of *Sulking Crow* once the Comanches had figured out he had betrayed them.

Cord had no option left but to leave Brett there in the brush. He could not stay with the man until his last breath, besides he had nothing to bury him with. He could only hope his friend would die before the vultures began to feast. He couldn't even fire a mercy round into his skull, as it would give away that he was alive and armed to boot.

Cord worked his way down the canyon wall, tracking the mangled trail over the next hour. At the bottom, the tracks became clearer again, especially those of the unshod Comanche ponies who rode on the outside of all the others. Cord could only count three of these, but he was pretty sure he'd had counted four atop the canyon's rim. He thought that one of them was doing as he had long heard they would - trailing one brave behind their traveling party. If so, that brave was behind him and would soon enough see Cord's footprints trailing the others.

Cord looked to the sky, and found no circling buzzards. He assumed their feast had begun. He removed his hat and prayed for Sumner's soul.

Well, Brett, I don't 'spect ya' got any of them braves, my friend, so I best prepare for some company to drop in.

Cord followed the creek that flowed through the bottom of the canyon. He then waded into its waters to hide his own tracks, and sloshed another quarter mile in the same direction along the muddle of tracks on the dry trail. He took off his duster and hid it crudely in a bush before climbing the fullest cottonwood he could find nearby.

Then, he waited. And waited some more. All the while his Baby Dragoon was gripped loosely in his palm. After a good spell, he heard an Indian pony sloshing through the creek's water. Then Cord saw him, a Comanche boy who had undoubtedly followed his tracks until they disappeared into the creek. The young brave was scanning the bank, looking for anything that showed where his prey had emerged back onto the dry earth. At one point, the boy looked in his direction up in the bough of the tree and Cord feared he had been seen. But then the brave spotted the duster at water's edge that Cord had left for him to find.

The Comanche boy rode over to it as Cord drew his bead on the child. *He can't be anymore than twelve or thirteen,* Cord thought, but then added, *plenty old enough to have killed Brett Sumner.* He thought this just as he spotted Brett's fresh scalp dangling, its hair tied tightly to the long strands of his pony's mane.

The boy wandered in close to the duster, but must have feared a trap as he drew an arrow into his bow. Leaning forward in the tree to fire, Cord repositioned his leg and a small slosh of water drained from his boots.

As the drops from Cord's boot rippled on the creek's surface below, the young Comanche brave reacted by firing off his arrow in the direction from which they had fallen. It twanged into the bark just next to Cord's head and the boy was already in the process of readying another.

Cord had no other option than to fire on the young brave. The Baby Dragoon's first ball hit him in the shoulder, causing him to drop the bow. He kicked his pony to run when Cord's second shot found his head, dropping him in flight. *Only fitting,* Cord mused, *a scalp for a scalp.*

Cord climbed down from the cottonwood. The Comanche boy was dead, sure enough, his skull shattered, but his mount had run off, Brett's scalp still danglin from its mane. Cord knew it wouldn't take long for his friends to understand the meaning of their companion's empty mount, given the echo of the two gunshots through the canyon.

As tempting as it was to do, Cord could no longer follow the tracks of the braves and their captives, as that would be what the Comanches would expect him to do. With three other boys, at least, and only two balls left in his Baby Dragoon, the odds were not in his favor.

Cord found a rock formation that looked to him like a parrot lying on its back, its beak pointing upward toward the sun. He knew if nothing else, it would afford him great cover from arrows and gunfire.

Cord recovered his duster and walked off an obvious trail back toward the creek for them to spot. Then he made his way to the Parrot Rock, covering his tracks as best he could. Again he waited, and waited more until his patience paid off as two Comanche boys cautiously came up the creek. They found their companion and loaded his body onto the back of one of their ponies.

Then Cord watched as one of the young braves followed the tracks he had left back into the creek. After some time with both braves talking, they continued back in the direction from whence they had come. One rode with the other walking alongside the horse carrying the body of their friend.

If those were two of the three remaining Comanche braves on horseback, Cord reasoned, *then we must be close to their camp. They wouldn't leave the three captives - Sulking Crow, Piotr and Midge - with only one boy left to guard them. No, they must be in the main village closeby.*

Cord stayed hidden behind the Parrot Rock as the sun began to drop over the western canyon's wall. His head had stopped throbbing, but his stomach rumbled with hunger. Long shadows stretched overhead, preceding the darkness he knew was his enemy. But at this point, he knew moving off in search of food would be too risky.

The shadows thickened into night. Cord stayed awake, vigilant, but for what he did not know. Then, when he finally gave into his fatigue and started to nod off, he heard a low growl coming from behind him. It stirred him, with his hair standing on the back of his neck. Then the growl came a second time, somewhat less threateningly.

"River?" Cord whispered. The shape in the darkness moved toward him, and Cord pointed his Baby Dragoon as he was unsure. He drew a bead on the approaching shadow, and began to tighten his finger on the trigger.

But as the shape drew slowly closer, Cord could see a wagging tail trailing behind it. He exhaled a sigh of relief and reached out for the animal.

"Good boy. Good boy," he whispered.

They huddled close together and rested from what had been a tiring day for them both. About an hour later, River growled lowly, almost inaudibly and moved to the side of the rock they hid behind. The dog stared off down onto the trail below them.

"What is it, boy?" Cord said in a hush after he raised himself to peek over the top of the Parrot Rock.

"I see him too," he whispered in an even lower hush. Along the trail below them lurked a figure, far too large to be a boy. He was clad in black, and as such was hard to pick out among the shadows and partial moonlight. It was not until that figure walked in front of a moonlit shimmer on the creek's flow that Cord made out the flared sleeves of the long leather coat. It was just as he remembered Doc Blevins describing it.

Chapter 32: Reverence of the Otter *"Puha"*

June, 1874

Lobo came back into the lodge from his night scouting, having found nothing along the trail. Inside, huddled around the fire, was Midge, Piotr and *Sulking Crow,* being watched over by three young Comanche braves. The half-breed looked glaringly at the Kiowa trader. The two natives spoke in the Comanche language, and as they did Midge and Piotr could not understand any of what they discussed.

"Tell me again, Kiowa, why you bring these golden haired people here," *Lobo* said, pointing at Midge and Piotr.

"I have told you over and over," *Sulking Crow* said. "I captured them, their man was very sick from the cholera. Your young braves looked at him. Very sick. Very sick. They agreed."

"So you say, yet you took this white man with cholera and was bringing him here, to this village?"

"No. I was not," *Sulking Crow* said. "I was only camped near the rim overnight on my way west with them to Santa Fe. Get big ransom for all of them there."

"Including the other man?" *Lobo* asked. "The one who was killed on the trail by the braves. He was not sick. You did not even have him bound. He still had a gun hidden on him. How do you explain all this?"

"I explained to you many times," *Sulking Crow* said with exasperation, "these two golden hairs, the boy and the woman, are looking for the girl you took. They hired other two men to help them. One sick man with cholera. The other badly wounded. Arm in sling - shot. I captured them all out on *the Llano,* not far from here. Your young braves killed and scalped that second man on the trail. I not know he hid gun. But the two golden hairs' family wants them back. Big ransom. In Santa Fe."

"Those young braves were defending themselves," *Lobo* said, "the fool should never have gone for that gun he had hidden in that sling. These men you bring to us had many guns. Some very strange guns."

He held up the LeMat revolver. Both Indians looked at it with confusion. Piotr gazed at it with a desire to kill.

"And this was found on you?" *Lobo* produced the black sack holding the two hundred dollars in gold coins.

"I take it from them," *Sulking Crow* feared he was a bit too fast to say. He was afraid that the half-blood in the long leather coat did not believe his story.

"But you never took over money from the saddle bag? From the horse of the cholera man? Much more money, yet you leave it there?"

"I knew it was there, it was safe there!"

"Well, my Kiowa friend," *Lobo* said, "you appear to be a most lucky brother. You come here and trade with our war chiefs just before big battle with the white men hunting the *cibolo,* then steal a very large sum from these sick and wounded white men as you head home. "

"Not home. To Santa Fe. You say I am lucky? Why?" *Sulking Crow* asked, "because I take gold from the white men?"

"No," *Lobo* answered him, "because the medicine man *White Eagle* has forbidden me from any killing while the great battle remains to be fought. And because you show up with these people just after I bring White Eagle golden hair girl here. Or else, I would kill you now."

"Your medicine man, *White Eagle,* is very wise," *Sulking Crow* said.

"Wise enough that he did not say I could not inflict pain upon you," *Lobo* responded. "Perhaps you are not so lucky after all. When the sun rises, I will send two young braves to the wagon on the canyon's rim. If your friend is not found inside, you will wish I had the freedom to kill you. For you will suffer much by my hand for telling lies!"

"Your braves will find the sick man there." *Sulking Crow* was lying, biding for time.

"No," *Lobo* said, "They will not. For your sick man has today already killed one of the young braves. He is in the canyon, somewhere, hiding and has a gun. And I will not forget that it was you who brought him and this death here. Now, these two golden hairs, what are their names?"

"Peehyatr and Meedge," *Sulking Crow* answered, blending the names in the rhythm of the Comanche tongue.

"She looks like sister of girl of the White Eagle medallion," *Lobo* said, referring to Midge about Kalina who was being kept in another lodge within the village.

"This one is the sister of the young girl's father," *Sulking Crow* explained, "and the boy is the young girl's brother."

"And the sick one you left in the wagon, who killed our brave, he is the young girl's Father?"

"No. He is only a hired trailhand. I am tired of defending myself to you," *Sulking Crow* said. "I will answer to *Quanah* and *White Eagle* when they return in victory over those who slaughter the *cibolo*."

"*Peehyatr* is a very strange name," said *Lobo.* "What does it mean?"

Sulking Crow said, "I must ask, I do not know…"

Lobo waved I his hand, as if to say, *then ask them…*

Sulking Crow spoke English to Midge and Piotr, but cautiously as he did not know how much of that language the half-breed understood. He decided to answer *Lobo* with Cord's joke, as he thought it something an Indian might understand.

"They say it is equal to the English term *Pee Otter*."

"Which means what?" *Lobo* asked.

"Water from the river otter," the Kiowa answered.

"What?" *Lobo* suddenly became very attentive. "Does this boy possess the *puha* of the river otter?"

"Yes," *Sulking Crow* lied, "the boy is said to have strong power, much otter magic."

"Bring him," *Lobo* answered. "All our medicine men are off to battle the white men. We have a woman with child tonight who needs his otter *puha*. Quickly."

"I must explain…" *Sulking Crow* said.

Lobo again waved his hand. Then great discussion in English occurred, of which *Lobo* understood very little.

"He says he will do it but only if the woman here assists him," *Sulking Crow* said, "and he must first see the girl, his sister."

"Bring them both - quickly."

Piotr was taken to the lodge where *She Who Runs Like The Trembling Wind* was preparing to give birth. Midge entered the tent and recognized that the woman was already having strong contractions and labor pains, and the child would come soon. But Piotr refused to enter the lodge until he was taken to see Kalina. He was led away by *Lobo* as Midge stayed with the delivering mother.

"I take you see sister," *Lobo* said in English. "No talk, no touch, only see."

The two entered another lodge, and the girl was there surrounded by the two young girls who kept watch over her. When she saw him enter through the flap, Kalina yelled out *"Piotek!"* But she did not move towards him.

His heart melted within his chest when he saw her. He almost did not recognize her. She was dressed out in buckskin clothes with colorful markings and beading. The two Comanche girls sat on either side of her, braiding her long blonde hair as if she were a doll.

"Kalina!" he answered, and ignoring *Lobo's* instruction, he quickly added in Polish, "Are you alright? Did they harm you in any way."

"No," she answered, "I am fine, but I am frightened. Very frightened."

"No talk!"demanded *Lobo.*

"Do not worry any longer, *Ciocci Mieczysława* is here with me. We will get you out, take you back home. And this one will pay dearly for ever having taken you!"

"I say no talk!" *Lobo* repeated and forcibly pulled him from the tent. Outside he added, "You go back now. Otter *puha!"*

"I will deliver the baby," Piotr said to him, "then, you will give my sister back to me."

"No!" *Lobo* said. *"White Eagle!* Only to him."

Then, *Lobo* all but dragged Piotr back to the lodge to deliver *Trembling Wind's* child.

That night, Piotr and Midge delivered the child of *She Who Runs Like The Trembling Wind.* Midge had assisted in the delivery of many children during her years at *Panna Maria,* and sadly had been present when more than a few were lost. But it was too late to object. Their failure to deliver the child that night would be their death warrant.

When Piotr rejoined Midge in the birthing lodge, the woman was squatting in her attempt to deliver the child. She appeared to be having great trouble and was in intense pain. Her face was heavily sweated and distorted in agony. Midge was fearful that the child was perhaps in the breeched position. She seemed to disrupt everything when she had the birthing mother assume a reclined position, which was not the Comanche way. She had two of the attending village women act as human stirrups, pushing in resistance to the woman's widespread legs.

Midge had told Piotr to keep out of the way, but to act as though he was invoking a spell of magic. She would do all the rest. Piotr had noticed the strange reaction from the young girls in Kalina's lodge when he spoke Polish to her. As he raised his arms over the birth mother, Piotr began to speak out loudly in his native tongue. At first, he started by rambling in Polish, but soon fell short of which words to say aloud next. So, he turned to stories from his youth.

Midge almost laughed, but managed to suppress it when she heard her nephew recalling passages from Henryk Sienkiewicz's Polish classic *Krzyżacy* about the Teutonic Knights. In that passage, the main character *Zbyszko of Bogdaniec* was in the woods hunting a bear to kill. His uncle, *Maćko,* was badly wounded, in need of bear fat to salve his wounds, to regain his health and strength.

The story told in Polish both relaxed Midge as she delivered the child, and seemed to invoke the feeling of a complex spell to the natives. Midge could only wonder just how similar to a Comanche story it might really be.

It took some time, but Midge was relieved to see the child's head finally crown. She instinctively commanded in English, *"Push,"* forgetting the birthing mother might not understand her.

Midge was greatly surprised to hear the mother-to-be answer through gritted teeth, "When?"

So she speaks some English, Midge thought before responding, "Now!"

The delivery thereafter was straightforward. After a few more strong pushes, the first cries of the baby girl could soon be heard. After a careful glance, Midge could see the daughter appeared to be healthy and perfect. Then, she was pushed away as the village women assisting her moved in to cut the umbilical cord with a special knife made from antelope sinew. They cleansed the child and wrapped the baby in warm skins of the namesake animal.

The news of the birth was greatly welcomed in the village. *Lobo* convinced the elders to declare that thanks to the *puha* of the river otter, no harm would come to either he who possessed it or she that assisted in the child's delivery. They would be free to wander the village, but not leave it.

It was only then that Piotr and Midge learned that the birthing woman was *Lobo's* own mother. She was very appreciative and thanked them over and over again in English as she held the newborn girl. She was happy to be alive, as she had been deathly afraid while in the throes of her labor pains that she would die, just as the absent village otter medicine man had predicted. Not only had he been wrong about that, but the child was not the son that he had predicted. Of course to *Trembling Wind,* this was a blessing, for she already had a son and greatly desired a daughter. But for her warrior husband, *Raging Anger,* it would be a great disappointment. But as it was clear to Midge, and even to Piotr, the newborn daughter brought great joy to her mother.

These two had saved *Trembling Wind's* life, as well as that of the infant girl. All in the village were told that these two golden hairs possessed great otter magic, powerful *puha.* In no way were they to be harmed.

Chapter 33: A Meeting at Midnight

June 26th, 1874

Following the birth of the child, Piotr was given his freedom to roam throughout the village, although he was warned not to go too far or he would be hunted down. That would cause *Lobo* to be forced to track him, something the half-blooded Comanche had no desire to do. Especially not after the boy had safely delivered the child of his mother. *Lobo* respected that his otter *puha* had saved his new sister's life, and more importantly, that of his mother, *Trembling Wind,* especially given the village medicine man's prediction of catastrophe.

That night and the next Piotr could not sleep. The second night after the moon had risen high and cleared the dark canyon walls, it glowed full against the indigo night sky. Despite the great success of his Aunt Midge having delivered the woman's child, Piotr found himself laden heavy with worry. What had become of Cord? Was he even still alive? Had the half-breed *Lobo* caught up with him and destroyed the man with whom he had been through so much? No one knew for sure, as *Lobo* would not speak to that topic, not even with the Kiowa trader *Sulking Crow.* All they knew was that neither Cord nor River had been seen since the rest of them were captured.

Piotr walked from the encampment to the nearby creek. It soothed him to hear the fast water running over the beds of rocks there. The glow of the moon skittered upon its ripples, as if refusing to be washed away into the night.

Then Piotr heard something skipping across the dry rocks along the shoreline. He was still in sight of the village, so he doubted it would be any of the Comanche youths following him. Even had it been, they likely would not have made such an obvious sound.

Then Piotr heard it again. Stone skipping on dry stone. He looked down river to see if there was any wildlife lurking in the darkness, but as he did so he felt a third stone strike him in the back between his shoulders. He spun to look upstream.

"Hey, *Pee Otter!*" he barely heard called out in a hushed tone no louder than a whisper. "Come here, I gotta talk to you."

It was Cord. Piotr walked slowly upstream into the darkness. "Ya' sure can be a slow witted son of a gun at times. I thought I was gonna have to send River down to drag ya' over here by yer backside."

"Cord, I am so glad to see you're in a good way!"

"Shhh!" McCullough hushed him. "We don't need any of them Injun youths coming after you, do we? I been watching the camp. I've seen them taking Kalina out when you were not about. She's here and safe, at least fer now."

"I know," Piotr whispered. "I saw her night before last. She's good, but very afraid. The half-breed says he's saving her for the medicine man, *White Eagle*. And what do you mean, for now?"

Cord laid his hand on the boy's shoulder. This was the part of the discussion he dreaded with the willful teen.

"Easy now. This is where things get tough. Before we left Adobe Walls, *Sulking Crow* told me he believes that when the dawn breaks after the next Comanche Moon, the Injuns will attack the buffalo hunters at Adobe Walls. That full moon up in the sky is a Comanche Moon. Tonight is its first night being full."

"Sulking Crow told you this back then?" Piotr asked. "He didn't say anything to me about it."

"I swore him not to," Cord whispered. "Ya' can't be tortured to tell what ya' don't know."

"But you trust *Sulking Crow?"*

"Yes, Piotr, I trust *Sulky.* I've known him for years. We've been through a hell of a lot together."

"You and me been through quite a bit ourselves..."

"And that's why I am here talking to ya'. *Sulky* believes that something is going to happen regarding your sister when the dawn breaks. He says the Comanche don't believe in human sacrifices, but doesn't trust what that half-breed might do. Thinks he's under some kinda spell of that medicine man, yeah, the one that calls hisself *White Eagle*. But don't ya' worry none, I'm keeping an eye on the half-breed. Should he take your sister from camp in the morning I'll be right on 'em. I'll bring her back in good shape. But as soon as they leave, ya' gotta sneak into that tent where they're keeping her and get Midge and the guns they took from y'all. Then ya' gotta stay here with *Sulky* and protect Midge till I get back with Kalina."

"How will we know they've left the camp, Cord?"

"I'll run River through the camp. That's the signal. If ya' hear the camp dogs going crazy, make for Aunt Midge and the guns."

"I will Cord, but then I'm coming after Kalina."

"No, ya' stay and look after yer Aunt Midge with *Sulky*. I'll can take care of that half-breed easy enough and come back with yer sister. Just y'all be ready to ride and ride hard once I get here. Make sure ya' get out Trouble from that remuda of horses. I spotted her over there. I ain't leavin' without the old gal."

"I didn't come through all this," Piotr objected, "just to stand aside when the rescuing of Kalina is to be done. What if *Lobo* gets the best of ya?"

"Damn it, *Pee Otter!* Stay in the camp. Kill the rest of them Comanche youths if ya' have to. Just look after Midge. I can't be in two places at once."

"Where do ya' figure he'll take Kalina?"

"Likely to the place I trailed him to today. About three miles in from here. I think he was doin' some sort of a dry run. But the good news is there's only one way in and one way out, so I'll surely get the drop on him."

"Okay. I'll stay and look after Aunt Midge, but what happens if them camp dogs tear River to pieces?"

"Don'tcha worry none, River can handle hisself. But if ya' need to shoot one or two of them mutts to even things up, go ahead and do so."

Comanche camps always had several dogs in them. The Comanches saw them as descendants of the mighty wolf, which they revered. They never would think to harm, let alone eat, any canine. Not even the devious coyotes.

"Okay, Cord," Piotr said, "that's what I'll do." While he said this, he thought to himself, *To hell with all that. Sulking Crow can protect Aunt Midge and take care of the camp dogs. I'm coming to make sure Kalina is safe.*

Chapter 34: The Attack on Adobe Walls

June 27th, 1874

During the overnight hours of June 26th into the morning of the 27th, Big Jim Hanrahan could not sleep. He watched the rise of the Comanche Moon in the velvet black sky and wondered when the attack would come. He was thankful that everyone was back in camp, but felt guilty for not sharing with the men Cord McCullough's warning of what the Comanche and their Kiowa, Cheyenne and Arapaho allies were planning. Now the hunters and skinners all slept soundly in their tents outside his saloon, easy prey for an Indian surprise attack.

Hanrahan had not shared Cord's warning because with only twenty-eight men in camp, he feared driving off even a single man. Normally, the camp town would have only ten or so men in it. But all the Indian activity as of late had drawn those who normally would be camping out on *the Llano* into Adobe Walls. No, there was nothing unfair in not telling them. They were all there to make their fortunes, he figured, and all these men would bear the brunt of the Indian savagery. That was all there was to it. No man would get to decide if he wanted to stay, they had decided as soon as they came to camp. *Share the bounty, share the burden.*

At two in the morning, Big Jim gave into his hunch. The Comanche would most likely attack on the first night of the full moon, making it a true Comanche Moon. But he knew he could not just wake his comrades and explain to them how he had withheld the critical news. Instead, he took to the plan he had devised ever since McCullough had pilfered his best bottle of Kentucky bourbon.

Hanrahan stood just in front of the entrance to his saloon. He had his Sharps Big Fifty in his right hand. With his left he mussed his hair to give the appearance of being roused out from a deep sleep. He then raised his rifle and held in his palm the guard housing the rifle's double trigger. He reached his index finger inside it and pulled back on the rear trigger. This was the "set" trigger that allowed the firing trigger to have a lower pull value. It was the feature that made a gun that powerful so accurate, because the hunters weren't require to "jerk" the trigger so hard to fire it. Then, Big Jim Hanrahan raised the rifle in the air, moved his finger onto the forward trigger and gently squeezed it.

The explosion of the Sharps Big Fifty echoed through the camp like a crack of lightning, although the night sky was calm. Hanrahan quickly went inside and placed his rifle behind the bar, then stumbled outside as the other men in the camp were roused and in a panic.

"What the hell was that rifle shot for?" asked the first buffalo hunter responding, one of the best, the man called Billy Dixon.

"Aw, shit!" replied Hanrahan, "that weren't no rifle shot."

"Sure as hell sounded like a Big Fifty going off to me," Dixon said. "God knows I heard enough of that sound to last a lifetime. If it weren't, then what was it?"

It might be a very short lifetime to last, Hanrahan thought, *if ya' don't buy and help me sell my story.*

"Billy, that *'shot'* was the ridgepole of the saloon roof cracking under the weight of all that sod. Ya' better get every man in camp up that drinks, and that's all of 'em, cuz if that damn ridgepole cracks clean through, every drop of booze we got is gonna to be buried under hundreds of pounds of sod. Get 'em bastards up, and quick."

Most of the men had already been roused by the "crack" of the ridgepole. Over the next several hours, near every man was motivated to help repair it to save their precious supply of booze. Big Jim oversaw the repairs and kept lookout for his feared Injun attack from atop the roof. He kept the men awake after they had replaced the "cracked" ridgepole with one hacked from a cottonwood taken from the creek by offering them all free booze, and not a single man refused his generosity. Only two men, the Shadler brothers, freighters out of Dodge city, failed to rise and help in the "repair," instead they slept in their wagon.

Hanrahan was just beginning to regret his ruse when the attack he feared came at dawn. An initial wave of Indian riders three hundred strong swept toward the camp, led by none other than *Quanah Parker* under a full headdress of eagle feathers. His body and face were colored yellow with ochre, highlighted with angry streaks of vermillion war paint, as were those of all the attacking riders. The medicine man *White Eagle,* once called *Isa Tai'i,* had promised that the yellow ochre paint would make their bodies immune to the bullets of the hunters. Even their war ponies were painted yellow. Yet, despite his boasts of his great magic, *White Eagle* was not among those warriors descending upon the camp. He stayed back nearly a mile away watching from atop a bluff.

As the drumming of the approaching horde of war ponies rolled like thunder over *the Llano,* the men in camp moved desperately for their weapons. They all knew the savagery awaiting them should they fail to get to their guns.

The wave of Indian riders crashed upon the camp like a storm's surf on an immovable clutch of coastal rocks. The invading savages carried repeating rifles, lances and tomahawks, some with only bows and thick shields of buffalo hides. The crush of the Indian wave pooled before the saloon, as others raced between it and the mercantile adobe-front of the Olds' Store. The Shadler brothers were caught out in their wagon and were cut down during that initial onslaught, but thanks to the "cracked ridgepole" of Big Jim Hanrahan, the remaining buffalo hunters began returning fire from within the saloon and the Olds' store.

What transpired next was as great a disappointment to *Quanah Parker* as he could ever have imagined. Not only did his party not catch the men sleeping in their tents as he had planned, but the firing of the revolvers and rifles emerging from inside the saloon quickly proved the medicine man *White Eagle's puha* to be nothing more than a hollow echo of *Isa Tai'i's* false magic.

The men in camp had barely enough time to gather inside the adobe structures and barricade the windows and doors before the Indians were upon them. Nine men took refuge in Hanrahan's Saloon, including Big Jim, Bat Masterson and Billy Dixon. Dixon had barely made it, having gone out to a wagon for his gun when the Indian attack was first spotted, he got to the saloon after the door was bolted. He pounded on it to be let in, which the others did just in time. They'd be glad they did, for with perhaps the lone exception of Bat Masterson, no man fought more bravely or killed more attackers than Billy Dixon.

Six men, seven if you counted Mrs. Olds, took refuge in her husband's mercantile across the street. Sadly one of those was Billy Tyler who ran up to the mercantile from the corral, and was shot through the lung as he waited for the door to be opened. He fell inside, but the wound would prove to be fatal.

The final eleven men were in the second Mercantile, called Myers & Leonard's, behind the saloon and closest to the corral of horses. With both of the Shadler brothers already cut down, that accounted for all twenty-eight men and Mrs. Olds in camp during the attack.

The first rounds of the buffalo hunters were fired into the concentrated mass of Indians pooling between the saloon and mercantile run by the Olds. These two structures acted as a choke point for the hundreds of Indians trying to gain access to the camp. Several had dismounted and were banging their rifle stocks against the saloon doors, as well as upon the sides of the two mercantiles. The .45 and .50 caliber rounds, used so effectively from hundreds of yards to drop buffalo, proved to be devastating against that mass of natives at near point blank range.

Some inside the saloon fought back with more conventional Winchester and Henry rifles. Even these at such close range ripped through the stacked layers of buffalo hide forming the Comanche war shields and severed limbs, penetrating the ochre painted torsos nearly in half. The attackers lost some thirty braves in that initial onslaught, their bodies lay scattered in the street. But perhaps the greatest Indian casualty was the invulnerability promised by *White Eagle's* yellow ochre war paint under the guise of his great *puha*. Under the withering fire from the three structures, *Quanah Parker* had no choice but to withdraw his braves back to a much safer distance.

Those not driven from their saddles soon withdrew. In order to get out of the range of the buffalo hunters powerful Sharps rifles, the natives had to retreat to beyond the range of their own less powerful repeating rifles.

Had the buffalo hunters still been asleep, they most likely would have been hatcheted to death before they knew what had hit them. As dastardly as it was for Big Jim Hanrahan to keep the news of the impending attack from them, his ruse that morning saved the life of every man in camp, but three: the two Stadler brothers and Billy Tyler. A fourth, Mr. Olds himself, would be lost due to an accidental discharge of his weapon, but it is hard to argue that his lethal clumsiness could have been avoided.

Throughout the first day, parties of Indians made stealthy advances on the camp, but in each case were discovered and driven off by the buffalo hunters. What followed over the next days was essentially a rare Indian seige, but the natives were forced to respect the range of the buffalo hunters' rifles. This gave those in camp the ability to come outside and move between buildings, which allowed the stockpile of some eleven thousand rounds of ammunition to be distributed between the three strongholds.

Over the next few days, hunters from nearby camps heard the news and came in small numbers to reinforce Adobe Walls. But their numbers never came close to matching the seven hundred to a thousand Indian braves they were up against. Thanks to the bravery and skill of buffalo hunters like Billy Dixon and Bat Masterson and others, the killing field was more than evened out.

Chapter 35: The Sacrifice at The Thunderbird of the Great Spirit

June 27th, 1874

The first arc of the Comanche Moon in the sky had set. The summer sun had just begun its rise into the stillness of the cobalt blue sky left behind. The morning of the great battle was upon them, and just as the opposing forces arrayed themselves against each other at Adobe Walls, so as well did two singular opponents ready themselves to pair off under the tranquil climb of that *Palo Duro Canyon* sunrise.

Overhead, the sky slowly sloughed away its veils of violet, crimson, and scarlet, to eventually reveal a turquoise expanse. Under this, Cord McCullough held watch over the quiet Comanche village from a vantage point high on its canyon wall. River sat patiently at his feet. Nestled in dawn's shadow of the cliff wall itself, the lodges below were enveloped only a diffused, passive haze of gray.

Cord watched one particular lodge, and searched for any signs of movement near it. In it, was the girl, Kalina. *It had all come down to this,* he thought. *Whatever was to happen over the next few hours, it would not be said that I did not do what my dear, departed Callie demanded of me. I will free that little Polish girl or die trying.*

Cord took his eyes away from the lodge briefly for only two reasons - to periodically scan his surroundings and to compulsively check and recheck the loading of his gun. It was the only weapon he had left, the old five shot cap-and-ball Baby Dragoon. In the middle of the night he would have loaded the empty chambers, even the one he usually kept empty for safety, with fresh balls. But he did not have any to load, nor any powder. He had traveled with one chamber empty as a safety, and had fired two rounds into the young Indian brave, which left only two remaining rounds. He wished desperately that he had more, even just one round more, but convinced himself that if he was careful, two shots should be all that he would need.

As he had committed to *White Eagle, Lobo* prepared to take the girl wearing the medallion in his image to the sacred rock formation. The Comanche knew there was a risk, because the white man who the Kiowa said to have cholera was not found in the wagon on the rim of the canyon. This only confirmed what *Lobo* already was sure of - that he was the man who had killed the young brave at the creek.

The news of the empty wagon came to him late the day before, and *Lobo* decided he would leave the captured Kiowa in camp to be dealt with after his trip with the girl. Given that the otter's *puha* had saved his mother, *Lobo* was inclined to allow the boy who possessed it and the woman who had assisted him to leave the canyon unharmed when he returned, but the lying Kiowa had to be punished.

Before *Lobo* would take the girl to *the Thunderbird of the Great Spirit,* he stopped in to see *Trembling Wind.* He wished to please her, and to do so wore her father's long leather coat, along with the black hat with the wide rolled brim. As he entered, his mother lay near the fire, his newly born half-sister curled comfortably high upon her chest.

This morning *Trembling Wind* insisted on adding something new to his outfit. Something to celebrate the birth of her daughter, and to thank *the Great Spirit* for her own spared life. She presented him with two beautiful eagle tail feathers that had been given to her to commemorate the child's birth. *Trembling Wind* took great delight in braiding these into her son's long raven black locks, and secured them such that the enormous feathers would lay boldly, proudly upon his shoulders and upper back.

"Mother," he said as she worked the strands of his hair tenderly, lovingly, "I did not tell you that in my travels I visited the home in Mexico from which you were taken."

"Oh, I see," *Trembling Wind* said, but thinking him surely to have been mistaken. But as her son described the house and the distance to the *arroyo*, she knew she truly had found it. Long lost memories flooded back to her.

"I went to the *arroyo* on the night of the full moon. I laid your father's coat in one of its many crevices. I am sure had you not cried out for your *papá, Dark Wolf* would never have found you. Even his eye was not sharp enough to discern black from black, darkness from darkness."

Trembling Wind focused on her hands, busily securing the tail feathers into his braids as dark and black as that night. Emotions rose in her like a fountain, and soon tears crept down her cheeks. *Lobo* sensed this, and turned to say to her how sorry he was for making her relive it all.

"Turn back around and let me finish my handiwork," she chided her son. "My tears are not of sorrow, except perhaps a few shed for the death of my own father. No, mostly, my tears show how happy I am for your safe return to me, for the joy of our reunion, and for the sheer fortune of ever having been taken in the first place."

"Truly, Mother?" he asked, still looking away from her as she finished her work.

"Truly, my son," she answered, "for had I not been taken, you would never have entered my life. You would not be here by my side this day. Your new sister would not be the great gift she is to me had you not found the boy with the otter *puha*. No, my tears are offered up to *the Great Spirit* for all he has bestowed on me. To show my gratitude, you'll wear these two feathers when you go to *the Thunderbird* to commune with him. In that way, your mother and her new daughter, your new sister, will be there with you. There! You are done."

He turned to face her. "It is time. I must go now."

"My son," she said, looking into his eyes, "what will you do with the girl?"

"*White Eagle* has only told me only to present her there, and to read the sun, and *the Great Spirit* will direct me."

"Be very careful," she said. "I fear that the white man is very dangerous. Please take a weapon with you."

"The elders have forbidden me to have one since I returned to camp. They took away my gun. But I still have my knife and I will take the horsewhip should I need it. Do not worry, no harm will come to me."

"And to the girl?" *Trembling Wind* asked. "Will you assure your mother no harm will come to her?"

"That is for *the Great Spirit* to decide," *Lobo* said.

"If only I was free of *Raging Anger,*" his mother said, "then, the young white girl could live here with you and me. We would raise her with your new sister. The white girl could grow here, much like *Quanah's* mother did at the side of *Peta Nocona*. I could raise her in the ways of our village, as I myself, being an outsider, was once raised."

"That is a very dangerous dream, my mother," *Lobo* warned, reaching up to stroke her face. "Remember when I wished for *Raging Anger's* death, how it drove me away for ten years, and instead it took the life of *Dark Wolf.*"

"All due only to the false magic of Isa Tai'i," she scoffed. "That 'Great Medicine Man' is a menace to us all."

"Do not worry, mother," *Lobo* said, "You will be free of your husband, *Raging Anger,* soon enough."

"I hope your word proves to be true, my son."

In his own lodge, Piotr lay on his side, feigning to be asleep. He watched through the opening of the flap the lodge across the village in which his sister was being held. He waited for the half-breed to come and take her away to the spot that Cord had spoken of. But in no way was he ready to do as McCullough had said.

"No, ya' stay and look after yer Aunt Midge with Sulky. I'll can take care of that half-breed easy enough and come back with yer sister." The words kept ringing in Piotr's ears. *I'll be damn if I intend to leave Kalina's life in the hands of that murderous drunken coward.*

Then he saw the half-blood in the distance, entering Kalina's lodge. He watched as the Comanche soon emerged and led her by the hand from the tent. She was still all dressed out in her Indian clothing - the hand painted and beaded buckskin tunic over a skirt of similarly tanned deer skin, and moccasins that rose high on her calves like boots. She even wore a tan hat, hiding her blonde locks.

This is it, Piotr thought to himself, *the time has finally come to rescue Kalina. I just need a weapon.*

Piotr raised himself and soon was walking through the village. He had seen the three young braves the day before handling the massive LeMat revolver. He wandered over to their lodge and was not surprised to see they were already up and no longer there. Piotr slipped quietly inside and rummaged through their few possessions. He found the LeMat, still loaded, but only with five of the nine revolving chambers filled. That would have to do he thought. However, he was pleased to see that the center shotgun barrel was still tamped full with buckshot.

Piotr prepared to leave the braves' lodge when he saw the three youths approaching. He was trapped, and wondered if he had time to crawl out under the sides of the lodge tent. He felt that he did not. If they caught him in their lodge, the freedom to wander the camp that he had been awarded would be stripped from him. If they caught him with the revolver, his troubles would be far worse.

He stood within the flap of the lodge, and the three braves stood talking just outside it, when a tremendous stir occurred. Every dog in the camp began to bark and growl and give chase to another animal as it darted through the gaps between the lodge tents. One of the braves pointed, and looking off in that direction, Piotr saw a familiar sight.

River darted out into the open, attacked one of the camp dogs, and then slipped away off into the brush. It was Cord's signal. The three braves gave chase, which allowed Piotr to slip out with the revolver, unnoticed amidst all the mayhem and commotion.

Cord followed the half-breed at a distance, as the trail began to climb. The girl, Kalina, hiked in front of the Indian. She was no longer dressed as she had been on the stage coach, he noticed, but instead wore the light tan of the Comanche buckskin clothing. Cord's initial thought seeing this was, *Poor kid. I wouldn't be caught dead in buckskin.*

Along the creek the trail was overgrown and as the sun rose, the June heat became offensive. Kalina tripped twice on the undergrowth, the second time she did not get up very quickly. Instead, she reached out her arms for the half-breed to carry her, which surprisingly to Cord, he did.

As the half-breed carrying Kalina climbed higher on the trail before him, Cord noticed another detail. Wound over the half-breed's shoulder was a horsewhip.

That has to be the horsewhip taken from the stage coach driver, Cord thought. *Doc Blevins said her hind quarters had been whipped. No tellin' how much skin that bastard took off her back and rump with it since then.*

But then Cord's thoughts turned on him.

Why on Earth would the savage carry her when he could be driving her forward with the whip? And why was Kalina so comfortable clinging to him so?

The rock formation rose high before them. As a boy, Cord had seen sketches of lighthouses along the shores of the East Coast. The rocky tower reminded him of these.

His pulse quickened as he felt a concern building within himself. He looked up at the elevated mesa, narrow as it was, and a dreadful thought came over him. *Did that half-breed intend to take her up there to sacrifice her? Will he whip her until she is driven off the edge and fall to her death? It doesn't seem consistent with the protective way in which he was carrying her.*

Cord reached in the pocket of his duster and laid his hand on the Baby Dragoon. *Only two balls left in it. Sure wish I had my Colt .45, if I ever needed it, this was the time.*

By the time *Lobo* and Kalina reached the elevated mesa, the sun had risen high in the clear blue sky. He released the girl to walk the rest of the trail on her own as the creek and its tripping growth had dropped away below them. The trail became rocky and barren. Cord followed them cautiously from a distance.

The small mesa was part of a much greater ragged rise of wind swept rock. The entrance to the mesa was narrow, as the path hugged the wall of the rise closely at that point. Cord had noticed it the day before. Once the two wandered out on the flat mesa, he would block it and they would have no way out. Except, of course, to go over one of its sides. That surely meant death for either of them. Cord still thought this was what the half-Comanche intended to do with the girl.

Kalina and *Lobo* climbed the ascending trail. As they made their way out onto the mesa, the girl had a look of wonder upon her face. She felt as if she was suspended in mid-air. Kalina had never been up so high in her entire life. Slowly she spun taking in the incredible view. As she did, she could feel the constant *Llano* wind rush over her. She had the sensation of being a bird soaring over the green, winding ribbons of *Palo Duro Canyon* below.

Lobo placed his hand on her shoulder and stopped her from twirling. "This special place," he said in his tattered English, "very special place."

He then placed his other hand on her other shoulder, and slowly moved her so that she looked directly ahead up at the vertical rise of *the Thunderbird.* It soared over them both and just above its apex, the sun was shining brightly. Not a cloud dared compete with it in the sky, which was painted with the blue tint of a most delicate hue of azure.

Lobo reached around her neck from behind and the fingers of his right hand reached down and fished out her medallion. She reached to grasp it for him, but he pushed her hand away. Then he said only one English word, "Still."

Lobo held the White Eagle medallion in his fingers. He lifted it, still around her neck, as high as he could toward the rock formation. He offered her as a gift on behalf of the medicine man, away in battle at Adobe Walls.

In his Comanche tongue, *Lobo* stared into the sun overhead and said aloud, "Oh *Great Spirit,* I bring before you this untouched offering of your medicine man, *White Eagle.* By now, he and war chief *Quanah* have your favor in destroying all the white men who slaughter the *cibolo.* "

Lobo looked upward, awaiting a message of some sort in response. But no message came forth.

The sun simply burned atop the rock formation, as if it were a flame lit atop a torch, but one which refused to illuminate the path before them.

Remembering her golden locks, *Lobo* stepped up to Kalina from behind and gently spun her round. He removed her hat, so that her blonde braided strands could fall free. He moved her hands until she grasped the hat with both, just in front of herself. He then turned her again to face *the Thunderbird* formation.

Kalina stayed in that position as *Lobo* continued aloud in Comanche, "This pure and golden crowned gift is to thank you for the powerful *puha* you have bestowed upon our warriors. By your power, they will be victorious not only today, but also again, when they next do battle with the white man's army of Blue Coats."

Lobo backed up ten paces. He faced the back of her as he removed the horsewhip from his shoulder to his hands. He took its grip with into his right palm. His left hand allowed its loops of braided leather to fall free. He followed *White Eagle's* instructions and gazed up directly into the sun, and awaited a vision from *the Great Spirit.*

Lobo was in intense concentration, attempting to sense any sign that might be used to communicate to him. He was oblivious to the long shadow of the white man in the duster that crept across the rock wall at the mesa's entrance behind him.

Circles of great light burned bright in his eyes and began to dance erratically, even after he could take no more and closed their lids. Soon, two words repeated over and over again in his mind, *behind you.* He looked at the girl, who still stood facing *the Thunderbird.* Then, he said aloud in English, *"Great Spirit* warns me of your presence."

"Well, he's a little too late," Cord McCullough said, "to be of much use, anyway. I already got the drop on ya'. So just go ahead and lay down that horsewhip."

Cord watched the girl's face as she spun around and he saw great fear in it. He knew that with only two rounds left to fire in his Baby Dragoon, he had to make them count. He sized up this man to be just as Doc Blevins had said, 6 foot or so, about 200 pounds. Bigger than your average Comanche. A skirmish would likely be a toss up, and if there was one thing Cord hated in a situation like this, it was even odds.

But *Lobo* did not lay down the whip, instead he walked slowly back to the girl. The move caught Cord unexpecting it, and he hesitated to fire, fearing the ball might pass through the Indian and lodge itself into the girl. When the half-breed reached her, he did a very curious thing. He stood before the girl, shielding her from Cord's view, but more importantly from his weapon's line of sight.

Cord called out to her, "Kalina, come slowly to me." Very tentatively, the terror stricken girl stepped from behind the brave and moved toward Cord. She took only two steps and then abruptly stopped in front of *Lobo.*

"Do not hurt us," she pleaded with Cord.

It took Cord a moment to realize what she was doing. She was shielding the Comanche, or trying to, anyway, with her undersized body. It was in that instant that Cord realized, the terror stricken look on her face was not from fear of the Indian, but from the strange white man pointing a pistol at them both.

"I will not hurt ya' girl," he said. "I've come to take ya' back to yer brother, *Pee Otter,* and yer Aunt Midge." But she gave no response, she only looked fearfully at him.

In fact, Kalina stared at Cord, frightened to death. "Do not hurt him, he has not hurt me." She did not move. Instead, she just stood protectively in front of her captor.

Lobo placed a hand on her shoulder and guided her to move behind himself. He then stood protectively in front of her again, as his face hardened in anger at Cord.

"How you dare come this place!" he said to Cord.

At that point a shot was fired off in the distance well behind Cord, quickly followed by another. Cord instinctively turned to spot Piotr walking up the trail toward them, having fired aimlessly into the air. Cord could not believe Piotr's carelessness, but then realized his own lack of control as he turned his head back toward the half-breed.

Cord turned his head just in time to have the fall of the horsewhip snap just below his right eye. The pain was crippling, searing along with the scream that came from Kalina's mouth as it landed. Cord fought to stay on his feet as purple streaks blurred his vision. He felt his balance leaving him and struggled to remain upright.

Another crack and the whip struck at his gun hand like a viper. The Baby Dragoon fell free before he could get off a shot. He could see through his blurred vision that it came to rest just before the edge of the mesa. Cord knew if the Indian recovered it, Piotr would be shot dead, and then himself. He moved toward it, but as he neared the gun, before he could realize fully what was happening, *Lobo* was on him, striking hard with his fists at his chest.

"I… drop… whip," he yelled through gritted teeth, "What… you… do? …No… gun!…Fight …like …man!"

Amidst the onslaught of blows from the half-breed's fists, Cord glimpsed the bandit's eyes, which were lit with a fury as fierce as he had ever seen in another man.

Figure 10: The Lighthouse at Palo Duro Canyon
Our Tale's "Thunderbird of the Great Spirit"

Cord absorbed the initial several punches to his body, but was able to collect his wits and block the last few blows. He did not have enough energy left, however, to land any blows of his own. His ribs ached horribly from the half-breed's punches, and as much as he tried to block out the pain, he couldn't. Then, the fall of the Indian's kick to his kneecap crumpled Cord to the ground.

Lobo stood over him a second, then said, "Now you die like white man." The Indian drew out his skinning knife and began to press its tip to Cord's chest. Cord was able to get a grip on his wrist with his right hand. He was just able to hold back the blade as he kicked at the Baby Dragoon in futility. It lay only inches beyond the sweep of his leg.

As the Indian fought with all his strength to overpower him and drive the tip of the blade into his chest, Cord used his left hand to reach for what remained inside the bottom of his duster. He felt it hard beneath the fabric and worked it free. Then, he positioned it for striking.

Cord slashed his left hand up into the face of the Comanche with every bit of might he could muster. The flint stone he used to counter the weight of his hidden gun ripped into the bronze flesh of *Lobo's* cheek. His skin gashed open, and blood spurted as Kalina's horrific scream reached a new peak of urgency. The bloodied half-breed pulled back in surprise, if only momentarily, from his assault atop the trailhand.

Cord felt the slight release of the Comanche and used his last remaining bit of energy to scoot his butt down toward the Baby Dragoon. He kicked at it with his boot, and with great satisfaction, felt the impact of his foot against it. He watched as it slid off the mesa and dropped out of sight. Piotr was then safe from its use against him.

The Indian saw his blood dripping from the hand he held to his cheek. The sight only enraged him all the more. Despite Cord having dropped the stone and placed his left arm under the half-breed's forearm, trying to block the knife, *Lobo* was still able to force the blade down hard. It penetrated into Cord's chest. Cord watched as its tip first pierced then sank into him. The pain he felt was immediate and overpowering. A burning explosion rippled throughout him. He knew this was to be the end for him. He thought that the Indian had done what no white man had been able to, up to that point. Then he thought of his Callie, and as he lay dying, he could hear her say, *So, Cordell, you failed even here in trying to save the girl and the boy. But you did your best. Come, join me and our son.*

Then, he heard another shot, and this time felt the *vifft* of a lead ball flying just overhead. Cord looked up to see Piotr standing just ahead of them both, with the massive LeMat revolver pointed at the Indian.

Lobo pulled the tip of the knife out of the white man's chest and, in a rage, lurched at the white otter boy. Kalina screamed again and pleaded with *Lobo* not to hurt her brother. The Comanche hesitated momentarily, glanced at her tearfully pleading so, and in that halting second, Piotr gazed closely upon his sister. Time suspended in that moment; the boy's heart filled with rage. He aimed the weapon at *Lobo*, at point blank range and pulled the trigger.

The hammer fell onto the firing cap of the next round. It ignited and fired, but the explosion of the round in the chamber sparked over into the next round in the revolver, igniting it also. The gun chain-fired, simultaneously shooting both remaining rounds left in it. The result was catastrophic, as the last two balls were expended, and Piotr, in shock, released the weapon.

As the gun chain-fired, the round in the firing chamber travelled through the barrel and exploded into *Lobo's* left shoulder. The other, ignited next to it in the revolver's cylinder and having no barrel to straighten its flight, went off in an erratic direction hitting nothing. Still, the kick and the flash of heat of the chain-fire in Piotr's hand was enough to force him to drop the misfired gun.

One round of lead had passed through *Lobo's* shoulder, but not cleanly. The lead ball shattered his shoulder blade before deflecting off and out of his back. The pain ripped through *Lobo* from deep him as the force of the impact spun his body to the ground.

Cord lay just behind where the half-breed fell, and could only watch all this as he seemed to fall deeper and deeper into a state of shock from his own stab wound. When the misfired LeMat was dropped to the ground by Piotr, all three men seemed to be lost in a moment stalled in time by shock and confusion. Cord lay disabled by his own deep wound; *Lobo* still breathed, but suffered from the bullet passing through him; and Piotr seemed frozen by the sheer naked truth that if this half-breed got back up, he would have to face him without any weapon whatsoever to defend himself.

The Indian was the first to come out of his shock. The boy he had been so willing earlier that day to set free had tried to kill him. There was no mercy left within his bronze skin, only rage. He grabbed the LeMat laying on the ground just before him. He rose and pointed it up at Piotr and squeezed the trigger over and over again. The strange gun, one with which the Comanche was completely unfamiliar, had no rounds left to discharge. It only clicked away hollowly with his nine trigger pulls. Having assessed the gun to be spent and useless, *Lobo* tossed it behind him.

He raised himself to his feet until his mangled frame towered in front of the defenseless otter boy. His slashed face and shoulder wounds bled freely, but still he moved slowly, toward Piotr, intending to kill the boy.

Kalina screamed, and ran, pleading, over to grab the hand of the Comanche. She attempted to pull him back away from her bother. Cord could only watch passively as he lay, his back on the mesa floor, as the girl tugged at the man in the blood stained black leather coat. She seemed stunned when the half-breed pushed her away hard with his right hand, driving her to the smooth, dusty floor of the mesa. She fell alongside the discarded LeMat revolver.

Cord looked at her and mouthed the words, "Bring it to me," but the girl was scared and refused to do so.

Above them both, the Indian and the boy were locked up with one another in a battle of life and death. *Lobo* had dropped the knife when he was shot, and no one saw it lying near the edge of the mesa. The two fought hand-to-hand, and though the Indian was larger and stronger, his shattered bleeding shoulder made him vulnerable to Piotr's blows. But given even this, *Lobo* was eventually able to overpower the boy and drive him to the ground. He knelt on the boy's shoulders and continued to rain blows down on him, pausing only to look for his knife.

Cord was too weak to drag himself to either the gun or the knife. Even had he grasped the blade, he was too close to death himself to attack with it. "Bring the gun to me," he said louder to Kalina.

She continued to watch as *Lobo* brutally continued to punch away at her brother. Kalina stopped sobbing and walked over to the LeMat. She picked up the heavy revolver with both hands and took it over to Cord.

Exhausted and himself injured, *Lobo* rested from assaulting Piotr with his fists. The boy was a bruised and bloody heap. *Lobo* stood, spotted the blade and walked over to the mesa's edge to retrieve it.

Cord took the LeMat from the girl, and said only "Good, good." With all the strength he could muster, he rolled himself over onto his stomach. The pain that accompanied that effort nearly made him black out, but somehow he held on, and focused his view on the half-breed who stooped to pick up the knife.

Cord grasped the LeMat and pointed it at *Lobo*. The Indian saw this and laughed, knowing the gun to be spent. He slowly walked with the knife toward him. Kneeling in front of Cord, the Indian lifted the knife and made its blade catch the sun, as if the resulting flashes were needed to pull the wounded trailhand out of his shock.

Lobo said in his highly fragmented English, through painful draws of breath, "Gun empty… I kill boy now… I was to let him live… Now I kill him…. Then I come back… And scalp you… Alive."

Cord cocked back the LeMat's hammer. *Lobo* defiantly opened both arms and smirked mockingly as if to say, *go ahead, cowboy, you can't hurt me with that.* Cord used his thumb to flip up the small switch on the hammer. *Lobo* looked inquisitively as he did so. He noticed it changed the orientation of the striking pad on the hammer. *Lobo* glanced at the larger but shorter barrel around which the cylinder turned, and realized too late what it all meant.

He reached frantically for the gun, but as he did, Cord, still lying on his throbbing chest in the dirt stained with his own spilled blood, pulled back as hard as he could on the trigger.

The explosion of the buckshot and black powder rammed down into that center barrel hit *Lobo* in the chest from only inches away. The force of the impact ratcheted the Indian's body several feet into the air. He landed with a thud on his back, writhing in pain. His lungs had been riddled by the buckshot, but amazingly his heart still beat.

Cord passed out from the effort expended to fire the massive gun. His face pressed flat against the mesa floor. His chin and cheek were covered in the stain of its red chalky blood-soaked dirt.

Lobo lay only a few feet away on his back, staring up at the sun. His life too drained from him. Only Piotr, who was badly beaten but not incapacitated, could garner enough strength to raise himself to his feet. When he did, he was shocked at what he saw. His little sister, Kalina, who had begun to move toward him slid to her knees over the fallen Comanche. She sobbed over him, who was heaving as he could no longer breathe normally. Only the last remnant's of life remained in his riddled carcass. Piotr stood stunned.

"Why do you cry for this man who stole you from us?" he asked her in Polish.

"He never hurt me," she sobbed. "He only protected me."

"He whipped you," Piotr said.

"Only because I ran from him," she answered. "You don't understand. He had no one. He was alone, and now he is dying."

As she said these words, three warrior teens came out onto the mesa behind Piotr.

Figure 11: Thunderbird of the Great Spirit
(The Lighthouse at Palo Duro Canyon)
By Kellen Churchill

Chapter 36: Long Shots

June 29th, 1874

On the third day of the seige of the camp at Adobe Walls, after the buffalo hunters had successfully driven off the Indians, there was great consternation among the amassed natives as what should be the next step. On a bluff overlooking the camp from some three-quarters of a mile away, a meeting of war chiefs took place.

"The white men have more coming to their aid each day," *Quanah Parker* said. "And every white man brings another *cibolo* rifle with him. We cannot get close enough to fire our weapons at them."

"We wait until nightfall," *White Eagle* advised, "and attack them while they sleep."

"We have done that," a Cheyenne chief who called himself *Little Robe* argued, "and still they wait for us. Even in the darkness, they kill our braves. Even when we get close, we cannot shoot through their walls, we cannot burn them out."

White Eagle raised his hand to get them to stop. He had something important to add.

"Tonight will be different," he said. "I will make magic to make them sleep. Our braves will walk in and club them where they lie."

"Your magic has failed us, *White Eagle!*" the Cheyenne chief *Little Robe* jeered. "You say your yellow war paint make the buffalo bullets bounce from our skin, but instead they tear our braves apart. No, your *puha* has no power. It is bad magic."

"Only because your Cheyenne braves broke the forbidden taboo the night before our attack," *White Eagle* said. "They killed a skunk and displeased *the Great Spirit.* They are to blame for all the dead."

White Eagle knew the Cheyennes had indeed killed the skunk, a forbidden thing. But was that alone enough to cause his magic to have failed? He did not think so. He had yesterday received word of the death of the half-blood at the base of the *Thunderbird* rising from the mesa, and took that to mean that *the Great Spirit* had rejected his untouched gift. But why? Was the girl crowned with golden hair not as pure as the half-blood had said? What about her displeased *the Great Spirit?* Why had the prophecy failed?

As the Indians continued to quarrel amongst themselves on that bluff, below them, off in the distance a few buffalo hunters had come out of doors and watched. It was safe to do so given the mighty range of their weapons.

"Billy, I would have to say you are the finest marksman I have ever seen," Bat Masterson said. "I sure am damn glad we unbolted that saloon door for you."

"Thanks, Bat," Dixon replied, "but don't sell ya'self short. Ya' did well yerself in the thick of things. We all did, or we wouldn't be out here congratulatin' each other."

Masterson shrugged his shoulders and looked up at the bluff full of Indian chiefs. "My point being, Billy, is that I think with your skill, you could hit one of them savages from here."

"Naw," Dixon said. "They're a good three-quarter mile off, maybe more. Certainly couldn't hit 'em with this .45/90 from here. Had I a .50/90, I might have a chance."

Dixon referred to the models of the Sharps rifle.

"Here, Billy," another buffalo hunter said, "take my big fifty and give it a shot. Whatcha' got to lose in tryin'?"

Billy Dixon took the .50/90, the so-called 'big fifty,' and sighted it on one of the distant Indians. He adjusted it for yardage and windage, and pulled back the rear set trigger. He made some final corrections, then squeezed the forward trigger.

On the bluff, a violent disagreement had broken out, and the chief opponent of *White Eagle* was none other than the Old War Chief *Raging Anger.*

"You and your excuses, *White Eagle!*" he accused. "Do not put the failure of your *puha* on our brave Cheyenne brothers. No, this is your failure. You have mislead us. You have ever since the days when you were called by the name *Isa Tai'i.* Your lies have cost us a great many lives. You lied regarding the theft of the long leather coat then. You lie about the great *puha* you have now. Many warriors are dead. I refuse to call you by the name *White Eagle* any longer. You are *Isa Tai'i.* I never believed that you had communed with *the Great Spirit …*"

Figure 12: Quanah Parker

Figure 13: Bat Masterson and Billie Dixon

It was no where near simultaneous. First the war chiefs heard the ring out of Billy Dixon's shot. A full second and a half later his round drove through *Raging Anger's* skull, killing him instantly. He was dead before his body fell from his war pony. When the War Chiefs saw from where the blast had been fired, they could not believe their eyes. They all scurried off to the woods behind the rise before another shot could be fired. They sent out two braves, crouching low, to recover the lifeless body of *Raging Anger.*

"Now they have guns that shoot this far?" *Quanah Parker* asked. "We are finished here. We will leave only a small number of braves to harass them until we pull out all the others. We will return to *Palo Duro* before we lose many more of our brothers."

The other chiefs all agreed. *White Eagle* was disgraced, but given what had befallen *Raging Anger,* no one else was prepared to call out the failed magic of *the Great Spirit.*

Down below, Bat Masterson and the others congratulated Billy Dixon on his fantastic shot. He said he couldn't claim it by his marksmanship, cause it was only a "scratch shot," meaning it was lucky.

Luck or not, that shot may have saved many more lives as it convinced the natives to give up the siege. It lasted five days in all, but after Dixon's scratch shot on the third day it had all but ended. Just as the Mountain Howitzers had saved Kit Carson and his men, these Sharps rifles had saved these buffalo hunters.

After it was over, they had lost only four men out of twenty-eight: the two Shadler brothers who were caught in their wagon sleeping; Billy Tyler shot through the lung in the doorway of the mercantile; and tragically Mr. William Olds, who had slipped on the ladder coming down from a lookout position and accidentally discharged his rifle into himself, leaving young Mrs. Olds a poor widow.

Word came to *Palo Duro* by rider on the night of the third day. It was said that *Raging Anger* had fallen and that the braves would return soon. Both *Lobo's* body and Cord McCullough had been brought back to the village by travois two days earlier after the fight on the mesa.

Even though still recovering from childbirth, *Trembling Wind* had them both brought into her lodge, where she prepared her son for burial. She also attended to Cord's wounds. She allowed Midge and Kalina to stay there as well. Piotr was kept in another lodge with *Sulking Crow,* where they were guarded by the young braves.

As *Lobo* had died on the mesa, *Trembling Wind* was denied the honor of caring for him over his last moments. Still, she lingered over his lifeless body for hours those days, wondering what her life would have been like had he lived. Especially as she was now freed from *Raging Anger.*

Over the two days since his death, Cord McCullough somehow barely clung to life. *Trembling Wind* cared for him. While he never regained consciousness, his body stabilized somewhat. Still, Midge realized that despite this, if they did not get him to a doctor, Cord would die.

Trembling Wind and Midge had begun to communicate in English, but due to the limitations of *Lobo's* mother, they quickly found it easier to do so in Spanish. The Polish woman had picked the language up from Latino hands on the Trinity Quarter Ranch. She was skilled in that way. New tongues came easily to her.

"I have received news that my husband was killed at Adobe Walls," *Trembling Wind* told her matter-of-factly.

"I am so sorry," Midge responded, "first your son, now your husband." She had only learned that *Trembling Wind* was *Lobo's* mother after she had delivered her child.

"I accept your sorrow for the loss of my son," she replied, "but not for the death of my husband *Raging Anger.* I never had anything but dark feelings for him. Yet it now explains my son's last words to me."

"What did he say?" Midge asked. "I thought his life was gone from him before his body was brought to you."

"So it was," *Trembling Wind* said, "but before he left for the mesa, he told me that I would soon be free. When I asked, *'free from what?'* he said, '*Raging Anger.*' Now, the husband I did not love is dead, but so too is my son who lived with so many troubles."

"Well, his spirit is free from all of its troubles now," Midge said.

Trembling Wind went on to tell Midge of how, like Kalina, she had once been taken against her will. She told the story of her having been ridden across *the Llano* as a young girl, even younger than her niece. She spoke of her father's long leather coat, and of its being taken by the brave who scalped his body in front of her. The same man who later became her unwanted husband. She explained how her son stole it back from him just to make her happy.

The two women paused their conversation for a bit, then *Trembling Wind* asked, "How is the young girl?"

She seemed to do so with no malice, only deep concern over the health and state of mind of Kalina. Midge sensed her question was fueled by the sympathy of having lived a similar experience.

"Kalina?" Midge asked. "Physically she is fine, but she seems very confused, and greatly troubled by all she witnessed up on that rock mesa. I assume there is also the trauma of her being abducted. She will need a lot of time to get over all this. What troubles her most, I think, is the loss of your son. I cannot understand it, but she keeps saying how well he protected her on their journey. There is certainly a part of her heart that is broken. Not that she loved him, but it is crushed by the loss of the chance to be with him. It seems they had bonded very closely. "

"As I did with my *Dark Wolf* out on *the Llano.* That journey has a powerful influence over someone so young. I was fortunate, as I fell in love with the man who protected me. I was his wife for many years. Together we had a son."

Midge hesitated awkwardly, as she sensed a great sorrow wash over the woman. *Trembling Wind* then began to cry over the bloodied and bullet-pierced long leather coat that two days earlier she had stripped from her son's lifeless body before he was buried that first day just before sunset.

Midge said to her, "This coat has caused you much sorrow. Would you like for me to destroy it for you?"

Tears streamed freely down *Trembling Wind's* cheeks. "No, you do not understand. This coat tells the story of my life. Like all lives, it has stitched many sorrows to many joys. One day it shall shroud my own body when I go to rejoin my son under a great Comanche star."

"Now, about your man," *Trembling Wind* continued. "I have treated him as well as my medicine can do. He needs to be taken to Santa Fe, for white man doctors to treat him, before he also dies."

"Cord will never make it to Santa Fe," Midge said. "It would be a long shot if he survived the ride, even in the Kiowa's wagon. His body is just too weak."

"I only know that when our warriors return, they will surely kill him. You and the girl will be given away to the Comanche braves. No, I cannot bear for that to happen to you both. You have saved my life and given me a beautiful daughter, who I love. I cannot allow those you love to be taken away from you. Just as you and the girl must not be taken from your own people and from your own way of life."

Midge was moved by this woman who held such sympathy for the man who had killed her own son. She did not understand how there could be anything but hatred stored in her heart toward Cord.

Trembling Wind read the confusion in her face.

"I told my son not to go there," she said. "Too dangerous. He too had a head much too hard. Very hard. Yes, your man killed my son, but my son tried to kill him as well. And the boy, also. You must take them both away, along with the Kiowa trader. Leave here before the warrior braves return from Adobe Walls."

Midge's first instinct was to tell the woman she did not love Cord, but decided that maybe deep down, she had all along. She had to admit to herself that it pleased her ears to hear *Trembling Wind* call him "your man." All she knew was that she dreaded losing him. Especially after all he had given to get her niece back, as he had promised he would.

In any case, she would not lose him without a fight. "Well, he is a stubborn man," Midge said, a smile creasing her face. "A very hard-headed and stubborn man at that. Perhaps he'll survive the ride after all."

"He clings to life to be with you," *Trembling Wind* surprised her by saying. "You must take him from here. His wounds are beyond what we can care for. Take him to the fort of the Blue Coats at Santa Fe."

Midge agreed. They would leave on the rise of the morning sun westward to Santa Fe. She heard Cord say once he might never make it to that town. Perhaps, just perhaps, he would after all.

Finally, Midge asked *Trembling Wind* if she had decided on a name for her newborn daughter.

"Yes," she said. "I will ask the medicine man to name her after my son, whose life spirit has now been silenced. Even if he refuses, I will always call her *'Silent As A Hunted Owl'*. It is only fitting, given her life has come in the waning hours of his own."

Chapter 37: After Adobe Walls
1874 and Beyond

After what became known as the Second Battle of Adobe Walls in late June, the rest of 1874 became highly eventful for the buffalo hunters and their Comanche adversaries.

Billy Dixon had become famous far and wide for his "scratch shot" which toppled an Indian dead from his saddle over three-quarters of a mile away in June. This was not the end of Dixon's claim to fame for the remainder of that year. On September 12th, he and five other riders were carrying army dispatches across the plains when they were caught out in the open by a group of about one hundred and twenty five Comanche and Kiowa Indians. They fought off the initial attack and took cover in the only thing available nearby - one of the large depressions in the earth on the plains known as a buffalo wallow. It was a ten foot circular shallow swale where buffalo would roll, or "wallow," in the moisture which collected there. Dixon and his compatriots used their knives to "burm" up any dirt they could, behind which they held off the circling Indians. They were saved by the onset of a "Blue Norther," a prairie storm with a prodigious drop in temperature. The next morning brought the arrival of the cavalry. It proved to be an incredible feat, but once again the Indians failed to press their advantage.

All in all, only one of the men died, but in the end, the other survivors of "The Buffalo Wallow Fight" had fought so heroically, that the men became the only civilians ever to be awarded the Congressional Medal of Honor.

Dixon and his fellow scouts had been assigned to an army expedition of three thousand men that headed off in search of *the Quahadi* Comanches and any other tribes still out on *the Llano.* The army converged in five columns: from Fort Concho under overall expedition leader Colonel Ranald S. Mackenzie, with additional columns from the East (Fort Sill and Fort Richardson), from the North (Fort Dodge) and from the West (Fort Union in the New Mexico territory). The intent was to encircle the natives in the Red River tributaries. The fighting very quickly became fierce.

In September, the army defeated the *Quahadi* in the Battle of the Upper Washita River. The natives had attacked a supply wagon train, which formed into a defensive circle and held off the attackers until they were rescued by the US Army's sixth cavalry.

The Army employed Tonkawa scouts to track and locate the Comanches. The Comanche and Tonkawa tribes had long been enemies, even before the latter took to scouting for the Army. For one thing, the Tonkawas had long practiced cannibalism, acts taboo to the Comanche culture. By late November, the Tonkawa had located *the Quahadi* in their wintering camp in *Palo Duro Canyon.*

Palo Duro Canyon, the second largest canyon in the United States, was cut by the headwaters of the Red River. It is more a maze of canyons than just one massive geological feature. It is 120 miles long, and can be up to 20 miles wide in places. It was a favorite camping site for *the Quahadi,* although even finding a large village of lodges in its extensive area could pose a very significant challenge.

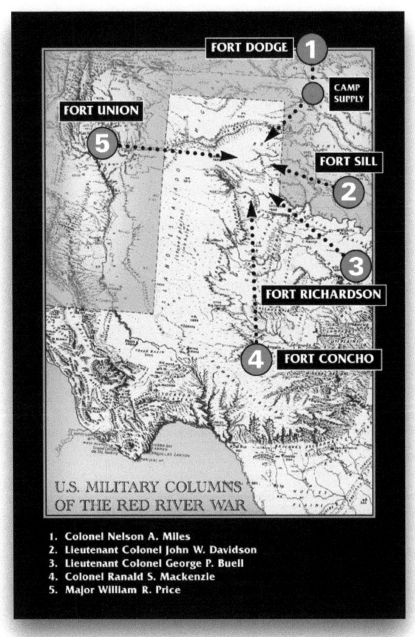

FORT DODGE **1**

CAMP SUPPLY

FORT UNION

5

FORT SILL

2

3

FORT RICHARDSON

4 FORT CONCHO

U.S. MILITARY COLUMNS OF THE RED RIVER WAR

1. Colonel Nelson A. Miles
2. Lieutenant Colonel John W. Davidson
3. Lieutenant Colonel George P. Buell
4. Colonel Ranald S. Mackenzie
5. Major William R. Price

Figure 14: Army Columns in 1874 Red River War (Courtesy of The Texas Historical Commission)

Colonel Mackenzie decided to strike on the morning of September 28th. They raided the Comanche corral of 1400 horses, most of which were destroyed to deny them to the natives. Then the US Army proceeded to burn out the village of 450 lodges. The braves under *Quanah Parker* fought valiantly to cover the escape of their women and children, whose only recourse was to flee on foot. However, all attempts failed. Amazingly, perhaps thanks to *Quanah Parker's* leadership, very few Indian lives were lost in the attack in the canyon.

After their surrender, *Quanah Parker* had no choice but to lead these noble warriors on to the reservation at Fort Sill in the Indian Territories. This opened up for settlement not only the Texas Panhandle around *Palo Duro,* also the entire *Llano Estacado* and all of *Comancheria.*

On the reservation, *Quanah Parker* became the undisputed leader of the Comanches at Fort Sill. He met and was befriended by the US President Theodore Roosevelt, even attended his inauguration in 1905. Parker lived with his many wives in his impressive ten room "Star House." Later in life, he and Ranald Mackenzie, by then promoted to General and appointed overseer of the reservation at Fort Sill, became close and respected friends.

Isa Tai'i remained with *the Quahadi* even after the humiliating exposure of his *White Eagle* "powers" during the Second Battle of Adobe Walls. Somehow, this medicine man retained his ability to attempt to rival *Quanah Parker* for leadership of *the Quahadi* on the reservation, although he never took the mantle away from *Quanah*. And as fond as *Quanah Parker* had been of his white mother, he never betrayed the Comanche spirit that lived and breathed within him until his death in 1911.

Chapter 38: One Last Flourish of Fiction
The End of the Trail

Trembling Wind would forever remember the morning she watched as the white woman departed with the otter boy, his young sister and the Kiowa, *"Sulking Crow."* They took the older one called Cord, so badly wounded by her son, away on the wagon headed toward Santa Fe. After they had left, she retrieved the skinning knife that had belonged to her son, *Kills Owls.* She used its razor sharp edge to cut free from her father's long leather coat the knotted ends of the fringes that held the Comanche beads. With several slashes they all fell free to the ground, where she collected them into a carved wooden cup to preserve them as a future gift for her infant daughter. *The two worlds of my life are no longer connected in conflict. I may now live and die in peace,* she thought

She moved later to the reservation at Fort Sill, as they all did, after their defeat at *Palo Duro.* She watched as her daughter grew, and as *Quanah* became very famous. There, she lived for many years in a lodge not far from his renown Star House. When asked, she would interpret words written in Spanish and English for him. *Trembling Wind* endured her life there, but became very sad when she thought of the loss of their freedom living out on *the Llano.*

In 1905, when her age was many years, she became very sick. Her daughter, *Silent As A Hunted Owl,* draped her in her father's long leather coat, the one with some missing fringes to keep her body warm, but still her it could not stop her shivering. Finally, she was taken into the great house of *Quanah,* who was away in Washington DC riding proudly for their people in a parade for his friend, the great white father. Under the roof of his house, her spirit left her.

Silent As A Hunted Owl had long lived on the edge of the white man's world. She, like others, had been forced to adopt many of their customs. This included marking the dead they buried in the ground.

She rummaged through her mother's possessions and found the knife that had long ago belonged to her half brother, *He Who Kills Owls,* after whom she was named. She took the knife to an old elder who was skilled in carving wood. She had him carve a marker made from many small pieces of Juniper taken from Palo Duro and skillfully laid side by side. The marker read:

Here Lies the Remains of
She Who Runs Like the Trembling Wind
Who Died Wrapped in her Father's Long Leather Coat
Under the Great Comanche Star
Just as She Had Long Ago Foreseen.

Next to it, in the dirt of her mother's grave, *Silent Owl* left a small carved wooden cup containing the Comanche beads gifted to her so many years ago. She prayed some other, perhaps a young Comanche girl, might find them to be lovely, and take them for her own…

The End of
"The Untouched"

Proudly Published by

ASSOCIATES

Authors' Notes

Let us begin by thanking you, the reader, for sacrificing your precious time to read this fictional but historically accurate tale of ours. We hope you enjoyed it, and we will take the time for a few more pages of notes to share with you what was factual within it and what were embellishments of our imagination.

This novel was originally intended to be just a simple tale of adventure as told from the perspective of the trail hand Cord McCullough. However, after attending a writers conference in Rapid City, South Dakota and listening to a riveting keynote address by a prominent Native American who spoke of the need for portraying all perspectives, we decided to add the backstory of the Comanche character "Lobo". We hope our doing so brings another level of understanding to the conflicting cultures and their beliefs that drive our many characters.

First, our hero, Cord McCullough, is obviously fictional, as are Father Jerzy, Kalina, Piotr and Midge, and to be accurate, most of the characters in this work. However, it is factual that the first Polish permanent settlement in the United States was indeed at Panna Maria founded on Christmas Eve in 1854 just south of San Antonio, Texas. There still exists a thriving community there today. We recommend a visit to it by all means.

In the Fort Worth sequence, Augustus Mueller is a fictional character, but the site of his home spread, as we portray it herein, did actually later become that city's first Catholic Church in 1876. Interestingly, it was named Saint Stanislaus Kostka after the Polish Jesuit Patron Saint. Whether this was influenced by the community of Poles at Panna Maria, we are unsure. But it confirmed our understanding that Polish immigrants were throughout the state of Texas in some number by the timeframe of this tale.

In any case, the church and the grounds were later absorbed as part of the grounds of the town's first Catholic Cathedral named Saint Patrick's, opened in 1892. The original St. Stanislaus church building was reconfigured as the cathedral's school house. Eventually, the original Saint Stanislaus building was razed completely for the construction of the Saint Patrick's Rectory in 1908. Of course, the Saint Patrick Cathedral stands and actively serves Fort Worth to this day.

Both Saint Stanislaus Church and Saint Patrick's Cathedral were located just on the edge of Fort Worth's bawdy and raucous "Hell's Half Acre" district. In it, the Keg Saloon was a real enough place, and was known to keep a caged Panther within it. Occurrences of that mascot swiping inebriated patrons is real and well documented in newspaper columns from the period. The owners likely kept the animal because the town had earned the nickname "Panther City," derived from the comments of a lawyer from rival Dallas. He had said upon a visit to Fort Worth that the "cowtown" was so vacant that he saw a panther sleeping on the sidewalk. Fort Worth residents laughed off the obviously fictitious slight and soon accepted the name "Panther City" as their town's badge of honor.

When Piotr inherits the LeMat revolver in "The Acre," he landed one of the most interesting handgun designs of the Civil War, and later, the Wild West. It has been used in many novels and movies, and we decided for it to become the featured weapon around which this story "revolved." Its deficiencies are well documented, including its propensity to chain-fire. In fact, in doing research for this novel, we came across a video of a cap and ball expert firing a current day replica of this gun. The demo had to be stopped after the shooter himself experienced a chain-fire.

Another gun featured in this story is the Sharps Big Fifty buffalo rifle. It is critical to the story because without it, the Second Battle of Adobe Walls would most certainly have ended much differently. But, the Big Fifty was notable in another, much more somber way. It was the gun, along with its .45/.90 and other variants, that were most responsible for the near extinction of the buffalo. The plains were swept clean of the massive herds that once roamed upon them. Devoid of these bison, the plains no longer nourished the nomadic Comanche lifestyle.

The town of Weatherford was used as a setting for this novel for several reasons, most notably the documented robberies of stage coaches traveling from Fort Worth during this period. Secondarily, even as early as in 1874, it was very much home to some of Texas' most prominent quarter horse ranches. While the Trinity Quarter Ranch is fictional, it is representative of Weatherford during that era. The town was also very much ravaged by Comanche raids over this time. Many were by Comanche braves coming off of Fort Sill just outside the state. They would raid Texas ranches and return to the reservation. Finally, we have to admit, having lived not far from the town for nearly a decade, we used Weatherford as it was one of our favorite Texas towns.

As our storyline progresses, we make many references to the Texas Rangers. We have the highest regard for these lawmen, originally founded over a century ago in 1823, to "range" across Texas and protect settlers and homesteaders from the "depredations" of the Comanche, Kiowa and other Native American tribes. The Rangers, to be successful, had to learn how to fight as the Comanche did, on horseback with ferocious hostility. Our research also suggests that sometimes the brutality shown by these lawmen was equal in many ways to that of the Native Americans. The Battle of Pease River is presented in that light, and we believe it very accurate to portray it as a massacre of the Comanche. Chief Peta Nocona was slain during it as were most other Comanches. His wife Cynthia Ann Parker "was rescued," and their two sons, Quanah and Pecos, indeed somehow, miraculously, escaped on horseback.

The references to President Ulysses S. Grant and Secretary of War William Tecumseh Sherman in the Warren Wagon Massacre and its aftermath are historically accurate. The hunting of the three Chiefs and their fates are well documented, including Jacksboro being the first city where Native Americans were tried in a white man's courtroom.

This novel is split into three parts. Most of what is seen from a white man's perspective occurs in the first part - A Trailhand's Tale. But in an attempt to give the story an alternative perspective of Native American life (at least as well as we could present it from our research), the second part - "A Comanche's Story" was added. Derogatory and offensive terms to Native Americans such as "Squaw" and "Half-Breed" used intermittently in Part I as historical perspectives of the white man are not found here.

We attempt to tell the backstory of the character "Kills Owls/ Lobo" in terms of his being raised among the Quahadi Comanche, and how much of a feeling of despair and loss descended upon this young brave after being exiled from amongst "The People." Some of his antics including the sewing shut of the smoke lodge vent are representations of childish pranks known to occur among the Comanches.

Finally, "Part Three - The Pursuit" is a tragic clash of cultures. We used Polish characters for several reasons, as their families had been driven from their lands as a result of Eastern Europe's "*Kulturkampf.*" With Poland's emblem being the White Eagle, it fit seamlessly into the true history of Isa Tai'i recreating himself as "White Eagle." As we see it, the Comanches and Poles both had their lands stolen away from them by nothing more than greedy neighbors armed with superior weaponry.

The Polish names used are traditional ones. Piotr's Aunt Midge's native name of "Mieczysława" is the female form of the Polish name for Milton. In fact, my own mother's name was Mieczysława, named after her father, and everyone called her either Mildred, Millie, or Midge. Kalina is a traditional Polish girl's name meaning "flower" which we thought appropriate given the focus on being "untouched" throughout the narrative.

The sequence of the Second Battle of Adobe Walls is described weighing heavily on our research, with much of the action sequence based on the auto-biography of Billy Dixon ("The Life and Adventures of Billy Dixon" published in 1914.) The roles of the buffalo hunters, including Billy Dixon and Bat Masterson, are accurately portrayed. The details of the Battle of the Buffalo Wallow are also drawn from Dixon's own accounting. The references to Three Finger Jack - Colonel Ranald S. Mackenzie - at The Battle of Palo Duro Canyon are accurate as well. Surely this last battle opened up the land known as "Comancheria" after the Quahadi had no option left to them but to take up life on the Comanche reservation at Fort Sill.

Perhaps the two historical figures in this novel most intriguing are none other than Quanah Parker and "Isa Tai'i," later to reinvent himself as "White Eagle." Quanah Parker was only twelve years old when his mother put him and his younger brother, "Pecos," on horseback to escape the massacre at Pease River in 1860. The two youths outran the pursuing Texas Rangers and survived, although Cynthia Ann Parker would never come to know that. It is likely that she died wondering what might ever have become of them.

Years after Quanah Parker escaped from Pease River, he joined the Quahadi band of Comanches. These were the last Comanches to roam the lands of Comancheria, after all others had taken up residence at Fort Sill. Quanah soon became their main war chief and leader. He demonstrated great prowess against the US Army during the Battle of Blanco Canyon in 1871. His great defeats would come at the Second Battle of Adobe Walls and The Battle of Palo Duro Canyon, both in 1874. But even after their resettlement onto the Reservation at Fort Sill, Quanah Parker led his people and became a national figure. He was invited to attend Teddy Roosevelt's inauguration in 1905 (Along with the Apache Warrior Geronimo), and afterwards even hosted the president in his magnificent Star House at Fort Sill. Quanah was proud of his mixed heritage, and was adamant that he be respectfully addressed fully as Quanah Parker.

If there is any one character in this novel who is a mix of historical accuracy and pure imaginative fiction, it is our rendering of "Isa Tai'i." His Native American name we diluted to mean "Coyote Dropping," but in reality it translates to something much more vulgar. Obviously, his interactions with "He Who Kills Owls" or "Lobo" are pure fictional works of our creation. But his later renaming himself as the medicine man "White Eagle," and claiming to have communed in the sky with the Great Spirit is historically accurate. He indeed did predict the coming and disappearance of a comet in the night skies of 1873. He also did promise the braves at The Second Battle of Adobe Walls that the magic of his yellow ochre war paint would keep the bullets of the buffalo hunters from doing any harm to them. And when that "puha" so disastrously failed, he in fact did blame it on the Cheyennes who had killed a skunk - a taboo to both the Comanche and Cheyenne cultures. We could not resist fictionalizing this character, creating a mix of romantic mysticism and historical accuracy, as one of the central figures of our tale's storyline.

We hope you enjoyed this rollicking adventure, full as it is of larger than life characters and clashing cultures. We offer it with the greatest of respect for both the Comanche and the Texan cultures. It is one of our land's greatest losses that the two could never quite be reconciled to peacefully coexist in a manner fully benefitting both.

David and Marie Trawinski

Research Sources/Suggested Reading

1) **"Comanches: The History of a People,"**
   by T. R. Fehrenbach, 1974, Anchor Books.

2) **" The Comanches:Lords of the South Plains,"**
   by Ernest Wallace & E. Adamson Hoebel, 1952,
   University of Oklahoma Press.

3) **"Empire of the Summer Moon,"**
   by S.C. Gwynne, 2010, Scribner

4) **"Hell's Half Acre,"** by Richard F. Selcher, 1991, TCU Press

5) **"The Life and Adventures of Billy Dixon,"** by Billy Dixon,
   Copyright Olive Dixon, 1914, Public Domain, Presented by Project Gutenberg

6) **Texas State Historical Society Website**

7) **Texas Historical Commission Website**

Attributions for Cover Figures

Front Cover Layout by David Trawinski, featuring Original Artwork
"The Lighthouse at Palo Duro Canyon" by Kellen Churchill

> Composited with Licensed Adobe Stock Image # 553966108
>> "Cowboy and cows in a shadow," by 2ragon
> Licensed Adobe Stock Image # 568137236
>> "back of a traditional native american," by Noel Cook
> Licensed Adobe Stock Image # 189629532
>> "Set of Western Silhouettes" by miloskontra
> Licensed Adobe Stock Image # 336803702
>> "Girl with Long Blonde Hair" by Lapidus
> Adobe Stock Image # 641886596
>> "Photo portrait of a sad beautiful blonde" by whitecityrecords

Rear Cover Layout by David Trawinski,

> Stagecoach Image Courtesy Booth Western Museum of Cartersville, Georgia
>> over photo of Palo Duro Canyon by David Trawinski 2023
> Composited with Licensed Adobe Stock Image # 553966108
>> "Cowboy and cows in a shadow," by 2ragon
> Licensed Adobe Stock Image # 568137236
>> "back of a traditional native american," by Noel Cook
> Licensed Adobe Stock Image # 588499467
>> "Watercolor clipart of cowboy portraits," by flipper 1971
> Licensed Adobe Stock Image # 57239826 Rider and Horse by Michael
> Licensed Adobe Stock Image #604053713 Cowgirl in Leather Hat by Gizmo
> Licensed Adobe Stock Image # 626509838 Cowgirl's face by jechm
> Background Photo: Palo Duro Canyon by David Trawinski 2023

Attributions for Interior Figures

Part One - A Trailhand's Tale Image

Licensed Adobe Stock Image # 594099450
"Semi-silhouette illustration of a cowboy on a horse in a desert" by Gary

Part Two - A Comanche's Story Image (and watermark p.195)

Licensed Adobe Stock Image # 522696353
"Portrait of a fictional Comanche Indian Man" by designprojects
Composited over Licensed Adobe Stock Image # 268141991
Native American Scene by Daniel Eskridge

Part Three - The Pursuit: A Clash of Cultures Image

Composited with Licensed Adobe Stock Image # 553966108
"Cowboy and cows in a shadow," by 2ragon
Licensed Adobe Stock Image # 568137236
"back of a traditional native american," by Noel Cook
Licensed Adobe Stock Image # 588499467
"Watercolor clipart of cowboy portraits," by flipper 1971
Licensed Adobe Stock Image # 57239826 Rider and Horse by Michael
Licensed Adobe Stock Image #604053713 Cowgirl in Leather Hat by Gizmo
Licensed Adobe Stock Image # 626509838 Cowgirl's face by jechm
Background Photo: Palo Duro Canyon by David Trawinski 2023

Interior Figure Images

Figure 1: Colt Navy Six and Slim Jim Holster - Courtesy of Mr. Jim Dunham
Overlaid on Licensed Adobe Stock Image #61052282
"Leather floral pattern background" by Irina Ukrainets

Figure 2: LeMat Cap & Ball Revolver
Composited from Wikipedia Image Le Mat-IMG 1761-gradient.jpg
Hammer Insert Wikipedia Image - Public Domain
Overlayed Text Added by David Trawinski

Figure 3: Kalina's Polish White Eagle Medallion
Composited Adobe Stock Image # 33255393
"Metal eagle - military symbol" by Jaroslaw Grudzinski
Composited With Polish Eagle Crown by David Trawinski

Figure 4: Republic of Texas Map (1839) Licensed Adobe Stock Image # 495664126
"18-19th Century Vintage German Map of the State of Texas"
by Steve Estvanik/Wirestock Creators
Additional Overlays added by David Trawinski

Figure 5: Cynthia Ann Parker Photo - Public Domain

Figure 6: Colonel Christopher "Kit" Carson Photo - Public Domain

Figure 7: Two Photos of Palo Duro Canyon - Copyright 2023 by David Trawinski

Figure 8: Cord McCullough's Wanderings
Composited Adobe Stock Image # 483292244 by EmLion
Overlays Added by David Trawinski

Figure 9: _Isa Tai'i /White Eagle_ - Public Domain

Figure 10: "Palo Duro Canyon Lighthouse at Sunrise"
Licensed Adobe Stock Image # 250135440 by Kip

Figure 11: "The Lighthouse at Palo Duro Canyon" Original Artwork
by Kellen Churchill Copyright 2023

Figure 12: _Quanah Parker_ standing and on horseback - Public Domain

Figure 13: Bat Masterson and Billie Dixon - Public Domain

Figure 14: US Military Columns of Red River War,
Courtesy of the Texas Historical Commission

Other Novels by David and Marie Trawinski:

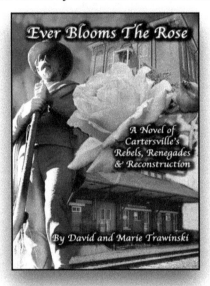

<u>*"Ever Blooms the Rose," 2019*</u>

Two Confederate soldiers, Virgil Clay-Harris and Willet Blackwell, return to the small town of Cartersville, Georgia after each being wounded severely at the Battle of Chickamauga. Virgil tries desperately to eke out an honest living, while his friend Willet resorts to setting up a group of murderous marauders upon nearby Three Sisters Mountain. When the girl they were both raised with, Deekie, comes between them, and the niece of an Irish carpetbagger, Ever, comes to town, tensions flare until a climatic showdown ensues.

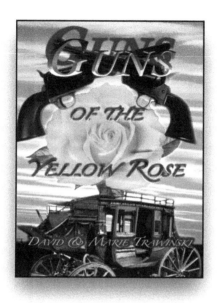

"Guns of the Yellow Rose," 2022

Clay and Deekie return, only to be taken on a cross-country journey by
an ambitious riverboat gambler, Armistead, to Nashville nd Memphis.
When things go awry, the couple heads by stagecoach for Fort Worth,
Texas, and its notorious *"Hell's Half Acre"* district in search of Clay's
gunsmith *"Diddy."* Along the way they become ensnarled in a game of
cat & mouse with a vigilante enforcer of rustlers along the historic
Chisholm Trail named Cord McCullough, and an unscrupulous
Pinkerton agent sent to trail him from Chicago.

Visit our website at DavidTrawinski.com